THE GIRL IN TIMES SQUARE

By the same author

Tully
Red Leaves
Eleven Hours
The Bronze Horseman
Tatiana and Alexander

PAULLINA SIMONS

THE GIRL IN TIMES SQUARE

HarperCollins*Publishers*

HarperCollins*Publishers*
77–85 Fulham Palace Road,
Hammersmith, London W6 8JB

www.harpercollins.co.uk

Published by HarperCollins*Publishers* 2005
1

First published in Australia and New Zealand by
HarperCollins*Publishers* 2004

Copyright © Paullina Simons 2004

"Lost in the Flood" by Bruce Springsteen. Copyright © 1972
Bruce Springsteen. All rights reserved. Reprinted by permission.
"Fire" by Bruce Springsteen. Copyright © 1978 Bruce Springsteen.
All rights reserved. Reprinted by permission.
"Across the Border" by Bruce Springsteen. Copyright © 1995
Bruce Springsteen. All rights reserved. Reprinted by permission.

HarperCollins*Publishers*
A catalogue record for this book
is available from the British Library

ISBN-13 978 0 00 711891 5
ISBN-10 0 00 711891 0

Typeset in Goudy by Palimpsest Book Production Limited,
Polmont, Stirlingshire

Printed and bound in Great Britain by
Clays Ltd, St Ives plc

For my sister, Elizabeth, as ever searching
And for Melanie Cain, who has been to the crying room

In the Vatican after they have chosen a new pope, they lead him to a room off the Sistine Chapel where he is given the clothing of a pope. It is called the Crying Room. It is called that because it is there that the burdens and responsibilities of the papacy tend to come crashing down on the new pontiff. Many of them have wept. The best have wept.

PEGGY NOONAN

JUST BEFORE THE BEGINNING

Lily Quinn

What happened to love? Lily whispered to herself. Has someone else taken all that was given out for the universe, or have I just not been trying hard enough? What happened to overwhelming, crushing love, the kind of love that moves earth and heaven, the kind of love my Grandma felt for her Tomas half a century ago in another world in another life, the kind of love my father says he felt for my mother when they first met swimming in that warm Caribbean Sea? Doesn't anyone have that kind of love anymore? Isn't anyone without armor, without walls, without pain? Isn't anyone willing to die for love?

Obviously not tonight.

They called her Lil. Sometimes when they loved her they called her Liliput. She liked that. And sometimes when they didn't love her they called her Lilianne. Tonight nobody called her nothin'. Lily, hungry and broke, stood silently with her back against the wall watching Joshua pack his things while she remained just a stoic stain on the wall, eyes the color of bark, hair like ash, dressed in black—somewhat appropriately, she thought, despite what he had said: "It's only temporary, just to give us a short break. We need it."

He was leaving, he was not coming back, and she was wearing black. She would have liked to clear her throat, say a few things, maybe convince him not to go, but again, she felt that the time for that had passed. When, she didn't know, but it had passed all the same, and now nothing was left for her to do but watch him leave, and maybe chew on some stale pretzels.

Joshua was skinny and red-haired. Turning his muddy eyes to her, he asked, running his hand through his hair—oh how he loved his hair!—if she had anything better to do than to stand there and watch him. She replied that she didn't, not really, no. She went and chewed on some stale pretzels.

She wanted to ask him why he was leaving, but unspoken between them remained his reasons. Unspoken between them much remained. His leaving would have been inconceivable a year ago: how could she handle it, how could she handle *that* well?

She stepped away from the wall, moved toward him, opened her mouth and he waved her off, his eyes glued to the television set. "It's the Stanley Cup final," was all he said, one hand on his CDs, the other on the remote control with which he turned up the sound on the set, turning down the sound on Lily.

And to think that last week for her final paper, her creative-writing professor, as if the previous week's obituary flagellation were not enough, gave them a topic of, *"What would you do today if you knew that today were the last day of your life?"*

She hated that class. She had taken it merely to satisfy an English requirement, but if she knew then what she knew now, she would have taken "Advanced Readings on John Donne" at eight in the morning on Mondays before creative writing on Wednesday at noon. Oh the merciless parade of self-examination! First memory, first heartbreak, most memorable experience, favorite summer vacation, your own obituary (!), and now this.

All Lily fervently hoped at this moment was that today— breaking up with her college boyfriend—would not be the last day of her life.

Her apartment was too small for *Sturm und Drang*. The hall-way served as the living room. In the kitchen the microwave was on top of the only flat counter surface and the drainer was on top of the microwave, dripping the rinsed-out Coke cans into the sink, half of which also served as storage for moldy bread—they did not eat on regular plates, they barely ate at home. There were two bedrooms—hers and Amy's. Tonight she went into Amy's room and lay down on Amy's bed, consciously trying not to roll up into a ball.

During the commercial, Joshua got up off the couch for a drink, glanced in on her and said, "You think you could sleep with Amy? I'm going to have to take my bed back. I'd leave it, but then I'll have nowhere to sleep."

She wanted to reply. She thought she might have something witty to say. But the wittiest thing she could think of was, "What, doesn't Shona have a bed?"

"Don't start that again." He walked into the kitchen.

Lily rolled up into a ball.

Joshua paid a third of the rent. And still she was broke, her diet alternating between old pretzels and Oodles of Noodles. A bagel with cream cheese was a luxury she could afford only on Sundays. Some Sundays she had to decide, newspaper or bagel.

Lily used to read her news online, but now she couldn't afford the twenty bucks for the Internet connection. So there was no Internet, no bagel, and soon no Joshua, who was leaving and taking his bed and a third of the rent with him.

If only she had had the grades to get into New York University downtown instead of City College up on 138th Street. Lily could walk to school like she walked to work and save herself four dollars a day. That was twenty dollars a week, $80 a month. $1040 a year!

How many bagels, how much newspaper, how much coffee that thousand bucks could buy.

Lily was paying nearly $500 a month for her share of the rent. Well, actually, Lily's mother was sending her $500 for her share of the rent, railing at Lily every single month. And coming this May, on the day of her purported, supposed, alleged graduation,

Lily was going to get her last check from the bank of mom. Without Joshua, Lily's share would rise to $750. How in the world was she going to come up with an extra $750 come June? She was already waitressing twenty-five hours a week to pay for her food, her books, her art supplies, her movies. She would have to ask for another shift, possibly two. Perhaps she could work doubles, get up early. She didn't want to think about it. She wanted to be like Scarlett O'Hara and think about it tomorrow—in another book, some fifty years down the line.

The phone rang.

"Has he left, mama?" It was Rachel Ortiz—Amy's other good friend, maybe even best friend, she of the *sudden* ironed *blonde* hair and the perpetual blunt manner. Someone needed to explain to Rachel that just because she was Amy's friend, that did not automatically make her into Lily's friend.

"No." Lily wanted to add that watching the Stanley Cup was slowing him down.

"That bastard," Rachel said anyway.

"But soon," said Lily. "Soon, Rach."

"Is Amy there?"

"No."

"Where is she? On one of her little outings?"

"Just working, I think."

"Well, tomorrow night I don't want you to stay in by yourself. We're going out. My new boyfriend wants to take us to Brooklyn, to a nightclub in Coney Island."

"To Coney Island—on *Monday*?" And then she said, "I'm not up to it. It's a school night."

"School, schmool. You're not staying in by yourself. You're going out with me and Tony." She lowered her voice to say *TOnee*, in a thick Italian accent. "Amy might come too, and she's got a friend for you from Bed-Stuy, who she says is a paTOOtie."

"Oh, for God's sake!" Lily lowered her voice to a whisper. "Joshua's still *here*."

"That bastard," said Rachel and hung up.

4

"What, is she trying to fix you up already?" Joshua said. "Rachel, wasn't it? She hates me."

Lily said nothing.

That night, after the Stanley Cup was over, up and down the five flights of stairs Joshua traipsed, taking his boxes, his crates, his bags to Avenue C and 4th Street, where he was now staying with their mutual friend Dennis, the hairstylist. (Amy had said to her, "Lil, did you ever ask yourself why Joshua would so hastily move in with Dennis? Did you ever think maybe he's also gay?" and Lily replied, "Yes, well, don't tell me, tell that to Shona, the naked girl from upstate New York he was calling on my phone bill.")

Who was going to cut Lily's hair now? Dennis had always cut it in the past. Why did Joshua get to inherit the haircutter? Well, maybe Paul, who was Amy's other best friend, and a colorist, knew how to cut hair. She'd have to ask him.

Joshua had the decency not to ask her to help him, and Lily had the dignity not to offer.

Around 3:00 a.m., he, with his last box in hand, nodded to her, and then left, rushing past her *The Girl in Times Square*, her only ever oil on canvas that she had done when she was twenty and before she met Joshua.

"There are things about you I could never love," he had said to Lily two days ago when all this started to go down on the street.

"If I knew that today were the last day of my life, I'd want to be like the girl in the famous postcard, being thrown back in the middle of Times Square, kissed with passion by a stranger when the war was over.

Except—that isn't me. That is somebody else's dream of a girl in Times Square. Perhaps it's Amy. But it's a fraudulent Lily.

The real Lily would sleep late, until noon at least, with no classes and no work. And then, since the weather would be warm and sunny on her last day, she would go to the lake in

Central Park. She would buy a tuna sandwich and a Snapple iced tea, and a bag of potato chips, and bring a book she was re-reading at the moment—Sula by Toni Morrison—slowly because she had time, and her notebook and pencils. She would spend the afternoon sitting, eating her food, drawing the boats, and Sula's Ajax—with whom she was perversely in love—reading, thinking about what to render next. She'd have a long sit-and-sketch on the rocks and on the way home at night she would go to Times Square pushing past all the people and stand against the wall, looking at the color billboards animating and the towers sparkling, red green traffic lights changing and blue white sirens flashing, the yellow cabs whizzing by. The naked cowboy standing in the street, playing his guitar in his hat and underwear, and the families, the children, the couples, the young and the old, lovers all, taking pictures, laughing, crossing against the lights.

This girl in Times Square stands by the wall while others cross against the light."

Lily turned away from the door and stared out the open window into the night, on Amy's bed, alone.

Allison Quinn

There once was a woman who lived for love. Now she stood and stared out her window. Outside she saw green palms and red rhododendrons and a blue sky and an aqua ocean and gray cliffs and black volcanoes and white sands. She did not look inside her room. She was waiting for her husband to come back from buying mangoes. It was taking him *forever*. She moved the curtain slightly out of the way to catch a movement outside, and sighed, remembering once upon a time when she was young, and had dreamed for the sky and the sea and plenty.

And now she had it.

And once a man put on a record on an old Victrola and took her dancing through their small bedroom. The man was handsome, and she was beautiful, and they spoke a different language then. "*The look of love is in your eyes . . .*" Now the man went for walks by himself under the palms and over the sands. He wet his feet in the ocean and his soul in the ocean too, and then he walked to the fruit stand and bought the juicy mangoes, and the perky salesgirl said they were the best yet, and he glanced at her and smiled as he took them from her hand.

The woman stepped away from the window. He was always walking, always leaving the house. But she knew—he wasn't leaving the house, he was leaving her. He just couldn't *stand* the thought of being with her for an hour alone, couldn't stand the thought of doing something she wanted instead of everything *he* wanted. When she didn't do what he wanted, how he sulked— like a baby. That's all he was, a baby. Do it my way or I won't talk to you, that was him. Well, could she help it if mornings were not the best time for her? Could she help it that in the mornings she could not get up and go for a walk and a swim in all that sunshine. It depressed her beyond all sane measure that at eight in the morning the ocean was so warm, the sun was so strong. If only it would rain, just once! She was done with that damn ocean. And that sun. Those mangoes, that tuna sashimi, that volcanic ash. Done with it.

She bought heavy room-darkening curtains and drew them tight to keep out the day, to make believe it was still night.

She made believe about a lot these days.

She couldn't understand, where was he? When was he going to grace her with his presence? Didn't he know she was sick, she was hungry? Didn't he know she had to eat small meals? That's just it, he didn't care what she needed, all he cared about was what *he* needed. Well, she wasn't going to put a single bite in her mouth. If she fainted from low blood sugar and broke a bone, so much the better. She'd see how he felt then, that he was out all morning and didn't make his sick wife breakfast. She'd see how he'd explain that one to her mother, to their kids. She'd be damned if she put a spoon of sugar into her mouth.

The bedroom door opened slightly. "I'm back. Have you eaten?"

"Of course I haven't eaten!" she spat. "Like you even care. I could croak here like a rat, while you're glibly walking in your fucking Maui without a single thought for me!"

. . . a look that time can't erase . . .

Silently the door closed, and she remained in her darkened room with the drawn shades in the ginger Maui morning, alone.

A Man and a Woman

It's late Friday night and they're in her apartment. They had been to dinner, she invited him for a drink and dancing in a wine bar near where she lives. He said no. He always says no, drinking and dancing in wine bars is not his strong suit, but you have to give it to her—she's plucky. She keeps on asking. Now they're in her bed, and whether this is his strong suit, or whether she has no more attractive options, he doesn't know but she's been showing up every Friday night, so he must be doing something right, though he'd be damned if he knows what it is. The things he gives her, she can get anywhere.

And after he gives them to her, and takes some for himself, she falls contentedly asleep in the crook of his arm, while he lies opened-eyed and in the yellow-blue light coming from the street counts the tin tiles of her tall ceiling. He may look content also—in tonight's ostensible enjoyment of his food and his woman—to someone who has observed him scientifically and empirically, wholly from without. But now in a perversion of nature, the woman is asleep and the man is staring at the ceiling. So what is in him wholly from within?

He is counting the tin tiles. He has counted them before, and what fascinates him is how every time he counts them this late at night, he comes up with a different number.

After he is sure she is asleep, he disentangles himself, gets up off the bed, and takes his clothes into the living room.

She comes out when his shoes are on. He must have jangled his keys. Usually she does not hear him leave. It's dark in the room. They stare at each other. He stands. She stands. "I don't understand why you do this," she says.

"I just have to go."

"Are you going home to your wife?"

"Stop."

"What then?"

He doesn't reply. "You know I go. I always go. Why give me a hard time?"

"Didn't we have a nice evening?"

"We always do."

"So why don't you stay? It's Friday. I'll make you waffles for breakfast."

"I don't do waffles for Saturday breakfast."

Quietly he shuts the door behind him. Loudly she double bolts and chains it, padlocking it if she could.

He is outside on Amsterdam. On the street, the only cars are cabs. The sidewalks are empty, the few barflies straggle in and out. Lights change green, yellow, red. Before he hails a taxi back home, he walks twenty blocks past the open taverns at three in the morning, alone.

PART I
IN THE BEGINNING

*You call yourself free? Free from
what? What is that to Zarathustra!
But your eyes should announce to
me brightly: free for what?*

FRIEDRICH NIETZSCHE

1

Appearing To Be One Thing
When it is in Fact Another

1, 18, 24, 39, 45, 49.

And again:

1, 18, 24, 39, 45, 49.

Reality: *something that has real existence and must be dealt with in real life.*

Illusion: *something that deceives the senses of mind by appearing to exist when it does not, or appearing to be one thing when it is in fact another.*

Miracle: *an event that appears to be contrary to the laws of nature.*

49, 45, 39, 24, 18, 1.

Lily stared at the six numbers in the metro section of *The Sunday Daily News*. She blinked. She rubbed her eyes. She scratched her head. Something was not right. Amy wasn't home, there was no one to ask, and Lily's eyes frequently played tricks on her. Remember last year in the delivery room when she thought her sister gave birth to a boy, and shouted 'BOY!' because they all so wanted a boy, and it turned out to be another girl, the fourth? How could her mind have added on a penis? What was *wrong* with her?

Leaving her apartment she went down the narrow corridor to knock on old Colleen's door in 5F. Fortunately Colleen was always home. Unfortunately Colleen, here since she was a young lass during the potato famine, was legally blind, as Lily to her dismay found out, because Colleen read 29 instead of 49, and 89 instead of 39. By the time Colleen finished with the numbers, Lily was even less sure of them. "Don't worry about it, me dearie," said Colleen sympathetically. "Everyone thinks they be seeing the winnin' numbers."

Lily wanted to say, not her, not she, not I, as ever just a smudge in the reflected sky. I don't see the winning numbers. I might see penises, but I don't imagine portholes of the universe that never open up to me.

She was born a second-generation American and the youngest of four children to a homemaker mother who always wanted to be an economist, and a *Washington Post* journalist father who always wanted to be a novelist. He loved sports, and was not particularly helpful with the children. Some might have called him insensitive and preoccupied. Not Lily.

Her grandmother was worthy of more than a paragraph in a summary of Lily's life at this peculiar juncture, but there it was. In Lily's story, Danzig-born Klavdia Roza Venkewicz ran from Nazi-occupied Poland with her baby, Lily's mother, across destroyed Germany. After years in three displaced persons camps, she managed to get herself and her child on a boat to New York. She had called the baby Olenka, but changed it to a more American-sounding Allison, just as she changed her own name from Klavdia Roza to Claudia Rose and Venkewicz to Vail.

Lily lived all her life in and around the city of New York. She lived in Astoria, and Woodside, and Kew Gardens, and when they really moved up in the world, Forest Hills, all in the borough of Queens. Her dream was to live in Manhattan, and now she was living it but she had been living it broke.

When George Quinn, who had been the New York City correspondent for the *Post*, was suddenly transferred down to D.C. because of cost-cutting internal restructuring, Lily refused to go and stayed with her grandmother in Brooklyn, commuting to Forest Hills High School to finish out her senior year. That was some wild year she had without parental supervision. Having calmed down slightly, she went to City College of New York up on 138th Street in Harlem partly because she couldn't afford to go anywhere else, her parents having spent all their college savings on her brother—who went to Cornell. Her mother, fortunately guilt-ridden over going broke on Andrew, paid Lily's rent.

As far as the meager rations of youthful love, Lily, too quiet for New York City, went almost without until she found Joshua— a waiter who wanted to be an actor. His red hair was not what drew her to him. It was his past sufferings and his future dreams— both things Lily was a tiny bit short on.

Lily liked to sleep late and paint. But she liked to sleep late most of all. She drew unfinished faces and tugboats on paper and doodles on contracts, and lilies all over her walls, and murals of boats and patches of water. She hoped she was never leaving the apartment because she could never duplicate the work. She had been very serious about Joshua until she found out he wasn't serious about her. She read intensely but sporadically, she liked her Natalie Merchant and Sarah McLachlan loud and in the heart, and she loved sweets: Mounds bars, chocolate-covered jell rings, double-chocolate Oreos, chewy Chips-Ahoy, Entenmann's chocolate cake with chocolate icing, and pound cake.

One of her sisters, Amanda, was a model mother of four model girls, and a model suburban wife of a model suburban husband. The other sister, Anne, was a model career woman, a financial journalist for *KnightRidder*, frequently and imperfectly attached, yet always impeccably dressed. Her brother, Cornell having paid off, was a U.S. Congressman.

The most interesting things in Lily's life happened to other people, and that's just how Lily liked it. She loved sitting around into the early morning hours with Amy, Paul, Rachel, Dennis, hearing their stories of violent, experimental love lives, hitch-hiking, South Miami Beach Bacchanalian feasts. She liked other people to be young and reckless. For herself, she liked her lows not to be too low and her highs not to be too high. She soaked up Amy's dreams, and Joshua's dreams, and Andrew's dreams, she went to the movies three days a week—oh the vicarious thrill of them! She meandered joyously through the streets of New York, read the paper in St. Mark's Square, and lived on in today, sleeping, painting, dancing, dreaming on a future she could not fathom. She loved her desultory life, until yesterday and today.

Today, this. Six numbers.

And yesterday Joshua.

Ten good things about breaking up with Joshua:
10. TV is permanently off.
 9. Don't have to share my bagel and coffee with him.
 8. Don't have to pretend to like hockey, sushi, golf, quiche, or actors.
 7. Don't have to listen to him complaining about the short shrift he got in life.
 6. Don't have to listen about his neglectful father, his non-existent mother.
 5. Don't have to get my belly button pierced because he liked it.
 4. Don't have to stay up till four pretending we have similar interests.
 3. No more wet towels on my bed.
 2. Don't have to blame him for the empty toilet roll.

And the number one good thing about breaking up with Joshua:
 1. Don't have to feel bad about my small breasts.

Ten bad things about breaking up with Joshua:
10. There
 9. Are
 8. Things
 7. About
 6. You

16

5. I
4. Could
3. Never
2. Love.

Oh, and the number one bad thing about breaking up with Joshua . . .
1. Without him, I can't pay my rent.

1, 18, 24, 39, 45, 49.

Her hair had been down her back, but last week after he left she had sheared it to her neck, as girls frequently did when they broke up with their boyfriends. Snip, snip. It pleased Lily to be so self-actualized. To her it meant she wasn't wallowing in despair.

Barely even needing to brush the choppy hair now, Lily threw on her jacket and left the apartment. She headed down to the grocery store where she had bought the ticket. After going down four of the five flights, she trudged back upstairs—to put her shoes on. When she finally got to the store on 10th and Avenue B, she opened her mouth, fumbled in her pocket, and realized she'd left the ticket by the shoe closet.

Groaning in frustration, tensing the muscles in her face, she grimaced at the store clerk, a humorless Middle Eastern man with a humorless black beard, and went home. She didn't even look for the ticket. She saw the mishaps as a sign, knew the numbers couldn't have matched, *couldn't* have. Not *her* lottery ticket! She lay on Amy's bed and waited for the phone to ring. She stared out the window, trying to make her mind a blank. The bedroom windows faced the inner courtyard of several apartment buildings. There were many greening trees and long narrow yards. Most people never pulled down the shades on the windows that faced inward. The trees, the grass were perceived to be shields from the world. Shields maybe from the world but not from Lily's

17

eyes. What kind of a pervert stared into other people's windows anyway?

Lily stared into other people's windows. She stared into other people's lives.

One man sat and read the paper in the morning. For two hours he sat. Lily drew him for her art class. She drew another lady, a young woman, who, after her shower, always leaned out of her window and stared at the trees. For her improv class, she drew her favorite—the unmarried couple who in the morning walked around naked and at night had sex with the shades up and the lights on. She watched them from behind her own shades, embarrassed for them and herself. They obviously thought only the demons were watching them, judging from the naughty things they got up to. Lily knew they were unmarried because when he wasn't home, she read "Today's Bride" magazine and then fought with him each Saturday night after drinking.

Lily had drawn their cat many times. But today she got out her sketchbook and mindlessly penciled in the number, 49, 49, 49, 49, 49, 49, 49, 49, 49, 49, 49. It couldn't be, right? It was just a cosmic mistake? Of course! Of course it was, the numbers may have been correct, but they were for a different date: how many times has she heard about that? She sprung up to check.

No, no. Numbers matched. Date matched too.

She went into Amy's room. She and Amy were going to go to the movies today, but Amy wasn't home, and there was no sign of her; she hadn't come home from wherever she was yesterday.

Lily waited. Amy always gave the appearance of coming *right* back.

Lily. Her mother forgot to put the third L into her name. Though she herself was an Allison with a double L. Oh, for God's sake, what was she thinking about? Was Lilianne jealous of her mother's double L? Where was her mind going with this? Away from six numbers. Away from 49, 45, 39, 24, 18, 1.

18

She had a shower. She dried her pleasingly boyish hair, she looked through *The Daily News* and settled on the 2:15 at the Angelica of *The Butcher Boy*.

While walking past the grocery store she thought of something, and taking a deep breath, stepped inside.

"Excuse me," she said, coughing from acute discomfort. "What's the lottery up to at the last drawing?" She felt ridiculous even asking. She was red in the pale face.

"For how many numbers?" the clerk said gruffly.

Not looking at him, Lily thought about not replying. She finally said to the Almond Joy bars, "All of them."

"All six? Let's see . . . ah, yes, eighteen million dollars. But it depends who else wins."

"Of course." She backed out of the store.

"Usually a few people win."

"Uh-huh."

"Did your numbers come in?"

"No, no."

Lily got out as fast as she could.

18 was one of the numbers. So was 1.

That was in April. After Joshua Lily swore off men for life, concluding that there wasn't a single decent one in the entire tri-state area, except for Paul and he was incontrovertibly (as if there were any other way) gay. Rachel kept offering her somewhat unwelcome matchmaking services, Paul and Amy kept offering their welcome support services. They went to see other movies besides *The Butcher Boy*, and *The Phantom Menace* and sat until all hours drinking tequila and discussing Joshua's various demerits to make Lily feel better. And eventually both the tequila and the discussions did.

Lily—making her lottery ticket into wall art for the time being—affixed it with red thumbtacks to her corkboard that had thumbtacked on it all scraps from her life: photos of her together with her brother, some of her two sisters, photos of her grandma, photos

19

of her six nieces, photos of her father, of her cat who died five years ago from feline leukemia, of Amy, and drawings of some of her neighbors from the courtyard, report cards from college (not very good) and even from high school (not much better). The wall used to have photos of Joshua, but she took them down, drew over his face, erasing him, leaving a black hole, and then put them back.

And Amy, who had prided herself on reading only *The New York Times*, never read a rag like *The Daily News*, and because she hadn't, she didn't know what Lily's grandmother knew and brought to Lily's attention one Thursday when Lily was visiting.

Before she left, she knocked on Amy's door, and when there was no answer she slightly opened it, saying "Ames?" But the bed was made, the red heart, white hand-stitched quilt symmetrically spread out in all the corners.

Holding onto the door handle Lily looked around, and when she didn't see anything to stop her gaze she closed the door behind her. She left Amy a note on her door. *"Ames, Are we still on for either The Mummy or The Matrix tomorrow? Call me at Grandma's, let me know. Luv, Lil."*

She went to Barnes & Noble on Astor Place and bought June issues of *Ladies Home Journal, Redbook, Cosmopolitan* (her grandmother liked to keep abreast of what the "young people were up to"), and she also picked up copies of *National Review, American Spectator, The Week, The Nation,* and *The Advocate.* Her grandmother liked to know what *everybody* was up to. In her grandmother's house the TV was always on, picture in picture, CNN on the small screen, C-Span on the big. Grandma didn't like to listen to CNN, just liked to see their mouths move. When Congress was in session, Grandma sat in her one comfortable chair, her magazines around her, her glasses on, and watched and listened to every vote. "I want to know what your brother is up to." When Congress was not in session, she was utterly lost and for weeks would putter around in the kitchen or clean obsessively, or drink bottomless cups of strong coffee while she read her news-magazines and occasionally watched C-Span for parliamentary news from Britain. To the question of what she had done with herself before C-Span, Grandma would reply, "I was not alive before C-Span."

She lived in Brooklyn on Warren Street, between Clinton and Court in an ill-kept brownstone marred further not by the disrepair of the front steps but by the bars on the windows. And not just on the street-level windows. Or just the parlor windows. Or the second floor windows, or the third. But *all* the windows. All windows in the house, four floors, front and back, were covered in iron bars. The stone façade on the building itself was crumbling but the iron bars were in pristine shape. Her grandmother, for reasons that were never made clear, had not ventured *once* out of her house—in *six* years. Not once.

Lily rang the bell.

"Who is it?" a voice barked after a minute.

"It's me."

"Me who?" Strident.

"Me, your granddaughter."

Silence.

"Lily. Lily Quinn." She paused. "I used to live with you. I come every Thursday."

A few minutes later there was the noise of the vestibule door unlatching, of three locks unlocking, of the chain coming off, and then came the noise of the front door's three dead-bolt locks unbolting, of a titanium sliding lock sliding, of another chain coming off, and finally of the front door being opened, just a notch, maybe eight inches, and a voice rushing through, "Come in, come in, don't dawdle."

Lily squeezed in through the opening, wondering if her grandmother would open the door wider if Lily herself were wider. Would she, for example, open the door wider for Amanda who'd had four kids?

Inside was cool and dark and smelled as if the place hadn't

been aired out in weeks. "Grandma, why don't you open the windows? It's stuffy."

"It's not Memorial Day, is it?" replied her grandmother, a white-haired, small woman, portly and of serious mien, who took the bags out of Lily's hands and carried them briskly to the kitchen at the back of the house.

Grandma's home was tidy except for the newspapers that were piled on top of the round kitchen table, *The New York Times* first, then *The Observer*, then *The Wall Street Journal*, and then the tabloids, *Newsday*, *Post* and *News*.

"Do you want a cup of tea?"

"No, I'm going to have to get going soon."

"Get going! You just got here."

"Last week of finals, Grandma. Perhaps you've heard." Lily smiled just in case her grandmother decided to take offense.

"I've heard, I've heard plenty. How are the subways this morning?"

"They're fine—"

"Oh, sure, you can't even fake a polite answer anymore. Did you stand far from the yellow line?"

"I did better than that," said Lily, putting milk in the refrigerator. "I sat down on the bench."

Her grandmother squirmed. "Oh, Lily, how is that better? Sitting on that filth-covered bench, how many of those people who sat on it before washed their clothes that morning? And they're sitting next to you, breathing on you, watching over your shoulder, seeing what you're reading, hearing your Walkman songs, such loss of privacy. All the homeless sit on that bench."

Lily wanted to remark that, no, all the homeless were lying on the steps of the 53rd Street church on Fifth Avenue, but said nothing.

"From now on, I give you money, you take a cab to see me."

Lily wanted to button up her jacket, if only she had one. "So what's going on with you?"

"I'll tell you what's going on," said her grandmother, Claudia Vail, seventy-nine years old, widow, war survivor, death-camp survivor, all cataracts removed, a new pacemaker installed, arthritis in check, no mysterious bumps, growths, or distensions, but widow first and foremost, "On Sunday a child fell out of his sixth-floor apartment in the projects and died. This is on a *Sunday*. What are the parents doing if not looking after their child on a Sunday? On Monday a five-year-old girl was stabbed and killed by her brother and his friend who were supposed to be looking after her. The mother when she returned home from work said, 'It's so unlike him. He's usually such a nice boy.' Then we find out that this boy, age eleven, had already spent three years in juvenile detention for beating his grandmother blind. The mother apparently overlooked that when she left her child with him."

"Grandma," Lily said feebly, putting up her hands in a defensive gesture.

"Last Friday, a vegan couple in Canarsie were arrested for feeding their child soybeans and tofu from the day she was born. That mother's milk must have been all dried up because at sixteen months the child weighed ten pounds, the weight of a two-to-three-month-old."

"Grandma," said Lily helplessly. Her grandmother was cornering her between herself and the fridge. Lily could tell by her grandmother's eyes she was a long way from done. "Did anything happen on Saturday?"

"On Saturday your sister and that no-good man of hers came over—"

"Which sister?"

"And I told her," Claudia continued, "that she was lucky not to have any children."

"Oh. That one. Grandma, if life is no good here, why don't you move? Move to Bedford with Amanda. Nothing ever happens in Bedford. Hence the name. City of beds."

"Who said life is not good here? Life is perfect. And are you

23

insane? With Amanda and her four kids? So she could take care of me, too? Why would I do that to her? Why would I do that to myself?"

"Did José bring your groceries this week?" The kitchen looked a bit bare.

"Not anymore. I fired him."

"You did?" Lily was alarmed. Not for her grandmother—for herself. If José was no longer delivering groceries, then who was going to? "Why did you fire him?"

"Because in the paper last Saturday was a story of an old woman just like me who was robbed by the delivery boy—robbed and raped, I think."

"Was it José?" Lily said, trying not to sound weary. Struggling not to rub the bridge of her nose.

"No, it wasn't José. But one can never be too careful, can one, Liliput?"

"No, one certainly cannot."

"Your door, is it locked? To your *bedroom*?" Grandmother shook her head. "Are you still living with those bums, those two who cannot keep their sink clean? Yes, your father told me about his visit to your abode. He told me what a sty it was. I want you to find a new place, Lil. Find a new place. I'll pay the realtor fee."

Lily was staring at her grandmother with such confusion that for a moment she actually wondered if perhaps she'd never spoken of her living arrangements with her grandmother, or whether there had been too many residential changes for her grandmother to keep track of.

"Grandma," she said slowly. "I haven't lived with those bums, as you like to call them, in years. I've been living with Amy, in a different apartment, remember? On 9th Street and Avenue C?" She looked at her grandmother with concern.

Her grandmother was lost in thought. "Ninth Street, Ninth Street," she muttered. "Why does that ring a bell . . . ?"

"Um, because I live there?"

"No, no." Claudia stared off into the distance. Suddenly her gaze cleared. "Oh yes! Last Saturday, same day as the old woman's battery and rape, a small piece ran in the *Daily News*. Apparently three weeks ago there was a winning lottery ticket issued at a deli on the corner of 10th and Avenue B, and the winner hasn't come to claim it yet."

Lily was entirely mute except for the whooshing sound of her blinking lashes, sounding deafening even to herself. "Oh, yeah?" she said and could think of nothing else. The sink faucet tapped out a few water droplets. The sun was bright through the windows.

"Can you imagine? *The News* publishes the numbers every day in hopes that the person recognizes them and comes forward. Eighteen million dollars." She tutted. "Imagine. By the way, they publish the numbers so often I know them by heart. Some of the numbers I could have chosen myself. Forty-nine, the year I came to America, thirty-nine, the year my Tomas went to war. Forty-five, my Death March." She clucked with delight and disappointment. "Do you go to that deli?"

"Um—not anymore."

"Maybe it's lost," said Claudia. "Maybe it's lying unclaimed in the gutter somewhere because it fell out of the winner's pocket. Watch the sidewalks, Liliput, around your building. An unsigned lottery ticket is a bearer bond."

·"A what what?"

"A bearer bond."

"What does that mean?"

"It means," said Claudia, "that it belongs to the bearer. You find it, it's yours."

Why did Lily immediately want to go home and sign her ticket? "What are the chances of finding a winning lottery ticket, Grandma?"

"Better than the chances of winning one," replied Claudia in a no-nonsense voice. "So how is that Amy? She's the one who spent last Thanksgiving with us instead of that no-good boyfriend of yours? How is *he*?"

25

Are there any men who are not no-good? Lily wondered but was too sheepish to ask, since it appeared that her grandmother was right at least about Joshua. It was time she told her. "She is fine, and . . . we're no longer together. He moved out a month ago."

For a moment her grandmother was silent, and then she threw up her arms to the ceiling. "So there is a God," she said.

Lily's face must not have registered the same level of boundless joy because Claudia said, "Oh, come on. You should be glad to be rid of him."

"Well . . . not as glad as you."

"He's a bum. You would have supported him for the rest of your life, the way your sister supports her no-good boyfriend." —and then without a break—"Is Amy graduating with you in a few weeks?"

"Not *with* me," said Lily evasively. She didn't want to lie, but she also didn't want to tell her grandmother that Amy was *actually* graduating.

"When is it exactly?"

"May 28, I think."

"You *think?*"

"Everything is all right, Grandma, don't worry."

"Come in the living room," Claudia said. "I want to talk to you about something. Not about the war. I'll save that for Saturday's poker game." She smiled. "Are you coming?"

"Can't. Have to work." They sat on the sofa covered in plastic. "Grandma, you live here, why don't you take the Mylar off? That's what people do when they live someplace. They take the plastic off."

"I don't want to dirty all my furniture. After all, you'll be getting it when I die. Yes, yes, don't protest. I'm leaving all my furniture to you. You don't have any. Now stop shaking your head and look what I have for you."

Lily looked. In her fingers, Grandmother held an airplane ticket.

"Where am I going?"

"Maui."

Lily shook her head. "Oh, no. Absolutely not."

"Yes, Lily. Don't you want to see Hawaii?"

"No! I mean, yes, but I can't."

"I got you an open-ended ticket. Go whenever you want for as long as you want. Probably best to go soon though, before you get a real job. It'll be good for you."

"No, it won't."

"It will. You're looking worn around the gills lately. Like you haven't slept. Go get a tan."

"Don't want sleep, don't want a tan, don't want to go."

"It'll be good for your mother."

"No, it won't. And what about my job?"

"What, the Noho Star is the only diner in Manhattan?"

"I don't want to get another waitressing job."

Claudia squeezed Lily's hands. "You need to be thinking beyond waitressing, Liliput. You're graduating *college*. After six years, finally! But right now your mother could use you in Hawaii."

"Why do you say that?"

"Let's just say," Grandma said evasively, "I think she's feeling lonely. Amanda is busy with her family, Anne is busy, I don't even know with what. Oh, I know she pretends she works, but then why is she always broke? Your brother, he's busy, too, but since he's actually running our country, I'll give him a break for not calling his own mother more often. Your mother is feeling very isolated."

"But Papi is with her. He retired to be with her!"

"Yeah, well, I don't know how that whole retirement thing is working out. Besides you know your father. Even when he's there, he's not there."

"We told them not to move to Hawaii. We told them about rock fever, we told them about isolation. We told them."

"So? They're sixty. You're twenty-four and you don't listen. Why should they listen?"

"Because we were right."

27

"Oh, Liliput, if everyone listened to the people who were right there would be no grief in the world, and yet—do you want me to go through last week with you again?"

"No, no."

"Was there grief?"

"Some, yes."

"Go to your mother. Or mark my words—there will be grief there, too."

Lily struggled up off the 1940s saran-wrap-covered yellow and yellowing couch that someday would be hers. "There's grief there aplenty, Grandma."

She was vacillating on Hawaii as she vacillated on everything—painstakingly. Amy was insistent that Lily should definitely go. Paul thought she should go. Rachel thought she probably should go. Rick at Noho Star said he would give her a month off if she went now before all the kids came back from college and it got busy for the summer.

She called her brother over the weekend to see what he thought, and his wife picked up the phone and said, "Oh, it's you." And then Lily heard into the phone, "ANDREW! It's your sister!" and when her brother said something, Miera answered, "The one who always needs money." And Andrew came on the phone laughing, and said, "Miera, you have to be more specific than that."

Lily laughed herself. "Andrew, I need no money. I need advice."

"I'm rich on that. I'll even throw you a couple of bucks if you want."

His voice always made her smile. Her whole life it made her smile. "Can you see me for lunch this week?"

"Can't, Congress is in session. What's up? I was going to call you myself. You won't believe who's staying with me."

"Where?"

"In D.C."

"Who?"

"Our father, Lil."

"What?"

"Yup."

"He's in D.C.? Why?"

"Aren't you the journalist's daughter with the questions. Why, I don't know. He left Maui with two big suitcases. I think he is thinking of un-retiring. His exact words? 'No big deal, son. I'm just here to smooth out the transition for Greenberger who's taking over for me.'"

"Meaning . . ."

"Meaning, I can't take another day with your mother."

"Oh, Andrew, oh, dear." Lily dug her nails into the palms of her hands. "No wonder Grandma bought me a ticket to go to Maui. She's so cagey, that Grandma. She never comes out and tells me exactly what she wants. She is always busy manipulating."

"She wants you to do what she wants you to do but out of your own accord."

"Fat chance of that. When is Papi going back? I don't want to go unless he's there."

"You'll be waiting your whole life. I don't think he's going back."

"Stop it."

"Where are you?"

"I'm home, why?"

"Are you . . . alone?"

"Yes." She lowered her voice. "What do you want to tell me?"

"Are you sitting . . . listening?"

"Yes."

"Go to Maui now, Liliput. I can't believe I'm saying this. But you should go. Really. Get out of the city for a while."

"I can't *believe* you're saying this. I don't see you going."

"I'd go if I weren't swamped. Quartered first, but I'd go."

"Yes, exactly."

"Did I mention . . . gladly quartered?"

29

After having a good chuckle, Andrew and Lily made a deal—he would work on their father in D.C. in between chairing the appropriations committee and filibustering bill 2740 on farm subsidies, and she would go and soothe their mother in between sunbathing and tearing her hair out.

"Andrew, is it true what I heard from Amanda, are you running for the U.S. Senate seat in the fall?"

"I'm thinking about it. I'm exploring my options, putting together a commission. Don't want to do it if I can't win."

"Oh, Andrew. What can I do? I'll campaign for you again. Me and Amy."

"Oh, you girls will be too busy with your new lives to help me in the fall. Leaving school, getting real jobs? But thanks anyway. I gotta go. I'll call you in Maui. You want me to wire you some money?"

"Yes, please. A thousand? I'll pay you back."

"I'm sure. Is that why you keep buying lottery tickets every week? To pay me back?"

"You know," said Lily, "I've stopped buying those lottery tickets. I love you."

"Love you, too, kid."

2

Hawaii

Hawaii. Hawaii was not Poland. It was not the wetlands of north-ern Danzig, rainy, cold, swampy, mosquito-infested Danzig whence Allison had sprung during war. Hawaii was the anti-Poland. Two years ago Lily's mother and father had gone on an investigative trip to Maui and came back at the end of a brief visit with a $200,000 condo. Apparently they learned everything they could about Maui in two weeks—how much they loved it, how beautiful it was, how clean, how quiet, how fresh the mangoes, how delicious the raw tuna, how warm the water, and how much they would enjoy their retirement there.

Lily knew how her father was taking to his retirement, enjoy-ing it now in his only son's congressional apartment in the nation's capital.

How her mother was taking to Hawaii Lily also could not tell right away because her mother was not there to pick her up from Kahului airport. After she had waited a suitable amount of time—which was not a second over ninety minutes—she called her mother, who had come on the phone and sounded as if she had been sleeping. Lily took a taxi. The narrow road between the mountain pass leading to the Kihei and Wailea side of Maui where her parents lived was pretty but was somehow made less attractive by Lily's crankiness at her mother's non-appearance.

She rang the doorbell for several minutes and then ended up having to pay the cab driver herself ($35!!! —the equivalent of all tips for a four-hour morning shift). After ringing the bell, Lily tried the door and found it open. Her mother was in the bedroom asleep on top of the bed and would not be awakened.

Some hours later, Allison stumbled out of her room. Lily was watching TV.

"You're here," she said, holding on to the railing that led down two steps from the hallway to the sunken living-room.

Lily stood up. "Mom, you were supposed to pick me up from the airport."

"I didn't know you were coming today," said her mother. "I thought you were coming tomorrow." She spoke slowly. She was wearing a house robe and her short hair was gray—she had stopped coloring it. Her face was puffy, her eyes nearly swollen closed.

Lily was going to raise her voice, say a few stern things, but her mother looked terrible. She wasn't used to that. Her mother was usually perfectly coiffed, perfectly made up, perfectly dressed, perfect. Lily turned her frustrated gaze back to the TV. Allison stood for a moment, then squared her shoulders and left the living room. Soon Lily got up and went to bed in her father's room. Of course Grandma was right—something needed fixing. But Lily was the child, and Allison was the mother. The child wasn't supposed to fix the mother. The mother was supposed to fix the child. That was the natural order of things in the universe.

The next morning Allison came out, all showered and fresh, with mascara and lipstick on her face. Her hair was brushed, pulled back, her eyebrows were tweezed. There was even polish on the nails. She apologized for yesterday's mishap, and made Lily eggs and coffee as they talked about Lily's life a little bit, and it was then that Lily broke the bad news that she didn't think she would be graduating this year because she didn't think she had enough credits.

"How many credits are you short?" asked Allison.

"A few."

"Wait till your father finds out."

"Mom, you can't still be threatening me with my father. I'm twenty-four."

"Have you noticed by the way that your father isn't here?"

Lily coughed. "I've noticed. Andrew told me he's in D.C."

Now Allison coughed. "Yes, whatever. He said he was going on freelance business. He said Andrew asked him for help in preparation for the fall campaign. It's all lies. That's all they both do, is lie." Turning away, she got up and went away into her bedroom. When Lily knocked to ask if she was coming to the beach, Allison said she wasn't feeling up to going.

The Mauian beach couldn't help but erase some of the bad taste in Lily's mouth. She imagined being here with Joshua, having money, a car, snorkeling, whale watching, biking at dawn to volcanoes, hiking in rainforests, swimming in water that in her great enthusiasm felt like liquid gold. It was enough to get her good and properly depressed about her own situation and to forget her mother and what more could one want from paradise, but to forget your mother's troubles and remember your own?

Strangely, Hawaii was able to overcome even romantic disillusionments, for it looked and smelled and felt as if God were watching from up close. She had never seen water so green or the sky so blue, or the rhododendrons so red. She had never seen anyone happier than a guy who was swinging on a hammock in his backyard on the ocean and reading his book. Lily didn't know how he could be reading. You couldn't look away from that ocean. She was not hot, and when she walked into the water she was not cold. The water and the air were the same temperature. When she finished swimming and came out, she did not feel wet. She thought she could not get a suntan in weather that felt so mild, yet when she pulled away the strap of her bathing suit, she saw white underneath it, and next to it skin that was decidedly not white. That made her incredulous and happy and when she returned she was ready for *rapprochement.*

33

But in the darkened condo, Allison was still lying down, and Lily, not wanting to disturb her mother, went into her own room. It was only four o'clock in the afternoon.

She had a nap, and at six when she came out, her mother, her hair all done, and her make-up on, was ironing a skirt in the living room. "Come on, do you have anything nice to wear? Or do you want me to lend you something? I'll take you to a wonderful oceanside café your father and I go to sometimes. It's dressy, though, can't go there in that little bikini you're wearing."

"I have a dress."

"Well, let's go. They have great lobster."

All dressed and perfumed they went. Watching her mother walk in so elegant, so slim, so tall in her high-heeled shoes, smile at the host and be escorted on his arm to their beachside table, Lily thought that her father was right—when Allison was on, there was no woman in the room, regardless of age, more beautiful. Anne, Amanda, Lily, they inherited some of their mother's remarkable physical traits, but parceled out, not in total, whereas their mother had all her remarkable physical traits to herself. The thick, wavy, auburn hair, the wide apart, slightly slanted gray eyes, the regal nose, the high cheekbones, the perfect mouth, elegant and slender like the rest of her. Amanda got the hair and the nose, Anne got the height and the cheekbones and the slimness. Anne got a lot. Lily got no height, no cheekbones, no hair, and no gray eyes. She got the slant of the eyes and a certain fluid grace of the mouth and the neck and the arms.

Before the water was poured, Allison said, "I'm not feeling well, Lil. This medicine I'm taking for my stomach is making me feel awful. I don't know why I'm taking it."

"Why are you?"

"Why, why. Because the doctor told me to, that's why. I have a great problem with my stomach. You know how sick I am."

Lily stared straight ahead. Ten years ago, Allison had an emergency operation for a perforated ulcer.

Ten years ago!

"You didn't ask about Joshua, Mom."

"How is that Joshua?"

"We broke up. Rather, he broke up with me."

"He did? Why? I thought you got along so well." She managed to inflect but just barely.

"Not really. I wasn't a good enough listener for him, I think. All he wanted to do was talk about himself."

"Ah, well. You'll find somebody else. You're still so young." She sighed operatically. "Not like me. I'm so depressed, Lily."

Of course you are. "Mom, how can you be depressed in a place like this? Look all around you." Where depression was loss of color, Hawaii was color's surfeit.

"Oh, what's Hawaii to me? I'm so unhappy. Don't you know you carry what's inside you wherever you go?"

Lily supposed. For Hemingway, Paris was a moveable feast. For her grandmother it was Poland—one word synonymous with apocalypse and iniquity and kielbasa. Lily's mother's moveable feast was misery.

Not this conversation *again*. "Why are you unhappy?" she said, trying herself to inflect, trying and failing, trying not to let life-long impatience creep into her voice. "Why are you unhappy? You have a beautiful life. You don't have to work. You don't have to worry about money. You can travel, you can read, you can swim, fish, snorkel. You have all your faculties, plus a husband who loves you."

Allison sighed again.

"Mom, Papi loves you."

"Oh, Lily, you're so naïve." She shook her head and looked into her food. "What is this love you talk about? Once, your father and I, true, we had love. But that was such a long time ago." She gnashed on her teeth. "Your father is very cruel. You don't even know."

Their lobster was brought. Lily tried to remember her first sixteen years of life with her mother and father. "Papi's not cruel." Papi was too passive to be cruel, she wanted to say.

"This is what I mean about naïve! How can I even talk to you about this if you won't listen to me."

"I'm listening," said Lily, but wished she weren't. She kept picking at her lobster with a fork. Her mother stopped eating completely.

"Your father is very controlling, very unkind. And he doesn't understand my depression, he doesn't understand how unhappy I am, and worse, he doesn't care. He is like you—he says, what do you have to be depressed about."

"Mom," Lily said quietly. "Answer me. Answer him. What do you have to be depressed about?"

Tears appeared in Allison's eyes. "My whole life is a complete failure."

"Why do you say this?" Lily wished she were more outraged. She wanted to be outraged. If this were the first time she was hearing it, she might be. Soon her mother would wave off mention of the four children she had ably raised, of the six grandchildren she had, of the various happy lives of her offspring, of her son, the congressman! She would bring forth mention of a job she didn't get when she became pregnant with Lily, as if that job would have been the panacea for the ills of the currently afflicted. She would bring forth Lily's father, and how Allison's whole life had revolved around him. "He was the tree under whose shadow we all fell."

Did Allison just say that, or was the voice inside Lily's head so frigging loud?

She looked up at her mother, who nodded. "Yes, yes, it's true, you, too, Lily, you, too, were under his shadow. Under his and Andrew's. I don't know why you girls love Andrew so much, he was never there for you. Especially for you. He would take you out once a month to the movies, and you just thought he was a gift from God, why? I would spend all day, every day with you, parks, bike rides, ice skating, movies, book stores, and I never got you to look at me with a hundredth of the affection you looked at him. And you ask me why I'm bitter."

36

"I didn't ask," Lily said.

"My son—is he all right, by the way? Now that his father is not here he stopped calling."

"He doesn't call anybody."

"What's your excuse? Or your sisters'? None of you ever call me. Amanda has more kids than anybody and she calls me the most, and that's hardly ever. Just you wait, wait till you're my age. I hope God will give you daughters as ungrateful as yourself."

To say Lily wished she were anywhere but here would have been like saying she preferred to sleep in a comfortable bed rather than on a bed of rusty nails.

"Mom," she said, "you could be in New York, seeing us every week. But you moved to Hawaii. What do you want?"

"To die," said Allison. "Sometimes that's all I want, relief from the blackness." She took Lily's hand. "Daughter, I think of killing myself sometimes, but I'm too afraid of God. I think of killing myself every day."

Lily took her hand away. Did this, or did this not, count as psychological abuse? She thought it did. "I can't believe you're telling me this."

"Daughters are supposed to be friends to their mothers in their old age."

"I think they're supposed to be daughters first. I can't believe you're telling me you want to die. Do you understand how wrong that is?" If only it had been the first time she were hearing it. But she had a vivid memory of being thirteen years old when her mother took her into the bedroom and told her calmly that she only had three months to live. Still, every time Lily heard it, it sounded like the first time. It felt like the first time.

"I'm not telling you to upset you. I'm telling you so you can be prepared. So you know that it wasn't out of the blue. Your father, if he was a different man, maybe my life would be different. If only he understood me, sympathized with me."

"Ma, Papi put food on our table for over forty years. Fed us, clothed us, paid for our college."

"Could barely afford City College for you," said Allison. "Didn't have anything left for you."

"City College is fine," said Lily.

"And you're repaying his kindness by refusing to graduate. You know we can't afford to keep you. We pay for your apartment and for your grandmother's house, and taxes and maintenance for this condo. We're completely broke because we're keeping three different homes."

"I'll get more hours at Noho Star. I'll be fine."

"Yes, but your grandmother, what about her? She's not going anywhere, is she?"

"Guess not. Guess your mother is not going anywhere."

Allison said nothing, but busied herself in pretending to pull out pieces of her lobster. "I can't believe you haven't graduated. Six years completely down the toilet. Six years of college so you can wash dishes at a diner. Well, I hope you're a good dishwasher. Certainly you've had enough education to be the very best."

Lily did not eat one more bite of her lobster. What had Andrew said, she should go to Maui and soothe their mother? Had anyone in the history of the universe ever had such a dumb idea? She was the exact wrong person for that sort of thing. Lily couldn't soothe her mother into a massage.

And the next afternoon when she knocked on her mother's door to ask her to come to the beach, Allison was lying down. "I've been to the beach. I don't want to go anywhere."

"You haven't been to the beach with me. Come."

"Leave me alone, will you?" said Allison. "You're just like your father. Stop forcing me into your pointless regimens."

Lily went alone. How could she manage even another day?

But it's Hawaii, Hawaii! The rainforests, the volcanoes. What would she prefer, yesterday's dinner conversation, or the beach by herself? The choice was so clear.

And so it was the beach by herself, and lunch, and walks

through the palms, and the sunsets, and the community pool at the condo.

Days and days went by. Concentration drained out of Lily. She was unable to focus long enough to sketch. She kept rendering the same palms over and over. Charcoal was an insult to Hawaii, watercolors did not do justice to Hawaii, and oil paints she did not have, nor a canvas for them. All she had was her charcoal pencils and her sketchbook, and there was nothing to draw in Maui with charcoal except the inside of her mother's colorless apartment and the numbers 1, 18, 24, 39, 45, 49.

Andrew had not called to tell her how it was going with Papi. Amy had not called. She had not heard from Joshua.

For hours during the day, Lily busied her mind with being blighted with the lottery ticket. Cursed.

Simply, this is what she believed: she believed that the universe showed each of us certain things, that it made certain things open.

Most people lived a peaceful life with nothing ever happening to them. But into some families other things fell. Some families were afflicted with random tragedies—car accidents, plane accidents, hang gliding accidents, bus crashes, knifings, drownings, scarves getting caught under the wheels of their Rolls Royces, breaking their necks. The lovely girl in the prom dress standing in the dance hall and suddenly a titanium steel pipe from above breaking, falling on her, impaling her through the skull on her prom night! The valedictorian high school graduate headed to Cornell, standing on the street corner in New York City, suddenly finding himself in the middle of a robbery. A stray bullet—the only bullet fired—hitting him, killing him. Lily was not worried about old age or hereditary illness, she was worried about portholes of the universe opening up and demons swallowing her.

Lily believed that the portholes that allowed random tragedy to fall in were also the portholes that allowed lottery tickets to fall in. Out of control SUVs at state fairs. A sunspot in your eye, and wham, your child is dead. Plane crashes, ten-car collisions, freak lightning storms, fatal infections from a harmless day at the farm, and 1, 18, 24, 39, 45, 49. All from the same place. All leading to the same place—destruction.

And Lily Quinn prided herself all her life on being exactly the kind of girl who'd never won a single thing. Her karma had been being not just an un-winner, but the anti-winner. In fact, she could be sure that if she picked it, it would never win. She couldn't win so much as a pack of cigarettes on a free tour of the Philip Morris tobacco factory in North Carolina. She couldn't win a no-homework weekend when there were only ten entrants and the professor picked three names. She didn't win the short or the long straw. She didn't get to lose and clean the toilet, or come up to the headmaster and ask for more gruel, any more than she got to win a prize at a baby shower contest. She played a game at her sister's shower called, "How well do you know your sister?"—and came in third!

49—for the year her mother and grandmother came to America.

45—for the end of the war that changed the world.

39—for its beginning.

24—for her age. Last year she played 23.

18—Because it was her favorite number.

1—because it was the loneliest number.

She bought herself a lottery ticket every single week for six years, playing the numbers that meant something to her not because she had hope, but because she wanted to reaffirm the order of her quiet universe. Because she truly believed that the Force that let her numbers *never* be pulled out of a hat at Saturday night's drawing was the same Force that did not place the titanium rod in her two feet of life.

Unable to draw or read or focus, Lily concentrated all her efforts on getting a tan. In a secluded part of a small semi-circle of the local beach near Wailea, Lily took off her bikini halter and

40

sunbathed topless, getting a very thorough tan indeed. After almost three weeks her breasts looked positively Brazilian and even her nipples got dark brown.

In the first week of June, Lily was sitting outside on the patio, home from the beach, thinking about what to do for the rest of her day—for the day was so loooong—when the phone rang. The phone never rang! Lily was so excited, she nearly knocked over a chair getting to it.

"Hello?" she said in an eager-lover voice.

"Lilianne Quinn?" said an unfamiliar man's baritone on the other end.

"Yes?" she said, much more subdued, in a voice unfamiliar to herself.

"This is Detective O'Malley of the NYPD. I'm calling about your roommate, Amy McFadden."

Excitement was instantly supplanted by something else—worry. "Yes? What's happened?" From his tone, she thought Amy might have been in a car accident.

"Have you heard from her?"

"No." She paused. "I'm here in Hawaii."

"Well, I know," said the detective. "I'm calling you there, aren't I?"

That was true. "What's happened?"

"She seems to have disappeared."

"Oh." Lily immediately calmed down. "Hmm. Have you checked with her mother?"

"Her mother is the one who reported her missing, which is why I'm calling *you*. According to Jan McFadden, Amy hasn't called home in three weeks. Their repeated attempts to reach her at the apartment have failed. Do you recall the last time you saw her?"

"I don't know," Lily said, deflecting. "I'd have to think about it."

There was silence on the other end. "Are you thinking about it now?"

41

"Detective, I don't know. I've been here three weeks. I guess I saw her right before I left."

"When was that?"

"I . . . I can't remember now." Dates had been singed out of her head by the Tropic of Cancer sun. "Can I think about it and call you back?"

"Yes—but quickly."

"Or . . ." Something occurred to Lily. "Do you think I should come back? Is this something you need to speak to me about in person?"

"I'm not sure. Is it?"

"Yes, yes, I think I should come back. I'll be able to give you much more detail."

"Well, I appreciate that, Miss Quinn. This seems quite serious."

Lily didn't think so, but then this detective didn't know Amy.

"You need me to come back right away? The sooner the better?"

"Well—"

"Of course. This is an emergency. I'll be glad to be of any help. I'll fly back tonight. Is that soon enough?"

"Yes, I think that will be fine. I apologize for having you leave Hawaii. You don't really—"

"No, no, I do. It's really no problem. I want to help. Where do I go?"

"Come to the 9th Precinct on 5th Street between First and Second Avenues. Ask for me."

"Who are you again?"

"Lieutenant-detective O'Malley. Spencer Patrick O'Malley."

She called United Airlines to find out about the next available flight: it was in four hours. It took her forty-five minutes to pack, then she called a cab.

She carried her suitcase out with difficulty. Her mother was on the patio, smoking, drinking cranberry juice.

"I have to go back to New York. Something . . . something's happened," she said, and didn't want to give voice to anything more. "That was the police on the phone."

42

"Police? What's happened? What did you do?"

"Nothing, but . . . no one can find Amy. The police want to talk to me."

"They can't talk to you on the phone?"

"No. I guess it's serious." She said it, but didn't believe it for a second.

She wasn't worried about Amy. She thought Amy's disappearance was a karmic ruse to get her out of Maui.

She threw herself into the cab with relieved haste. When the plane was in the air heading back home she found herself exhaling for the first time in three weeks. She was sure Amy would have turned up by the time she got home.

3

An Hour at the 9th Precinct

Amy hadn't turned up by the time Lily got home, but their apartment looked as if the police expected to find Amy in Lily's closet. A copy of the warrant was plastered to the wall in the hallway. Nothing obvious had been disturbed in Lily's room—though she had the feeling that all her things had been looked at, even touched—but Amy's room had been turned upside down.

Without even unpacking, still in her traveling clothes—a white spaghetti-strap tank top, a small cropped cream cardigan, and a denim mini-skirt, she dropped her suitcase and left for the precinct. She gave her name and waited for ten minutes before a heavy, out-of-breath man came out. "Detective O'Malley?" she said, sticking out her hand.

"No, no, my partner always sends me. He thinks I need the exercise," the man puffed.

His hand was wet and clammy and unpleasant. She pulled hers away. "How thoughtful of your partner," said Lily, warily eying him, a little bit relieved that this detective wasn't the lead detective. He had a sour, greasy look about him, his thin, long, scraggly hair needed washing, or at best combing; he was very tall, but was ungainly about his limbs, listing slightly to the right, his head bobbing slightly to the left. His paunch was so large that the white dress shirt he was wearing couldn't contain it, and both, the shirt and the belly, were spilling over the top of the pants, onto the belt and downwards. Lily almost felt like telling him to tuck himself in. He didn't look jovial and jolly though, he was not a happy fat man.

"Detective Harkman," said the panting man, motioning her to follow him. As he walked by her, she smelled what she knew unmistakably to be uric acid. Detective Harkman had gout—his body couldn't metabolize the nitrogenous wastes properly, hence the sour smell emanating from him. Her paternal grandfather had had it at the end of his life. Involuntarily she held her breath as she followed him three flights up ("What, no elevators?" she quipped. "It's either elevators or our salaries," he unquipped back.) and was out of breath herself when they entered a high-ceilinged plain open room with a dozen wooden cluttered desks, behind one of which sat a man, who was not heavy or out of breath.

"Lilianne Quinn?" He stood up and extended his hand. "I'm Detective O'Malley." He did not have gout.

She looked up at him. Her handshake must have seemed formal, uncertain, and mushy compared to his, which was casual, certain and un-mushy. Despite the moist heat in the room, his hand was dry.

Lily was usually good with ages, but Detective O'Malley she couldn't quite place. He moved young—he had a wiry build that came either from sports or from not eating—but his eyes were old. He looked to be somewhere around forty, and somewhere beyond a sense of humor, though that could have been an affect— affecting to be serious in front of her. He had lots of light brown hair, graying slightly at the temples and was wearing black metal-rimmed glasses that he took off to greet her. His gray suit jacket was hanging evenly on the back of his chair. His nondescript gray tie was loosened, and the top two buttons of his tucked-in white dress shirt unbuttoned. All the windows in the open room were flung ajar and there was a hot breeze coming through in the early evening. He buttoned his shirt after he stood up, fixed his tie and put his jacket back on; she noticed the massive black pistol in his holster. "Why don't we go in here," he said, point-ing to a door that said *Interrogation #1*.

He was half the width of his partner though Lily couldn't tell if O'Malley seemed thin simply by comparison. No, he was definitely thin, and he didn't look like he had time for sports. His desk was stacked a foot high with files and papers. Maybe he played a little baseball. He looked fast like a shortstop. Did shortstops wear glasses? Perhaps soccer? Thus occupying her slightly anxious brain with idle observations and impressions, she followed him with Detective Harkman panting behind. She hoped the room would be air-conditioned, but she found it to be heated by a whooshing large fan that spun the hot air around her in a clammy vortex. She resisted the impulse of sticking her head out the open window and panting like a Labrador. Her cardigan was too hot for this room, but she wasn't about to take it off in front of two police officers, leaving herself in a barely-there top.

Detective O'Malley, his glasses back on, invited her to sit down (she did) and asked her if she wanted something to drink (she said no, though she did). He began without waiting. Drumming a pencil next to his notebook on top of the table, he put up his feet on the chair next to him, "Okay, tell me what you know."

"Well, nothing." She nearly stammered. What kind of a ques-tion was that? "About what?"

"About where Amy is."

"I don't know that."

"Why aren't you concerned? Her mother is out of her mind with worry. Amy didn't go to her college graduation. You—didn't attend either, I take it?"

"Um—no." She wasn't going to be telling a stranger, was she, why she had not attended. But the detective knew she was in Hawaii, he knew she couldn't have attended. Her eyes narrowed at him. His eyes widened in response. They were extremely blue. They seemed to know things, understand things without her

46

opening her mouth. Then why were they staring back at her, expecting an answer?

"Why not?" he asked.

Oh here we go. "Unlike Amy, I'm not officially graduated." Lily cleared her throat. "I have some credits still to take."

"You're not a senior?"

"Yes. Just not a"—she lowered her gaze to study the complexities in the grain of the wooden table—"a graduating senior."

"I see."

She wasn't looking at him so she couldn't tell if he did see. Oh, she bet he understood everything. He just wanted to watch her squirm.

"How old are you, Miss Quinn?"

"Twenty-four."

"Did you two start college late? Amy is also twenty-four."

"I didn't start late, I just . . . kept going."

He was observing her. "For six years?"

"For six years, yes."

"And still not graduated?"

"Not quite."

"I see." He switched subjects then as if they were file folders lying on his desk. "So—you didn't go to your graduation, because you weren't graduating. Fair enough. But Amy didn't go either, and she was graduating."

"Hmm." That *was* surprising. Lily had no answer to it.

"Were you and Amy close?"

"We were, yes. Are I mean. Are." She paused and decided to take the direct approach. "You're confusing me."

"Not deliberately, Miss Quinn. So what were you doing in Hawaii?"

"Sunbathing looks like," said Harkman from behind her.

Detective O'Malley didn't say anything, but in between the blinks of his eyes behind his black-rimmed glasses, his flicker of an expression made her blush, almost as if . . . he could see her sunsoaked brown nipples.

47

Pulling the cardigan closed, she looked down at the table and bit her lip. "My parents. I went to visit my mother."

"You left when?"

"On the Thursday morning, very early. My flight was at eight. I took a cab to JFK at six in the morning."

"Was Amy up?"

"No."

"Was Amy home?"

"I think so. I didn't check her room, if that's what you mean."

"So she could've not been home?"

"She could've not been, but—"

"So the last time you actually saw her would be . . ."

"Wednesday night, May 12."

"Had time to recall some dates since our phone call?"

Lily lifted her gaze. Detective O'Malley's eyes stared at her unflinchingly from his clean-shaven, calm, angular face, and she suddenly got the feeling that the firm and casual handshake *was* a ruse, was an affect, that she should be very careful with the things she said to this detective because he might remember every syllable.

"Yes." She crossed her arms. "Initially I had been taken aback by your phone call."

"That's understandable. Did she seem normal to you that Wednesday?"

"Yes. She seemed the same as always."

"Which is how?"

"I don't know. Normal." How did one describe a normal evening with Amy? She became flummoxed. "She was her usual self. We drank a little, talked a little."

"About what?"

"Nothing. Everything. Movies. Finals. Really, just . . . regular girl things."

"Boyfriends?"

"Mmm." She didn't want to tell this detective about her pathetic love life, and since that's all the boyfriends they talked about, she couldn't tell the detective anything. "We talked about our mothers."

Detective Harkman stood behind Lily and every once in a while, Detective O'Malley would glance at him for a silent exchange and then look back at her. Now was one of those times.

"Then you left . . ."

"And I haven't heard from Amy since."

"You never called to tell her how you were getting on in Maui?"

"I did, a couple of times, I left messages on the machine, but she never called me back."

"How many times would you say you called her?"

"I don't know. Maybe three?"

"Three?"

"Around three."

"So possibly two, possibly four?"

"Possibly." She lowered her head. She didn't know what he wanted from her.

"Does she have a cell phone?"

"No."

"Do you?"

"No. I can't afford one. I don't know why she doesn't have one."

"So you called a few times, she didn't call back, and you gave up?"

"I didn't give up. I was going to call again. I was even thinking of calling at her mother's house."

"But you didn't."

"I couldn't remember the number."

"Did she tell you of her plans to visit her mother the weekend you flew to Hawaii?"

"I don't remember her telling me anything like that, no. Did she go visit her mother that weekend?"

"No," said the detective. "What time did you call her?"

"In the evenings, I think."

"Your evenings?"

"What? Yes. Yes, my evenings. Midnight Hawaii time. Before I went to bed, I'd call."

O'Malley paused before he said, "Hawaii is six hours behind New York."

Lily paused, too. "Yes."

"So your midnight would be six in the morning New York time?"

"Yes." Lily coughed. "I guess I should have been more considerate."

"Maybe," O'Malley said non-committally. "What I'm really interested in though, is Amy not picking up the phone at six in the morning."

"She could have been out."

"Out where?"

"Well, I don't know, do I? Perhaps she was sleeping."

"Perhaps she could have called you back, Miss Quinn. Would you like to know how many times the caller ID showed your Hawaiian phone number on the display? Twenty-seven. Morning, noon and night is when you called her. The answering machine in your apartment had nine messages from you to Amy. The first one was on Sunday, May 16, the last one was after you and I had spoken, on June third."

Lily, flustered and confounded, sat silently. Was she caught in a lie? She did call a few times. And she did leave some messages. But nine? She recalled some of those messages. "*Ames, ohmigod!!! I can't take another day. This mother of mine, call me, call me back, call me.*" "*Ames, how long have I been here, it feels like five years, and I'm the one who is sixty. Call me to tell me I'm still young.*" "*Amy, where in hell are you? I need you. Call me.*" "*I'm going home, home, home, I can't take another minute. My dad is not here, just me and my crazy mom. If I don't talk to you I'll turn into her.*" "*Amy, in case you've forgotten, this is your roommate and best friend Lily Quinn. That's L-I-L-Y Q-U-I-N-N.*"

She was profoundly embarrassed. Strangers, police officers, detectives, these two men, *this* grown up man listening to her sophomoric jabberings, her tumult and frustration on an answering machine!

Harkman panted behind her, sneezed once, she hoped it wasn't on her. Detective O'Malley at last said, as if speaking directly to her humiliations, "Let's move on."

Yes, let's. But Lily didn't know what to say. Harkman's gaze prickled the back of her neck. She felt intensely uncomfortable. O'Malley's hands were pressed together at the fingertips, making the shape of a teepee as he continued to study her. She couldn't take it anymore, she looked away from him and down at her own twitching hands and noticed that a small cut near her knuckle was oozing blood.

"Miss Quinn, are you bleeding? Chris, can you please get this young lady a tissue. Or would you prefer a first-aid kit? When did you cut yourself?"

Lily didn't want to be evasive, considering the amount of fresh blood that was coming out of an old wound, but she couldn't tell him when. "It's an old thing," she muttered. "It's nothing."

Harkman came back with cotton wool and a bandage. Lily dabbed at the cut, feeling ridiculous.

O'Malley said, "You might want to get that checked out."

"No, it's fine."

"Well, Miss Quinn, it may seem *fine* to you, this ability to bleed spontaneously, but you weren't bleeding when you first came in here, and the bright color of your blood tells me you may be anemic."

"Yes, I've always been a little anemic." She emitted a throaty laugh. "Never could donate blood."

He wrote something down in his notebook, not paying attention to her. "Okay. I just have a couple more questions, if you think you're all right to go on."

"I'm fine."

"Tell me, did Amy have any enemies?"

"Enemies? We're college girls!"

"The answer is no then? You can just reply in the negative."

"No." In the smallest voice.

"What about a boyfriend?"

"No."

"Was she seeing anyone at all? Casually?"

Lily said, "What kind of a question is that?"

O'Malley stopped looking into his notebook and looked up at her. "I'm not interested in passing judgment. Now was she or wasn't she?"

"Well, she's single, so . . . yes."

"Did she ever stay overnight somewhere else?"

"Once in a while."

"How often?"

"I'm not sure."

"Where?"

"I don't know that either."

O'Malley exchanged another look with Harkman. What, she wanted to exclaim, what are you looking at each other for? What am I not telling you? She glanced back at Harkman herself. She started to actively dislike his eyes, which she realized were like two small, round, ugly drill holes. They were lost on his big, round, double-chinned face, but boy did they manage to bore into the back of her friggin' head.

"How did you meet Amy, Miss Quinn?"

"We met in an art class at college almost two years ago."

"Did you become good friends?"

"We moved in together, didn't we?"

"Don't get testy with me. I know it's been a long day. You could have moved in for financial reasons. You could have hated Amy's guts. I don't know. That's why I'm asking you."

"Yes, we became friends, then we found this apartment, and moved in together." Just to make sure there was no wrong impression, she said, "My boyfriend lived with us for a few months."

"Three of you in that tiny apartment?" O'Malley whistled. "Why did Amy get the larger bedroom then?"

"Why? Because when we were moving in, we drew for it, and

I got the short straw." She let that sink in—Lily never got the long straw, but sometimes she got the short straw.

"I see. And during your living together, has Amy had many boyfriends?"

"I don't know. What do you consider many?"

O'Malley raised his eye brows. "What I consider to be many, how is that relevant, Miss Quinn?"

Why was he flustering her! "Like I said, she would see people sporadically, on and off. No one serious."

"Not a single serious boyfriend?"

"No." Why was that strange? It wasn't strange. Amy was always looking for love. She just wasn't lucky like good old Lily with good old Joshua. But there was a formless memory wedged in there of something—Lily didn't even know what. A sense of something that Lily could not then or now place. She didn't know if it actually involved Amy, or love, but for some reason she thought so—and cold damp and flashing lights. What a strange thing to think of at a time like this. She shook her head to shake off the oddness of it.

"That's interesting. Because while we were waiting for you to return from Maui, we interviewed a number of people, among them a girl named Rachel Ortiz, do you know her?"

"Yes, I know Rachel." Was her response too clipped? Judging from the look on the detective's face, yes, it was.

"No love lost there?" he asked. "Well, Miss Ortiz stated flatly and for the record that Amy *told* her she had been seeing someone for some time but it was all over with now."

Lily rubbed her eyes. "Detective, I apologize, I'm jetlagged and exhausted—but I just don't see how this is relevant."

"I will allow for your jetlag and tell you how it's relevant. I see you're not particularly worried about her disappearance for your own peculiar reasons. But it's been over three weeks since Amy was last heard from or seen by anyone. It is no longer a simple mishap with dates and schedules, and little things like college graduations. This is a missing person investigation.

Perhaps if we find the person she had been seeing, we'll find out where she is."

"I understand, detective, but I don't know what to tell you— I just don't know who she was seeing."

They had been tape recording the whole conversation, though by the sharpshooter look in O'Malley's eyes, Lily didn't think an electromagnetic recording would be necessary. She signed the missing person's report, threw away her bloodied cotton wool, took his business card and stepped to the door. O'Malley remained sitting behind the table, his feet up on a chair.

"Still, though, doesn't it niggle you a little bit, Miss Quinn," said Detective O'Malley, placing his hands behind his head, "just a tiny bit, that your friend wouldn't tell you about her love life? I mean, why would she keep that a secret from you?"

She didn't know what he was getting at, and so she didn't reply. Did he think Amy wasn't into boys? Did he think Amy was into her boyfriend Joshua? She didn't want to think.

O'Malley didn't get up, telling her to call the station or the beeper number on the card any time if she learned anything, or thought of anything. She left the room without glancing at Harkman. She would have preferred him interviewing her. She would have preferred Robespierre interviewing her.

Home wasn't nearly far enough to walk off the gnawing sense of malaise around her nerve endings.

4

Lily Goes Back to Work—in a Fashion

The Noho Star on Bleeker and Lafayette was short people, so Lily came in the following day and was working the graveyard shift, thirteen hours, from eleven in the morning until midnight. Her hours, as per her request, had been increased to fifty. She hoped she could handle it.

When she got home from the precinct the night before, she had found Rachel, Paul, and to her greatest surprise, *Joshua!* camped out on her front stoop. They followed her up the stairs to her fifth floor crawl-up. By the third floor, Lily was so out of breath, she had to stop and rest. How did old Colleen do it? When she finally got inside, she collapsed on the futon.

Joshua had been calling the last two weeks, he said, because he needed to pick up his guitar case. "What happened to your hand?" he asked Lily. Unhappily she didn't want to talk to him in the presence of all those other people.

Paul, small, slender, perfectly groomed, perfectly dressed, perfectly Italian-looking and calm as a small pond said, "Are you all right, Lil?" Then, "What happened? Where's Ames?"

She opened one eye from the futon. "Is that a trick question?"

Rachel, once a kinky-black-haired Puerto Rican fourth runner up in a San Domingo teenage beauty pageant, now a Puerto Rican bleached blonde with hair thinner and straighter than Lily's, was making retching noises in the kitchen sink after drinking three-week-old apple juice from the too-warm fridge. Lily couldn't keep her eyes open. Suddenly there was a tree in front of her eyes, and an animal hiding behind it, and there was a whirl of red color, and patches, and small bits of dialogue, and here came that cold damp and Amy again, and Hawaii, the red flowers, and her mother saying *everything I go through I go through completely alone*, and here were the sounds of Rachel swirling her mouth out with water, irritating Lily. She wanted them all to leave, especially Joshua. So she kept her eyes closed and pretended they did, and fell asleep, just in that position, on the futon, still sitting up, slightly hunched over to one side, and Amy away, her mother away, her father away, perhaps Amy was with her own father? Perhaps she went down to Florida to visit him? She must mention it to the detective, what was his name? Joshua away, Joshua, who was supposed to be the real deal, now coming for his guitar case, and when Lily woke up fourteen hours later, her body was stiff, the phone was ringing, and her knuckle was seeping blood through the bandage.

Today, the jetlag was getting to her. During her break, instead of eating Jell-O with whipped cream like always, she put her head down on the waitresses' table in the booth in the back and was instantly asleep. She didn't fall asleep, she went to sleep. When she awoke, Spencer O'Malley sat looking at her from across the table.

"Your hand is still spontaneously bleeding, I see," he said.

She looked around groggily. His partner was not with him. "Did you come here to tell me that?" She felt disgusting.

"You called me this morning. I thought you might have remembered something important."

"Yes. Yes." She struggled to remember anything at all, much less why she called him nine hours ago.

"Something about Amy?"

"Something about Amy." She nodded, rubbing her eyes. He

56

pushed a glass of water toward her. She drank from it, came to a little. "Her father lives down in Islamorada, I think. Or Cape Canaveral?"

"St. Augustine perhaps?"

"No, that's not it."

"Yes, that's where he lives. St. Augustine."

"Okay then. Maybe she went to visit him."

O'Malley was quiet. "That's what you called to tell me?"

"Yes."

"You must think I just started this job. You're going to have to do better than that. He was the first one we called. He hadn't heard from her. But besides, Miss Quinn, you're missing the point about Amy. She told her mother she would be coming home. She didn't. She told her family she would be graduating. She didn't. Hasn't called, hasn't shown up, and no one's heard from her, not even her father in Islamorada."

She struggled up. "Would you excuse me? My break is over, I think."

"Break?" said O'Malley. "I think your shift is over."

"Ha." She left to wash her face. He was still sitting in her booth when she returned.

"Detective, I really must . . ."

But he wasn't moving. "Just two more minutes of your time. There were a few things I forgot to mention yesterday, after all, we had so much to cover. During our search of Amy's room, we discovered her house keys and her wallet on her dresser, leading us to suspect that she didn't go far."

"As I told you, that's probably true."

"Was she generally in the habit of leaving the apartment without her wallet or keys?"

"I guess," said Lily. "I'm not trying to be evasive," she added, seeing his face. She smiled wanly, but O'Malley didn't smile, in fact, studied her extra carefully, as if she were a word on the page whose meaning he was trying to decipher. "She used to go running and didn't like to weigh herself down. She usually took what little money she had with her. Crumpled up into a ball, or change stuffed into her pants pocket."

"Where did she go running?"

"Central Park. The reservoir."

"Far to go for a run all the way from the East Village."

"Far, but worth it."

He made a note on his pad. "What about other times? When she would disappear overnight? Did she also leave her wallet and her keys then? Running for days at a time, was she?"

"She was very fit," Lily said, a feeble attempt at a joke. During those days too, she would leave her wallet. Why did she strongly *not* want to tell the detective that? "You know I didn't always notice. I tried not to go into her room when she was gone unless I needed something. So I don't know if she always left her wallet. I'm sure sometimes she took it."

"Where's her driver's license, by the way?"

"I don't think she had one," Lily said hesitantly.

"Really?" With obvious surprise and a glance at her hesitation.

Lily averted her gaze, trying to think of the thing that turned her face away from him. Some vague confusion, some vague inconsistency regarding the license, but she couldn't quite place it, hence the averted gaze. "She didn't know how to drive. We live in New York. I don't know how to drive either."

"Interesting," said the detective, stroking his chin. "Fascinating." He stood to go. "Well, you'll forgive me for not sharing in your relaxed and easygoing attitude about your best friend's whereabouts, but I'm finding it odd, to say the least, that she's been gone for three weeks, with her cash card, her Visa card, her Student ID, her MetroCard, and her door keys all serenely on her dresser. And she doesn't know how to drive. So where did she go? When we searched your room, we found your MetroCard there. But we didn't find your keys or your wallet or your ATM card. You went to Hawaii and took them with you. That seemed normal to us."

Their eyes locked for a moment. Detective O'Malley with clear eyes that didn't miss a thing said, "So where's your bed?"

"Boyfriend took it."

"Nice."

"Yeah, well."

Presently he slapped the table, sitting back down. "Damn! I just figured it out. I just understood why you are so cavalier about Amy."

"I don't know what you mean. I'm not cavalier."

"Of course. You are not concerned for her, because she has been disappearing with constant regularity. She would leave her life on the dresser, vanish, and then come back, as if she'd just been for a long run. You thought nothing of it then, and you're thinking nothing of it now."

"Incorrect detecting, detective. I am thinking something of it now. She'd never been away for three weeks before."

"She would leave her wallet and ID and keys on her dresser, when she went out, and you never asked why?"

Lily didn't know why she didn't ask. "I figured when she was ready she'd tell me."

There was a long pause. "Still waiting, are you, Miss Quinn?"

She hastily excused herself and went to finish her shift. Everybody at work had noticed that a suited-up detective flashing his badge had come looking for Lily. They asked her, they teased, they prodded, she equivocated, they pursued and pursued. Rick, the manager, watched her carefully and then called her over. "Are you in trouble of some kind?"

"No, no."

"It's not drugs, is it? Because . . ."

"It's not drugs."

"He's a cuuutie," said Judi, another waitress, pixie and not yet twenty. "Is he single?"

"I don't know and he's twice your age!"

"You say it like it's a bad thing."

5

Spencer Patrick O'Malley

He came home that night and sat at his round dining table. He lived in a small apartment close to work and in a perfect location—on 11th and Broadway. From his microcosm of a kitchen and adjoining dining area windows, he saw a dozen traffic lights on Broadway, all the way down south past Astor Place. The wet, red lights burst in Technicolor in the gray rain; the grayer the rain, the brighter the reds and greens. From the entry foyer that was his library *and* bedroom he overlooked the courtyard of a small church. He continued to live alone, certainly not for lack of trying on the parts of some of the women he had been with. What attempt has this been for you, detective, to live with another human being, his last girlfriend had asked him right before she left him. He was convinced they had not been living together; shows what he knew. Certainly he was spending a lot of time at her place, and she had been asking him to leave his things, insinuating. He was seeing a social worker now, Mary. He quite liked her—they had been together a year—but couldn't help feeling that he was really just another one of her more complicated cases. Once she fixed him she would go. He couldn't wait for that day. He just wasn't sure: to be fixed or for her to go?

The place belonged to his oldest brother Patrick who had been a bad boy and was kicked out by his wife, so he bought an apartment in the city, where he could be single on the weekdays and on the weekends have his kids. Soon his wife saw that living alone with the kids was not all she imagined and decided to give the wandering Patrick another chance. And so Spencer sublet Patrick's apartment that he could barely afford on his NYC detective's salary. But no one in New York could afford their apartments, so there was no use complaining. He complained only because he was constantly broke.

When he came back to the Suffolk County Police Department after leaving his job as a senior detective at Dartmouth College up in New Hampshire, he stayed in a room above the garage in his brother Sean's house. But then being a patrol cop on Long Island had become enough for Spencer and besides he wasn't too crazy about Sean's wife (she was too tidy for his liking), so he transferred to NYPD. His brother's wife's freakish neatness drove him to New York City, that messy kettle-pot of vice.

New York was quite different from changing tires for women on the Long Island Expressway and administering the DUI test fifteen times on a Saturday night. Spencer was first assigned as a detective third grade to the Special Investigations Division of the Detective Bureau. He was one of four local squad detectives working on the Joint Robbery Apprehension Team. He was moved across—at his own request—to Missing Persons after the MP senior detective was at the wrong place at the wrong time and was fatally shot by a perp fleeing the scene of a robbery at an all-night deli on Avenue C and 4th Street. Spencer thought he might be ready for missing persons again. He was made senior to the dead man's partner, Chris Harkman, who'd been in Missing Persons for twelve years, remaining at third grade, because as Harkman said, "It's such a low-pressure job." He had had three heart surgeries, gout, arthritis, and was set to man the missing persons desk just two more years, long enough to retire at forty-eight with nearly full pay and full benefits.

But Spencer wasn't ready to retire or die. He didn't mind

coasting, and, like Harkman, would have coasted also, but it just so happened that he, by accident or by fate, or by virtue of his own nitpicky character and peculiar memory, found a boy who had been missing since 1984, living years later in a crack den off Twelfth Avenue and 43rd Street. He was picked up by the narcs, but when Spencer saw his name on the books—which he checked daily and religiously—he recognized it. Mario Gonzalez. Spencer obsessively checked the photos and the names of every person detained by the NYPD exactly because of a case like Mario Gonzalez. Turned out the boy—who had been twelve when he had disappeared—did not want to be found by his inconsolable parents, but that wasn't the point, for in his department Spencer was a hero. He was promoted to lieutenant first grade—and put in charge of the entire MP division—while Harkman, by virtue of being partnered with him, got a second grade promotion and a raise. That the boy killed himself a few weeks after being found didn't dampen anyone's joy at a, finding an MP that long gone, and b, finding an MP *alive*.

After that, results were expected of Spencer in a department that was notoriously low on results. It wasn't like other departments in special investigations where the detectives were constantly getting patted on their backs for jobs well done, collars made, perps caught—in credit card and con games, larceny and extortion, airline fraud, arson and art theft—and especially homicide. If only Spencer cared a whit about the other divisions he might have been a captain already.

But Spencer's heart, for reasons unfathomable even to him, remained with finding people that had been long missing. No, not even that. *Looking* for people that had been long missing.

Since Gonzalez, he had found six or seven more hopeless cases and become somewhat of a mythological maverick at the department—a favorite of his chief, Colin Whittaker, and a homeboy of the homicide division next door with whom he was loosely associated. "Give it to O'Malley," the saying around the station went. "He'll find anything." He became tight with a couple of guys in homicide, one particularly, Gabe McGill, whom he liked so much he wished he could be partnered with him, except Spencer didn't want homicide, and Gabe didn't want MP.

The apartment was dark, he hadn't turned any lights on, and that was just the way he liked it in the first few minutes after he got home from work. Work was frenetic and boisterous, and the apartment was blissfully mute; work had glaring fluorescent light contrast, and the apartment was soothingly dark. Only the changing traffic lights from Broadway flickered through the open windows. He poured himself a J&B—blended with 116 different malts and 12 grains—and kept it in front of him as he palmed the glass with both hands, turning it around and around like a clock, counting the seconds, the minutes of time passing, looking at the drink, smelling it. He threw off his shoes. He took off his shirt and tie. He used the bathroom, he came back to the table. The drink was still there. Spencer was still there. He sat in the dark, facing the open windows and palmed the drink again.

He had interviewed the panicked mother, the people this Amy McFadden girl waitressed with at the Copa Cobana, her clique of friends, all confounded but eager to help. He searched the apartment, he checked her bank records, her credit card accounts, the Department of Motor Vehicles.

And then he met Lily.

The girl seemed so self-possessed, so unconcerned—and so tanned. No histrionics, no whining from this girl, he liked that. Unlike the other one, Rachel Ortiz. She was an emoter. But Lily had herself and the matter in hand. Unlike the mother, Lily was not unduly anxious. She should talk to Amy's mother, calm her down. Perhaps Lily was right. Perhaps her missing roommate would just show up.

Lily was smooth and chocolate bronzed and young, her little spaghetti strap tank top, her short short denim skirt. Fleetingly he imagined her lying on the white sand in Maui, all moist and hot from the sun, eyes closed, on her back, browning, burning, topless.

Spencer needed to pour the drink back into the bottle. He never drank on the days he worked, because Spencer knew that his mind played tricks on him when it told him he could do it, could have just one, when it intellectualized and rationalized the glass in his hands. He imagined bringing the whisky to his mouth and downing it in three deep swallows. No dainty swilling, smelling, sipping of the blended malt for him in a quaint dram.

If life had taught Spencer Patrick O'Malley anything it was that the missing never just showed up, and there was no such thing as having just one.

6

Conversations with Mothers

"Detective O'Malley . . ." She wished she could ask him to stop, tell him to stop coming to the diner. He'd been to see her three times in ten days. "People are starting to talk," was all she said.

"Really? What are they saying?"

She shook her head. "What can I do for you today? Can I get you a cup of coffee? A donut?"

"Very stereotypical of you, Miss Quinn. No, thank you to both. I am not a donut person. Have you spoken to Amy's mother?"

"No, not yet."

"You should call her. She would like to hear from you. I think it will be good for her to hear from you. She's always just this side of hysteria. She calls me four times a day. And I've got no leads besides you."

"I'm not a lead," said Lily, taken aback, but then saw he was half-joking. "Detective," she said, almost pleadingly. "I'll call her, and I'm going to tell her what I've told you. I think she's worried for nothing. I think Amy just left for a while and will soon turn up safely and everything will be all right. My hunch is that Amy went with whoever she was seeing on vacation."

"Oh, so a minute ago you didn't think she was seeing anyone at all, and now you think she's eloped?"

Lily squeezed her hands together. She could not do this any more, she had to go back to work, she had other customers!

During her silence, Spencer said, "And do you think she would leave on vacation for four weeks without telling anyone and miss her graduation, to which she invited her whole family? Is she that unthinking, that inconsiderate? Wouldn't she realize her parents would be worried sick about her?"

"Not unthinking, not inconsiderate, just in love, detective. You know? We forgive people who are in love for their short-term inconsideration. It's such bad form to deny them."

"So a minute ago, no boyfriend whatsoever and now so wildly in love, you're defending her on grounds of temporary insanity? Please, pick a side of the fence, Miss Quinn and keep to it." He tipped his proverbial hat as he left.

Judi came over and whispered, "Ooooooh," from behind.

"Just stop it," said Lily.

Why wasn't she able to call Amy's mother? Why couldn't she make that call? On the surface it seemed so easy, as easy as talking to the detective. Easier—she knew her, she liked her. Hi, Mrs. McFadden, how are you, and the other children . . . ugh, right there. The *other* children? Yes, Mrs. McFadden, I know it's terrible about Amy, she's gone and no one knows where she is, but the other children that you still have, how are *they?* Are they safe? That was the whole problem. Imagining the conversation filled Lily with such itching discomfort that she just couldn't bring herself to pick up the phone.

She called her grandmother instead.

"Have you been reading the papers?" said Claudia. "An Amtrak train struck a log truck at a crossing this morning, derailing all ten cars and the engine and injuring ten people. Two people were seriously hurt."

"Grandma . . ."

"A microphone stand impaled a pregnant mother, who fell in her own house while getting her two boys ready for school.

She fell from the second floor to the first and was impaled through the chest on her microphone stand. She was a musician."

"Grandma, please!"

"Think about those boys. It's terrible seeing your own mother get hurt in such a freak accident."

"Yes. Yes it must be. Well, thanks for talking. I gotta run."

Andrew hadn't called Lily since she got back. She had called him at home last week, but Miera said he was in Washington. "Lily, his schedule is posted online. Clearly says, Washington. Call him there."

She called him there, but he was still in session. And he didn't return her call. Typical of him. He would get so busy, sometimes she didn't hear from him for weeks. She called Andrew's apartment to speak to her father, but there was no answer. She walked around her bare room, looked at her watercolors, her photographs, her words, pictures of her as a child, held by her sister Amanda, hugged by her brother—their youngest, Lilianne, good girl, dark girl, smart girl, walking early, smiling early, clever, funny, holding up a picture of a perfect lotus flower she drew when she was three, laughing at her mother, who took the photo. Suddenly she stopped walking, her gaze darkened, her eyes blinked, blinked again, closed.

Spencer who saw everything. Could he have looked at her walls and missed the lottery ticket? It was small and tucked in, part of a collage, covered by a photo on one side, and old American Ballet Company tickets on the other, but could he have seen? She came closer to the ticket. Oh, so what if he did? He didn't know by heart the drawing from that day, April 18, 1999.

When the phone rang, she absent-mindedly picked it up.

"Lil?" It was her mother! That caught Lily unawares. Had she been caught awares, she never would have picked up the phone. The modern conveniences of caller ID—call screening. Maybe if she cashed in her lottery ticket, she could afford the six extra

bucks for caller ID-while-call-waiting, that would be *most* useful.
Ha! This she was thinking while trying to decipher the tone of
her mother's voice which seemed rather chipper for a woman
who had found herself recently and unexpectedly without a
husband.

Suddenly her father picked up the other extension. "Lil?"

"PAPI?"

"Yes, why so shocked? I do live here, you know." And he
laughed.

Her mother said, "I barely spoke five seconds to my own child.
Could I have her first, and then you'll have her when I'm done?"

"Mom, let me speak to Papi quick now."

As soon as Allison slammed down the phone, George said,
"Yes, honey?" in his most casual, most unconcerned, most I'm-
in-Hawaii-and-I'm-so-happy voice.

"I don't understand. I thought you were staying with Andrew?"

"Oh, I was just in D.C. on a little business. That's all. Not a
big deal."

"So you're . . . back?"

"Everything is fine, great even. I was just getting the jitters,
you know, having worked non stop for forty-five years. Well, you
wouldn't know. But someday you'll work."

"I work now. Fifty hours a week. Papi, what's going on? Talk
to me."

"Nothing to talk about. Do you know your mother has been
coming to the beach with me every single morning? She loves
it. She wasn't feeling well when you were here. She is much
better now. And she is cutting down on her smoking. She is looking beautiful, by the way, your mother."

Allison came back on the line, and both she and George were
on the phone now, clucking, joking, chuckling. "Lily, this is like
a second honeymoon with your father," her mother whispered
conspiratorially. "I can't tell you how happy we are."

Could Lily hang up fast enough? She didn't think so.

Now she had the strength to call Amy's mother!

The voice on the other line was groggy and slightly slurred.

"Oh, Lily," said Mrs. McFadden. "Where is she? Where is Amy? Why haven't we heard from her?"

Lily wanted to say a few hollow words, and did, petering off, trailing off, she wanted to say so much more, about how she wasn't that worried—which was less and less true—and about how Amy liked to be independent and she hated accounting to anyone for her actions. ("That's so true," said Amy's mother. "So true.") She said that she would call as soon as Amy came back, but she said it feebly, and it didn't matter anyway, it wasn't heard over Mrs. McFadden's crying. There was no getting through to the mother, just as Lily had suspected, and she didn't have anything in her arsenal with which to get through. Maybe Amanda would know how. After all, she had four children. Maybe if one of them went missing she would know what to say to Mrs. McFadden who had had Amy with her first husband, and was now remarried with two brand new children. She must have thought she was so close to not having to worry about Amy anymore.

Jan continued to cry, and Lily continued to sit on the phone and not know what to say except intermittently and impotently, "*I'm really sorry.*"

Paul and Rachel, who were Amy's friends and whose nucleus was Amy, only wanted to talk about—Amy. The conversation with Paul inevitably went something like this:

"Lil, where do you think she is?"

"I don't know. What about you?"

"Have no idea. But then I didn't live with her, I don't know her everyday habits."

"Paul, I might know how many times a day Amy brushes her teeth but I don't know where she's gone to."

"I understand. No one is blaming you, Lil. Why so defensive?"

"Because everybody seems to think I have answers that I just don't have. You don't know how often that detective asks me where she is."

"Where *do* you think she is?"

"I don't know!"

"Do you think something happened to her?"

"No! Like what?"

And with Rachel:

"God, Lil, what do you think happened to Amy?"

"I don't know. What about you?"

"I have no idea. But then, I didn't live with her."

Lily formulated her doubts. "Rach, the detective told me you told him that Amy was definitely seeing somebody."

"That's what she told me. Don't *you* know? I thought you'd confirm for sure. Who was it?"

"I don't know."

"How could you not know?"

"She didn't tell me, Rachel."

"Why would she keep something like that from you? I thought you were close."

"We were close. We are close."

"By the way . . . is the detective married?"

"I don't know. Why would I know that? And what do you care? How is *TO*-nee?"

"Tony is great," Rachel said cryptically. "Never better."

"So what are you asking about the detective for then?"

Lily fell back on Amy's bed. Did she have the answers? Should she have the answers? That was even worse. Should she, and she just doesn't because Lily Quinn doesn't have the answers to anything? Not to why she hasn't graduated in six years, not to what she wants to do with her life, not to what's wrong with her mother, not to just what it is that Joshua can't love about her, not to where Amy is. Not to 49, 45, 39, 24, 18, 1.

MISSING: Amy McFadden
DESCRIPTION:
Sex: Female
Race: Caucasian

Age: 24
Height: 5'8"
Weight: 140 lbs.
Build: Medium
Complexion: Fair
Hair: Red, long, curly
Eyes: Brown
Clothing/Jewelry: Unknown.
Last seen: May, 1999, in the vicinity of Avenue C and 9th Street in Manhattan, New York, within the confines of the 9th Precinct.

Lily and Rachel and Paul walked around the neighborhood and tacked the 8¹/2 by 11 posters with Amy's photo on the lampposts of every block from 12th Street down to 4th and on three avenues, A, B, and C. Lily couldn't help but be reminded of thumbtacking her lottery ticket to her wall, and every time she thought of it she felt stabbed a little in the chest, and walked on to the next lamppost without raising her head, careful not to look at her friends, nor at the homeless on the stoops who gazed at them from underneath their rags. Paul tied shiny yellow ribbons above the posters. Amy missing. 49, 45, 39, 24, 18, 1. Amy missing. 49, 45, 39, 24, 18, 1.

7

Birds of Paradise

Allison showed up for their new conjugal bliss of a honeymoon three days straight. She went to the beach with him gladly the first day, reluctantly the second day, and on the third morning with hostility, complaining about the wetness of the water, and the sandiness of the sand, and the sunniness of the sun, and the steepness of the hill, complaining about his shoes, which as far as he could see weren't bothering *her*. Complaining about the omelet he had yet to make ("I'm sick of your omelets.") and the coffee ("You never make enough.").

The fourth morning she didn't get out of bed, telling him in a mumbled voice that she had had a late night and needed to sleep. The fifth morning, she said she wasn't feeling well. Her legs hurt from all the walking. She was developing corns and calluses on her feet. She was getting a chill from the cold (??? 79°F!) water so early in the morning. Her bathing suit was dirty and needed to be washed. The towels weren't dry and she wasn't going without the towels.

"Allie, want to go to the beach?"

"No. How many beaches can we go to? I've seen them."

"You've seen a volcanic beach?"

She paused. "Sand and water, right?"

"No, volcanic pebbles."

"You want me to walk barefoot on rocks? Don't you remember how I cut my foot?"

"Allie, let's go, for an hour."

"I'm not going. I have to put the towels in the dryer, they'll smell if I don't. Why don't you go?"

"I don't want to go by myself."

"Well, I'm not going."

George went by himself.

How about Hamoa Beach with gray sand and 4000-foot-high cliffs hanging over the ocean?

"*Gray* sand? I'm supposed to be tempted by that?"

George went by himself.

Big Beach, Wailea Beach, Black Sand Beach?

"Big Beach, just bigger than ours? And *black* sand? That's attractive. Now white sand beach on the Gulf of Mexico, that's attractive, that's nice. It doesn't get hot, and it's so fine, it's like flour. Why didn't we get a condo in Florida?"

"Because you said there were too many storms and it was too hot and humid."

"I never said that, never. It would have been a beautiful life."

George went by himself.

Lahaina, the Road to Hana, the rainforest?

"You want me to go see trees, George? Walk along the road and into the trees? Poland had forests. And roads. Is it going to rain in the rainforest? I don't think so."

George went by himself. Allison came with him to Lahaina once because there was shopping in Lahaina.

"Maui, the god of sun, the cursed god of sun. He cursed this place with perpetual long days of sunshine," said Allison.

George tried a different tactic.

"What about if we go to the mainland, Allie? Let's fly to San Francisco, and we'll drive down south to Las Vegas. Wouldn't that be something?"

"Something hot, yes. Do you have any idea what the temperature is in Las Vegas in July? It's a hundred and twenty degrees.

And what are we going to do, rent a car? We can't afford such
an expense. You're retired now, George."

He suggested bringing their own car on a ship to San Francisco.

"What, our car, with no AC, in July? We'll suffocate before
we leave California. Look, get it out of your head. I'm not going
to the mainland in the summer. You know I don't feel well, I
can't be traveling in such heat with all my problems. It'll set me
back ten years."

He suggested making plans to go in the fall when the weather
became cooler. He was playing on her love of the slots. On her
love of getting dressed up and like a proper civilized person giving
her money away willingly and happily to a small steel machine.

Viva! Las Vegas.

But she couldn't face the thought of traveling anywhere with
George, of spending every waking moment with him and sleeping moment, too, for they could hardly get two hotel rooms,
could they? The thought of not having a room of her own to
retire to where she could close the door, and when no one would
see her, was too difficult even as a thought to Allison. She
couldn't imagine it, how could she ever live it?

"Would you stop pestering me already! What's this compul-
sion with always going, going, going? Why can't you sit still for
a moment? And if you wanted your beloved continent so much,
why did we buy a condo in Maui, then, huh? Why did you push
me to buy one here?"

He reminded her she was the one who had wanted to live in
Maui.

"Oh, that's right, blame it all on me. Well, fine, we're here, and
I'm paying plenty for this condo, I'm not leaving it for three months
to go somewhere else. What an idiotic waste of money. You always
were a spendthrift. That's why you don't have any money now."

Slowly, very slowly, he suggested selling the condo and moving
back east. To North Carolina, perhaps, where there was fishing
and gardening, and seasons, and lakes—where his brother lived.

"We just got here and you want to move already? You're sick,

75

that's what you are. You need professional help, why can't you be happy anywhere, why? It's beautiful here, what the hell is wrong with you? You have too much time on your hands, that's your problem."

And then she started falling down.

After the first time she fell, he asked her about it, and she said, "Cough syrup. Haven't you been paying any attention to what's going on with me? I'm very sick." She coughed for emphasis.

"Maybe if you left the apartment *once* for five minutes in a whole month, you'd feel better."

"Oh, that's great! Go ahead, scream at a sick woman!"

The next morning when he came back from his constitutional walk and swim at eight-thirty, she had fallen again in the sunken living room.

"It's my osteoporosis," she said later. "My knees buckle. They don't bend anymore like they used to."

He found her on the floor clutching the mail in her hands.

"The cough syrup," she told him. "Mixed with anti-depressants. The doctor said it's a very dangerous combination. I could die."

"Then why do you take them in a combination?"

"Oh, I suppose that's what you want, your depressed wife to cough herself to death!"

In the mornings she was always in a terrible mood, and in the afternoons he didn't see her because she was sleeping. He hated cooking only for himself, hated eating alone. But what could he do? He would have tuna sashimi, with some soy sauce and wasabi. He had never had tuna of the kind he bought in Maui, or pineapples. He ate them in the afternoon, while he planned his dinner menu, read cookbooks, went on the computer, emailed his friends, called one of his children and sat on the patio, smoking and waiting for his wife to awaken. The sun was bright, the wind high, the trees sparkling green, and twice a week the rolling lawns in the condo units were mowed and the air smelled so green and fresh and cut-grassy as he ate his dripping mangoes.

Allison got up hours before George, despite the black blankets she hung on her windows to keep the light out. As soon as the Hawaiian sun shot an arrow of light over the horizon at five, Allison was up. She didn't want to be up. She wished she could sleep soundly through till midday. When the children were small, isn't that what she had dreamed about? Isn't that what her oldest daughter dreams about now, with four little ones of her own? To sleep and not be awakened? Why won't Allison's body sleep past the squinting sunrise?

It's that Hawaiian sunrise.

At night she stayed up until two or three in the morning, watching old movies, infomercials, the psychic network, the shopping channel, and had big plans for herself for the next day. Big plans. She would get up, and go for that cursed beach walk with him, and she would clean and do laundry and then maybe they would go out for the afternoon, go for a drive, into the fucking rainforest, into the fucking volcano. To Lahaina maybe where she could do a little shopping, a little window browsing. They would find a restaurant right on the ocean and have dinner while watching the sunset. Oh, and she would read. She had the time. Her older daughters kept sending her novels to read. Her small condo was overwhelmed with their packages. It's not that she didn't try to read. She did. She just couldn't read a single sentence through to the end. Not one. Her mind would start wandering, she would lose track of her thoughts, she would start examining her hands, dotted with age, darkened with the years. Her nails, thinking about polish, red or clear? She would—

Nothing held her interest, not a single word in anybody else's life. Don't they know what's happening to me, she wanted to cry. I'm old. My skin is sagging, and the corners of my eyes have turned down. I'm bloated and I've got skin where I shouldn't have any.

The look of love is in your eyes . . .

Sometimes music played from the past in the quiet condo.

I want to be young again, she cried, standing by the window. I want to be young and to swim in the sea, and fall in love, I want to be beautiful and watch him fall in love with me.

She told this to George and he flung out his hand and said, "Swim in the sea every fucking morning, Allison."

"You don't understand anything," she said. "I said swim in the sea *young*."

She wasn't growing old gracefully.

The day was so long, there was so much of it, and there was nothing she wanted to do, there was nothing she needed to do. Was Hawaii beautiful? Yes, so what. Peaceful? Still so what. She constantly wished for rain. Rain! Sky be cloudy! Be gray.

Every day was like every other. The morning was crisp, in the afternoon there were winds, and the evening was all gold hues and still waters. Come another day and another and another. After living in seasonal New York so many years, after coming from damp northern Poland as a little girl, Allison had said all her life that what she wanted was somewhere warm to rest her weary bones. They came to Maui when they heard it was paradise. And here it was.

Allison had never been more miserable.

She cleaned the condo, but that took all of an hour. She showered. She made her bed. She made coffee. She smoked. She pretended to read the paper, she pretended to read books, she thumbed through catalogs, she indifferently watched TV. She didn't know how to make her life right. If only she hadn't had all those children. They sapped, sucked what young life she had had and weren't any comfort to her in her old age either. She never heard from them. Even from youngest to whom she still sent money. Allison didn't hear from Lily the *most*. The ungrateful youngest child. The noose around the neck of Allison's thwarted ambitions.

But it wasn't the non-existent career she lamented the most.

It wasn't the children. It wasn't the husband. It was the loss of youth, the loss of youthful beauty, the loss of skin tone and smoothness, the pert freshness of her young legs, her arms, her flat stomach; it was the vertical lines, the horizontal lines, it was the neck that no amount of Creme de la Mer could fix. Youth. In the war against Time, her minuscule armies were being defeated, and it wasn't an even fight. Time knew she wasn't a mythical creature that sloughed off its old skin as it went into the sea and came out fresh to her daughters and granddaughters as the young girl inside the old woman. This was no time for myths. The whole day time toyed with her, laughed at her.

And at five in the morning when she woke up with the sun peeking promise through her room darkening blankets, time mocked her the most.

8

The Disadvantages of
Walking to Work

Spencer was outside Lily's door. It was the end of June. She was wearing her work uniform—black pants and white shirt. Her short hair was slicked back and still wet.

"Detective . . . if Amy comes back, don't you think you'll be the first one I'll call?"

"I don't know, will I be?"

"Isn't there some other vice in this city besides missing persons? Isn't anyone committing crimes out there? I know the mayor's 'Clean Up New York' program has been a considerable success, but there must be something else for you to do." They turned the corner and continued down Avenue C.

"There isn't." He looked dispirited. "These missing person cases . . ."

"Is this a standard case, then?" Lily wished she hadn't said that. It sounded so flip. What if he said yes? Yes, this is just one of our regular, run-of-the-mill, nothing-special-about-it cases. In one month it won't be a case anymore. It will be a statistic. Lily shivered in the heat. Why did she ask?

But Spencer to his credit said, "Amy is not a standard case." And when Lily was afraid to look at him, lest she see the lying in his eyes and he see the skepticism in hers, he repeated, "Really. She is not. Missing person cases are in many cases misunderstandings. Someone moves away and doesn't leave a forwarding address. Or someone goes for that planned two week trip to Europe and decides to stay for three months. Or the teenager runs away with her boyfriend whom her mother forbids her to see. The family hires a private eye, and with luck finds them in two weeks."

"There's no private eye for Amy." She said that wistfully.

"Oh, but there is."

She stopped walking and looked at him in surprise.

"Jan McFadden is paying for him. Lenny, the muckwader, sacked after twenty years on the force. We sacked him, now suddenly he's indispensable."

"Is he a gumshoe, Detective O'Malley?" Gumshoe was such a funny word.

"Gumshoe is one way to describe him. He is an unhealthy version of my partner, with less fashion sense. Lenny hasn't turned up anything. And that's saying something because Lenny trudges up dirt we don't even ask for." Spencer paused. "Lenny is . . . shall we say, a bottom dweller."

"Oh. Well, that's good then. Amy is obviously not at the bottom."

"Who knows? She's made herself impossible to trace. But don't you see, in the discarded identification is everything. She didn't leave her identity behind every time she went out. You said so yourself. *Sometimes she left it,* you said. When Amy left the apartment without ID, it meant one of two things: either she was trying to protect herself, or she was trying to protect whoever she was with."

Lily was quiet. "She wasn't that calculating. Maybe she's working somewhere. What about a check of some kind, Social Security maybe?

"Last Social Security entry dates back to the second week in May, when the tax was taken out of her paycheck at the Copa Cobana."

He had already been so thorough. "Anything else to check?"

Without looking at her, he said, "In New York State there

81

have been no reports of deceased unidentified young women either in hospitals, morgues or funeral parlors. There have been no reports of unidentified young women found in crashed cars, train wrecks or public parks. And believe me, we have men combing through every bush around the Central Park reservoir. It should only take us another three or four years to search every acre."

She was storming for other ideas, trying to be helpful, walking briskly. Lafayette Street never seemed so far away. He walked alongside her. "Maybe," said Lily, her voice weakening with the slowing of her heart, "Amy doesn't want to be found."

"Maybe," said Spencer, "Amy wants to be found but can't be."

9

Ignorance in Amy's Bed

Lily was awake at three in the morning. She was lying in Amy's bed, staring at the ceiling, thinking about Amy, trying to trick her mind into not thinking about Amy. There was something bothering her terribly. She kicked off the covers, she spread her arms and legs, pretending to fly. Her limbs felt a peculiar aching, and her heart wasn't letting go of the needles. A water faucet dripped in the bathroom, she could hear it clearly through the open door. She wanted to get up and close the door but couldn't.

Something was wrong inside her. Her weakness, her sadness, her exhaustion. Maybe Spencer was right, maybe she should go talk to somebody. But who?

She could not go to sleep. An inner beast was gnashing its teeth on her spleen, sucking out her bone marrow—Oh God!

She jumped up off the bed. Where did she get the energy to do that? She was so tired. But she jumped out of bed and stood for a moment, panting, looking down at Amy's quilt, Amy's pillows, Amy's sheets.

She went into the bathroom and then into the kitchen to get some water. Afterward she sat cross-legged on the floor in her own empty bedroom and dialed 1-800-m-a-t-t-r-e-s, leaving the last S off for savings. In fifteen minutes at four in the morning she bought herself a full-size mattress with a frame, all for five hundred bucks—her last week's earnings—and it was going to be delivered just hours later at eleven. What a country.

After she hung up with the bed people, she lay on the futon in the living room/hallway and turned on the miserable middle-of-the-night TV, channel-surfed for a few nightmarish minutes—cream on your face, psychic on the 900 line, lose weight fast with our successful formula—then picked up the phone again and called the precinct. The night-time officer asked if it was an emergency, and she didn't think it was, but she couldn't be sure.

"Detective O'Malley is not on call tonight, miss. I can tell him in the morning when he comes in that you called. Are you in trouble?"

She thought she was. But to the officer she said no, and hanging up, lay on the futon, turning the sound off on the TV and staring at the flickering screen. She thought of calling the beeper number on his business card, but didn't. Words from an almost forgotten Springsteen song kept going round in her head. *Hey man, did you see that?/His body hit the street with such a beautiful thud/I wonder what the dude was sayin'/or was he just lost in the flood?*

She played around with the remote and adjusted the colors to black and white. Now she was watching the Psychic Network in black and white and as she stared into the TV all she kept thinking about was the weeks and weeks she had spent sleeping in Amy's bed without ever bothering to get her own, as if she knew in her deepest, blackest heart that Amy was not coming back.

They had plans to get jobs together. They were both artists, they both painted. Lily liked to paint people, she had a facility with faces and bodies. Amy liked to paint still life—chairs, pots, trees. They sketched together in Washington Square Park and in Union Square Park, and in Battery Park, and even in the homeless-addled, heroin-addled Tompkins Square Park. They sketched the nightlines of Broadway and Fifth Avenue and later painted in

84

the colors. But in many sketches, particularly of late, Lily had been noticing that while she continued to add color where color was needed, Amy left her own work black and white, gray, tonal, uncolored. There were no yellows of street lights, no reds of traffic signs, no blues of police cars. Amy's night-time Statue of Liberty, night-time World Trade Center, night-time Empire State Building remained dark and colorless. One sketch was all black tones, and when Lily asked what that was, Amy replied that it was Times Square from Broadway at midnight. Where are the billboards, Lily asked. They're always lit. *It's foggy*, said Amy, sounding so empty. *It's a blackout. Can't see them.* Why was Lily remembering all that now?

She slept on the futon and remembered Amy, and when she woke up, Amy was so vivid as if she were still in bed sleeping.

And Lily cried.

The mattress came, the iron frame. She tipped the two Hispanic delivery guys twenty bucks for being young and flirty with her, showered, got dressed and went to work a double. After making one-hundred-and-seventy dollars, she took a cab back home. She paid ten bucks to take a cab home from work every night now, the days of no cabs long behind her. One evening it had occurred to her that if only she cashed in her 49, 45, 39, 24, 18, 1, she could have a limo and a driver waiting for her every night when she finished her shift as a diner waitress. She had laughed and walked home that night.

Tonight Spencer was waiting for her on the front stoop. "How long is that shift, anyway?" he said, closing his police notebook.

She couldn't help a small smile. "Detective O'Malley, it's nine thirty at night. Don't you ever *not* work?"

"Not when I have a mother who calls me every day wanting to know if I've found her child," said Spencer.

Lily stopped smiling and was silent. Silent or defeated. She made to move around him but he took her arm. "Why did you call me in the middle of the night, Lilianne?"

"I—" she stammered.

"Did you have something to tell me?"

"I just—I got worried about something."

"About what?"

"I don't remember now."

They sat down on the stoop. It was a New York night in July, still dusky out, still hot out.

"I'm not Miss Quinn anymore?"

"When Miss Quinn calls me in the middle of the night she automatically becomes a Lilianne. City regulation 517."

When does Lilianne become a Lily? She wanted to ask but didn't. It sounded too flirty.

He said, "The Odessa Café on Avenue A and 7th has very good stuffed cabbages, and I'm starved. Can I work *and* eat?"

"Will eating count as working?"

"Of course. Dining with witnesses. It's called canvassing. Come. While you eat, you can try to remember what you were thinking about at four in the morning. But you know, don't you, that if you're calling me at that time of night, I'm going to think Amy has come back."

"Unfortunately, no." She struggled up from the stoop and saw he struggled with resisting helping her. She wanted to ask if she could call him Spencer. Seemed odd to be so formal. "You must see quite a bit on these mean streets, no?"

"Yes, especially in your neighborhood."

"Did you say you drove a patrol car on the LIE before coming to New York?"

"Yes."

"You went from being a traffic cop on the expressway to manning a special division?"

"Before that I was for years a senior detective up in Dartmouth College."

Lily perked up. "That must have been some great job! I actually took a tour of Dartmouth in my senior year in high school. It sure looked like an awesome place to go to school."

"Hmm," he said. "I didn't go to school there. I wouldn't know."

"But what kind of investigative experience was that for you? Arresting frat boys on Saturday nights for underage drinking?"

"If only," said Spencer.

Lily glanced at him with curiosity. "More?"

"A little more."

Was he clamming up? "Detective . . . does Ivy League Dartmouth have a steamy underside?"

"I don't know if steamy is the right word. Maybe wicked."

"Oh, do please tell. I *love* wicked stories."

"Another time. Though I do like your faith in the things you believe to be true. It's very youthful." He smiled. "I'm slightly less youthful."

At the diner after they sat and ordered, Lily said, "I remember what I wanted to tell you."

"Is it something about Amy?"

"Yes. She took two years off between high school and college. Right after high school she went traveling cross country with some friends of hers from Port Jeff. Eventually I think she got tired of the whole thing and came home."

Spencer became interested in Amy's sabbatical. He asked about the people she traveled with. Lily told him what she knew which wasn't much. Lily didn't know any of the other kids. Paul might've though, having gone to the same high school.

"What happened to them all? Did they come back to Long Island, like Amy?"

Lily wasn't sure. The only thing she thought she knew for sure was that one committed suicide, one OD'd, one was killed in a drunk driving accident, smashing their traveling van, and two were still at large. But she wasn't sure.

Spencer stopped eating his stuffed cabbage.

Lily coughed. "She was evasive when she talked about this period in her life. She told me some anecdotes, of Kansas, or New Orleans, but she hardly volunteered information other than to tell me a little about her friends, and to caution me against using drugs." She looked into her cold cabbage. "She was like you with Dartmouth. Cagey."

Spencer tapped on the table to get her attention. "You better hope she wasn't like me at Dartmouth. But are you telling me that of the six people that went in one beat up van—three of them are dead?"

"If you put it like that."

"How would you put it?"

"Just life, detective. Car accidents, drugs, suicides. What else kills the young these days?" Lottery tickets?

Spencer quietly studied Lily. "Aren't you wise. I'll tell you what else kills young people. Unlawful killing. Homicide. Manslaughter. Killing with depraved indifference to human life. Murder. But two more people missing? Paul must know about these kids. They all went to the same high school. Tomorrow you and I will go talk to him."

"Spencer—I mean Detective O'Malley . . ." she turned red. He smiled. "I don't know if Paul knows anything. But these kids aren't the important thing."

"You don't think so? Six people in one car meeting with extreme fate? Not important?"

Lily wondered if their birthdays or significant digits were 49, 45, 39, 24, 18, 1. But why would she wonder that? What did *her* six numbers have to do with six people she did not know?

She knew Amy. Amy was 24.

Lily was 24, too.

This was a stupid line of thinking. Lily wished Spencer hadn't led her to it with his talk of fate.

When he went to pay and took his cash out, a stash of lottery tickets fell out of his wallet. She laughed. "Aren't you an optimist. Are you collecting them?"

"Yes, when I get to twelve, I check them all at once. But what, you just collect the one on your wall?"

Her heart skipped a beat, another. "So is there anything at all that you don't notice, Detective O'Malley?"

"Obviously, Miss Quinn, or I wouldn't be still looking for your roommate."

They met the next afternoon in the downstairs reception area of the precinct to go see Paul at the salon. Spencer had on a suit jacket in which he looked boiling hot, while Lily had practically no clothes on at all, and still had glistening arms and legs and neck. New York City in July. Hot.

"A little warm in that jacket, Detective?"

"I am, yes. But who's going to take me seriously if I wear skimpy shorts and a tank top, Miss Quinn?"

Lily squinted. Another tease from Spencer? She didn't want to draw attention to the fact that he noticed her summer outfit. He didn't seem to be the kind that noticed that sort of thing. He noticed everything, as an officer of the law, but not *that* sort of thing. Yet he said *skimpy* shorts. When she walked in front of him to cross the street she wondered if he was watching her.

"Your partner doesn't come with you?"

"On little errands like this? Nah. You've seen Detective Harkman. He likes to save himself for the big trips. Most of the day, he's just a housemouse."

Lily laughed at the terminology.

At the salon, Paul declared that he knew "nothing about nothin'." That period of Amy's life, he told Spencer, was a two-year hole from which Amy emerged intact, as if the two years had never existed. She graduated high school, she disappeared, she went to find her wild and new self, she came back, her wild and new self found, and re-entered life. She enrolled at Hunter, became a waitress at a cocktail bar, transferred to City College where she met Lily, re-established her friendships, and did not talk about the two years on the road.

"I'm not asking about the two years on the road. I'm asking about the people she traveled with."

Paul didn't know them.

"You and she weren't friendly in high school?"

89

"Best friendly."

Spencer waited.

"We lived on the same block but we didn't hang out with the same people, all right. She hung out with some real losers, and I didn't. They weren't musicians, they weren't jocks, or nerds, or in choir. I don't know who they were. I don't know them, don't know their names, don't know what happened to them. Like I said, we didn't travel in the same circles back then."

"I see. Could you point them out in your high school year-book?"

"God! I don't see what it matters. It was six years ago. What does high school matter now?"

"Could you point them out in your high school yearbook?" repeated Spencer.

"No, I don't think I could."

"Did they belong to a club?"

"I don't know. I don't think so."

"Were they political maybe?"

"Maybe. I don't know about them. Political! They were just a bunch of going-nowhere potheads."

"Amy too?"

"No, not her! She just got mixed up with the wrong people, all right?"

"Well," said Spencer, "it would be all right, if Amy weren't missing for two months, but since she is, it's not all right, no. Your friend here seems to think it was something stronger than pot."

Paul shot Lily a withering look, standing clutching his colorist's chair. "Does Harlequin know this for sure?"

"Harlequin knows nothing for sure," said Lily.

"Exactly," said Paul.

Spencer led her away, his hand momentarily pressing her between her bare shoulder-blades.

Talking to Spencer about Amy was getting to be bad for Lily's ego. It was like being with Joshua. It was occurring to Lily with startling alarm how many things she ought to have known that she didn't know.

Did Amy live a life that was more troubled and troublesome than Amy let on, coming from white, middle-class, peaceful Port Jefferson? Did Amy have secrets she kept *so well*? Or was Lily less interested than she realized? She didn't know and didn't want to know.

How long had Lily not been able to speak normally to her mother? When did her mother so thoroughly and completely check out of Lily's life? She didn't know and didn't want to know. Ten years ago after that blasted emergency ulcer surgery? Nine years ago in Forest Hills when she fell out of a chair (!) in the apartment and broke her arm, and her father said, "Mommy is fine, she's fine, don't worry, she just fell."? Lily thought it was an aberration, a Polish accident, it was so long ago. But there had hardly been a mother since then. What had her mother been doing *for nine years*?

One more layer of bottomless ignorance.

10

Thinking About the Ungrateful Child

It was five in the morning, the sun was barely up, while Allison, who *was* up, was up seething.

She never called, never, Allison thought, as she meandered from her room to the kitchen, wondering if she wanted something to eat. She didn't even call when Allison sent her half her rent plus a little extra. Since Amy went missing, the entire $1500 has been on Lily's shoulders, and Allison wanted to help her daughter, who didn't even call to say thank you! Not even a thank you for sending nine-hundred dollars, as if the money was a given, a birthright.

Typical of her. Lily always took everything for granted, as if it all were just handed down on a large platter for the youngest child. Allison heard George snoring behind the louver doors of his small room. Hear that? He sleeps as if he doesn't have a care in the world. Nothing fazes him. Not my ill health, not my depression, not my unhappiness, nothing. He doesn't need me either.

She glanced at her bills, in a pile on the desk, at the unopened packages from Amanda and Anne. They kept sending those damn books. You'd think they'd call once instead.

Nobody calls.

Oh, Andrew calls every week, to say the quickest hello to her and to then to speak for half an hour to his father. Andrew, who's got no time for anyone, speaks to George for half an hour every week! They pretend they're talking politics, hockey, but what they're really doing is ignoring her. And even Andrew has been calling less and less lately.

She went into her bathroom, and examined her face in the mirror. It was bloated and swollen. She examined her graying teeth (because of all the smoking and coffee) and her yellowing skin. She looked for the cranberry juice. She wasn't feeling well. The cranberry juice would soothe her. Make her feel better. She poured herself a drop of cranberry juice into a highball and stared at it. All she wanted was relief from being awake at dawn. She couldn't sleep, she didn't want to eat, and there was nothing at all in the whole world she wanted to do. All she wanted was relief from this.

She went to her closet that was piled high with clothes on the floor, winter clothes that she no longer wore because they were in Hawaii. They weren't needed the same way she wasn't needed. She could be lying in a heap in the closet. Her hand deep down inside the sweaters, she rummaged for something, down below, layers hidden, to the right and at the bottom. It wasn't hard to find. She struggled a bit and then pulled out a gallon, half-empty, of Gordon's gin. Before she pulled it out, she felt around the bottom to make sure she still had another full gallon left. She did.

She brought it to the countertop where her cranberry juice waited for her. She stared at the highball for a moment, and at the bottle in her hands. She decided the hole inside her was too big today to fill with such a little glass. Tomorrow she would get herself in control. Tomorrow she could sleep past five, and maybe go for a walk with George . . . though what for? Really, what for? Why should she get herself in control even tomorrow? Like she had somewhere to go.

She unscrewed the top of the gallon of gin and with shaking hands lifted it to her mouth. The hands could barely hold such a heavy bottle. She opened her throat and poured the gin in, barely even needing to swallow. The bottle was much lighter, that was good. And her heart was much lighter. That was good too. So good.

She had to put the bottle away before she lost—

11

Spencer PATRICK O'Malley and LiliANNE Quinn

To get out of the heat of her broiling apartment, Lily was sitting in air-conditioned Odessa at eight on a Sunday evening having dinner when Spencer walked in. The diner was nearly empty, but she was hidden in a booth a few tables away from the front door and he didn't see her. He went to the cash register, where Jeanette helped him. He was in jeans, and was wearing an incongruous denim jacket. Lily was nearly naked, she was so hot. Looking at his jacket only made her hotter. She didn't want him to see her, so she slid down in the seat and surreptitiously watched his exchange with Jeanette.

He ordered a turkey club.

"Will that be to go or to stay, Detective O'Malley?"

Jeanette was twenty nine and a waitress for eleven years.

He said it would be to go.

"Why don't you stay for once? I'll be glad to take care of you." And she giggled!

He said no thank you, just a turkey club no mayo, a large coffee, a large Coke, and a cup of coffee while he waited.

Jeanette, all breasts and batty eyes, said she would be right back and went to the kitchen. Spencer turned away from the counter to look at the patrons in the diner. Lily slid down further in her seat.

He saw her.

She sort of smiled and waved, and closed her sketchbook as he walked over. She had been sketching the empty countertop of the diner on a Sunday night with herself not Jeanette standing behind it.

"Hello, Miss Quinn," he said.

Lily said hello.

"Jeanette, I'll have that coffee now, while I wait," he said to the waitress, who brought him a cup, eyeing Lily with extreme displeasure as Spencer sat down in the booth across from her.

Lily asked if he was on duty today.

"No, I try not to work weekends," he said.

He should have looked better for not working weekends. He looked wiped out, like he hadn't slept in days. He was unsmiling until he surveyed the food in front of Lily—a BLT, a Greek salad, a slice of cheesecake, Jell-O, and bread pudding.

"Hungry today?" He smiled slightly.

A little sheepishly she told him she never knew what she was going to feel like until it was right in front of her.

Jeanette brought Spencer his brown paper bag, placed it in front of him and said, "Here's your stuff, Detective O'Malley. Would you like me to ring you up now?"

Spencer said, "On second thought, I will stay and have it here. Could you bring me some mustard, please?"

They ate their food quietly. She was a bit more chatty than he. She asked him why the jacket in the heat and Spencer pulling it open and revealing the holster with a weapon in it, said, "I prefer not to brandish the Glock when I'm off duty. Makes people nervous."

She asked why he carried a piece if he was off duty.

He said, "The gun may be smaller, but I'm required to carry it at all times. Off duty is just for pretend. To deceive us into believing we're fairly compensated for our trouble. We're never off duty. New York City would go broke if they had to pay us for 24/7 of service."

She asked if he lived around here, if this was his local diner. He seemed to be so well-known by Jeanette—though she didn't say that.

"No, I live on 11th and Broadway."

Oh, she said, that's so close to Veniero's! that sublime bakery.

"I wouldn't know. Never been there. Don't care much for sweets." He eyed her dessert buffet. She shrugged, and said that she did care a little bit for sweets.

They finished eating and paid their separate checks. Jeanette seemed pleased by the separateness. Spencer opened the door for Lily, and Lily was pleased by that.

"You spell your name oddly," he said, as if making a statement of extreme importance and fascinating fact.

"Oddly, why?"

They were walking back from Odessa. It was dark now and warm; they were full. Spencer slowed down a bit, Lily slowed down a bit, they were sauntering. From a bar they passed on Avenue A, loud music blared. Bruce Springsteen was *out in the street/walking the way he wanted to walk.* Spencer hummed part of the song before he answered. "I don't know. Lily-Anne. I've heard of Lilian with one 'el' and Lillian with two. But Lili-ANNE?"

She couldn't tell if he was teasing her, she didn't know whether to tease back or proceed with solemn caution. In the end she opted for caution. "I was born sixteen years after my brother was born, and my mother, having forgotten that she already named my oldest sister Anne, wanted to name me Anya, or Anita, or something like that. My father said they already had an Anne, but my mother didn't see his point. They didn't have an Anita. My father asked if they were Hispanic. That's when my mother came up with Anya. No Anya, my father said. No Anastasia, no Anika! They had an Anne. No more Anne. So my mother's *valiant compromise*, as she calls it to this day, was to name me Lili*anne*. So she could still get that Anne in there. I don't know how he agreed."

Spencer smiled and when he looked at her, he looked at her differently, with more familiarity. "I know how he agreed. The way *my* father agreed. When I was born my mother put on my birth certificate Patrick O'Malley, and never told my father. She called me Baby for the first three months of my life, so my father never even knew the truth, and never asked, God bless him, until I started to smile."

"You didn't smile for three months?"

"Would you smile if you were called Baby for three months?"

"Good point. What was wrong with Patrick?"

"They already had a Patrick."

Now it was Lily's turn to look at Spencer differently. "They named you Patrick and there already was a Patrick?"

"Yes."

"How many of you were there? Please tell me more than two."

"Eleven."

Lily's eyes widened. "You might want to forgive your mother," she said. "Eleven kids."

"Who said I didn't forgive my mother?"

"So did she nickname you Spencer for Spencer Tracy?"

"Correct." Again looking at her with friendly approval.

"Spencer is a nice Irish name." She stared at the pavement.

"Quinn is a nice Irish name. Why does your friend Paul call you Harlequin?"

Lily was discomfited. "Once he saw a clinch novel in my room. Has never let me forget it."

"Oh, yeah? My sisters read those and never stop torturing me. According to them the only way I'll get hitched is if I become more like the man from one of those novels. From which series was your book? Temptation or Intrigue?"

"Blaze," said Lily, flushing with embarrassment and then laughing when she saw Spencer's amused face. They were at her apartment, and she had a tinge of regret that the stroll was over so soon.

"So why did your mother like the name Anne? Who is Anne?"

"I don't know. My mother just likes that name."

"Likes that name a *lot*," Spencer said thoughtfully.

Lily glanced at him at the top of her stoop. "Detective O'Malley," she said, teasingly, "I'm sorry to inform you but my mother's preference for the name Anne is not one of your MP investigations."

"Don't be so sure. What about your other sister? She's just plain Amanda."

"That was my mother's continued subterfuge over my father. AmANNEda."

Spencer grinned. "Your brother? Was he spared?"

"ANNE-drew."

"Ha!" And then he said, "Oh, of course, your brother is *the* Andrew Quinn, the congressman for the first district?"

"Yes. *The* Andrew Quinn."

"Well, congratulations. He was just re-elected last year, wasn't he? I remember it vaguely. That was a squeaker."

"You can credit me for that squeaker, I campaigned for him. Me and Amy. And it was a landslide compared to his first election against Abrams."

She opened her front door, while he remained at the bottom of the stoop. "Very, very interesting, Lily Blaze Harlequin. Well, good night. I still say you might want to look into your mother's regard for the name Anne."

"Thank you, Detective O'Malley, in my copious free time I'll do that."

"Miss Quinn, you can call me Spencer."

She had a smile on her face the entire five flights of stairs.

12

A Little Rented Honda

Lily was having a rare and desultory conversation with her mother and she could tell it was desultory by the amount of quick, sloppy black circles she was dashing off on her sketchpad, wearing down her nub of charcoal, getting black all over her fingers and her quilted bedspread. She had just come out of her bath—she had been taking baths for a while now, she found herself too tired to stand in the shower.

Now she was feeling relaxed and sleepy and her mother was keeping her on the phone. Lily was on her new comfy bed, with the sky-blue curtains behind her tied in a bow, billowing in the hot breeze. Black circles, black. Blah blah blah. Then her father came on the line and said, "Did your mother tell you she drove the car into a ditch?"

There was silence.

"Can you get off the phone?" said Allison. "Can't you see I'm talking to my daughter?"

"What ditch?" said Lily incongruously.

"Oh, a little ditch by the house," said Allison.

"Your mother means a ravine, Lil. She crashed the car into a ravine, left it there, and now has to go to court to explain to the judge why she would leave a perfectly good Mercedes in a ditch without notifying either a tow company or the police."

Allison had nothing to say to that.

And the only thing Lily said to it was, "Is that the first time Mom drove the car into a ditch?"

"Yes, it's just an aberration," Allison said.

"Oh, yeah?" said George. "Tell that to the stop sign you plowed through and knocked over on Wailea Drive last month."

"It doesn't count," said Allison. "That was a rental car. A Honda."

"Your mother is on a lot of medication, Lily," said George, realizing perhaps how this was all sounding. "Sometimes it knocks her out. Makes her shaky behind the wheel."

Lily called back the next morning when she was pretty certain her mother was asleep. "Papi," she said, "You can't let Mom drive a car. The first time was a stop sign, the second time was a ditch, but the third time is going to be a woman with a baby carriage."

"I know, you don't think I know? I know! Who lets her? I don't let her. I tell her all the time I'll drive her anywhere she needs to go. What else do I have to do? But she says she wants to run out for fifteen minutes to the drug store. And Lily, think about it, what am I, her policeman? Did I retire so I could police your mother? She is a grown woman. She knows when she should and shouldn't drive."

"I don't think she knows. I don't think she should drive at all. At the best of times she's a bit . . . erratic."

"I don't know this? I know this better than you, daughter."

"What's wrong with her, Papi?"

"Ah. You know your mother. She loves her histrionics. She loves for everything to be about her. Look at me, I'm sick, I'm depressed, I'm not well, I'm going to court. What a sham it all is. There is nothing wrong with her."

Lily waited. "Nothing?" she said.

"There is one thing wrong with her. She keeps falling down. She can't walk down the one step to the sunken living room, or up one step to the front door to get the mail without falling down. You should see her legs. You wouldn't believe what they look like. And her arms. They're covered with black and blues. You almost can't imagine how terrible and bruised her legs look. And your mother has such nice legs, as you know." He chuckled. "If someone didn't know any better, you'd think she was a battered wife."

Listening, falling in her sadness for her mother, Lily said, "A person who can't walk down one step into the sunken living room should not be driving."

"Don't tell me. Tell her." He paused. "She's sleeping now. Is that why you called? But you know, she doesn't go out that often. Not often at all. Maybe once a week. She suddenly rushes out. And usually it's after a good week."

"'Good' meaning . . . ?"

"Meaning, she's not screaming, or upset, or incoherent. She even goes walking with me. Then suddenly she rushes out, and things turn bad again for a few days, for a week. I think those meds she keeps taking are no good for her."

"Papi?" Could she get the words out? She took a deep breath. "Something is wrong with mom. She . . . could she be . . ."

"What?"

Lily said nothing. She was such a coward.

"What? Drinking, you think?" he said finally.

She let out her breath. "Yes." What relief. Yes! Drinking. And she didn't even have to say it.

"No, no. I don't think so."

Lily waited. George waited. "Papi, could she be running out of alcohol and then driving to go get it?"

"I don't think so. She comes back with bags of stuff: shampoo, soap, lotions, bleach, her pills. I carry the bags in for her. I know what's in them. There is no liquor in the bags."

"Okay, Papi."

Lily thought on the way to work that she hoped Spencer was a better investigator than her father, because otherwise Amy was doomed.

13

Lily and the City of Dreams

One late Friday night Lily was wandering the streets of the East Village looking for the posters they'd hung up of Amy, wandering from Avenue C, Avenue B, Avenue A, First Avenue, Second Avenue, Lafayette, and on Broadway, in front of Dagostino's she ran into Spencer who was with a thirtysomething woman, her arm through his. He was casually dressed in slacks and an NYPD light jacket, the woman was wearing a skirt and blouse. Her hair was long and brown. She was tall. Pretty.

Lily's mouth had opened into a gleaming Hi! she had been so happy to see a face she knew, and then she saw the threaded arms and didn't know what to do or say. Spencer said *Hi, Lily,* not gleaming, and—

Lily felt so unbearably awkward she wanted magic powers that would let her fall through the sidewalk and down into the firepit of hell. On a Friday night she runs into Spencer, grins like an idiot, and now the smile is cemented on her face, and she doesn't know where to look, and how in the devil's name is he going to introduce her, a lumbering oaf—

Spencer said, "Mary, this is Lilianne."

That's all he said. Lily shook hands with Mary, who smiled politely, so well-mannered, so groomed, like a smart poodle.

"Nice to see you," said Lily, detaching herself. "Listen, gotta

103

go, sorry," waving and running into Dagostino's to hide in the frozen food section. Oh, God!

After an unreasonable time in the French Fries and the Lean Cuisines, she left the store, and meandered back home, so absent-minded she nearly walked through Tompkins Park.

She was disgraced. She couldn't think straight. She bumped into Spencer while by herself on a *Friday night*! What kind of a loser was she, roaming the streets of New York at midnight on a Friday? She was loser number six, that's what kind, Amy knew six deadbeats, of which Lily was the last.

But also . . . while *alone* on a Friday night, she accidentally and surprisingly—even to herself—felt joy at seeing Spencer, a familiar face, a familiar person, and less joy when she realized he was not alone.

It was days later when she finally calmed down long enough to resign herself to the slight aching left by the memory of the female arm through his male arm. But not because . . . no, not at all because . . . it was nothing like that, he was too old and not her type, and she was too young and not his, obviously. She knew herself, she knew she was telling the truth—there was nothing untoward in her aching. It wasn't because of him in the particular. It was seeing the warm familiar female flesh through warm familiar male flesh—the companionship of coupledom that wounded Lily. They were all around her, she realized belatedly—on Friday nights, couples, arm in arm, walking through Greenwich Village in the summer, happy to be alive. And even Spencer, harassed, glum, overworked Spencer, who almost didn't seem like he was a man, and yet, decidedly—a man! Not a detective, not a cop, not a professional, but a *man*, walking with a woman, who was touching him, and he was not objecting. That was the aching in Lily. The wanting of the wanting to feel. The envy and piercing sadness at the realization that someone, who she thought was her kindred spirit in this—who she also didn't think felt—felt.

* * *

Rachel, ever at the ready as a matchmaker, promptly fixed her up on three dates, crash and burn all. One barely spoke English, here from Morocco on a student visa wanting to become a professional basketball player—this at barely six feet tall. Even Lily had more sense.

One was a senior management accountant with Deloit. He was thirty-one, short and square, but wore clothes that were too hip for him, and drove a flashy car and hung out in bars trying to pick up younger girls. He spent the entire dinner advising her to change her choice of future profession from "something in art" to something more sensible, and take a course to become middle management for a large brokerage firm. ("That's where the money and the security is.") Lily was surprised to find herself thinking how different Spencer seemed from this man, how sturdy and un-middle-aged, even though there was something slightly grave about Spencer, as if he walked around carrying the feeling that life had already passed him by.

The last one was a mixed-race kid from Coney Island, who was adorable, but was obviously on drugs from beginning of the date to the end, and possibly went into the men's room to take another hit of whatever he was on (coke? heroin?) during their dinner on bar stools at a cheesy Mexican take-out in Clinton Hill. He was disjointed and could not focus on anything she was saying, which admittedly wasn't much. But was he ever *cute!*

She asked Rachel not to set her up on any more dates. Rachel thought she was being too picky. "You've built a wall around yourself, a forcefield, and you're not letting anyone near."

"Thank you, doctor."

"You can't let Joshua have so much power over you, Lil."

"He doesn't have any power over me," Lily protested.

But Paul, who had heard about their exchange, called the following day. "He has all the power. You gave it to him during your relationship, and you're giving it to him still. Keep going out with the boys, be happy."

She had gone out with the boys, but how could she be happy?

She felt something slipping away from her, but didn't know how to fix it because she didn't know what it was.

Just to show what kind of power he had over her, Joshua called, hemmed and hawed, asked a few perfunctory questions, and then asked for his TV back. Apparently Dennis's broke. He came over for five tongue-tied minutes and took his TV! He asked Lily to open the door for him, and she crossed her arms and refused.

Paul stopped calling her Harlequin. She missed that. He stopped calling her as often. She missed that, too. He said he was busy, Rachel said she was busy—to think that Lily would care if Rachel was busy! But she did care, she did. Lily couldn't help feeling a prickle of judgment coming from Paul and from Rachel, characterized by their uncharacteristic and displeasing aloofness—judging Lily for losing Amy and not knowing where she put her.

Spencer told her the yearbook had proved to be a dead end: Paul could not recall a single one of Amy's other friends, not even visually. He pointed to three that looked familiar, but upon being checked out, they all turned out to be alive and well, and teaching or mothering on Long Island. Amy's mother also was drawing a blank. The rest of Amy's friends she could not recall, but Paul she knew well. Amy's friendship with Paul was really, *really* well corroborated.

Chris Harkman remained behind the desk, plowing through Lily's phone records. Despite thorough checking, Harkman could not find a smoking gun in the phone numbers. 90% of the calls were placed by Lily to her siblings and grandmother. In April, calls were placed to an upstate New York number. That damn Shona, still repeating like a bad taste in Lily's mouth! Amy's phone calls included ones placed to Paul, Rachel, Copa, to ask for shift switches, and that was *all*. Spencer said to Lily that Amy's use of the phone seemed just like her ID on the dresser and her lack of mementoes from her two years on the road—all suspect because they were so circumspect. She was so careful that Amy.

106

"There is something that I'm overlooking," Spencer said. "I'm sure of it. I just don't know what it is." Amy left no clues behind because Amy meant to leave no clues behind. But did Amy mean to vaporize? Or was that the unplanned thing? One thing was certain: after May 14, and until Lily returned on June 4, there were no phone calls placed from the girls' apartment. Wherever Amy was, she was no longer at the apartment after May 14.

After being seen with a grown-up woman on his arm, Spencer turned professional with Lily, careful and circumspect himself. The two of them would stand at the precinct, or at Noho Star, chat for a few minutes about yearbooks and phone records, and then he would be on his way. He stopped coming around or calling nearly as often—maybe twice a week, Lily would hear from him, about Amy. She missed him a little bit, missed something calming about him, something supportive, and sensible, and true.

New York, the city of dreams, the city of nightmares. New York for the poor, for the rich, for the homeless, for the multi-aboded, New York for the eight million people who roamed within. New York when it rained, they all went into the bookstores, and when the sun shone they sat on the grass in Central Park with their books. They complained that it was too noisy, too overpriced, too amphetamine-charged, too multicultural, too dusty. They all lived single in the great city, and when they got married and had children many left. Lily's friends, Erin and Michael, he a 24/7-admitted workaholic stockbroker for Shearson Lehman, moved out of New York when they had kids. They moved to New Jersey. They bought a high-rise apartment in the Palisades so Erin could look at New York whenever she wanted. He didn't have to look, spending all his days there, in the World Financial Center, making millions, losing millions, clogging his arteries with stress and bad coffee.

But Lily wasn't married and had no kids. There was nowhere else for her to go. She lived close to Lower East Side where her mother and grandmother first lived when they came to America, and every time she wanted to walk off a part of her life she walked the streets of New York until she walked herself out of it.

She couldn't walk far enough to rid herself of the persistent nagging caused by Amy's persistent, unending absence.

"It's because you're depressed and broke," said her sister Anne. "The depression is depleting you from the inside out. Being broke sucks. But I gotta go, Lil."

"It's because you can't walk off something like your roommate missing," said her other sister Amanda. "Go dancing. That will cheer you up. Go ahead, like you used to. Everything will be okay. You're young. But I gotta go, Lil."

But Lily didn't have the energy to go dancing.

Once I had been clarified by Joshua, by Amy. He's not coming back, and until she returns I'm in limbo. Amy, come back and tell me what I'm supposed to do at twenty-four in the middle of my life. Define my life for me, Amy.

How long was she going spend all her earnings on Union Square Café's exquisite calamari and yellow cabs? Until Amy came back.

How long was she not going to cash in her lottery ticket?

Until she found out who she was.

Until Amy came back.

As if not cashing it were insurance against the unthinkable.

Her exhaustion got worse. Got so bad that she had to cut her hours from fifty to forty, to thirty-five, to twenty-five. She would sit down on her break and fall asleep, and once they couldn't wake her. They got so scared, they had almost called 911. Turned out she had walking pneumonia. She took antibiotics and ate calves' liver for dinner every day until she lost her appetite for everything, not just calves' liver. She was afraid to get on the scale. Even Yodels didn't tempt her. Though they tempted her in the Associated supermarket down the street. She had big plans for Yodels, for Chips Ahoy, for Mallomars, for Double Chocolate Milanos, for German Chocolate cake, for strudel, for Krispy Kreme donuts. Then she would come home and put her goods on top of her microwave. She would balance them delicately atop the microwave and once she sneezed and the top six boxes of Entenmann's and Pepperidge Farm ended up on the floor. She didn't pick them up for . . .

Well, they were still on the floor, and unopened.

It was warm, but she felt cold, bundling herself in a thick cardigan that belonged to Amy, and going to the movies to sleep.

Her mother sent money for August, threatening that it was going to be the last time. When Lily cut her hours down she asked for a little extra, but Allison refused to send it. She yelled into the phone for ten minutes, while Lily, phone cradled to her ear, sketched with her soft charcoal a large black mouth perpetually open in a screaming O.

"Your father is telling you venomous lies about me, I know. While I sleep, so sick, my body old, shaking, bruised, full of medicines that keep me alive, I know he calls you up and complains about me, tells you I'm drinking, but what about him, does he tell you about himself, how he refuses to be a man to his wife—"

"Got—To—Go—Mom. Got—to—go."

She burned her forearm at work, and over days it became so infected it required emergency medical treatment and more antibiotics. She was a walking mold spore. She tried to eat yogurt to counteract the Ph imbalance in her body, but found that she had gone off yogurt. She kept bandaged the burn that wouldn't heal. Not so much kept bandaged as kept hidden.

14

Grandma Helpfully Worried About Lily

On Thursday, August 5, Claudia sat Lily down and said, "I'm not going to beat around the bush. The family is worried about you."

Lily squeezed her hands together, realizing they were numb, released them and said, "Don't worry, Grandma, I'm just tired, that's all."

"That's not it," said Claudia. "You're not too tired to find a job, are you?"

"Oh, that." Yes, too tired for that, too.

"Yes, that. The family wants to know if you're looking for work. For meaningful work."

"Tell them all, from me—no."

"Stop wringing your hands. You're not helpless. You're a college graduate."

"Not quite."

"Well, that's deliberate, you know it is. What, you didn't know you needed one more class to graduate? One more. Three hours a week, three credits. You didn't know that?"

I didn't know that. Did she have enough energy to say it? "I didn't know that." Good, Lil.

"Puhlease."

"Grandma, I was already taking eighteen credits last semester, the maximum you can take."

"You could've gotten permission."

"In case you don't know, I work to pay my rent."

"Your mother sends you half your rent. Your boyfriend, and Amy—they pay the rest."

"Perhaps you didn't hear me speaking to you these last three months, but Joshua's been gone since April. And believe it or not but Amy has not paid her rent since she went missing in May."

Claudia continued as if Lily hadn't spoken. "I think you kept three credits, consciously or subconsciously, so that you could hang on to something, hang on and not move forward. I think you want to feel that you're still unfinished."

She wanted to tell her grandmother that she *was* still unfinished. Unfinished, unanswered, unformed. "I can't have this conversation again. Here are the magazines." She stood up from the couch and swayed.

"You're not getting any younger, you know. Only you think your time is infinite. But you're twenty-five next month. And then youth is gone. Ask your mother how she feels about her youth being gone."

"I know how she feels. She's told me enough times. And you know what, my mother has bigger problems than her youth being gone."

"What kind of problems?"

"Never mind."

"By the time I was twenty-four, do you know what I'd done?"

"Yes, I know, Grandma. You've told me—"

"I'd been in one concentration camp, Ravensbruck, and one death camp, Sobibor. I walked two hundred kilometers carrying your mother on my back. I lived in DP camps near Hamburg, sleeping on the ground for three months, and then in typhoid barracks. All this by the time I was twenty-four."

"—A thousand times," Lily finished quietly.

Claudia remained sitting. "What are you waiting for? You want to turn out like that young woman in Iowa?" She said nothing

111

more, as if Lily should have intuited, or perhaps known the rest.

"What woman in Iowa?" Lily finally said in a flat drone.

"The woman, thirty-four years old, was riding in the passenger seat of her car and a landscaping block fell from an overpass and crashed through the windshield. It hit her in the face. A two-foot-square concrete block struck this woman in the face. What does this tell you?"

"She shouldn't have been riding shotgun?" offered Lily.

"Exactly. Lily, don't be caught in a passenger seat with a concrete block in your face."

Lily wanted to tell her grandmother to stop, to desist for a moment, to remember Lily, to remember Lily's life, that Amy was missing, that her mother was missing, that Joshua, yet another supposed constant, was missing. That even she, Lily, was missing. But no way to talk about that when her hands, her thighs were going numb, *numb*! No way to talk about anything. She left.

Friday night, August 6, Paul asked her to come watch him perform his music at Fez on Lafayette. She was happy to be asked, so she went but found it nearly impossible to remain upright. The noise, the smoking was debilitating to her in ways she could not explain. She left as soon as Paul's set was over. At home the machine was chockfull. Rachel asked her to go to the movies tomorrow. Amanda called to invite her for Sunday dinner. Anne called just to find out how she was doing. Her mother called, spoke in some sort of code. "Your father will be the death of me," was all Lily could decipher. The coke-addled cutie-patootie called asking her for a drink but in Bedford-Stuyvesant. "I don't do Manhattan, baby," he said, "but boy do I do Bed-Stuy. Come out, I'll show you a good time . . . like before." She smiled. He had been such a good kisser.

But Lily didn't do good time in Bed-Stuy anymore, not with the bruises that appeared on her legs, on her lower arms, on her shoulders. Bruises on her thighs, on her shins. She refused to notice them a week ago, thinking they would go away, not recalling when she had banged herself, but over the last weekend, she hadn't banged herself at all, yet they appeared and stayed. The older ones weren't turning yellow either. They remained black and blue, and new ones came, and grew while Lily slept. Did she fall and not know it? Did she bump into futons, furniture, flowerpots and not know it? Was she sleepwalking? Indeed, indeed she felt as if she were sleepwalking.

15

Spencer Gets to Twelve

Thursday, August 12, Spencer asked her to come to the diner. They walked in clipped silence, she slowly. The numbness and heaviness in her legs made it difficult for her to keep up with him. It was a scorching New York evening, but she wore jeans and a long-sleeve Gap shirt to cover her bruises. No more skimpy shorts for Lily. He walked alongside her, and once she thought he was going to offer her his arm, but he did not. Would she have taken it if he did? She would have taken it and pretended for a warm second she was a Mary on a Friday night.

At the Odessa, they had barely sat down and ordered soup and stuffed cabbage before he said, "So I got to twelve."

"What?"

He pulled out the stack of lottery tickets out of his wallet. "Twelve. Remember I told you, when I get to twelve, I check them all at once?"

"Yeah . . . did you win?"

"No, believe it or not."

"Hmm."

He took out his notebook, flipped back several pages, and showed her the numbers 1, 18, 24, 39, 45, 49. "But guess what? As I was checking mine, I came across these, from April 18, and they rang a small bell in my head, because I'd seen them before, you see, and I couldn't remember where, but having searched your apartment, I had written these numbers down in my blotter."

Lily was quiet for a long time and didn't look at him. "All right. So? So, there's a lottery ticket. So what?"

"So what? Lily . . ." Spencer put his hands, his notebook on the table, staring at her. "Did you . . . win the lottery back in April?"

"I don't know," she said. "I didn't know if it was the right date."

"Oh, it's the right date, all right."

She didn't answer. There was no question.

"What's wrong with you?" said Spencer, and Lily for a moment, just like with her grandmother, didn't know what he was referring to, so wrong was the feeling of malaise in her own body. "Don't sit there, *please*, and pretend that you have no earthly idea what I'm talking about when I say what's wrong with you?"

"Did you come to deride me? Because I have no energy for it."

"You have no energy for a lot of things."

"And how's that any of your business?" Her face was harsh, angled. "Are we done here? I don't owe you an explanation, do I?"

Spencer shook his head. "You don't owe me an explanation, though I would like one."

"Oh, Spencer." Lily resisted the impulse to cover her face. "I have no explanation."

"Did you win the lottery and not claim your ticket? Do you understand why that might seem slightly off the wall to a broke cop making seventy grand a year, talking to a waitress making maybe thirty?"

The sausage soup came. The stuffed cabbage, the Coke, the coffee. They remained untouched between them, as Spencer and Lily sat, she with her hands squeezed under the table, he with his fingers intertwined tensely above it.

"I don't know what you want me to say."

"Look," Spencer said. "It's normal for you to be down on

yourself. There is no denying that something terrible's happened in your life. A young girl disappears, and despite a concerted effort of the New York police, involvement of the FBI, and a private detective, there is no evidence of her. She fell into the earth, she vanished into the air. She left the country. She is dead. She called no one, took no money out, packed nothing, left no note. One day she simply vanished. And we keep going over the same unfertile ground. We have nothing new to say, yet we keep picking at it like an unhealed sore, like the burn on your arm."

"Detective," said Lily and broke off. She was hoping her voice would be steady. "What if . . . How can I go on with my life if Amy—God help me—lost hers?"

"I don't know." Spencer wasn't looking at Lily. "I don't know how I went on when I lost my wife at twenty-three in a car accident. I didn't win the flipping lottery, I can tell you that."

"I'm sorry about your wife."

"Don't be sorry. It's been many years, I've moved on. But why are you sitting in your room, looking at the four walls, at the six numbers on your cork board?"

"I don't know," she said.

"So? Make yourself feel better. Paint. Did you do that oil on canvas I saw in your apartment? Of the girl in Times Square? It's very good. Paint some more."

"Don't feel like painting."

"So go out with your friends, go to a club, go to the movies. Go to dinner. Forget the guy who took your bed, he isn't worth it. Go out with other guys."

She shrugged. "Well, look, I've just decided that I'm single for a reason and that's nothing to worry about. Annoying when I have to take the garbage out every Monday and Thursday night. But hey, some poor, desperate soul will find me in the end. That's the thought I can cling to. And then you get into all the drama of having to be nice to people . . . who me?"

"Lily . . ." he said soothingly, reaching over to touch her hand.

"I admit I'm a little bit stuck. But what about you, detective?"

"What about me? *I'm* not the point. I have a grown-up life. I'm not twenty-four. I haven't won eighteen million dollars."

And she wanted to say that she didn't feel like she was twenty-four either.

49, 45, 39, **24**, 18, 1.

"Is it because of her that you haven't claimed it?"

"Not really." She didn't want to look into his face.

"Why then?" he asked. "It goes against human nature. It goes against everything I understand about human beings and I make my living off my gut feelings."

She couldn't tell him that at the moment she was having some small spiritual difficulties, and she refused to muddle further her already muddled free choices by the temptation of an unsought—and unwanted—miracle. She did not know what kind of life she was supposed to, or even wanted to live but claiming the lottery would remove the choice from *her*, and even though she was wallowing and foundering and maybe even a little drowning, she didn't want her Grandma-given, God-given freedoms trampled on in this way. An enslaved heart could not choose wisely—or unwisely. So even though these days she was mostly sleeping—she still wanted to reserve her rights for the just in case.

That is what she was *thinking*, but to Spencer what she was *saying* with a careless shrug, was, "I don't know what to tell you. I just didn't, that's all."

"Why would you not collect your money?"

Lily said nothing.

"Answer me, why?" He raised his voice a little.

Lily touched the cup of coffee. It was now cold. She motioned the waitress for another cup. But Spencer was still, and still waiting for an answer. "Why are you yelling at me?"

"I want you to give me an explanation I can understand."

"Detective O'Malley," said Lily dryly, "no matter how much you want it to, the lottery ticket is not going to figure into Amy's disappearance."

Undrunk coffee, uneaten soup, Odessa, August, numb legs, humid heat, noise, feebleness. And Spencer leaned across the table, and said, "I'm just trying to talk to you, and you're missing my point entirely. Do something besides work and fret. Claim your money, move to another city, give it to the downtrodden, pour it into your brother's senatorial campaign—anything—" He broke off suddenly, stopped talking, stared at her.

She didn't know how she got up every morning. She had no idea how she was going to make good on her words to Andrew back in spring, when she said she would help him with his campaign.

Spencer was still considering her intently, his mouth mulling. "What's the matter?"

He blinked, came out of it. "Nothing. I'm going to have to leave you here. Get back to the precinct ASAP." Standing up and taking out two twenties, he threw them on the table. "I thought we were a little bit friendly," he said coldly, "could talk about things." He walked out, leaving Lily alone at the diner.

The next morning, Friday, August 13, Lily was still asleep when the phone rang. She didn't pick it up. It was Detective Harkman. He called again five minutes later. She didn't pick it up.

Half an hour later, her door bell rang. That was just unfair. Through the intercom, Harkman's voice sounded, "Miss Quinn, can we talk to you a moment, please?"

Unbelievable. She asked him to wait downstairs, while she quickly (molasses slow) got washed and dressed.

Outside, Spencer and Harkman were both waiting for her. Spencer didn't look her way. Harkman said they wanted to talk to her for a few minutes at the precinct. They drove her back in their patrol car. She sat in the back like a perp.

Back in Interrogation room #1, she was across the table, but from Harkman this time. Spencer stood in back of her with his arms crossed. She didn't understand what was going on. Spencer was silent and cold.

"Miss Quinn," Harkman said brusquely, his little eyes beading into her. "Something Detective O'Malley and I wanted to talk to you about, something we needed to ask you. Just a couple of questions really about one tiny inconsistency."

Spencer said nothing. Lily wondered why he was letting Harkman question her, as if he were deliberately removing any personal connection between them, as if he were saying to her, fine, you treat me like I'm nobody, I'm going to treat you the same way—like you're nobody. She felt a pang of guilt. Harkman was asking her something, but she was so flushed with remorse, she didn't hear.

"Miss Quinn!"

"I'm sorry, what?"

"Did you say you worked on your brother's reelection campaign last year?"

"Yes." She frowned.

"Did you tell Detective O'Malley that you and your friend Amy both worked on his campaign?"

"Yes, I probably mentioned that. We helped at the Port Jeff office. We got a college credit for it, for our political science course. Why?"

Harkman and Spencer exchanged glances. "In my notes," and Harkman leafed through some papers, "in my work on the background of this case, I spent many hours calling the numbers on your phone statements. One of the numbers was your brother's congressional office in Washington."

"So? I call him there all the time."

"Yes, yes. It took him a while to call me back, it says here in my report that I had to call him three or four more times before he would speak to me."

"He's always like that. I haven't spoken to him in months."

"Our conversation was very short. I just asked if he frequently got phone calls from your apartment, and he said, once or twice a month, you would call him, and the phone records do confirm that, as well as his phone calls back to your apartment. Sporadically regular I would say, lasting for twenty to thirty minutes."

"Yes."

"We had a very short chat and hung up, but not before I asked him if he knew Amy McFadden, and do you know what your brother said?"

Why did Lily's heart start to beat so fast? What could he have said?

"He said, Miss Quinn, that he could not recall."

In a voice that was not hers, Lily said, "Could not recall what?"

"Amy McFadden."

They sat mutely, Spencer behind her, Harkman panting in front of her, while she herself thought she stopped breathing.

"I don't understand what you're telling me," she said at last. "I don't understand what you're asking me."

"I asked him if he knew that she was your roommate, and he said, he thought so, but he said it vaguely. He said he really could not recall her. He said it twice. Then he had to go and we hung up. And do you know, we thought nothing more of it, because it was nothing, until yesterday when Detective O'Malley came in to the office, and brought it to my attention, this small contradiction."

Nothing moved on Lily, except her head, which slowly and desperately turned to look at Spencer, her eyes pleading with him to help her, to explain, to make it clear and all right. "I don't understand what you're saying," said Lily in a shaken voice.

"Miss Quinn." That was Spencer. He finally spoke. His voice was like he did not know her. He came around the table and stood at its edge. "In light of what you've told me, it seems peculiar that your brother would say he didn't recall your roommate when you and she helped him with his reelection. Either he doesn't recall her, or she helped him with his campaign, not both. Both cannot be true. Either you are not telling us the truth—

120

Amy did not help with his campaign. Or he is not telling us the truth, and indeed he does recall her."

"Please," whispered Lily. "I don't know what you're saying." Her palms down on the table, Lily leaned forward, hyperventilation attacking her lungs. "Detective," she said, trying to breathe slower, to keep her voice calm. She failed. "I'm sorry, I really don't know what you're implying . . . I don't know what you're asking me."

"Could it be true, Miss Quinn," said Harkman, "that Andrew Quinn does not recall Amy?"

"I guess so, it can be true, yes," she said with breathless panic, placing her hand over her chest to still her heart. It was *Impossible!* Perhaps an interrogation room was not the place for such exclamations of the soul. Her voice lost its fight and got progressively weaker. She was whispering now. "It can be true." She was nearly inaudible.

And then the three of them were silent. Spencer watched her, Harkman watched her, and Lily stared at the table. Her whole body felt to be suddenly emptied and re-filled with nerve endings, all shooting electrical anguish into her skin.

"Miss Quinn . . ."

"Please." She jumped up. "If we're done, I have to go. I do, I can't sit here another minute." Lily groaned in the middle of Interrogation room #1 and ran out. Spencer followed her. They stopped on the street outside the precinct.

"Lily," he said, slightly panting. "Are you running away from me?"

"Yes," she blurted. "No." She tried to push past him but he stood firm in front of her. "Just let me through. We're done, aren't we? Let me through."

Spencer took her by her arms to stop her from moving. She was shaking.

"Please," she said. "Leave me alone."

"Lily," he said gently. He was still holding her arms, he almost brought her to him in an embrace, she was too stirred up to

121

know what it was. "I'm sorry, I am. We're just trying to find Amy."

"Oh, giving out traffic tickets on the LIE gives you experience in missing persons, does it?" she exclaimed, trying to wrest from him. Her knees were buckling from sadness. "No," she said, furiously shaking her head. "No!" Even more adamantly. "Whatever it is you're thinking, there's a simple explanation."

"I'm not thinking anything." He let go of her, and she stood still, but went to lean against the dirty wall of the building. "You're the one doing all the thinking. Because you're the only one who knows whether his statement is true." Spencer looked at the pavement. "And from your reaction, it seems to me that you know it can't be."

Turning her head to look inside a window pane, the glass reflecting off her own filmed over glass eyes, Lily put her hands over her face, struggling to keep the tears back.

When Spencer got back to his desk, he sat down heavily, looked around the office, and thought it was time to go—perhaps permanently. Harkman sitting across from him was by contrast jubilant. "Finally! A break in the immovable case. A lead."

"Yeah, a lead." After a few minutes Spencer said, "I think Sanchez and Smith can handle it from here." He turned to Harkman on the swivel chair. "I'm going to give this to them. I can't do it, Chris. I have to get off this case."

"Which case? The McFadden case?"

Spencer nodded.

"What the hell are you talking about? We finally made some headway. A U.S. Congressman!"

Blood ties. Brother and sisters. How Spencer craved a drink. "I know. That's just the thing. I can't do it."

"O'Malley, what's gotten into you?"

Spencer thought back to the white, wet buildings of Hanover, New Hampshire, to Dartmouth College, to the black shutters on his soul; thought back to Greenwich, Connecticut and the tangled web he had once weaved investigating another missing girl and the duplicity and manipulation of the ones closest to her. Their squalid story swallowed him. He couldn't go back to that place twice. It took him years as a traffic cop on the Long Island Expressway before he could face being a proper investigator again. There were some things in life for which once was enough. There weren't many of them. Many of life's offerings were renewable pleasures, like sex, or renewable miseries, like alcohol. But this drowning in shallow waters was not something he wanted to relive even while saturated in Scotch.

"O'Malley, you're overwhelmed. Give your smaller cases to me. Concentrate on this one."

"I'm not overwhelmed. Stop psychoanalyzing me. This is precisely the case I don't want. I'll keep the smaller ones. I got plenty else I need to be doing, and you too. Sanchez and Smith are more than capable of taking over for us."

"I don't want them to take over for us! This is a big case. A Congressman, O'Malley! There might be another promotion here for me and for you, too. I've got a family to think of. I've had three heart operations. What the fuck is the matter with you?"

"Chris, I'm sorry. I just don't want to do it. What can I tell you?"

"But you're the one who came to me with this!" Harkman exclaimed. "You're the one who remembered reading what Andrew Quinn had said. I mean, what the hell? Why are you doing this?"

He wasn't about to explain anything to Harkman. "You can't change my mind. I don't want to get mired in this. There's too much baggage here for me. I'm putting Sanchez and Smith on it."

"No, you're not, O'Malley."

Spencer's clouded gaze cleared slightly.

Harkman stood and came over to Spencer's desk, leaning over him. Spencer moved away, and it must have seemed like wariness, thought it was nothing but distaste. "You selfish bastard,"

Harkman said. "You think you're the only one who knows things. But I know things, O'Malley, I know things about you, the kind that NY Internal Affairs would be very interested in hearing. I've been very good to you, but don't fuck with me on this one, because I need this case. As always, you're only thinking of yourself."

Spencer looked steadily at Harkman's small angry eyes, at his swollen, contorted face. "Don't come any closer to me," he said, standing up himself, and pushing his chair away. "What could you possibly know about me?"

Harkman backed away, half a step. "O'Malley, I promise you. You fuck me over, I'm going to fuck you over, and good. You want a leave of absence? I'll make sure you get a nice long one." Harkman stormed out of the office—like a wounded woman.

Spencer sank back down at his desk. What the hell was Harkman talking about? *Was* he being selfish? Probably. He did not think of how giving this case to Sanchez would affect Harkman. He only thought of how it would affect him—whether he could handle it. He didn't think he could. He couldn't tell Harkman that what he wanted was . . . not to get personally involved, not to hurt Lily. If she was going to be crushed, he didn't want her crushed at his hand. His recusal would be the kindest thing, the best thing for her, and certainly the best thing for him. Spencer felt the murkiness, instinctively sensed the muddy and shallow waters, the swamp of design instead of the ether of accident on Amy's vanishing.

His feeling for his partner changed for the worse. Even more than most people, Spencer hated to be threatened. Of course Harkman was just bluffing. Spencer did have some secrets to keep, and he kept them, certainly from his relatively new partner, practically a stranger. He grabbed his jacket and left.

16

Reality: The Actual Thing
that it Appears to Be

Lily let him in, but so reluctantly she didn't even open the door all the way. "I don't know what you want from me," she said coldly, but couldn't help noticing his drawn face, the somber twist of his mouth.

"I want you to come with me," he said, pushing the door open and walking in, "I want to go talk to your brother."

"I'm not going anywhere."

Spencer took a deep breath. "Do you want to help him or don't you?" He walked into Amy's room.

She followed him. "How is talking to him going to help him?"

He was looking around, swirling his hand through the air. "Lily, perhaps you're deliberately misunderstanding me. You and I can go and talk to your brother right now in his home or my partner and I will have to pay him a police visit."

"Detective O'Malley," she said, wringing her hands in supplication. "Don't you understand? My brother, Andrew Quinn, is a U.S. *Congressman*." She lowered her voice. "He is married. He has two school-age daughters. He's just about to begin a campaign for election to the Senate. It's not just talking as you put it, it's his career and family. Don't you see that? You're a detective, you can't be that thick!"

"Excuse me, yes, I wish I were as sharp as a tack," said Spencer.

He was looking at the walls, in the closet. He was opening the drawers of Amy's dresser. He got on his knees and looked under her bed. "Didn't she keep a journal?"

"She did. I thought you read it."

"Oh, that wasn't a journal, it was a day planner. It had nothing in it. I mean a real journal. Dear Diary, you won't believe what happened to me today, I kissed a boy, that sort of thing. All girls keep one."

"I don't."

"Of course, you do. Your little sketchbook you don't go anywhere without. The one that has your lottery numbers doodled all over it. What do you think that is?"

"I don't know what you're talking about." She crossed her arms. "Do you want to go, or not?"

"She must have had something," he muttered. "She must have kept something somewhere."

"I want you to know I don't want to go," said Lily.

"Believe me when I tell you I want to go even less than you." He straightened up. "I've been down this way before." Spencer glanced away before his gaze became steady again. "This way corrupts the soul. I want to take myself off the case, but—I can't. Perhaps I should have chosen a different line of work. Chances are about even that after this case I just might. But right now, let's go. Perhaps like you said, there's a simple explanation." He paused. "Perhaps like you said Amy will be walking through that door any minute."

In the car, he asked again about the lottery, and this time she told him. He was incredulous and disbelieving.

"You're Irish, you're Catholic," she said. "Don't tell me you don't understand. Half my family is like yours. The other half was across the North Sea from you, living in northern Poland, in the wetlands, praying Hitler wouldn't come up to the parts near Danzig, near the Polish corridor. This stuff can't be all foreign to you." Lily shook her head.

126

"Irish and a Catholic, yes, but not crazy. What, you think because I say the Lord's Prayer I would let a ticket worth eighteen million dollars sit on my wall amid my family photos? And besides, Lily, your *not calling* New York State Lottery does not change the order of things, it does not change the fact that the numbers came up and your name was on them."

Lily looked away from him to her passenger window, to watch the Long Island Expressway rush by, her lids heavy, her legs aching, her fingers slightly trembling. "That, Detective O'Malley," she said, "is exactly what I'm afraid of."

Spencer asked Lily to tell him about her brother.

He was married. Twice. The first time was for love, and lasted eleven days. They were together prior to the wedding for seven years, but the marriage itself lasted eleven days. It produced nothing but a scar from deflecting the knife that was aimed for his heart. The second and current one was . . . who knew. For her love? She loved him, so he married her. And she had a little money. So far so good. Fourteen years later they were still married. And she still loved him. And she loved being a congressman's wife, and she would love being a senator's wife. And perhaps . . . somewhere down the road . . . a president's wife. For anyone who knew Andrew since he was a child knew this about him—he was a born leader of men, and to continue to be one at higher and higher levels was his only stated ambition in life.

He was the president of every club he had ever joined, the president of the National Honor Society, the president of the Law Club, the president of the Student Council. At Cornell, he was the president of the student union, and the captain of the All Ivy Big Red football team in the fall and of the crew team in the spring.

Andrew never failed to get a single thing that he wanted.

So at thirty-four, he ran for the congressional first district in Suffolk County and after a bloody battle and a bitter recount with accusations of wrongdoing by both sides, won by fifty-two votes. In 1998 he won his fourth re-election by a few thousand—he called it his "landslide victory."

"So, Lily, tell me, how well did Andrew know Amy?"

"I introduced them. He knew her through me," she said, gripping her arms. "Not only did we campaign for him, but he took us out to lunch, to dinner. Amy and I came to D.C. once or twice to visit him. We went shopping with him in D.C. last Christmas, we had such a good time." She lowered her head. "Amy came to Thanksgiving with me last year, she came to our Fourth of July barbecue. She was my friend, she came with me. He knew her like Anne, Amanda, Grandma know her. You see? It was just a misunderstanding what he said to Harkman."

The Quinns lived in a large colonial off Old Post Road in Port Jefferson. It almost looked like a regular house if you discounted that it was set about a hundred yards away from the sidewalk, with well-positioned, perfectly-trimmed shrubs on the outside so you couldn't get a good view from the street of any of the windows or doors. Regular if you didn't count the American flag on a twenty-foot pole flying in the middle of the front yard, and an old campaign poster still stuck into the ground near the sidewalk: "Re-elect Congressman Quinn—he is good for Long Island and for your family". Regular if you didn't count the unmarked car across the road with two Treasury agents inside.

The Quinn home was spotless, masterfully decorated, marbled, with hardwoods, and drapes that matched the upholstery, and lamp shades that matched the drapes, with not a paper out of place or a glass in the sink. Miera took care of that for Andrew. She was a good politician's wife. She took care of the house, took care of the girls, and looked great at parties and even better on the campaign trail. Back in 1992, Andrew credited his small margin of victory to Miera's polish, for his opponent's spouse was not nearly as glamorous or attractive. "I'm fully aware of what she has done for me," he said of his wife in his acceptance speech.

Nobody in Lily's family liked Miera. She had a weird name for starters. No one could pronounce it and she hated you for not pronouncing it correctly. People would call her Mee-YE-ra, or MEE-ra, but it was simply MY-ra. Why couldn't she have spelled it that way? She was always testing people—Lily told Spencer—by this first.

Miera opened the door. She was tall, blonde, manicured, frigidly good-looking. Showing his badge, Spencer said, "MEE-ra Quinn, right? Detective O'Malley. You know Lily. We're here to see Congressman Quinn."

Lily tightened her lip to keep from involuntarily smiling.

They waited in the hall, peering into the formals. Spencer noticed that the door was made of thick impenetrable metal, and the windows were tinted, and he would bet they were bullet-proof. He commented quietly to Lily that the home looked well fortified.

"Yeah. It's the politician's life. He's had . . . well, you know . . . a few years ago somebody shot at them as they were coming back from the movies on Route 110. They were just driving down the road and boom. They shot out the windows, scared the girls and Miera half to death."

"I didn't hear about that. Anyone hurt?"

"Yeah, the glass cut them up a bit. Miera had to have surgery, a glass splinter stuck in her eye."

"Who was it?"

"Oh, just some pranksters. No one knows. Stupid kids with nothing to do but make trouble. But once, a small bomb was found by police dogs in his executive suite in Washington. They were searching the whole hotel and found a bomb in his suite. So he became a little more careful."

"So how were you able to go to dinners, lunches out?"

"Andrew is only worried for his family, but he himself won't live in a prison. He takes chances, what can I tell you. So far so good."

They still had not been shepherded inside the kitchen, or

inside an office, or a dining room. They were left standing without a drink, without a seat. Lily raised her eyebrows and whispered, "What did I tell you? She hates me. And after how you mispronounced her name, forget it, you'll never get a drink in her house."

Before Spencer could answer, Andrew came down the hall to greet them. He had a clean-shaven, open, happy, friendly face, a strong handshake. He had height and girth. He had gone gray prematurely, which in politics gave him an edge over his youthful and inexperienced-looking opponents. He smiled, he looked right at Spencer as he shook his hand, he put his hand on Spencer's back and ushered him inside. He gave his sister a bear hug. That was Andrew, a bear hug of a man.

"Lily, forgive me for saying this, I love you like a brother, but you gotta get some sleep. And eat some food. Look at you. Are you hungry?"

She shook her head. They sat on padded cast-iron stools in the granite kitchen, while Andrew himself got them some lemonade. Spencer downed the lemonade, got up from the stool and said, "Can we talk in private for a few minutes?"

In the dark-paneled, cherry-wood office overlooking the coiffed and cleansed green and floral backyard, Andrew sat behind his desk and Spencer and Lily in the chairs in front.

Lily was so uncomfortable that she wasn't able to look up from the floor. There was an unusual pain in her upper legs traveling up to her stomach that she'd never experienced before, a pain that was dull and sharp at the same time, possibly from the bruises on her thighs. If she didn't have such an open pit in her stomach she could see how she might find the pain in her legs and abdomen breath-catching. Certainly she couldn't catch her breath now. She looked over at Spencer, who was completely calm and his hands were not tensely strung together like Lily's to shield him from pain. He looked almost relaxed when he said, "Congressman, do you know why I'm here?"

Andrew smiled pleasantly and shook his head.

The pain in Lily's legs got stronger.

"It's about Amy McFadden."

"Uh—" Andrew paused, glanced at Lily. "What about her?"

"You know we've been investigating her disappearance."

"Yes, yes, your partner, Harkman, was it? He mentioned it before. Has she been found?"

Spencer was silent. "No. But—this is the thing. You know who I'm talking about, don't you? Amy McFadden?"

"What do you mean? She was my sister's roommate." Andrew continued to look at Spencer.

She tried to smile, but she couldn't through her hammering heart.

"Well, that's right. Congressman, why did you tell my partner that you could not recall who Amy was?"

"What? I don't think I said that."

"You did."

"I couldn't have said that. I'm sure I said I knew her in passing."

"No, Congressman. The records of his conversation with you are very clear. You said you did not recall her."

Andrew laughed. "Then I must have misunderstood his question. It was very loud in my office. I couldn't hear. I thought he was asking me about phone calls. I could never have said I didn't recall Amy. It would've been untrue."

"So what did you say?"

"I was perhaps responding to a question he did not ask."

"He was very specific. Do you know Amy McFadden was his question."

"I don't think I heard him properly. Obviously it was not the question I answered."

"No, it obviously wasn't." Spencer glanced at Lily. "So what were you answering?"

"I don't know. But Amy was Lily's friend, and they came to my house for family parties, they came to see me in Washington. I mean, this is just absurd. It's so patently a simple misunderstanding. Either I misspoke, or he misheard."

131

"You did not say, *I do not recall her?*"

"Of course not!"

But, Miss Quinn, doesn't it niggle you just a little bit why Amy would want to keep her love life a secret from you?

Oh my God.

Lily groaned. Both men stared at her. "Would you excuse me," she said. "I'm not feeling well." She hobbled out without even drawing breath into her lungs until she was in the bathroom, where she sat, rocking on the john, with her hands covering her aching legs. The pain was akin to the needles your legs had after they woke from forced sleep. Something like that, except these weren't needles, these were knives, and the legs didn't wake, and the pain did not stop. She sat in the bathroom and groaned and rocked.

Andrew and Spencer remained in the office.

"Is my sister all right? She looks terrible."

"I don't think she's feeling well. She's been a bit under the weather lately."

"She looks it. Detective, is there anything else I can do for you? I'm very happy to help. I didn't know Amy very well, but like I said, I knew of her through Lily. They were very close. My sister was always talking about her."

"Congressman, did you ever go up to visit your sister at her apartment?"

"Yes. Not often. But I've been there once or twice."

"You won't object then if I take a hair sample from you? We have a couple of unknown hairs we've been trying to match." Spencer took a plastic bag out of his jacket pocket, a scraper, and a pair of small scissors.

"Of course, that won't be a problem at all." Andrew bent his head so that Spencer could cut some hair from him. "But it won't show you much. I've been to the apartment."

"Absolutely. We just want to eliminate all the family and friends to see what we're left with."

Spencer thought Andrew was a charming man. He was neutral toward charming men. Their charms were not lost but wasted on him.

"Did Amy ever come to visit you by herself?"

"What?" He took a step away from Spencer and narrowed his eyes.

"Congressman, it was a simple question. Did Amy ever come without Lily, to visit you by herself?"

"Visit me where?"

"Anywhere. Here in Port Jeff. In Washington. In New York City. The question was did she ever come by herself to see you?"

"I don't know," Andrew said. "I can't recall. You have to understand, detective, I deal with hundreds and hundreds of people a week. I can't remember each and every one who comes to see me. I just don't recall. She may have come to my office here, perhaps stopped by, to say hello. Doesn't her family live in Port Jefferson?"

"Yes."

"Well, then. Perhaps she did. I have no memory of her doing that, but it doesn't mean she didn't. It's just something I didn't keep track of." He smiled politely.

"When do you think was the last time you don't recall Amy stopping by?"

"What?"

"You have not answered one single question I've asked you directly. Not even this one."

"If you'll pardon me, this one was particularly convoluted."

"Meant to be ironic. When was the last time you saw Amy?"

"I don't know. It's been a while since I saw my sister, so a while ago."

"When was the last time you saw Amy on her own, without your sister?"

"I told you, I can't recall."

"Would anyone in your office be able to confirm Amy's visit

133

to your Port Jeff office? Your office manager perhaps? Your assistant? Your receptionist?"

"I don't write down impromptu visits from my constituents in my log book, detective."

"Amy was not your constituent. She lived in New York City."

"You know what I mean."

"How often did Amy stop by . . . *impromptu?*"

"Detective, she didn't. What is this?"

There was a knock on the door. "Andrew?" It was Miera. The door opened. "Sorry to interrupt. But something is wrong with your sister. She is . . . I don't know what's the matter with her. She's in the bathroom, and she sounds like she's being cut open."

In the car on the way back, after miles of miles of flat Long Island around them, miles and miles of the Long Island Expressway, somewhere around Westbury, after fifty minutes of silence, Lily spoke. How did Lily manage to suppress a groan, how did she do it? The pain in her legs was unrelenting. In as calm a voice as she could manage, she breathed out, "You see, Detective O'Malley, I told you there was a simple explanation."

Watching him grip the wheel and say nothing made the agony inside her only more acute.

Her brother and Amy flew above Lily, piercing her with their separate life, separate sharp trials. Lily's trials were in her bed, where she lay hurting so badly, screaming to Andrew, to Amy, to Joshua, to Spencer, and to the empty walls, screaming for her mother, for relief. What was it in her body that was shooting her up like this, what was that in her abdomen? Her stomach felt like it was repeatedly being punched by a steel ball from the inside.

Finally, after hours of twisting, she called her sister Amanda, who never called her back, and she called her sister Anne, but she was away and not answering, no one was answering, yet she needed somebody desperately. She could not call her grandmother, who could not go out of her house and could not help her, and she could not call her mother, who could not help her and didn't want to. Lily called the one person she knew would not come. She called Joshua. "I'm sorry, Lil," he said. "I'm still at work and then we're going out. Can it wait till tomorrow?"

She called the only person who would come.

She called Spencer.

It was the deep of a Friday night. She rang his beeper and he called her back within minutes.

"What's wrong?" He sounded like he'd been sleeping.

"Spencer," she whispered, "please could you come and take me to the hospital?"

"I'll come, what's wrong?"

"I don't know. But something is the matter with me." She dropped the phone. "Please come now . . ."

He came now. With his arm around her she got herself downstairs, and slowly, supported by him, they flagged a cab and went to St. Vincent's Hospital on 12th Street.

As the triage nurse was hooking up the blood pressure cuff to Lily's arm, she said, "What are you in here for?"

"Have a stomach ache," breathed out Lily, her left arm still clutching her abdomen.

"Hmm. Blood pressure's low," said the triage nurse.

"How low?" asked Spencer.

"Are you the husband?" The nurse glanced skeptically at Spencer and Lily's unadorned ring fingers.

"Just answer the simple question," he snapped. "How low?"

"Eighty over forty. I'll get the doctor."

She left, and they waited.

"That's low, Lil."

"I know."

Spencer wiped his forehead. Lily was wearing blue sweats. "Aren't you hot?"

135

She was bent over her knees. "I don't know."

The triage nurse came back. "Let me weigh you. Take off your shoes."

Spencer helped her. She got up on the scale. The nurse moved the weights down from 120 to 100. Lily was 102 pounds.

"How tall are you?"

"Five-four."

For the first time the triage nurse glanced at Lily with a note of what may have been concern. "Are you taking any controlled substances?"

"No."

"They're going to give you a blood test, they'll find out, you know."

"I want them to find out."

Finally they took her to a room. Spencer stepped out until she put on a hospital gown. When he came back she was lying on her side, eyes closed, arms entwined around her stomach.

"Lily," he said in a shocked voice. "What in God's name happened to your legs?"

Her thighs had bruises the size of grapefruits. "I don't know."

"Did you fall?"

"No."

"Did someone . . . hit you?"

"Of course not," she whispered.

"So what is it?"

"I don't know. Black and blue?"

"From what?"

Soon the doctor came in, middle-aged, thin, short, indifferent. "I'm Doctor Mladek. What seems to be the trouble?"

Lily was screaming. The pain had come back.

He put a hand on her. "Stop screaming, just tell me what's going on."

She was screaming and couldn't stop. Mladek asked her if she was pregnant. Lily shook her head. Spencer sank down in a chair by the curtain separating her cubicle from the rest of the emergency ward.

"When was your last period?" Mladek was reading her pulse. She had to think about it. "May, I think."

Mladek let go of her wrist. "This could be an ectopic pregnancy," he said to her.

Lily shook her head.

"When was the last time you had intercourse?"

She hadn't been with Joshua since early April and this was August. She narrowly escaped first date sex with the cutie-patootie from Brooklyn. Was she four months pregnant and didn't know it? She didn't think so. Didn't ectopic pregnancies happen in the first few months?

"Let me feel your stomach please." She turned on her back. "How long have you had this pain?" He was feeling through her hospital gown.

"Since this afternoon," she replied.

"Could it be a ruptured appendix?" asked Spencer.

"Could be," Mladek said without stopping his examination. "Quite likely, in fact."

"That would be a miracle," Lily said when she could speak. "Because the appendix was taken out twelve years ago."

Mladek asked her if she could walk to X-ray. It turned out she couldn't. They put her in a wheelchair.

Her bones were fine. But . . . they saw something in her lungs and refused to tell her what it was. They took her blood, they asked for a urine sample.

Finally they made her drink a quart of blue sickly sweet water. "For a CT scan." She couldn't, she kept throwing it up.

Mladek performed his own ultrasound exam, and said in a pensive voice, "That's odd. Looks like you may be bleeding internally. Which would explain the abdominal pain."

"Why would I be bleeding internally?"

"Were you hit? In an accident?"

"No and no."

Mladek left. She was still on the ultrasound table. Spencer was silent by her side.

"I don't have a doctor," she said. "I don't even have insurance. How am I going to pay for this? ER, X-rays, ultrasounds, doctors' fees."

"Self-pay," said Spencer.

"With what?" she whispered.

"With eighteen million dollars."

"I told you I'm not cashing in that ticket until she comes back."

"All right, Lily."

They waited.

"What do you think it is, Spencer?"

"I'm a detective, not a doctor." He fell mute.

The pain inside her abdomen came in waves. Internal hemorrhaging, what, why?

Mladek came back with a nurse. "I'm going to administer a morphine drip," he said. "You need some relief."

She didn't care for a moment what happened to her, all she heard was the word *relief*. "Thank you," she whispered. "Relief from what?"

"Look, we're going to have to transfer you to another hospital. We're going to move you to Mount Sinai."

"Why?"

"They have better facilities."

"Facilities for what?"

"For a bone marrow biopsy." His face was no longer indifferent. "Your white blood cells are out of control. Have you been sick?"

"I haven't felt well."

"Your astonishing numbers of white blood cells, depleted red cells and barely any platelets . . . your leg bruises . . . how long have you felt not well?"

She didn't answer. For months?

"Why didn't you go to a doctor?"

138

"I thought it was just a cold." She stopped to take a breath. The wave crashed into her abdomen again. Where was that morphine? "Then I thought it was psychological. I've been . . . under some stress lately."

"Have you had a cold that you just could not shake?"

"A little pneumonia last month. Is that what's on my lungs?"

"No blood tests?"

"For pneumonia? No. I went to a clinic. They listened to my chest, gave me antibiotics."

"Have you had any cuts or bruises that have not healed or that took a long time to heal?"

She glanced at Spencer, recalling from months ago the cut on her finger that oozed blood for days, her infected burn a few weeks ago. "Yes. I thought it was psychological," she replied quietly.

"Oozing blood is psychological?" Mladek asked. "Exhaustion, loss of appetite, loss of weight, irritable bowel, headaches, those can be psychological. But bleeding?"

"I had a lot on my mind," she said. "I've been sick before. I thought I would just get over it."

The nurse was starting an IV, as Lily lay there with her arm outstretched.

Mladek raised her gown slightly to expose her thighs. He stared at her black grapefruit bruises, silently, and then and walked out of the tent.

They were left alone. Spencer wasn't looking at her.

"Spencer?" she said. "What do you *think*?"

"I'm not thinking," said Spencer.

They remained side by side, glucose slowly dripping into her veins, her left arm still around her crushed abdomen; Spencer sitting on the chair, slightly hunched over, looking at his hands.

"Thank you for staying with me," she whispered.

"You're welcome."

"Were you sleeping when I called?"

"Something like that."

"Were you with . . . Mary?" she asked.

"Yes. Lucky for you I was."

She didn't know what he meant by that—and suddenly there was commotion and Spencer had to get up and leave. She extended her hand to him, but he didn't see.

She didn't remember getting to Mount Sinai. She hoped they took her by helicopter; how cool would that have been. The hospital halls, the walls, the smells were all filtered through the fog of morphine. The stomach stopped hurting. She heard someone say they were going to administer a general anesthetic. "A little oxygen for your leg," a doctor said to her, with a smile, and she felt the knives in her leg again. Catching her breath, she said, "What is that, what is that?" and fell away.

. . . Into blackness, from which she came up an eternity later, she woke slowly and was groggy. Nurses mutely fussed around her, lifting her arm, checking her blood pressure, her pulse, adjusting her IV, refilling her plastic bag, straightening her pillows. Something hurt in her hip, a new pain despite the morphine, through the morphine.

One nurse was black and looked as if she enjoyed her food. She smelled faintly of burgers and Milky Ways and cigarette smoke. She smiled at Lily. The other was Filipino and Lily could have been tuna for all the compassion in her eyes. She wanted to ask for Spencer, but was afraid that he had left. Please, be here. She was not thirsty but her mouth was cracked, her throat was parched. She asked for a drink; the black nurse brought it to her lips. There was no pain anymore, except for the discomfort in her hip. She whispered, "The pain is gone," and the black nurse said, "It's not gone, with morphine everything is hidden." And it was true, everything was hidden.

Everything.

And in the hidden space, between the blackness and the hospital room, in the recesses and nooks of senseless pain, Lily remembered the cold damp—it was in Times Square, it was so rainy, so cold, she wasn't alone that time, she was with Amy, they were waiting for Andrew a long time ago—finally Lily was going to introduce her new friend to her brother. She saw him walking down Seventh Avenue to them. The brilliant billboards were behind him and his raincoat was wet. A black umbrella was over his head, and he was smiling. And when Lily turned to Amy—she was smiling, too.

Libera me Domine. Free me from having to think about it again. Lead me down my way, with no numbers, no steel pipes, no concrete blocks in my bridle path. What joy it was. My whole life on metaphorical morphine.

Libera me Domine.

PART II
THE MIDDLE OF THE ROAD

I said to Life, I would hear Death,
And Life raised her voice a little higher and said,
You hear him now.

KAHLIL GIBRAN

17

The Biggest River in Egypt

"There is something wrong with you. No, no, don't argue. There is. You're sick. You are. You think you're well, you think you can lick it, but it's got you licked. You think you're in control, but it's got you in control. You think you have the power, but you don't have any. I always thought human beings were stronger. When we wanted to, we could just stop doing what was killing us. But I was wrong. You can't."

"I don't know what you're talking about," she said.

"You don't know? What about what's been happening? The screaming, the ranting? What about that?"

"I don't remember any of it."

"You were screaming as if you were being cut open."

"I wasn't. I was fine."

"You're pretending now. You're lying to me."

"I don't know what you're talking about."

"You're taking advantage of me. You're taking advantage that all I want is a peaceful life."

"I'm not taking advantage of you. You're taking advantage of me! I'm sick, and you're yelling at me."

"Look at yourself. Look at what you've done to yourself. What are people going to think when they see your legs covered in black bruises? I've never seen anyone bruised like that."

"My stomach medicine makes me very weak."

"Your stomach medicine? What about the liquor in your cranberry juice glass? Maybe that makes you fall down?"

"There's no liquor in the glass."

"I smelled the glass."

"Nonsense. It's fermented juice. It's been sitting out in your Hawaiian heat for two days."

'You don't think I know the difference between alcohol and fermentation?"

"No, I don't think you do."

"Do you think you're living a normal life?"

"Who can live a normal life in this hellhole. Of course I'm not living a normal life! I'm suicidally depressed. Perhaps you haven't noticed."

"Let's sell the condo and move back."

"You'll have to carry me out of here feet first," she declared. "There is no point in going anywhere. Don't you know you carry what's inside you wherever you go?"

"Yes, yes, you've told me," he said. "But *I'll* be happier in North Carolina."

"It's always about you! You, you, you. Never a thought for anyone else. What about all the money we're going to lose by selling it? It's not your money, so you don't care. You're very casual with my money. Living well now, aren't you, on the blood money I got for my health. I paid for this condo with my health, just so you could live in style, and now you want me to lose money? Never."

"You have to stop drinking, do you understand that? You have to have one glass of beer, one glass of wine, one small sip of cognac and then stop. I do it. I do it every day. Why can't you? I never drank during my forty-five years of work before five in the evening. Why can't you show an iota of self-control?"

"Yes, sorry, we can't all be perfect like you; if only I was more like you, I wouldn't have any problems."

"You have to stop drinking."

146

"I don't know what you're talking about."

George said quietly, "You crash the car, you get your license suspended, and twice a month the neighbors call the police because you're screaming so hysterically they think you're being beaten. I have to hide you in the bedroom because if they saw your legs they'd arrest me for sure."

"Maybe they should arrest you, the way you treat me."

At first he had tried to help her by regulating her, by drinking with her.

He gave her a little wine. She drank the whole bottle.

He bought a six-pack of beer. It was all gone by the evening.

It was all gone by dinner. It was all gone by the time they sat down to watch a movie.

He bought a twelve-pack.

It was all gone by movie-time.

He bought a twenty-four-pack.

It was all gone by the end of the movie.

He stopped buying the beer, the wine, and hid the cognac out in the trunk of the car and went outside at night to grab a quick swallow, like a criminal, a hobo, a drunk. How he resented her for it! Drinking—the balm of civilization. The lubricant of culture. To sit, to read the paper, to watch the news, a little baseball, and to have a small glass of cognac. And now he had to sneak out of his own house for a drink! He never hurt anybody, never ranted, never yelled, the police were never called on his account.

Was it his imagination or was his drink disappearing too quickly in the bottle of Remy Martin he was hiding near the spare tire in the trunk of his car?

18

The Doctor is In

Her doctor at Mount Sinai was a tall WASPian man named bizarrely Lawrence *DiAngelo*, though how he could look so white-bread and have a last name like DiAngelo, Lily didn't know. He said nothing while he looked over her medical chart. He was in his sweats and running shoes and a dark blue Adidas nylon jacket. He looked either on his way to, or coming from, something un-doctorly. Perhaps it was his day off.

"Where is Spencer?"

"Who?"

She sighed, wishing for Spencer and his impassive support. She could never tell what Spencer was thinking, and that was perfect at a time like this.

"It says here you're twenty-four. Is that right?"

"That's right. Why?"

He whistled, shook his head. "You look about sixteen."

"Give it to me straight, doctor," said Lily. "But not until I can sit up." He adjusted her bed so she could sit up. She watched him with the clipboard in his hand.

"You have leukemia," he said, giving it to her straight. "Acute myeloid leukemia. Acute promyelocytic leukemia to be precise."

It's cancer? She breathed out. Cancer!

"Do you know what leukemia is?"

"Yes . . . it's what Jenny Cavilleri had." She had no idea what leukemia was. She was going numb inside.

"Who?"

"Jenny Cavilleri. Oliver Barrett. *Love Story*."

"Oh, that's right."

She sat on her bed and looked at him, and he held the clipboard and looked back at her and she tried to focus on what she was thinking, but at the forefront of her brain, the prevailing thought was, HOLY SHIT, and also, is that why I have gone off Double Chocolate Milanos?

"You must have a million questions."

"I do . . . yes." She couldn't think of a single thing.

"I know this is difficult . . ."

This wasn't difficult. This could not be happening to her. And yet, why wasn't she surprised? All the visions in her head, of shock, of disbelief, of fear, were reduced to Jenny Cavilleri sitting by Wollman's rink watching Oliver Barrett skate before her. She could think of nothing else. Why? She waited for a suitable question to come to her, and she saw the doctor in his Adidas tracksuit and Nike cap waited too. He looked like a decent-enough man. But really, she was fresh out of questions.

The doctor sighed perceptibly. "Do you have any questions for me?"

She said nothing. CANCER.

The doctor read from the report. "You are grossly hypercellular. The cancerous cells in your bone marrow cannot mature into healthy blood cells. They grow big, like blasts, but are vacuous and do you no good. They are lazy and they do no work. They do, however, spill by the millions into your bloodstream. What they don't do is clot your blood, or fight infection, or transport oxygen. They slowly kill you, they don't heal you."

"What about my regular blood cells?"

"No room for them."

"Some room?"

"No room."

"Any?"

"No."

"What am I living on then?"

"Ah, good question. On three red-cell transfusions. On one platelet transfusion. One white-cell transfusion. Someone else's blood in other words."

"I mean before that?"

"I'd guess you weren't doing much living."

She didn't even nod.

"Your veins became thin due to the illness. Finally they burst. That's why you hemorrhaged internally. That's the pain in your stomach, that's the bruising."

"So painful."

"Yes."

"What about the pneumonia?"

"Yes. You've almost reached blast crisis."

"What?"

"That's the term we use for those whose blood has been completely replaced by the rapidly dividing cancer cells. No red, no white, just blasts. You have no choice but to begin chemotherapy immediately. Blast crisis patients do not go home."

"Is that me?" she said in a small voice.

"Nearly."

Lily didn't know what else to say. She breathed out shallowly. "I have to go home for just a minute, doctor," she said. "I have to do a couple of things, tie up a couple of things . . . you know . . . just for a day or two . . ." She had to call her brother. She had to call her Grandma. She had to . . . just see her bed for a second. Is leukemia a bad cancer? It sure wasn't so good for Jenny Cavilleri back in 1970. What does she ask the doctor now? Does she ask if they can cure it? Does she ask for her odds? She doesn't want to know. She wants to ask . . . has the cancer spread? She doesn't want to know. She wants to know . . .

"Why?" But she knows. 49, 45, 39, 24, 18, 1.

"There's no why. People just get sick." They sat. She could see the doctor wanted to get up and leave. "Do you want me to get Spencer? Is he your husband? Maybe we should go through the rest of it with him in the room."

"Through the rest of what?"

"Your treatment. Your protocols. Your therapy. Your care. Your prognosis. Your future for the next four months, and beyond. Your fertility options."

"My *fertility* options?" She clasped her hands tighter. "Spencer is not my husband. He is not even my boyfriend. He's just . . . a police detective who brought me here. What fertility options?"

He clasped the clipboard tighter. "Isn't there anyone I can call before we do this? Isn't there someone you want here with you during this time?"

"*Fertility* options?" she said in an empty voice. Her whole life she had never considered that question except in the contraceptive negative. She thought she had plenty of time for the fertile positive.

"Oh, God. Marcie!"

The black nurse with a yen for Yodels and burgers and cigarettes came in.

"You've met Marcie, your critical-care nurse. Marcie, meet Lily. You'll be spending quite a bit of time together. Now, Lilianne, who can Marcie call for you?"

Her hands squeezed and released the pillows underneath her as she shook her head.

He unbuttoned his nylon jacket. He was sweating. He looked up at Marcie helplessly. "I'll be back, all right?" he said. "I need some air."

"Me, too," Lily called to his leaving back.

"You giving the doctor a hard time, child? Don't you know he hates to see young ones like you get sick?"

"How would I know that? Can you tell me . . . please . . ." Lily became afraid she wasn't going to be able to get the words out. All of a sudden she felt monumentally small, monstrously alone. Her voice broke. "Is there anyone in the waiting room for me?"

Marcie went to look.

Marcie came back.

"No," she said.

When the doctor returned, she said in a defeated voice, "What about finishing college, what about painting, work?"

The doctor put his clipboard down. "Listen to me," he said. "For the next four months of your life forget school, forget work. Forget everything. I can't imagine you've been doing much of work lately the way you must have been feeling. Didn't you hear what I said? Blast crisis, Lily. Your blood looks like Beluga caviar, nothing left in it but black cancer."

"So what now?"

"Now we try to kill it. I'll let you go home until Monday. You've got a day and a half to sort yourself out. But Monday, you'll be with me for a month. In-house chemo. Then for three months we'll try the outpatient way, see how you do."

"Why such a long time?"

"Four months? I know this has to sink in, but you have cancer, don't you understand that?"

"I understand." She didn't at all, though. She may not have been surprised but she didn't understand either. "What about . . . the other thing you talked about . . . the fertility options?"

"I'm sorry, Lily." He shook his head. "We have to begin the chemo on Monday, and egg fertilization takes time. Since you don't have a boyfriend, perhaps even longer—you'd have to go to a sperm bank, find a donor." He paused. "It's not for you. The only thing remotely left is Lupron."

"What's Lupron?"

"It's a drug that makes your body think you're going into menopause. It stops your egg production temporarily. It's only about twenty percent effective in preventing sterility."

"Oh God, stop, stop, please . . ."

He stopped, stopped.

Finally she said, "Twenty percent is better than nothing."

"Before I tell you about Lupron, I'm going to tell you about cancer. The only point of it is to kill you. That is its sole objective. It doesn't want to do anything else, it does not moderate itself, it does not weaken when you weaken, it just gets stronger, and perversely, if you manage to get stronger, it gets stronger, too. It literally eats your healthy blood. Which is why we throw all our men in front of its tanks. Which is why we fight poison with poison. We put poison drugs into your body to try to kill the thing that's killing you. And sometimes that works. Sometimes. But in the meantime, for the duration of the battle, it poisons you too, it poisons everything healthy inside you. It makes your vital organs sick, all of them. The cancer and the chemo do battle inside your body, and it's a vicious bloody battle, Lilianne. You are going to feel very sick. And now about Lupron— I can give you the fertility drug, but Lupron is a division in your cancer's army, not yours. Lupron is a weapon against you. It will give you sweats that will make you feel like you're burning from the inside out. I advise all my patients against Lupron, but I have to inform them of it anyway. Do you understand?"

"And either way my hair falls out?"

"Right."

Lily said nothing for so long. Finally she said, "Who wants to live bald?"

Larry DiAngelo laughed, and took off his baseball cap, underneath which he had a shiny bare hairless skull. Lily smiled.

"And after four months I'll be all better?" she said, in a voice so hopeful and small she was embarrassed for it.

"You have advanced acute pro-myelocytic leukemia. I hope you'll be better."

"Or . . ."

"Or Oliver Barrett is sitting on that bench by himself."

The hospital room was private with beige curtains and beige walls, and smelled slightly of alcohol and bleach. Through the window was sunlight, the TV was attached to a wall bracket above the doctor's head. Lily sat and looked at her white sheets, at her blue specked gown, at the window, at the TV, at anything but DiAngelo. Finally she closed her eyes. "That's just the thing, doctor. Don't you see? In Central Park there is no Oliver Barrett."

Spencer had stepped out to make some work calls. He asked a grumbling Harkman to meet him at the precinct later in the afternoon.

When he came into her room and saw her in the bed, he summoned his strength and smiled. She looked a little better after the blood transfusions. He sat by her side.

"Did you hear?" she said. "I'm sick."

"Yes, DiAngelo spoke to me. You're in good hands with him, I can tell. You'll be fine." He tried to sound bright himself.

"Can you believe it?"

"I can't believe it." He tried not to look away from her.

She had a pale look about her. "Looks like you were right, Detective O'Malley. Looks like I'm going to have to claim that lottery prize."

"Looks like you are, Lily. I can think of worse things than claiming eighteen million dollars."

"Yes, you're looking at them." Self-consciously she reached for his hand. She felt like a little girl, holding his grown man's hand. They were quiet by each other. "Spencer, please," she whispered. "I need my brother, I need him now."

He pulled away from her. "Lily, every day Amy's mother calls me to ask if I have found her daughter. My job is to find her. Wouldn't you want someone to find you for your mother?"

"I'd like someone to find my mother for me."

"Oh, Lily."

She closed her eyes.

In an hour she was provisionally discharged until Monday.

* * *

154

In his unmarked Buick he drove her home where she pulled her lottery ticket from the wall while he waited.

"So what do we do, just go in and get my money?"

"How would I know? I've never won a single thing."

"Lucky you," she said.

He drove her downtown to the World Trade Center where the New York City Lottery office was located under one of the twin towers. She felt like fainting.

"Are they going to ask me how I would like my money?" she asked him.

"Yes," Spencer replied. "Tell them you want seventeen million singles and the rest in twenties."

She wondered if afterwards they could get a hot dog and sit near the fountain in the square in the fresh air space between the towers. She always liked sitting there. It was so peaceful. But she didn't feel like a hot dog today. She could barely remain upright. She sat in her chair, with her head back against the wall, until it was her turn.

When she went to validate her ticket, the lady behind the glass looked at it, looked at her ID, at her signature, punched the number of the ticket into her computer, and raised her gaze at Lily. She studied Lily. "We've been waiting for you for three months." It wasn't like she was curious, it was just beyond her. Some people.

The cashout amount on the $18 million ticket was $11.34 million. After federal and state taxes, the amount was $7.3 million. From $18 million to $7.3 million in a matter of five seconds. The wind was taken out of her. Even the unflappable Spencer seemed surprised by the reduction. Shrugging finally, he said, "So you might as well get the whole thing in singles then. It's barely anything. Laundry money."

She was told she would get a check in three weeks at a press conference at the Waldorf Astoria Hotel. She didn't know what to tell them. "Can I get some of my money now?"

"This isn't a bank, Miss Quinn. You do not withdraw from

your account," said the dull-eyed woman in the cash cage.

She didn't know where she was going to be in three weeks but she was pretty sure she wouldn't be able to gallivant about luxury hotels. She asked if New York State could just mail her the check.

"We have a press conference. Anything over a million dollars, we have a press conference at the Waldorf. It's policy. That's just what we do."

Spencer asked Lily to go sit and wait for him in the chair and talked quietly to the cashier woman.

When Lily struggled back to the window, the lady had a look in her eyes that said, well, well, this is how it all shakes out—given with one hand, taken away with the other. She became satisfied and pleasant. "I'll take care of it. Don't worry about a thing. We'll make an exception, we'll send the check by mail. Do you have a beneficiary? You have to put that on your claim form, a beneficiary name. You know, a husband, a child, a brother, a sister?"

"What's your Social Security Number, Spencer? I'd like you to sign as my witness. Go ahead. Sign. Right over here." As they were walking out of a malodorous, unclean, badly lit lottery office, he gave her his arm; gratefully she took it.

"Can I spend it all before Monday?" she said to him.

"I'm sure you can spend it all before Monday. What do you want to buy?"

"Another sixty years," said Lily feeling a pang of regret for her wasted summer.

19

Fibers of Suspicion

After he dropped Lily off at home, Spencer sat in the car for fifteen minutes looking at his hands, and then went back to the precinct to pick up Harkman, who was grumpy about being called in to work on a Saturday, but it made no impression on Spencer, who was even grumpier. They drove out to Port Jefferson to have a more formal talk with Andrew Quinn, who turned out to be the grumpiest of all. Spencer felt there were some things the honorable congressman just didn't have a chance to divulge during yesterday's informal interview which had had to be cut short because of Lily. He was going to give him that chance now, to come clear.

"Come on, guys! On a Saturday? My whole family's home."

"I'm sorry, congressman," said Spencer. "Procedure. We'll keep it short."

"Fine, but I'm not talking to you without my lawyer present," said Andrew. And Miera, who came to the hall to stand beside him, said, "He's definitely not talking to you without his lawyer present."

Harkman shrugged at Spencer, who shrugged too and unhooked a pair of handcuffs from his belt. "Fine, if that's how you want it. In that case, I will have to arrest you and take you in for formal questioning at our precinct. You have a right to an attorney. You have the right to remain silent, for everything you say can, and will, be held against you."

Andrew raised his hands. "Stop. Stop," he said. "I will waive my right to a lawyer, if we can just settle this amicably right here."

"Andrew! You cannot talk to them without your lawyer."

"Be quiet, Miera! Go back to the family. Be calm. This way, gentlemen."

"No, Andrew."

"I said be quiet, Miera."

In his office, Andrew sat calmly behind his desk while Spencer stood across from him. Spencer was too keyed up to sit.

Harkman stepped in before Spencer began. "Congressman, you can say what you want now, and you're obviously saying it, but I know and you know what you said to me in that phone call. I asked you if you knew her and you said you didn't."

"No, I said, I didn't recall, and I was obviously answering another question."

"I asked if you knew her!"

"I didn't hear you properly! And don't raise your voice to me, I won't stand for it."

"Congressman, were you having an affair with Amy McFadden? Did you hear *that* question?" said Harkman.

"Yes, I heard, and no I wasn't."

"You did not in any way have a relationship with Amy that was outside of her friendship with your sister?"

"As I told Detective O'Malley, she may have come into my office here in Port Jeff. I don't know, I don't remember. She may have. Do you consider that outside the friendship with my sister?"

"What about your offices in D.C.?"

"No, she was never there."

"That you're sure about? That you recall?"

"She didn't live in D.C., gentlemen. Obviously it's easier for me to imagine—even though I have no recollection of it—that she could have come here."

"When did you meet her?" Harkman asked.

"I met her through Lily."

"When?"

"I don't know. I can't recall."

Spencer was watching him very carefully. "There seem to be a lot of things you can't recall."

"About this girl, yes. I have a photographic memory about things that are important. I'm sorry she's missing, I wish you well in your investigation. I want to help as much as I can, but I wasn't friendly with her, and more to the point, I don't know where she is."

"Would you be willing to take a lie detector on this?"

"On what? Knowing her? Of course."

"Not on knowing her. On having an improper relationship with her. On not knowing where she is at the moment."

"Yes, we did not have an *improper* relationship."

"Would you be willing to take a polygraph?"

"I am absolutely, one hundred percent willing, but I will have to consult with my lawyer on that one. I myself don't see a problem with it."

Spencer waited to speak, kept quiet, formulated his thoughts. To take the plunge or no?

Andrew tapped tensely on his desk with his fingers. "Listen, will that be all? Because I've got a houseful—"

"Congressman, you've been in the girls' apartment."

"As I told you."

"Yes, you told me. But what you didn't tell me," said Spencer, "is that you spent most of your time inside Amy's room. That's where we found the hairs that match yours." .

Andrew stopped drumming, glancing from one detective to the other. "I don't know what you're talking about," he finally said. "I don't know how that could be."

"No? Me neither."

Harkman glanced at Spencer, who looked only at Andrew.

"I don't know what you're talking about," said Andrew, and

his voice was slightly shaking. "These intimidation tactics won't work on me, detective, and I'm going straight to your superiors to tell them how you are treating an innocent man."

Spencer glanced at Harkman.

"Congressman, I don't know what you're getting so rattled about. I'm asking you to explain how not only your hairs but your fingerprints could have been found all over Amy's room."

Andrew sat. "I don't know how. I didn't go into Amy's room."

"Were they perhaps all over Amy?"

Harkman sat.

Spencer stood.

Finally Andrew, his hands unclasped, slumped back on the chair, and rubbed his face, as if he wanted to rub his eyes away. His demeanor faltered. "Look," he said. "I'm not under arrest, I'm not under suspicion.. I don't want to do anything to impede your investigation so I'm divulging information to you willingly." He gathered himself for a long time before he spoke again.

"It is true . . . I have to admit . . . Amy and I *once* had a relationship that was not . . . entirely proper." He clenched and unclenched his fists as Spencer, holding his breath, waited. "But it's been over and done with a long time ago. We ended it and I haven't seen her in months."

Now Spencer sat down. Spencer and Harkman just stared at each other. The office was heavily quiet.

Very slowly Spencer said, "Congressman, you were involved with a girl who has vanished."

"The two are not connected."

"Congressman! Let me repeat—you have just told us you had an affair with a girl who has *vanished*."

"I heard you! I know! But one is one thing, the other is the other. The affair, as you call it, ended. I haven't seen her in months."

"Well, that's appropriate because she's been missing for months. When did it end?"

"When did it end?"

"Why are you repeating my questions?"

"I can't recall when."

"Did it end two weeks ago? In July? In June? Are we playing twenty questions? When did it end?" Spencer hated raising his voice as if he were speaking to a misbehaving child.

"Detective, you're hounding me."

"Congressman, you don't know what hounding is. Wait until the newspapers get a hold of this. Now when did it end?"

Andrew rubbed his face. "Perhaps March. I can't quite recall."

"Why did it end?"

"Why? What can I tell you, it ran its course. These things do sometimes, they run their course."

"It ended in March?"

"I think so. Sometime in the spring."

"So possibly April, possibly May? Perhaps it ended then? On the day she went missing?"

"This conversation is ludicrous."

"Do you know where Amy is, congressman?"

"I told you, I do not."

"Would you be willing to take a lie detector on *that?*"

"I already told you, I have no problem with it, but I will have to consult with my lawyer."

"You'll be consulting with him from jail when you get your one phone call," snapped Harkman. "Answer the detective's question. When did it end?"

"I told you."

"No, you told us you don't remember when. But you are sure, absolutely positive, it wasn't in May. Not sure when, but pretty sure it wasn't when she disappeared. Interesting," said Spencer. "Don't you think?"

"It was in April, all right?" said Andrew loudly. "Around the middle of April. When I did my taxes, we weren't together any more."

Spencer, Harkman, Andrew, all remained silent. Everything they said could and was held against them.

"When did it begin?"

"I don't know."

Spencer was amazed at how much the congressman said he did not know.

"You don't know? Did you see her only once in her apartment? Did you meet every week? Were you seeing each other for a month, three weeks, forty-seven days?"

"No, a few months."

"Before or after the reelection?"

"Around there, I think."

"Where would you meet—at the apartment?"

"Of course not!"

"You're *indignant*?" asked Spencer, widening his eyes. "Did I offend your sensibilities, congressman? Pardon me."

"I came to that apartment rarely and only for Lily, never for Amy." He lowered his eyes. "This is just devastating. For my wife, for my sister, for my children."

"Indeed." And his sister could not endure this news at the moment. The fire of his compassion for Lily froze any compassion Spencer might have felt for her brother. "You didn't answer my question. You have a knack for doing that. Where would you two get together?"

"I don't know. Wherever."

"On the street? In the alleys? Did she come to Washington to see you?"

"Sometimes yes."

"Did she stay overnight?"

"Sometimes yes."

Spencer nodded slowly. "So this is why she was leaving all her identification behind at home. You're the one she was trying to protect."

"I know she did that, but I never asked her to do it, that was all Amy, not me. What can I tell you, she was a very cautious girl. She didn't want to hurt Lily, I think. We both didn't."

"What about hurting your wife, your children?"

Andrew raised his hand. "Can you just spare me the moralizing. I have no stomach for it."

"Why did you end it? Your wife find out about you?"

"No."

"So why?"

"I told you. It just ended. It was time." But Andrew did not look at Spencer when he said it. Did not, or could not. Spencer never took his eyes off him. "It wasn't working."

"Your clandestine superficial affair with a girl young enough to be your daughter wasn't working?"

"That's right."

But that was spat out, that did not come out offhand.

Spencer's brain was swirling into focus. "Did you break it off with her when you realized you were going to be running for the Senate seat, and you were concerned about the chances of a successful outcome of your campaign if the details of your affair became known?"

"Oh, can you stop calling it an affair already!"

That took Spencer by surprise. "What would you call it?" he asked, frowning.

"It's over! It's done. It's finished. I don't know why you keep *belaboring* this point."

"Produce for me Amy, and I will stop belaboring this point. Until such time, this will remain a criminal investigation and the point will continue to be belabored." Spencer didn't know much about how politics worked, but he was pretty certain that if Andrew Quinn decided to press on with his senatorial campaign, his margin of victory wouldn't even be 52 after a bitter recount.

Andrew was instructed not to leave the country, not to talk to the press, not to hinder a government investigation, and was informed that all of his phone and bank records would be subpoenaed. As they were walking out, they saw Miera ushering the pre-teenage daughters into another room past two other glowering women—perhaps Andrew's sisters. They looked a little like Lily, yet nothing like her. One was tall and prickly, the other smaller and maternal. Everyone looked so grim, eyeing him with dour disapproval.

As they got to the front door to leave, Andrew hit the wall with his fist. "I just got it. There was no hair in Amy's room. No hair, no fingerprints?"

Spencer didn't reply.

"Bastards." Andrew slammed the door behind them.

Spencer shrugged, but the tension of his muscles made it seem more like a shudder.

"Nice one, O'Malley," said Harkman, as they walked to the car. "Forensics better come back with some fucking Quinn hair in her room, or you're going to be sweeping the sidewalks for New York next week."

"Harkman," Spencer said when they were on the LIE headed back to the city. "So what do you think of him?"

"I can't tell. The affair alone is unpleasant business. Young girl, sister's roommate, I mean, a bit slimy, if you ask me. I don't know about anything else. What do you think?"

"Hmm." Spencer was lost in the road. "What I think is that the *Titanic* is at the bottom of the sea."

20

Just Another Saturday Night for Lily

After Lily had slept away the afternoon, she took a cab to see her grandmother. The cabdriver got out and helped her up Grandma's stoop. How she was going to climb her five flights of stairs upon returning home, Lily could not and did not want to think about.

On Saturday nights Grandma held her crooked poker game. Obviously no one cared that it was rigged, because five ladies had been getting together for twenty-five years to play. Four other widows came each Saturday determined to outcheat each other. No one could bluff well, no one had a poker face, but they took the phone off the hook, and played for hours, and drank wine, and ate to bursting, and even smoked cigars. One of them had fallen on the way out, having had too much wine, and the ladies all left an empty chair for their convalescing friend, but continued to play and drink as if death and old age weren't right outside on Grandma's stoop.

So when Lily came to the cabal, she was asked—required—to take the place of Zani from Albania, who had been out the last six weeks. The ladies suspected she might not come back, since she was eighty-eight and her hip was not healing. The first thing Grandma said upon Lily's arrival was, "Dear God, Lily, you look like death warmed over. Come here, eat something, will you? Dana, look at her, this is what kids today do to themselves to look attractive to the opposite sex."

Dana said, "They don't understand men like a bit of flesh." They were talking as if Lily were not in the kitchen. Lily sat and pretended to play, to cheat, even to drink. She tried to have some food, some stinky French cheese, some imported crackers, some pâté. But the smell of food at her mouth made her retch and she stopped trying. No one noticed.

After she lost twenty dollars in the first hour, she sat and watched them deal and cheat each other out of their twenty dollars.

"Lil, you're glum, what's wrong with you?" said Grandma. "Look at the size of you. Are you anorexic?"

"Leave her alone, Claudia. She's fine," said Hannah from Bulgaria, always Lily's defender. "She's a young girl living in New York. This is what they look like." She turned to Lily. "But you did used to have such nice round hips, Liliput. What's been happening?"

"Exactly," Grandma went on. "Young, single, nearly graduated, working, having fun, living in peace. Why so glum? Not having any fun? Are you bulimic?"

Soon, Lily wanted to say.

"I wish I had been young in New York," said Dana from Poland. "When I was Lily's age I was in Treblinka, waiting for my turn in the shower rooms. If the Soviets hadn't come, I'd be one of the piles of ashes the Nazis grew cabbages on."

The ladies grumbled their sympathy. All of them were first generation Americans, having come here because of The War that divided history into the before and after.

"Oh how my granddaughters whine and whine," said Soo Min from South Korea. "Born here, yet so critical. According to them everything is wrong with unromantic American men. I say to them, do you know that my fiancé was killed by the North Koreans in 1950? What I would give to have my Yung alive, not bringing me flowers, not remembering my birthday!

Unromantic." Delicately she snorted. She was so tiny, she did everything delicately, even smoke cigars. "How about just alive? Right, Claudia? Claudia here, married her Tomas in 1939, then he went to war as soon as Hitler invaded Poland and she never saw him again. The way she lives, you think she's still waiting for him. But at least she got a daughter out of it and now a whole family. She is so lucky. Yung left nothing for me."

Lily noticed her grandmother didn't nod, didn't comment. Her grandmother, Klavdia Roza Venkewicz, changed the subject away from her Tomas. "Your granddaughters don't mention Envy, don't mention Coveting," Grandma said instead, glancing at Lily who sat mutely, her hands flat down under her legs. Traces of morphine were still in Lily, and she had taken two oxycontin before she came here. Probably the glass of wine was not a good idea. She was feeling delirious.

The air in the room was stale, the ladies were smoking, their wine-infused nicotine and carbon dioxide mixing with their inexpensive perfume and the smelly French fromage. Somebody please open the window, Lily thought, and then struggled up to go open it herself.

"What are you doing?" said Claudia. "The AC is on."

"It is?" said Lily, dropping back down. "You're right, Grandma. In America we shouldn't covet, we shouldn't envy. We've got too much of plenty."

"That's right," said Dana. "But my daughter isn't satisfied. She's on her fifth marriage and she's only forty-nine. She's still looking for the right one, and I say *still* looking because apparently husband number five is not taking out the garbage without being told. I tell her, in Poland we were lucky if we could hold on to our one husband, who cared about the garbage."

The other ladies murmured their animated assent. Claudia said, "Most of the husbands back then weren't even that great. They drank, they beat their wives. But they were alive. That made all the difference."

167

"Come on, Claudia," said Dana. "Your young Tomas would have taken out the garbage."

"I wouldn't have let him," said Claudia. "I would have done it myself, the way it's meant to be done."

The ladies murmured.

"Why are girls so picky in peaceful times? Lily, do you have a boyfriend?" asked Soo Min.

"I had one, but we're not together anymore."

"You see?" exclaimed Dana. "That's what I'm talking about. So choosy. What was wrong with him?"

"He didn't love me."

A short quiet fell over the table then. But only short.

"What's not to love?" huffed Hannah, who loved Lily. "You're a beautiful girl, even if you are much too skinny. So you two weren't getting along. You should have tried harder. You just thought there were many other choices out there."

For him there were, Lily thought. All the way in upstate New York.

"It's not even the boyfriends," Claudia said. "It's the choices in everything. Here we have life, we're affluent and what do we do? We can't quit complaining . . ." Lily tuned out her grandmother's voice. For sure she watched too much CNN.

Mock-glaring at her granddaughter, Claudia continued. "You know why? Because we've lived in peace so long. We've taken it all, taken and taken for fifty years and we don't know how to stop. We don't know what we have. We've never been invaded, this whole century we've never known bombing and suffering and privation, and famine and genocide. We live as if we're going to live forever in peace, forgetting what three hundred thousand of our men have died for, what fifty five million people the world over have died for, forgetting what we fought for—"

"The right to complain when we wish, right, Claudia?" said Soo Min. "Whining is our luxury. The right to complain, under-appreciate, and disagree, and bitch and moan and gain weight

168

and commit suicide and marry five times. The right to love our peaceful life and to take it all flagrantly for granted! To live as if we have infinite time. That's not a bad thing. Better that than my youth. I had malaria, pellagra, dystrophy by the time I was Lily's age. I thought I'd never make it out of my twenties. I didn't give a whit about social programs or police brutality. I just wanted a hunk of meat."

"I was tattooed by the Nazis and had my skin nearly all burned off my body, inch by inch."

"I was raped on three separate occasions in Bulgaria by the advancing Russians. I could never have children because of it."

"I lost all my children and my parents in Sobibor. Here we grieve over the loss of one child. I lost all three of mine."

"My husband, my only heart, left for the war and never returned."

"I have cancer," said Lily.

And then everyone was mute, and this time for good.

She couldn't believe she was walking, by herself, moving, sitting, standing, going down the stairs. She couldn't believe she was moving. Somehow the blood transfusion, somehow someone else's platelets glued back together her bowels, her abdominal walls, her vena cava. She barely got to the garbage can on the corner of Court and Bergen before she threw up, in full view of the young couples coming home from their dinners on a Saturday night. Blood came out with the bile. She wiped her mouth, and continued walking to the Brooklyn Public Library, open late in the evening for young girls who wanted to look up their disease.

Her good life—her mother notwithstanding, her going broke notwithstanding. Her good childhood, her happy urban days. Her biking around Forest Hills Park, her college years, her passions, if one could call them that. Her slight painting, her small joys.

And into this soft-around-the-edges and soft-in-the-center life comes a cancer cell.

Why? One single cell, on steroids, a cell in the extreme, a baby blast cell, a single cell with granules in its cytoplasm enters Lily's life while she's still dancing and painting and dreaming of love and a future life. Why? Why the first one? What are these granules and where do they come from?

But in a body of ten billion cells that divide and replicate and oxidize and catabolize, perhaps the question should be not why do they malfunction but why don't they?

The library has no answers to that one. It has info and statistics.

The granulocyte divides and grows but doesn't mature. It remains a baby blast cell, dividing into another and another and another. These immature neutrophils can't do what they're supposed to—plug up holes in her system. So Lily gets a cold. And keeps the cold. And thinks no more of it. So Lily bleeds. And keeps on bleeding. And in the meantime, the myeloid blasts divide and divide in the bone marrow, they spill over into her bloodstream. They're stupid and large and they won't die. They push and shove their way all around her body, which has stopped producing red blood cells, which has fewer and fewer white blood cells. The cancer cells thicken her blood to heavy cream, then to treacle. She is like a poison candy inside. She is coagulant, she is syrup. Black syrup.

And still she tries to work, to run, to walk, to stand, to lie down, and she lies on her back, and she thinks, what the FUCK is happening to me?

Meanwhile cancer knows no language, does not speak English. The blasts, untutored in the dynamics of exclamation and declaration, just divide and divide and never die.

Blast crisis. One cell to start. One errant, mutant death cell, and suddenly there are millions in her body and suddenly Lily is one of 10,600 new cases a year of AML. She is rare. She is unique. Most of the new cases are people over sixty. AML is an old person's disease. Yet here she is, 24. Twenty-four. Lily's porthole opened to acute myeloid leukemia.

49, 45, 39, **24**, 18, 1

And now her favorite statistic.

Death stats.

The good news is that men die in greater numbers. Now for the not so good . . . AML causes a third of all deaths from leukemia. Acute myeloid leukemia has the lowest five year survival rate of all leukemias. The graphs are the worst. They offer Lily a seventeen percent chance of living after five years.

Seventeen percent.

And that's the number door *she* picked. 49, 45, 39, 24, 18, 1.

She scratched out those numbers with a lead pencil on a pink piece of paper, and paid one dollar for the privilege of getting cancer. Lily Quinn, which door would you like, the lady, the tiger, door number one, door number two or door number *cancer*!

She is getting nowhere with this. For solace she will try international comparisons.

Ah. There you go. She is lucky to be living in the United States. For females the highest survival rates for leukemia are Australia and the United States. Perhaps she should move to Australia. Warm weather, green ocean, and the best chance of surviving the granulocytes. Bring on the great white sharks, thinks Lily. She'll take her chances in the infested Australian waters.

It's a good thing she is not living in Iceland. Really bad for women in Iceland. Or the British Isles. No cold islands for Lily. The bundled-up people can't feel their bodies, they think they're just hibernating and don't notice something is wrong until it's too late.

You mean unlike her? Unlike her, who at the first sign of trouble ran to the doctor and said, doc, I'm sleeping all the time, do you think it's leukemia? How long had her blood been a candy apple in the making and she didn't notice?

When she sees her grandmother next, she must thank her for choosing America after the Death March (1945) and the refugee

171

camps in Belgium (1949). The statistics in America, no matter how bad, are still better than anywhere else.

Grandma would be proud of her. That's a good way to describe many things in the United States.

Days and days, months and months, the leaves, the flowers have grown and soon will be dying. There had been no barbecues this past summer, no family get-togethers. Amy had taken her ID out of her pockets, her credit cards, the keys to her house, and placed them on top of her dresser, neat, orderly, meant to be there. She walked out of the house and was gone, days and weeks and months, and Lily never asked. Andrew hadn't called her, hadn't spoken to her since Maui, and Lily never asked. She couldn't stand up, she couldn't eat, her legs numb, her burn infected, she was wounded from the inside out, and she never asked herself why. And now she sleeps and dreams of her oblivion and desperately wishes for it again. To lead a life so wholly happy, so wholly unexamined that she could be dying, could be betrayed, could be besieged on all sides and never even know it.

21

Just Another Saturday Night for Spencer

Spencer sat in front of his Saturday night special—magnificent and rare Speyside Malt Whisky. He didn't work on the weekends—though sometimes, like today, he could not avoid it—and he did not see Mary, citing either work or family obligations, but the truth was, even his ailing father could not lure him for long away. When there was a family function he had to prepare himself in advance. He would take sick days and vacation days ahead of time, sometimes after. His body counted the five days from Monday to Friday as if they were a metronome, a pendulum of sobriety. Five days to be sober, and by Friday his body could barely function. He could not eat, he could not be merry, his mind clouded, his body a tremor. On Fridays he would sometimes go out with the guys from Homicide, and he would begin drinking with them, drinking cheap-ass stuff neat and small to show everyone how normal he was, how jolly, how much like them, killing two birds with one stone: showing faux sociability *and* starting his weekend reward. He preferred going out with Mary on Thursdays, but it was hard to avoid seeing your girlfriend on both weekend days. She was bound to get suspicious. Either you broke up with her, or you kept her and paid your price. So he kept her and took her out some Fridays, ending up at her apartment on the Upper West Side. He never stayed over, thinking of only one thing—going—even as he was coming.

He was very well trained, he bought his drink ahead of time and from different stores, for since he drank until there was not a drop of Scotch in the house he became too ill-behaved and erratic to go out during. Too many people knew him around the neighborhood. He didn't want them to see him in such need. He was a senior NYPD detective-lieutenant. He had to be operational, he had to be in control, hence the whisky-buying in Chelsea or Soho, hence the grumpy sobriety Monday to Friday, hence the careful drinking around his friends. He did not know of Saturdays. Most Saturdays were lost days, gone days, by all definitions of reality nonexistent days for him. By Sunday morning all the Macallan and Chivas or Johnny Walker and Glenmorangie, and even the best, 25-year-old Highland Park, was gone and he remained home and confined and by necessity got slowly and painfully sober.

Then came Monday again and five days of being good, five days of penance. Five days of living for the weekend. Spencer liked Mary, he needed Mary, he liked work, he needed work, but there was nothing Spencer needed as badly as a drink on Friday night.

Why did his mother have so many children? Why couldn't he have been an only Irish Catholic child? The weekends he had to stay sober for communions, confirmations, baptisms, weddings were torture to him. Actual torture. His body, dehydrated and throbbing, was expressing outwardly its internal malcontents. He was sullen, silent, and shaking. He never drank a sip at the gatherings, because he knew there was no way to drink without eventually drinking to blackout. There was no way to take one sip, one glass, one beer, one cocktail. Spencer never fooled himself, never deluded himself, never pretended. He knew the truth fully and accepted it fully, but it was more important that others did not know, didn't even suspect, than it was for him to casually wet his throat with his drug of choice. So he didn't drink but

174

drummed out the dry hours on his fingers, on his napkins, on the tines of his fork.

After he returned from Port Jeff and dropped off Harkman, and signed in the patrol car, and came home, Spencer without even taking off his shoes drank a 70cl of Glenmorangie, while standing by the sink, straight from the bottle.

He had a long shower to wash the drink out of his pores, and was now hours later and a quarter sober, sitting in front of the carefully placed full bottle of Macallan and the accompanying highball glass. It was after midnight and he was wondering if he could throw it away and not drink from it. He tried watching TV, opening a newspaper. What to do with the afflictions? Just go on, try to go on, try to function in a world which has no patience for tremors, for weakness. He would lose his job in Missing Persons, he would be placed on disability and then retired from the force if Whittaker thought he was not in control of his life. Gabe McGill didn't know, though if he knew, he wouldn't have cared. If Harkman knew, Spencer would have been out of a job long ago. Perhaps this was what Harkman was threatening him with?

This Saturday there was something else as he sat in front of his bottle and contemplated his eternal conflict and struggled with himself in his losing battle. Tonight he thought of Lily. He thought of the girl with doe eyes and spiky hair, the wisp of a very young woman being taken down by things far worse than elective addictions, though Spencer wanted to say in his own feeble defense that there was nothing elective about his addiction.

He wasn't contemplating the bottle in relation to Lily's sickness. He was contemplating himself in relation to Lily. She needed him yesterday—and by luck he was with another woman, and was therefore sober. But tomorrow? And the next weekend? If she needed him again, he would not be there. He would not be able to pick up the phone, answer her page, come over, help her. She would call him, and he would not reply. She would ask him where he'd been and he would not respond.

175

And there was no question about it—he couldn't deny it, even to himself in his dark apartment in front of his solace, his soul, his spirit. Lily needed someone.

Maybe just this one Saturday, this one Sunday, he thought, finally and with effort getting up. I'll hang on for six more days. Think of it as an unexpected, protracted family function. Before he could talk himself out of it, he went and poured the bottle of $93.06 whisky into the sink, grasping the stainless steel side while bending over to inhale the fermented barley mash's intoxicating iodine scent as it swirled down the merciless drain.

22

In the Garden of the Barber Cop

Through the ebony sleep, the phone, the phone, rings rings insists on itself, on its rights in her life, pick me up, answer me, now, come, come, COME.

She crawled out of bed and yanked the cord out of the wall. Tomorrow she was going to the hospital. Grandma must have called everybody. Well, that's good. At least Lily didn't have to. She wasn't going to waste her time talking on the phone. But maybe she should talk to someone—who would take her to the hospital in the morning to admit her to begin her chemo?

She wondered if Grandma called her mother.

I hope so. I can't call her. She talks, complains, hurts, aggresses, pushes toward a conflict I don't want to give her, and I scream at her, I turn into the ugly thing she wants me to be, until I hate myself. Well, I don't want to blame my mother anymore for the person I am when I am with her. Joshua, bless him and his mother complex, cured me of that. I choose to become someone else, but to do that, I can't speak to her, I can't be drawn in to what I don't want to be. I'm not calling her.

Brave words from a young girl. But in the back of Lily's sick heart was the mother she wanted her mother to be, the mother, who upon hearing that her daughter was gravely ill, dropped everything, let everything go to pot, and flew seven thousand miles to take her daughter to the hospital on Monday for induction chemotherapy. Induction into the rest of her life. A mother, who came in, and cleaned up, and cooked weak chicken soup for her, and washed all her towels, dragging them to the Laundromat, a mother who talked no nonsense to the doctors, who read medical reports, who drew Lily a bath, even though Lily hated baths and waited for the day she could stand up long enough, be strong enough, to take a shower.

It was for the purple-rose, wishful, child-like vision of that mother that she so desperately craved that Lily called Maui. Her father picked up the phone.

"Hey, Papi."

"Hey, Liliput," he said, and Lily nearly broke down.

"How are things?"

"Oh, you know," he said, and her mother came on the other line.

"Lily?" she said in a slurred voice. "Get off the phone!" she screeched, and Lily wasn't sure who she was talking to until her mother added, "Iwantshoshalkshomydaurreralone."

"Papi, no, don't hang up, I have something to tell you."

"He izh driving me crazy," Allison said, "I'm going to kill myself. I'm going to throw myself out the window. Do you hear me? DO YOU HEAR ME??"

And George in a gritted voice, said, "I hear you, I hear you. The whole world hears you."

Her mother dropped the phone and started screaming at her father. Her father started screaming back. Lily waited for an impolite moment, then another, and hung up.

The phone calls were unending. News of the lottery was drowned out by news of Cancer, news of Andrew. Amanda, Anne, Grandma, Rachel, Paul, Dennis, Joshua! Rick from the diner, Judi, Jan McFadden. Amanda and Anne didn't know what to do—cry for Lily or cry for Andrew as they told Lily about her brother being interrogated in his own house on a Saturday

178

afternoon by intrusive and objectionable NYPD detectives. "That Detective O'Malley needs some sensitivity training," Amanda said in a finger-wagging voice. "He'd put his own grandmother in jail."

The doorbell rang. It was one in the afternoon. She had to put Amanda on hold, tell Rachel she would call her back— again—and go to the intercom. "Who is it?"

"Spencer."

"Amanda, I gotta go." It's the jailer of grandmothers, she wanted to add.

She buzzed him in, running a hand through her hair, and changed into pants from shorts, to cover the bruises on her legs from him.

Spencer, looking beat and pale and red-eyed himself, brought with him electric hair clippers. "How are you feeling this morning?"

"Like I have cancer." She pointed to the razor. "What's that for?"

"I'm going to cut my hair."

"You came to *my* apartment to cut *your* hair?"

"Well, yes. I thought I'd cut mine, and then . . ." He smiled thinly. "Cut yours."

"What are you talking about?" she said, stepping away from him, touching her own hair. She was not finding him to be of sound mind this morning. "I'm not cutting my hair." The phone rang. They looked at each other. "I'm not picking up. I've been on the phone all morning. Hearing all about you at my brother's house yesterday."

He took a step to her. "I'm sorry about that. This is a terrible time. Don't read the papers."

"I don't intend to. It's all lies. Please put the clippers away, you're scaring me."

He came closer. "Lil, you're going to lose your hair."

"Not by your hand."

"Your hair is going to come out in chunks. You'll have bald

spots all over your head. But my way, I'll cut it all off evenly, snazzily even, and to show you I can do it, I'll cut mine off first."

"I'm not cutting my hair," she said, but less forcefully. Chunks?

"Fine," he said. "But I'm cutting mine."

She watched him in the kitchen, with a hand held mirror propped up on top of the dish-drainer rack. He had taken off his denim jacket and polo shirt and was suddenly and inexplicably undressed to the waist. His chest hair was still brown, barely graying at the edges. He was lean; there was not a scrap of fat on him as if he played soccer one time in his youth. Though well-formed he looked like he didn't eat well. Seeing a man even remotely naked in her apartment made her uneasy. Not bad uneasy. Just tense uneasy. He was crazy. He really was cutting his hair.

And now it was all gone. He turned to her. "What do you think? Good?" He looked ready for the army. He left himself with an eighth of an inch of brown fuzz.

"Frightening. And bald." But his eyes were large and blue and his full mouth looked sculpted on, drawn on as if in caricature with heightened lines all around, and he had a jaw line and cheekbones and eyebrows and ears. Everything on him was some-how made more pronounced through his absence of hair.

"Yes. You next."

"No."

"Lily."

"I don't care what you call me or what kind of tone you use. No."

He tilted his head to look at her with mock-seriousness.

"Stop." She left the kitchen. He followed her.

After fifteen minutes of trying to get away from him in her closet of an apartment, she relented. "I'm not getting undressed though."

"I think that's wise."

She sat in front of him on a chair. "I don't want you to do this."

"I know. But look at me. You think I wanted to do this? And I'm not even sick."

"I don't know why you did it. Clearly you're sick in the head. But besides, you're a man, what do you care about hair?"

"All right, fine, you've obviously never met a man before."

She sat uncomfortably as the razor whirred close to her ear and sheaths of her brown, highlighted hair fell to the floor. "Spencer," she said, "Didn't the doctor say all my hair is going to fall out?"

"Yes, he did." He continued cutting. His hand was holding her head to keep her steady. Lily closed her eyes. She was being touched by someone other than herself.

"Spencer."

"What?"

"*All* my hair?" She didn't open her eyes, because she didn't want to either smile or go red. She really shouldn't be making a joke like this to a police officer.

He leaned around to stare into her face. Now she opened her eyes and saw his expression and laughed. His eyes were smiling. "Would you like me to cut *all* your hair, Lily–Anne?"

"No, thank you." She turned red.

"That's what I thought."

Finally done, he ruffled her buzz head and dusted her shoulders off with a towel. Without hair she looked worse than him. Simply frightful. Her bark-colored eyes; bare forehead; half-asleep mouth and drawn oval facial bones were doing nothing for her. "You look much better bald than I do," she said in a disagreeable voice. "How is that fair?"

"I think it's hip. You look like Sinead O'Connor."

"That's just great. Well, my grandmother would be proud. I look like a survivor from one of the camps she keeps telling me about. All I'm missing is the pajamas."

He offered to take her for brunch at the Plaza. Lily had once said she'd always wanted to go, and so he offered. But she felt too self-conscious today with her porcupine head to go to a place like the Palm Court, she didn't even have a wig or a nice hat for cover-up, all she had were Amy's skicaps.

"Thanks, Spencer, but maybe I can take a rain check on that? I have no appetite anyway."

As if he knew why she didn't want to go, he said, "We'll get you a hat at Bergdoff's, if you want."

"I haven't been paid yet."

"I'll buy it."

"No. Really, it's fine. Another time, okay. I just can't today. You understand."

He understood. He stood silently, cleaning out his razor. "Well," he said after he was finished. "The barbershop's closed. So . . . do you want me to go?"

She didn't. Her mouth twisted a little bit, and not looking at him, she said, "Not really."

He asked her what else she wanted to do, and she said maybe walk a little bit in Central Park, and that's where they went, but she got so tired, she couldn't even get to the entrance to the zoo which was just off where the cab dropped them at 59th Street. It was a sunny, hot August Sunday. They sat on a low stone wall, in the shade. He bought her some water and an ice cream cone, while he had two hot dogs and an Italian Ice.

She was feeling weak and needed to go home and lie down in her bed, needed to but didn't want to. After a bit of energy returned to her, they strolled slightly west to Wollman's rink. There was no ice in August, but they went around to the bleacher seats and climbed up to perch high in the blue benches.

Quietly quietly they sat in the summer. There was much weighing so heavily on her, and she didn't want to talk about any of it. "Do you know who Oliver Barrett is?" she asked him instead.

"No."

"Jenny Cavilleri?"

He shook his head.

"Never saw *Love Story* when you were a kid?"

182

"Thirteen year old boys don't watch *Love Story*. *Night of the Living Dead*, more like it."

"You weren't thirteen in 1970!" exclaimed Lily, mining his face. Was Spencer older than her brother?

"Well, yes, there were thirteen year olds running around even in 1970."

"Did they even have moving pictures back then?"

"They had barely invented money."

"I thought so."

They continued to sit side by side, their domed round heads bobbing gently together like fishing floats in the swaying waters.

"So when did you join the police force?"

"In 1978."

"You've been a cop for almost as long as I've been alive?" How was that possible?

"Guess so. How long has Amy been leaving her ID on the dresser?"

"Ah. Please. Don't know, Spencer." She sighed. "Look, I know you want to tell me what you and my brother talked about yesterday . . ."

"I don't want to tell you."

"Good. Because I don't want to hear it. I *can't* hear about it, you understand?" She emitted a small groan.

He pressed against her shoulder lightly. "I understand."

"Did he say . . . he knew where she was?"

"He said he didn't."

"Do you believe him?" She didn't glance at him when she asked.

And he stared straight ahead. "Chicks. I thought you didn't want to talk about it."

"I don't. Let's go."

They took a cab to 11th and Broadway.

"I don't live here," she said as they got out.

"I do," he said.

They stood on Broadway in the late afternoon heat. Very

lightly he put his hand on her face. "You got nothing to worry about," he said. "Come upstairs. You can watch TV. Why don't you have a TV in your apartment?"

"Joshua took it."

"He's just a prince of a man, isn't he? Well, when you get out of the hospital and your money comes, you can buy yourself a plasma screen for every room, even the bathroom."

"Oh, that'll show him."

His place was clean. The newspapers were on the floor, the mail was on the table. The kitchen looked infrequently visited, like hers.

She liked his twelve-foot ceilings and Broadway right out of the ten-foot windows. Right across the street was Dagostinos in front of which she had run into him and Mary last month. The thought of Mary made her twitch for some reason and she backed away from the window, sitting down on his taupe-colored L-shaped couch and starting to leaf through *Sports Illustrated* while he was in the kitchen, possibly making her some tea. The leafing of the pages, the distant drone of Sunday cars outside, the clanging of doors, the occasional honking, the whistling of the kettle, the clinking of the silverware, and she was asleep, with the magazine on her lap, her hairless head falling back.

When she woke up she found herself covered by a blue cotton blanket with cats on it, while Spencer sat in the corner of the couch, watching something on TV. She tried to focus, couldn't. A movie and the music was familiar, and the faces . . . who was that? There was snow and a snowball fight and happiness and lilting waltzing music. She lay down, curling up under the blanket and went back to sleep. When she woke up, it was dark, and he was still sitting in the corner of the couch watching a baseball game this time.

"I'm sorry," she said, trying to get up.

He got up to help her. "Don't be sorry. I better get you home. It's late. You have to be up early tomorrow. What time do you have to be at the hospital?"

"Six in the morning for blood work."

"Come on, the nurses aren't awake at six. They're just messing with you." He watched her as she straightened herself out. "Do you . . . need me . . . to come and take you?"

"No, no. My sisters are drawing the short straw to see which of them will do it. Don't worry. I didn't mean to be so out of it. I'm such bad company." And in the foyer, Lily asked, "What were you watching? . . . When I was sleeping?"

"I went to Blockbuster and rented *Love Story*," he replied, holding the door open for her. "To see what all the fuss was about."

"No fuss," she muttered, unconditionally pleased by that. "So what did you think?"

"Eh. I liked *Night of the Living Dead* better." He grinned.

When he brought her to her apartment, he patted her shoulder, and she said, "I'm so scared, Spencer. Of what's ahead. What if I can't do it?" And he said, "You're going to do great, you're going to be all right," and she tiptoed up and kissed his stubbly cheek in the beige corridor.

23

Chemotherapy 101

On Monday at five-thirty in the morning her front door intercom rang.

"It's your grandmother," the voice said.

"Who?"

"Let me in."

"Grandma?" Lily buzzed her in.

Ten minutes later her grandmother showed up at the door, clutching the walls and panting.

"Grandma?"

"Oh my God, those stairs! Oh my God—what have you done with yourself, what have you done with your hair?"

"I cut it. It's all going to fall out anyway. Grandma!" Lily put her hand on her heart.

"What? Come on, ready to go?"

"Grandma!"

"What?" Her grandmother was looking at her as if she had no idea what the fuss was about.

"You left your house!" Lily said, trying not to cry. Left her house for the first time in six years.

"I didn't leave my house," said her white-haired little grandmother, opening her arms to her. "I left my house for you. Now get ready. But for the love of Mary and Joseph, do yourself a favor and don't read the newspapers. The news is terrible today and overwrought."

"Remember what Truman Capote said, Grandma. He said he didn't care what people were saying about him as long as it wasn't true."

"Well, let's just pray your brother feels the same way. Come on, let's go."

At Mount Sinai, at six in the morning, Marcie and Dr. DiAngelo were already waiting. He was wearing hospital whites, not a track suit this time, to impress her grandmother, Lily was sure, and he had on glasses, and didn't look like a kid. Grandma was not impressed. "He looks too young to be a doctor," she stage-whispered.

"Thank you for that," DiAngelo said, "but I'm fifty-four this year."

"*As* I was saying," Claudia whispered, but quieter. "A *child.*"

After DiAngelo explained what was about to happen to Lily, she got up off the bed and said, "I'm going to have a hole in my chest? She shook her head. I'm going home. Thanks anyway."

Marcie said, "A little Port-A-Cath, so we can administer the meds, take blood, give blood without having to scar up the veins on your arms. The Hickman catheter is nothing to be worried about. A central venous catheter is implanted just under your skin above your chest plate. It goes straight to your vena cava, which goes straight to the heart."

She would take Vitamin A once a morning by mouth, and then in the afternoon, bagfuls of liquid drugs would pour into her vena cava. She would do this for seven days. Then she would have three days to recover. They would then do a biopsy and start again. And then again. Three treatments, thirty days.

"Very very aggressive," said DiAngelo. "But we have no choice." He coughed slightly. "Just to let you know, these doses of Vitamin A, or ATRA as it is known in pill form, are associated with the potentially lethal pulmonary leukostasis syndrome."

187

"What?"

"White blood cells clump in your lungs and cause you to stop breathing."

"Oh."

"ATRA is very toxic."

"So what about chemo without ATRA?"

"Varying degrees of success and major morbidity. I don't recommend it. ATRA works very well, however, in combination with the other drugs."

"What are the names of these other drugs, young man?" said Claudia, officiously, as if she was going to look them up as soon as she got home.

A slight smile crossed DiAngelo's face. "Cytarabine, to kill the existing cancer cells, cerubidine, to stop the cancer cells from reproducing, and VePesid, which does both, for good measure." Cytarabine, or Ara-C as it was called, would be on a continuous drip for seven days.

"That sounds like a tremendous burden. Is this going to affect her?" Claudia asked.

"Oh yes, but not as much as dying would affect her," DiAngelo said.

Claudia gasped. Lily, in bed, in her ugly gown, patted her grandmother's pale hand. "Sit, Grandma. He's just joking with you."

"That's not funny, young man. We don't appreciate that kind of humor in my family. We survived the war, the death camps, we lived through too much to—"

"Grandma, Grandma." Lily was making serious eyes at her grandmother. "He is just *joking*. To lighten the mood. It's all right. He knows what he's doing."

"He better." Claudia turned to DiAngelo. "How long is she going to be in the hospital? After Wednesday I'm coming to take her home."

DiAngelo and Marcie exchanged a look. "Lily, you haven't told your grandmother everything, have you?"

"Not yet." She turned to her grandmother. "I'm going to be here a month."

"A month!"

"I can't release her if she's unable to stand up," said DiAngelo.

"Why can't she go home on her rest days? One of my friends had leukemia and she went home between treatments. Everybody goes home—to recuperate, to get strong, to eat."

"How's your friend doing?"

"Well, she's dead."

With a prolonged polite smile, DiAngelo leveled a look at Lily and at her grandmother.

"Give her something milder," said Claudia.

"Lily, you choose—mild or life."

"Life."

"I thought so."

Claudia sank into the chair. "And after a month?"

"You know what, let's all get through the next thirty days, and then we'll talk about what then. If we're lucky to have a what then, she'll be thirteen weeks on consolidation chemo as an outpatient. I'm not counting my chickens yet. Are you ready for that Hickman, Lily?"

"Absolutely not."

"That's my girl."

"Lilianne," said Claudia, "have you thought about getting a second opinion?"

"Lilianne," said DiAngelo. "I see you have not told your grandmother how sick you are. You didn't level with her."

"I leveled," she said. "It's just that no one can quite believe it." Least of all me.

"Don't treat your granddaughter as if she's got the common cold, Mrs. Vail. Treat her as if she has cancer."

Claudia grabbed on to her chest and started panting.

Lily squeezed her grandmother's hand. "You're going to be just fine, Grandma. Relax. You're going to pull through this, you'll see."

* * *

The insertion of the chest catheter seemed like it would hurt, therefore it hurt. They cut a hole in her chest and put a tube inside her! They gave her a local, but when the doctor asked her if it was hurting her, she said yes, even though there were other things in her body that were feeling worse. They asked her to rate her pain from one to ten. Nine, she said, and then downgraded it to four when she saw their raised eyebrows. But seeing the tube in the hole in her chest did something to her, she started to cry. Her grandmother started to cry too, which made Lily even more afraid.

Marcie calmed her down by pressing Lily's buzz head against her big black bosom. Lily was comforted. Why couldn't Grandma have breasts like this to be pressed against?

She worried about one thing—could she take the constant nausea, could she throw up and live through it? She hated feeling nauseated, always had, and had never in her life made herself be sick. She was a vomiting wimp. Could she tell them that? They'd only laugh at her. "Ho, ho, Lily, what's a little retching compared with your life." But she wanted to know: exactly how much retching would her new life entail?

The ATRA by mouth was quick, like Advil, and the bags of chemo wheeled to her bedside by the afternoon were so innocent-looking she couldn't believe they would make her bleed intestinally. She felt optimistic that she was going to be one of the ones that wouldn't get very sick, wouldn't throw up, wouldn't grow deaf.

By the afternoon, Amanda and Anne came. All were horrified at her haircut.

"Who did this to you? You paid money to get butchered like this, why?"

She didn't want to tell them who did this to her. She didn't think they'd understand. She hoped that if he came to visit he didn't come when they were all here.

Amanda held one hand, Anne the other, Anne was in a suit, Amanda in mother clothes, elastic pants, baggy sweatshirt. An hour was a long time to lie there and watch the cytarabine drip drip drip into her chest catheter. It was a clear solution; it could've been water, or a placebo. What a weird concept—an open hole in her body for things to drip through. Now they were injecting chemo into her, but potentially could they also inject chocolate? Or strawberry syrup? Or melted vanilla ice cream? How do you feel, how do you feel, Marcie kept asking, her grandmother kept asking, Anne, Amanda kept asking. Paul, Rachel kept asking.

Paul, Rachel were here?

"Oh my God, Lil, who did this to your hair?" Paul said. "This hurts me deeply as your personal hair stylist."

DiAngelo shooed them all out except one. Grandma stayed.

Lily was sleepy. How about a Cosmopolitan into the Port-A-Cath? Vodka, Cointreau, cranberry juice, lime, ahhhh . . .

The first bag emptied, Marcie hooked up a bag of VePesid. "I like the way you smell," muttered Lily. "Of Milky Ways and nicotine."

"I'll bring you a bagful of Milky Ways when you get through this," said Marcie.

"Hook me up—right into the Port-a-Cath," said Lily.

This second hour was longer because she started feeling . . . should she say? Nauseated. It was psychosomatic. They told her she would feel this, and so she did. The room, so plain and unadorned, almost like a convent room, began to change color, from more drab (was that even possible?) to hunter green, to pumpkin orange. The TV image overhead was doubling. She asked them to turn it off. Now the turned-off TV was doubling. She was on hallucinogens! They were giving her mescaline, magic mushrooms, morning glory seeds!

Marcie was no longer black, but green, with funny fish-eye glasses and freckles. She said, "Lil, you okay? You looking a bit white around the gills." Just to prove her right, Lily asked to be unhooked from the IV, which they wouldn't do, so she dragged the IV stand into the bathroom and threw up. She had to hold on to the toilet to have physical confirmation of the uncertainty before her eyes—the toilet was doubling. Did she throw up twice?

Her two grandmothers remained quiet; they may have nodded off in unison.

The third hour, a bag of cerubidine. The nausea decidedly not psychosomatic. Displeased with herself, Lily asked Marcie if she would get used to it, if she would get less nauseated as the chemo went on.

Marcie was quiet a moment. "Worse," she said. "The cumulative effect is what gets you. This is nothing."

This was nothing? The swirling wretchedness was nothing?

After three hours and three bags it was six in the evening, and she mumbled to her grandmother to go and get something to eat. She mumbled to Marcie, "What if I don't eat, will I be less nauseated?"

"More," replied Marcie. "Food absorbs some of the acid. Would you like to eat something?"

A resounding no. "Tell me a story, Grandma," she whispered.

"Want a story, Liliput? I'll tell you a story," said Claudia. Lily quarter-listened as Grandma told her that in her village south of Danzig when the Germans came in December of 1939, they took all the food for themselves, leaving only a small amount for the villagers, and some of the Poles during the morning head count, started pushing the Polish Jews forward out of line, so that they would be taken away and there would be more food left. Suddenly after centuries of living side by side as Poles, people became split up as Poles and Jews. Not Polish Jews, just Jews. It was only after the Germans came and annexed that part of Poland as their own that this trouble started. Hunger is a powerful tool at the hands of the enemy. "So eat something, Lily."

A new bag of cytarabine remained attached—permanently, for six more days.

"Tell me about you and Tomas," Lily breathed out.

"Not Tomas. Would you like me to tell you about your

mother? I think you might like to hear. I have some stories about her."

"No. I would like my mother, though . . ."

Lily didn't remember the rest of Monday.

24

Meet the Parents

Dear Mom and Papi,

It's been very hard for me to get you on the phone, but there is something I wanted to tell you. Two days ago, I was diagnosed with cancer. I have something called acute myeloid leukemia. I'm starting chemotherapy on Monday. Everything is up in the air depending on how I respond to the treatment. The doctor says I'm very sick.

I need your help very much right now.

Love,

Lily.

George Quinn sat on the lanai with Lily's letter in his hands. He sat for an hour, then he lit a cigarette, and then he cried. It was eleven in the morning, and he wished that he could tell his wife about their youngest child, but his wife was inside, ranting in the kitchen, dropping cups on the floor. She was irate over the lack or abundance of something in the house.

George wanted to call Lily, but he knew instinctively that he was not what she needed. And also, what she needed perhaps even from him—strength and support—he could not give her. Not knowing any of the facts, not knowing anything about myeloid leukemia, or the seriousness of Lily's condition, he instinctively understood that Lily was not getting over pneumonia or bronchitis, and suddenly in that hour outside on his shiny sunny lanai, George Quinn, at the age of sixty-five, learned something about himself. What George wanted from life, *all* he wanted from his newly retired life, was peace. He had been a beat reporter, then a section editor, had stress his whole life—stress, anxiety, deadlines every day for almost half a century. Now he wanted to have his walks, and to have his coffee and read his paper, and do his quiet shopping, and cook a nice dinner, and watch his sports at night. He wanted to smoke cigarettes, and have a drink of cognac later in the evening. It was so little from life he wanted, and it was constantly being denied him—first by the frenzied woman in his kitchen, and second by his last-born child. The shame was hot on his face. He couldn't really be sitting here blaming Lily for crashing into his reality! He wanted to put on his dark sunglasses to shield him from her letter—and then from himself. He wanted his wife of forty-two years in this hour. She didn't come out.

The evening came. And then he told her. On their lanai, where all matters of importance and trivia were discussed and discovered and decided, he said nothing when she sat down heavily, with fresh bruises on her upper arm and neck, with cuts along her jaw line. Her hand shaking she picked up her water glass. She had some of his noodles and tuna.

He let her eat in peace. He refilled her water glass but the rest of the time sat immobile, except for the cigarette from his hand to his mouth, staring out into the night. He was listening for the ocean. He still hadn't called Lily. He wanted to ask Allison if she remembered the day in September, nearly twenty-five years ago when she went to Booth Memorial Hospital to give birth to her. Allie ate too many pancakes for breakfast and her water broke—as if the two were related. She was at the hospital for six hours and then Lily was born and she was only six pounds and the nurse said to Allie, how did you gain sixty pounds when your baby is only six? The other three children came to look at her in the nursery. Andrew was a senior in high school, but the way he held Lily, you'd have thought she was his child. But George couldn't open his mouth to speak any of these words to the mother of his children. His voice was not strong enough.

When Allison was done eating, he said, "Lily sent us a letter. Here, read." And pushed the piece of paper toward her.

She didn't pick it up. She lit a cigarette and said, "I don't have my glasses. What does she want? More money?"

"She has cancer."

Allison did not stop smoking. "What did you say?"

"She has cancer."

"What are you talking about?" she said, raising her voice. "What cancer?"

"Read the letter, Allie. She is sick. She needs our help."

"Oh God! I'm so tired of hearing you talk and talk! Yak, yak, yak. What are you talking about, what cancer?"

He stood abruptly and walked back into the house.

She finished her cigarette, took the letter, came back inside, and slowly made her way to her bedroom where she'd left her glasses. He sat in front of the turned-off television and waited. In five minutes she reappeared. She stood to the side of him, by the couch.

"I don't understand this leukemia."

"Allie, what do you want from me? Call your daughter. Find out what's going on."

"Well, what is this acute myeloid? I've never heard of it."

"Me neither. We're not doctors."

"How serious do you think it is?"

"I don't know anything. If she needs chemo, it's probably serious."

"No, not necessarily. They give you chemo now as a preventive measure. They don't even care anymore if you need it or not."

"I can't imagine that's true."

"What, you're calling me a liar now?

She stood. He sat.

"Call your daughter. She needs you." George couldn't look at her.

She stood to the side of him for a few more minutes and then said, "Why don't you call her."

"She doesn't need me. She needs her mother." The words got stuck in his throat. He stopped speaking.

Slowly Allison turned and went up the two stairs back to her bedroom.

In the bedroom she sat at the edge of the bed, near the phone, with the letter in her hands, glasses on her nose, and she re-read it. The thing she responded to first, or rather most, was the *I'm sick and I need your help*. It was the *I need your help* that Allie's insides were responding to. What she wanted to do was call Lily and scream at her, the anger inside was so deep. *You need my help? My help!? What do you want me to do? I'm seven thousand miles away, what can I possibly do for you? You never call me, you never call your mother even to ask how I'm doing, and I'm doing horribly, I'm so depressed, I'm on medication, my teeth are falling out, I can't eat properly, I'm so sick myself and done with life, and you are asking me to help you! Why don't you help me? I need help too, do I call you up, do I write you letters and ask you for help?*

She held on to her stomach.

She tried to get control of herself. Cancer. Everybody has cancer. Lily is, as always, exaggerating. She probably has blood poisoning from all the drugs she's taking. I know, that's what I'm supporting, her drug habit. I know she wants money from me. She has no insurance, how is she going to pay for chemo? First she tells me she's sick, then she tells me she needs money to pay for her treatment. I know how this goes. Mom, my phone is being turned off. Mom, I can't pay my rent. I can't pay for my books, for my art supplies, for my crayons. I need a new winter coat, a new quilt, new pillows. It doesn't end. Now she's run out of excuses, so now she's got cancer. It's a ruse for my money. I know it. Cancer. A friend of mine at the bank, once had skin cancer, we were all apoplectic with worry, we sent flowers, we took her out to dinner, we had a collection for a present, I put in a hundred dollars. She went to the doctor and with a little local anesthetic he cut the thing out of her face, and with a bandage she was back to work on Monday. A hundred dollars I put in!

She looked at the phone. She didn't hear the TV outside. He's probably reading the paper, totally unconcerned but to me blowing it all out of proportion with his moist eyes. How he loves melodrama.

The phone was right at her hand height, two feet away. She barely had to reach over. I'm going to call, she thought, standing up, and heading for the bathroom. I am. But first I'm thirsty. I'm going to get a glass of cranberry juice. She poured herself a little, a drop of cranberry juice into her highball glass and brought the glass to her lips. This is the right thing to do, she thought, going to her closet, and rummaging in the pile of clothes until she pulled out her third-full gallon of Gordon's. This will help me take the edge off my anger. I can't talk to her when I'm this upset. I'll just end up yelling and she'll end up hanging up, like always because she has no respect for her mother. She poured the gin into the cranberry-juice glass, poured and poured, until the glass was full, and then she picked it up and opened her mouth and poured it in until the glass was empty. She waited a moment, and swayed. I think I need a little more, she thought. I'm still angry. I'll have one more and then I'll call her. She poured the gin into a now empty highball glass until the glass was full, and then she opened her mouth and poured it into her throat until the glass was empty. She waited. She swayed and this time she had to hold on to the countertop. Better. Better. She felt the warmth in her throat, in her belly, in her head. The warmth was all over her body, and it was so pleasing and *so* comforting. She wasn't angry anymore. It's all right now. Now I can call. But just a little more comfort. She tipped the bottle into her throat for the third time. And after that one she still managed to remember to stagger over to the closet and hide her now empty bottle, and to rinse her glass under water. She crawled back to her bedroom on her hands and knees, tried to pull herself up onto the bed, but failed and fell on the floor into the black abyss, still two feet from the telephone, now two feet above her head.

25

Chemo 202

Spencer came at eight, after work, to look in on her. Lily's grandmother was sitting by her side. They barely nodded to each other when he came in. He asked how Lily was doing. Claudia replied that she was sleeping and said nothing else. He asked how she had been during the day. Claudia stuck her finger out in a point. "You see. Like this." She glared at him, squinty-eyed. He sat down and Claudia said, "That's the nurse's chair."

Spencer looked around. "Is the nurse here?"

Claudia tutted and said nothing. Her posture was stiff, her fingers were drumming on her lap.

Spencer wondered if Lily was going to wake up. She didn't look as if she'd be waking up soon, as if she just didn't care that visiting hours were from six to eight and that he worked all day and couldn't come. After a few minutes, he got up and said he had to be going. "I brought her some Krispy Kremes. Would you give them to her and tell her I stopped by?"

"Oh, sure," said Claudia. She didn't tell Lily and ate the donuts herself.

On Tuesday, after a second day of chemo, Lily was sleeping again at six when Spencer came. Amanda was there with Claudia this time. Amanda was sitting in Marcie's chair.

Spencer stood for a moment, and then said, "That's the nurse's chair."

Amanda turned away from him until he left.

The following night, Lily was still unconscious. Claudia was there, with Anne and Amanda this time, and Spencer didn't stay even for a minute under their hateful gazes.

Voices kept coming at her, voices that belonged to her family, the deep resounding Slavic-accented Grandma voice, the no-nonsense, I-don't-take-no-for-an-answer Anne voice, and the calmer but no less righteous Amanda voice.

"He must be the densest cop in New York. Why would he still be coming? Doesn't he have any idea how it makes us feel to see him here?"

"We've made it pretty clear. He must be a terrible investigator."

"I'm not beating around the bush anymore. He obviously can't take a hint. I'm going to tell him to stop coming."

"Want *me* to tell him?"

"*I'll* tell him. You're going to garble your words like always."

"Stop it, Lily can tell him."

"She would definitely tell him if she was awake."

"She is sick, she can barely speak, she can't tell him."

"Can you believe she's won all that money? I mean, what un-believable luck, don't you think?"

"Look at her, she's sick. What luck?"

"I know. What luck though. God, what I could do with money like that!"

"Yeah, you'd blow through it, like you blow through every penny you ever made."

"But seriously though, what is he thinking? He's actively seek-ing the destruction of our family, of Andrew. You know how our Liliput feels about Andrew. If she knew that detective was coming around, she'd flip."

There was a silence.

"Why do you think he's got that crew cut? Just like her. You don't think *he* cut her hair, do you?"

"No! They don't know each other like that. For God's sake, it's our baby Lil and he's fifty! I'm telling you, he's here for information on Andrew. He's probably questioned her dozens of times. He knows he's got nothing on Andrew, so he's coming around trying to bilk a sick girl."

"You're so right. But we can't tell Lily. It'll just make her more upset."

" . . . Can you believe that about Andrew and Lil's roommate?"

"Can I tell you, if he didn't tell us himself, I would never believe it. I think Miera is still in shock."

There was a stifled chuckle. "Serves her right, that bitch. She hates us."

"I know—but look at our poor brother. He's had to abandon his Senate campaign."

"It's all right, he'll run again when the time is right. He'll sort this out, you'll see."

"He won't if Miera leaves him."

"Oh, yeah, that's likely. Where is she going to go? Poor Podunk where she came from?"

"Old Hartford, sadly."

"Whatever. Andrew's the best thing that ever happened to her. Let her go back to her posh little Hartford. She doesn't deserve him."

"No, I know, I know. But . . . you don't think he's had anything to do with . . ."

"Amy's disappearance? God, no. He just made a mistake, he's a human being, he's not perfect. I must say, I have no idea what he was thinking. Why take any chances at all when your whole career could be at stake. But it's nothing. So he had a meaningless fling, so what? Andrew said he ended it months before the girl went missing. It's got nothing to do with him, that part. The detective has no case and he knows it."

202

"Next time he comes, I'm definitely going to tell him to stop coming for good."

Suddenly Joshua came. That was a surprise. Lily was awake unfortunately, it was the early afternoon. What was he doing here? He seemed so shocked at her appearance. He couldn't even hide it and had nothing to say. She couldn't believe he was here! Who told you I was here? Was it Paul? Was it Rachel? Dennis?

Apparently it was her sister Amanda.

"It's nice of you to come," Lily said with a pasted-on grimace. And to her sister later, she said, "Are you actively working against my best interests?"

"I don't know what you're talking about."

"Amanda, what can't you see? He left me, he broke up with me, he left me to go out with bigger breasts from Corning, New York, and you bring him here when I look like this, when I feel like this?"

"I'm sorry. I wasn't thinking of you like that."

"No kidding."

Amanda came less after that, citing sore throats, the beginnings of school, parent orientations, school supplies, responsibilities. Anne, however, practically lived at the hospital, just like Grandma.

And Joshua blessedly did not come again.

Lily lay seven days with the voices filtering in and out. During her first day of rest between chemo treatments, when she was foggily conscious and not throwing up, when she could speak, she said, "Has Spencer been here?"

Claudia said, "I don't know who you're talking about." And then abruptly left the room.

So Lily hadn't dreamt it, those words that had been spoken by her family.

But here it was, day one, and now day two of her rest period and there was no Spencer, not even in the evening. And Grandma was always by her side.

Every time Lily picked up the phone, Grandma would say, "Who are you calling?"

"Paul, Grandma."

"Oh, how is that nice young man? He likes you, I think."

"He does. He likes boys more though."

"Oh."

During her third afternoon of rest, Grandma stepped out for a moment—thank God for bodily functions!—and Lily quickly picked up the phone to call Spencer, and to her horror discovered that she couldn't remember his beeper number. She couldn't remember the number of the police station. By the time she called information, and they started to check for her, Grandma returned. "Who are you calling?"

"Rachel, Grandma." Lily put down the phone. How could she have forgotten his beeper number?

She was fed through a tube and her Port-A-Cath, her port-a-life, her port-a-breath. When three days of rest passed and DiAngelo came to start ATRA and cytarabine again, she shook her head and said no more.

All through the following days she kept saying no more, no more, no more. Marcie was making her get up and walk, but Lily would stand up and fall down. Marcie had to carry her to the bathroom. They attached her to a catheter so she didn't have to get up if she didn't want to, but still every day after the morning ATRA and the afternoon chemo, Marcie would whisper, come on, come on, Spunky, don't just lie there, get up, walk a bit.

"Give me that Milky Way, Marcie."

"I told you—by the bagfuls when you're done."

"Give me a cigarette, Marcie."

"Forget it. Those things will kill ya."

Lily, in and out, up and down, weak and weaker, nauseated nearly non-stop, despite the anti-emetics they gave her to counteract the chemo, thought that perhaps her grandmother was right, perhaps a complete destruction of sanity would follow lying 24/7 in a bed. The room didn't turn purple anymore, not even for fun, and the toilets didn't double, and neither did Grandma.

"By the way," and this was Anne talking. "I just want you to know, I've decided to take a leave of absence from *KnightRidder* to be here full time, to help you, Lil, help you do whatever you need me to do. Get stuff, do stuff, be here for you 24/7."

"Don't talk nonsense, Annie. You need to work, pay your bills. I'm here all the time," said Grandma, "and I don't need to take a leave of absence."

"Yes, but you're not in the best of health yourself, Grandma. I don't want you to get sick as well. Do you know how many microbes are flying around in the hospital, how much bacteria from sick people? It's a wonder you're not sick already. I don't want to worry about you, too. No, it's done, I want to do this for Lily."

"Thanks, Annie," Lily said, "but the doctor seems to think I need a pro to take care of me."

"Oh, what does he know," Anne said. "I don't like him. He's got an attitude on him. Who's better for you than family?"

"Yes, Lily," said Amanda, a little too enthusiastically, "Let Anne do it. It's wonderful that you'll have someone right by your side at all times. You need her, Lil." As if she knew that if Anne were at the hospital she herself would be absolved from helping.

"But," said Anne, and here was the but! "It's unpaid leave. I'll need a way to pay my mortgage. Do you think you can take care of that, Lily? You have that money coming in, it'll be just like hiring a part-time nurse, the mortgage is only five grand a month. And maybe a little extra for utilities, and food, and transportation to the hospital, all those cabs do add up, you know. Maybe ten thousand a month. Say eleven. Does that sound reasonable?"

"Sounds reasonable, Annie. I'll have to check with the doctor, though."

On the sixth day of her second chemo/ATRA run, she was shuffling down the hall in her hospital nightgown and robe, as per Marcie's instructions to be Spunky, dragging her IV stand next to her, counting in her head, breathing to stave off nausea, and when she turned around to slump back to her room, Spencer was standing by her door.

She gaped at him, feeling every bit the wretch that she was, and there he stood, ironed, clean-shaven, black-rimmed, in a suit, his eyes twinkling with pity and compassion for her, his hair sheared in compassion for her, and Lily couldn't move from her spot in the corridor. When he walked up to her, she started to cry.

Cry!

"Lily . . ." he said, perplexed, opening his hands, and she came closer and pressed her head into his chest, and felt his arm carefully on her back, but her hours of being alone were stretched so long, and his arm on her back lasted but a moment. When she stepped away, Grandma was at the open door of her room, scowling at them.

She wiped her face. "I'm sorry. I don't know what just happened . . ."

"Don't worry. You're up. Every time I've come you've been so out of it. How are you feeling?"

They stood twenty feet away from the angry Grandma.

"Good, good. Fine. How've you been? The drugs are just awful. Amy was right when she told me not to do them."

"I don't think she meant these."

"I tried to call you but I didn't have your beeper number with me."

He took out his business card and stuck it into her hand. "You forgot my beeper number, Lil?" He sounded . . . surprised.

"It's these drugs, they've killed my brain. Anything

happening?" she asked, clasping the card. She wanted to look up at him, but suddenly found herself sinking into that Joshua mud. Into that I-can't-believe-anyone-who-is-not-family-is-looking-me-in-this-state mud. She stared at the floor.

"A bit's happening. Don't worry about any of it. You've got yourself to take care of."

"Lilianne! Let's go, Marcie's waiting!" Grandma called loudly.

She sighed. "I gotta go. I've got another bag of VePesid to get through. Can you stay?"

"I think your grandmother would shoot me if I stayed." He paused. "At night you're pretty bad. You're never awake."

"I know. In the early morning, or noon is better."

Spencer leaned to her a little. "Except that *she* is always here and I'm always working."

"Of course. I know. Look, I'm fine. I've got visitors here around the clock."

"Lily! Are you coming?"

"Just a minute, Grandma." She continued to be turned to Spencer, who was blocking her from Claudia's view with his body.

"Visitors around the clock?" he said. "Has your brother been to see you?"

She soaked that in under her skin, her small smile vanishing. "No," she said. "But now I really have to go."

"Why can't he face you?"

"I don't know, Detective O'Malley. I can't face myself either."

"He's hiding from you now the way he's been hiding from you since Amy disappeared."

"Please . . . that's not true." She was weak and her legs were buckling. "My family may be right about you. You are up to no good."

He mouthed, "I'm sorry, Lily," as she walked past, flicking his business card on the floor by his feet.

"Me too, Spencer." Her tears now coming from her heart and straight out the Hickman catheter in her chest, she shuffled by him, not lifting her eyes one more time to glance at him.

And when Marcie was hooking up the VePesid, Lily's eyes were closed, her head thrashing from side to side on her soaked pillow, wishing for the drug's retching oblivion, but after the VePesid was done dripping, Lily creeped back outside, and desperately searched the hospital linoleum for his card she had dropped. It wasn't there.

26

The Church on 51st Street

Claudia caught up with him at the elevator. "Young man, I want to talk to you."

He gave her his card. "That's Detective O'Malley of the NYPD, Mrs. Vail."

She frowned. "How do you know who I am?"

"Lily speaks about you frequently."

"You know what, I don't want you to be speaking to Lily frequently. You're a detective, can't you *detect* you're not welcome here? You're not family, you're not a friend. You're a hound, and you're coming to bother a very sick young girl."

The elevator wasn't coming. He had a dozen other open cases at that moment on his desk. Any of the others would be more fruitful. Ten of them were young kids—runaways, custody cases. One of them was a crack den mother, having disappeared for the fourth time this year. There was plenty he could be doing other than this.

He moved away from her, she grabbed his arm. She was feisty, well, she would have had to have been to get herself here from Europe. She was not afraid of him. But Spencer, even without the war-torn devastation, was not afraid of her either.

Her eyes were sharp as ice picks.

"She doesn't want me to come?" he said, buttoning his suit jacket. "She can tell me herself."

"You think she's going to remember something about her brother in the state she is in?"

"That's not why I'm here."

"You're barking up the wrong tree, you know. He doesn't know where that girl is."

"You have to think so. I'd be suspicious if you didn't."

"But he really *is* innocent of wrongdoing. He is my grandson. I lived with him, I nearly raised him, I know him from childhood. You don't think I can tell, you think I'd be lying to myself? I'm far too old and frail for that."

"Nothing frail about you," said Spencer. "And if he is so innocent, how come he's refusing the polygraph?"

"Because his lawyers advised against it. Innocent, I tell you. I will swear in a court of law on this one."

"No need, your grandson is swearing enough for both of you. But the question remains: where's Amy?"

They were standing in the impersonal, incongruous, fluorescently lit hospital hallway, with strangers walking back and forth, with the nurses at their station nearby, laughing, the phone ringing, an old man being wheeled by in a chair, looking at them with a blinkless gaze. Spencer was looking at them himself with a blinkless gaze. As Lily was lying inside door number 5547, struggling to stop retching, they were discussing her brother's connection in the disappearance of her roommate.

"I don't know," she said. "But his innocence I feel in my heart."

Spencer sighed. "All right then. Well, I'll go by what I feel in my heart, not having the advantage of being related to your grandson." The elevator finally came. "Now, if you'll excuse me."

Claudia called after him with angry frustration. "Why are you picking on him? Why don't you interview the hobos Amy was feeding every week, they have a better chance of knowing what happened to her."

210

Slowly Spencer turned around and walked out of the elevator. He came back to Claudia. "What did you say?"

"I said why don't you ask the homeless—"

"Wait, wait." He shook his head with incredulity. "What homeless?"

"What homeless? Some detective you are," she scoffed. "I met her a handful of times and even I know."

"That's a handful more times than I met her, so give it up. What homeless?"

"She spent Thanksgiving with us last year. She also came once with Lily to see me and stayed for dinner."

"So?"

"So, so. Both days were a Thursday."

"So?"

"She had to leave early both times, because she said she had to go to the soup kitchen to serve breakfast. We said, even after Thanksgiving? And she said, every Friday."

Spencer stood there stiffly. "What soup kitchen?" he said at last.

"How should I know? Now if you'll excuse *me*, I'm going to go back to my grandchild. But you heard me, don't come again."

On the way back to the precinct, Spencer had to fight to keep his mouth closed, to stop his dervish thoughts from whirling out like frenetic mendicants.

He had wanted a word that pointed him in the right direction, a word that made him feel that he wasn't chasing spiders up brick walls? There it was. Two words even.

But *soup kitchen?*

Who on earth could help him with this?

It was Paul's day off and Spencer couldn't find him. Rachel was also not in the salon. Lenny had no idea about any soup kitchen. What good was a private investigator who couldn't get these details out of the heap of remnants of Amy's life? Jan McFadden should fire him. She herself, unfocused on the phone,

211

had no idea that her daughter visited soup kitchens, it was as much of a surprise to her as it had been to Spencer.

The Copa Cabana where Amy used to work had got itself a spanking new staff, everybody had *heard* of Amy but nobody *knew* much about Amy or her affinity for the destitute.

Spencer called Joshua who said oh yeah, she did do something with them, but I can't for the life of me remember when or what or how or where. I may never have known it.

Lived with the girls for seven months and may never have known it? Lily was lucky to be rid of him.

Spencer had no choice. He had to talk to the one person who could help him. What day was it? It wasn't Friday, that was for sure. His hands were unsteady. It had been two weeks between drink. He had to keep holding something between his fingers: pens, pencils, backs of chairs, the wheel of the car, so that no one would notice.

After work he went back to Mount Sinai.

Marcie had gone, DiAngelo had gone, the night nurse didn't want to let him in since visiting hours were long over. He had to flash his badge and say he was here on police business. Why did he feel like such a heel saying it? Because it was true?

The grandmother wasn't there either. So there *was* a time to come when no one was around her. Trouble was, she wasn't around herself either. He sat by Lily's side in the quiet as the water dripped in the bathroom and the TV was on mute. He hated the TV on mute. He turned the sound up a little. She looked so helpless with the tube in her nose, under her covers, lying propped up slightly, with what little was left of her hair falling out in dark shavings onto her pillow. Through her chest catheter a fluid tube was connected, a glucose solution dripping in, like the bathroom faucet. Drip, drip.

After a while of watching her, he whispered her name, until she awoke, looking stranded. "What's wrong, what happened?" she mouthed.

"Nothing, all's okay."

"I keep dreaming people whisper my name over and over, and then I open my eyes and you're here."

"Whispering your name over and over." He gave her a drink, asked if there was something else he could get her. No, she said, sheepishly adding, maybe another business card? He took from his pocket the one she threw on the floor and put it inside her bedstand drawer.

"So what did your little policemen friends think about your hair?"

"The other kids made fun of me," he replied.

They fell quiet.

"Lily," he said, "What soup kitchen did Amy go to every Friday?"

Her eyes barely open, closed for sure. With a hurting sigh, her arms went around her stomach and she groaned. "A church on 51st and Seventh."

He couldn't help himself. He wished he could. "Why didn't you tell me? Why didn't you tell me three months ago she had somewhere to be every Friday?"

Lily didn't reply. A small tear rolled down her temple.

The nurse came in to take her vitals.

He sat with her for a while longer, and then he left.

27

Liz Monroe and 57/57

The next day after the morning meeting, Spencer was in the evidence room sifting through Amy's various empty shopping bags, receipts, papers, notebooks, textbooks, jackets, pockets of jeans, with a fourth cup of coffee in his hand, when Harkman stuck his head in and said, "Spence . . ."

Spencer decided to ignore him. He didn't like the tone of that whisper.

Harkman slowly brought his sour-smelling bulk over. Spencer resisted the urge to ask him if he had taken his gout medicine. This was just too strong a smell for nine in the morning. Harkman rested his rump on the table and with his bypassed heart panting an ostensible and unacceptable 137 beats a minute, said, "Spence, I gotta tell you something."

Spencer didn't look up from Amy's shopping bags. He was interested in their variety and their quality. "What?" He was studying a matchbook he had found in one of her jacket pockets. It was from the Four Seasons Hotel lounge bar, called Fifty Seven Fifty Seven. By itself it would have meant nothing, but the jacket was thrown into a Frederic Fekkai bag. Frederic Fekkai was also on 57th. Of course she also had matchbooks from the Caviar Bar on 58th and from Bombay Palace on 52nd. He was trying to put one and two together when Harkman said, "They want to see you upstairs."

Spencer looked up from the Four Seasons matchbook. "Who's *they*?"

Harkman didn't speak for a moment and then leaned his head forward and said in a low voice, "I swear to God, Spencer, I have no idea what it's about, it's got nothing to do with me."

"What the fuck are you talking about?" Spencer said, sharply getting up out of the chair, dropping the matchbook on the floor and coming toward him. "I was barely listening because I was trying to *work*. Who wants to see me upstairs?"

All Harkman could do was mutter an impotent, "IA."

"IA?"

He nodded.

"And you're sure whatever it is, it's got nothing to do with you? How do you know? Maybe it's got something to do with you. Maybe they want to ask me about that little bit of graft you receive from the drug dealers in Tompkins Square Park to look the other way, and not bring back the MPs that are strung out on the scag they're selling, huh, maybe it's got something to do with that?"

"Stop it, nothing to do with me, I'm telling you. Rumor mill has it that IA got an anonymous letter about . . . you . . ."

"What letter?"

"About Greenwich, Connecticut." Harkman was whispering. His lips were shaking. "But I didn't do it, I didn't send it."

Spencer grabbed Harkman by his jacket. "What the fuck do you know about Greenwich, Connecticut?"

"Let go of me, O'Malley." His voice was thin. "You don't want more trouble with IA, do you?"

Spencer shoved him hard. Harkman fell back against the rattling table, which slowed his tumble to the floor.

Upstairs, Spencer sat at the end of a long conference table across from three people whom he'd never met. One was an attractive woman in her early thirties, sharp, swift, efficient, in a dark blue business suit, with perfect make-up and without a mitochondrion of a sense of humor. Spencer saw it. The other two were men. Spencer did not pay much attention to men and so didn't notice what they looked like. They were older than the woman and in suits that were nowhere near as sharp or as ironed. Both their hair needed cutting. Spencer was displeased that he, breaking his own protocol, deliberately wore jeans instead of a suit today, preparing to go casual to the soup kitchen. Should have worn a suit.

Harkman was such a bastard.

The ironed-out woman introduced herself as Liz Monroe. "These are my colleagues." She pointed to her colleagues and Spencer was grateful she didn't tell him their names.

"Do you know why we're here, detective?"

"No."

She cleared her throat. Spencer thought she might have expected a follow-up, "Why?" But he wouldn't give her what she expected. Only the unexpected for her.

"We're here because inquiries have been made regarding your possible involvement in the death of a Nathan Sinclair."

Spencer said nothing. He had nothing to say.

"Do you know who Nathan Sinclair is?"

"Well, obviously."

"Inquiries have been made—"

"What inquiries?"

Monroe started looking through her notes. "What do you know about the circumstances of his death?"

"Nothing."

"Do you know who he was?"

"Of course."

"Who was he?"

"One of the witnesses in a murder investigation."

"This was in Hanover, New Hampshire?"

"Yes, this was in Hanover, New Hampshire."

"You were the senior detective there for ten years?"

"Yes."

"Why did you leave? Was it because of . . . Nathan Sinclair?"

"No, it was not because of . . . Nathan Sinclair." Spencer tried hard not to be too obvious with his mimicking. "I left because of a difference of opinion with my superiors regarding the murder investigation you mention."

"And then?"

"I came back home to Long Island and was rehired by the Suffolk County Police Department."

"What did you do for them after you were rehired?"

"That's not in my records? I was a traffic patrol officer."

"And then?"

"Then I transferred to the NYPD. Four years ago."

"Let's just stick with Suffolk County PD for a moment. You went from being a detective-sergeant in Hanover to being a traffic cop?"

"That's right."

Liz Monroe said nothing. "That's quite a demotion."

Spencer didn't respond as no response seemed necessary, or even possible. "Not monetarily," he finally said.

She looked down into her notes again. She was barely taking her head out of them. "It was brought to our attention—"

"By who?"

"That's not the issue."

"I'm sorry to interrupt. I'm afraid it *is* the issue."

"We received an anonymous letter, if you must know. All admissible evidence, as you also must know. The letter stated that witnesses saw you having lunch with Nathan Sinclair, at a Cos Cob, Connecticut diner."

"Ms. Monroe, surely you didn't need an anonymous letter to tell you this? It's in my file. Under O for O'Malley. Any time you wanted you could have found this information. And by the way, I've already dealt with the Suffolk County Internal Affairs on this issue in great detail. Four years ago."

"Yes, yes, I found this information. I have your records in front of me. Is this why you left the Suffolk County Police Department?"

"This is not why I left the Suffolk County Police Department. I didn't leave. I transferred to NYPD."

"You must understand—"

"Who are you talking to?"

She coughed, turning red. "Detective O'Malley, excuse me, you must understand that accusations of any kind are taken very seriously by our department and will be given weight and merit."

"Is the letter accusing me of having lunch with Nathan Sinclair at a diner? I'm guilty as charged."

"It's only significant because that was the last time anyone saw him alive. He was found by his gardener weeks later, the TV still on, long dead. It was summer, his body was gravely decomposed."

Spencer stared straight at Liz Monroe who stared straight back at him. "Perhaps you should speak to the gardener."

"Yes, thank you, detective. Why did you meet with Mr. Sinclair? Was it a police visit or a personal visit?"

"It was a . . ." Spencer hesitated. "I guess both."

"Were you on duty?"

"I was not."

"And you were no longer the investigating officer on that case, having taken yourself off it by resigning?"

"There was no case anymore. There was a conviction. The case was closed."

"So really your seeing Nathan Sinclair was more in a personal capacity, wouldn't you say?"

Perhaps Spencer did not answer in the first breath. "I suppose so."

"That part is not in your file, detective," said Liz Monroe, and this time she looked up from her notes.

"You're obviously a much more thorough investigator, Ms. Monroe."

"Thank you. Did you suspect that Mr. Sinclair was involved in the murder you had been investigating at Dartmouth College?"

"Not at all. I simply had questions that had not been answered."

"And what questions were those?"

"We discussed several topics. Music. Cars. We commiserated with each other about our wives both lost in car accidents."

Without a nod of sympathy, Monroe said, "You didn't seek him out just to talk to him about music and wives, detective."

"As I said, I wanted to catch up on old news. Idle chitchat."

"You were friendly then?"

"Glancingly friendly."

"What did you do after you left him?"

"I drove to Hanover, New Hampshire."

"Why?"

"For the same reason I sought him out. To catch up with old friends."

"But you didn't see anyone when you got to Hanover. At least that's what it says in your case notes."

"That's right. By the time I got there it was well after working hours and there was no one around. My old partner was on vacation. I walked around, and then drove down to Brattleboro mall down in Vermont, had some dinner, bought a carry-on bag, as I was thinking of visiting my sister in California. The receipt for that purchase is in the case file."

"Receipt's in here. Paid for in cash. But where's the bag, detective?"

"Long gone, Ms. Monroe. The handle ripped after much use and I had to throw it out. Is the bag of much interest to you?"

"Of some interest, yes. As in, why you would buy it, just then. Did the Suffolk IA ask to see the bag?"

"No, they did not."

"You do much traveling, then? I see here from your employment record that in the last seven years at SCPD and NYPD, you've taken your twenty-seven vacation days a year in dribs and drabs, not a single time, not *once* in any extended chunk."

"And your point?"

"After this frequently-used bag purchase, what did you do?"

"I drove home. As you know the ride is long, five hours, that time of night, I was tired, I drove carefully. I stopped several times. I must have gotten back around two in the morning or so. I was living in an apartment above my brother's garage at the time, and they heard me open the garage door; they said it was around two. It should all be in the file, Ms. Monroe."

The woman fell quiet looking into her notes. "It is, it is. You know it is our responsibility to look into any misconduct by our officers who are sworn to uphold the law."

"I know. You're doing your job admirably. I upheld the law. And moreover, I was not an officer of the NYPD during that time. I was an officer of the Suffolk County Police Department, off duty, and they already investigated this matter and resolved it to their satisfaction."

"Any misconduct?"

"No," said Spencer.

"Nathan Sinclair was shot once by a Saturday night special .22 directly into his femoral artery, and bled to death."

"So I understand."

"The police, upon coming to the scene of the crime, discovered that the TV was on mute." She paused. "As if Nathan Sinclair muted the TV because he wanted to talk to his assailant, plead for his life perhaps."

Spencer said nothing, since a response was not requested of him.

She continued. "The gun was never found. The bullet from the gun had been removed. Scooped out of his thigh by a gloved hand leaving no fingerprints."

Spencer felt something was required of him here. "I carried a Magnum in those days."

"Did you confiscate the specials during drug busts?"

"I have confiscated them from time to time, yes."

"There were boot-prints near him in his blood."

"I can't recall, were they police-issue boot-prints?"

"Um—no. But you weren't having lunch with him as an officer of the law, detective."

"The witness who saw us at a diner having lunch and so

220

helpfully wrote to you, did he remember if I was wearing boots? It was summertime, it's a kind of a thing that might stick out."

"There is no mention of the boots, no."

Spencer tightened and relaxed his fists on the cherry wood table in full view of Ms. Monroe.

"What size shoe do you wear, Detective O'Malley?"

"Size eleven. Me and seventy percent of the men in the United States."

"The boots were size twelve."

"Really?" Spencer tried to keep his voice even, but perhaps he inflected too archly into the middle of that *really*.

There was a pause. "You knew that already, didn't you?"

"Questioned *thoroughly* on this issue, Ms. Monroe."

"So you have no idea who killed him?"

"I have no idea who killed him."

"His murderer has not been brought to justice. And justice needs to be brought."

"I suppose."

Liz Monroe lifted her serious eyes at Spencer. "Detective O'Malley, do you feel that bringing murderers to justice is not something we should waste our time on, or is it just Nathan Sinclair's murderer that you think we shouldn't be spending our time on?"

"Is IA responsible for murder investigations now?"

"No, but IA *is* responsible for you."

Outside, Spencer, leaned against the wall for a moment to get his bearings. And then he slowly walked down three flights, resisting the impulse to hold on to the railing.

28

The Soup Kitchen

The First Presbyterian Shelter for the Homeless occupied the whole basement of an old church. Instead of bingo and church socials for newly divorced Protestants, the downstairs hall was used for alms—seventy beds, and food. Spencer finally managed to get there on Friday at dawn. He had nearly lost his will to pursue the McFadden case. The fight had gone out of him, but that didn't stop him from taking Harkman by his shirtfront when he came upon him in the empty hallway. He brought him hard against the wall, and stifling an urge to hit him, said, "You're such a fucking bastard. You better watch your back, Chris Harkman, because no one else will be watching it."

"Are you threatening me?" Harkman said. "Get away from me."

Spencer stepped back.

"I told you, it wasn't me. I told you that, why can't you believe me? But you know what, O'Malley, we all get what's coming to us. We all get exactly what we deserve, don't we."

"Yes, we do, Harkman," said Spencer, walking away and pointing an angry finger at the man's face, "and be careful that you don't get exactly what you deserve. What a sorry day that'll be for you."

Whittaker brought him into his office, Spencer thought to

chew him out over Harkman, but Whittaker said, "I don't give a shit about your schoolgirl fights, work it out between you and leave me out of it, and no, you can't be partnered with McGill, but O'Malley, lay off the congressman."

And suddenly the fight went right back into him.

"Did you just say to lay off a capital case, chief?"

"No, just lay off Quinn, O'Malley."

"Why?"

"Because he's got nothing to do with it, that's why." Whittaker was a good Irish cop, thirty years on the force, his no-shit-from-anybody character much improved in Spencer's mind by the fact that he liked Spencer. "He was banging her, not killing her. Do you see the difference?"

"He was banging her and now she's missing!"

"Oh, come on! He's not a politician if he doesn't have an affair. That's how you recognize them, their pants are around their ankles. What are you going to do—prosecute each and every one?"

"Yes, if their lovers end up missing four months on my watch."

"Look, O'Malley, I'll be straight with you—the congressman has powerful friends in the city of New York, and they've been leaning on me to either provide proof or lay off."

"He refused a polygraph!"

"O'Malley, what about you upstairs this morning? If that ball-buster Liz Monroe asked you to take a polygraph, would you?"

"Chief," Spencer said evenly and slowly, "I'd refuse just to piss her off."

"Exactly. People have all kinds of reasons for refusing polygraphs. Stay out of their heads. Their refusal is inadmissible as evidence, inadmissible period. Let it go." He pointed upstairs. "And watch out for the cohone buster. She's got a pair of her own and they're made of steel. Sergeant Vicario, remember him? The Jesse Ventura of the NYPD? The woman made him cry. Cry, I tell you."

"Thanks for the advice."

So perhaps Harkman, that son of a bitch, was telling the truth. It was entirely possible that the congressman hired a dick to dig up old, new, any kind of dirt on Spencer. Perhaps they thought it would make Spencer back down; but they didn't understand him, didn't know he was perversely invigorated by Internal Affairs, and zealously at five-thirty on a Friday morning, Spencer was at the soup kitchen.

He spoke to a man named Clive, a short heavy man in a suit with a bristly attitude. Spencer didn't know soup kitchen administrators dressed so well. He was wearing the pair of busted up jeans he'd thought appropriate to the occasion.

Clive told Spencer that indeed Amy McFadden had been showing up every Friday like clockwork for years, "until she wasn't showin' up no more."

Spencer explained that Amy wasn't showing up anywhere, she had been reported missing by her mother a couple of months ago and Clive's help would be appreciated in tracing Amy's movements in May. "So, Clive, do you recall if Amy was here on Friday, May 14?"

But Clive could not say. "Look, mornings swim together for me . . ."

Spencer pressed his palms together to keep his voice from lifting. "It is extremely *extremely* important that we find out if Amy came that day."

"Well, I got no idea!"

"Not good enough, Clive."

"All I got, I'm afraid."

"Clive, Clive. Would you like to come back to the police station with me? Anything that will help you remember the last time you saw her."

Clive was silent. "Wait. I remember the last time I saw her. She said she just finished with her exams, and that she was graduating . . ." Clive's eyes focused. "She said she was graduating in exactly two weeks. So when was that?"

"Her graduation was on May 28."

"Bingo."

Spencer stepped back.

Clive said, "I never did see her again after that."

Spencer looked around the soup kitchen. It was a dark room full of cafeteria tables and folding chairs. Every available seat was filled with men in rags who were eating something that must have once resembled eggs. "She talk to anyone here?"

"Well, sure, she talked to everybody. She was a friendly gal. Everyone liked her."

"Anybody in particular?"

Clive looked around the basement as if he were searching for someone.

"Hmm. He's not here, though."

"One guy she talked to in particular?"

"Yes. He hung around her. Wouldn't sit down. Disturbed her serving."

"What was his name?"

"He's not here, I tell you. He stopped coming some months back."

Spencer's shaved hair spiraled up.

"Clive . . ."

"I don't know. Hundreds of men a day, everyday. I don't keep track of them all in my head."

"Try."

"OK, let me think. I been here five years, started before Amy started. This guy used to come way back then, I remember. I paid no attention to him, but I did pay a little to Amy, because you know, I liked lookin' at her. Then he didn't come here anymore, not for a few years—suddenly bam! he was back again, loitering around Amy. I'd guess he could have been in a mental institution. Or jail. That was sometime in the spring, he reappeared, and then when she stopped coming, I'm pretty sure he stopped coming, too."

"What was his name?"

"Know nothing about him."

"What did he look like?"

"Like a homeless person. He wore rags on his body, skicaps to cover his head, cardboard on his feet. He smelled."

Spencer looked out the breakfast tables. All the men in front of him fit that description.

"Young, though," Clive added helpfully.

"How young?"

"I don't know. In his twenties? Thirties, maybe? He didn't shuffle, he had a bit of something in his step. A bit of youth. He didn't walk like an addict. Come to think of it, he didn't walk like someone who was mentally ill. You recognize them after a while by the way they shuffle, the way they hold their heads."

"And?"

"He was eerie. There was something wrong with him."

"What?"

"How should I know? Something not quite right. He had freaky eyes, like he'd pop you if you said a wrong word to him. He was repulsive too. Never took a shower, even when offered. We have showers here for the men. But he never took one, never shaved, never washed the dirt off his face. He was, I'd say, grimier than the others. He may have had tattoos on his face, I can't remember now. It could've just been filth . . ."

"Tall, short?"

"Average. Shorter than you. You might want to try the Bowery Mission. Perhaps he started going there after she stopped coming here."

"Why would he stop coming here? Does the Bowery offer better eggs?"

"I really don't know. Maybe because she stopped coming. He seemed pretty attached to her. He never ever spoke to nobody except Amy. Ever. Which is unusual—most of the people here have some connection to the others. Not him. Just to Amy."

"Anything else you can think of?"

Clive thought about it. "She used to give him stuff," he said at last. "I don't know what, but she had shopping bags full of things, I don't even know what. Something extra from her to him. I once asked her, and she said donations. But the bags were from nice stores, Guess, maybe? The Gap. What did she give him, clothes? God knows what he did with them."

Spencer gave Clive his card and told him if the man ever appeared again, to call him any time of day or night. Feeling hopeless, he walked over to the first table of diners in their uniforms of rags to find out how many of them remembered Amy and if any of them remembered her mysterious—freaky-eyed—admirer.

"Detective O'Malley!"

It was Clive, animated, pleased with himself.

"Milo!"

"Milo?"

"That's what I heard her call him once. I don't think it's his real name."

"You don't say."

Milo! was one word and a ray of light in an otherwise dark and sober Friday.

Lily was in her bed, pillows up when he came to see her in the early afternoon. She was in the middle of her third and last seven-day treatment, all the visitors now had to wear masks to see her and were not allowed to touch her. Spencer didn't know by the looks of her how she would finish this out, much less rear up for thirteen weeks of consolidation chemo. She looked as skeletal and gray as one could look and still remain upright. She didn't smile at him, she eyed him warily, though not as warily as her grandmother, who also in a mask, got up from her chair and said, "I thought I had made myself clear? You're not welcome here."

DiAngelo came in after Spencer. "Claudia, come with me," he said. "You know the rules—only one at a time in here."

"Yes, me. She doesn't want to see *him*."

Lily and Spencer stared at each other.

"Wait, Grandma," said Lily, looking accusingly at him, who had to avert his own gaze. "Give us a minute."

227

Claudia, extremely unhappily, left the room with DiAngelo, who said quietly to Spencer, "Ten minutes, okay? She can't take much more."

They were left alone, and at first they didn't speak. Then Lily said, "Here on police business again, Detective O'Malley?"

What could he say? He stood silently, wearing a mouth mask, wishing for a moment he was wearing an eye mask instead so he wouldn't have to see her disintegration. Summoning what he could of inspiration, of energy, of optimism, he took a deep breath under the hospital cotton and stepped up to the plate. "Both personal and business."

She stared into her blanket.

"How are you? Are you eating?" Two and a half courses of chemo and she was fading into the whites of her bed.

She shrugged. "Eating is overrated. If everyone could be fed through a hole in the chest, who wouldn't do it? New York would go out of business, though. Eighty percent of its economy is restaurants."

"Yes, but think how the medical-supplies business would boom."

"Hmm. I wish I could get a vanilla shake through this Hickman. Marcie says vanilla shakes are too thick. She says she can bring me a thin vanilla shake. Marcie, I tell her, that's not a vanilla shake, that's milk."

Under the mask Spencer smiled, while his eyes took in her sunken brows, her pale mouth, the translucent whiteness of her cheeks. "I brought you some Krispy Kremes. Do you want me to bring you a shake next time I come?"

"Nah. I'd only toss it. Don't waste your money." She leaned back on her pillows, while he sat six feet away from her in the chair. "Thanks for the donuts. My grandmother loves them." She paused. "So what do you want?"

"Nothing," he said. "I stopped by your building to pick up your mail."

"You did?" She frowned. "But you don't have a key to my mailbox."

"Well, I know. I'm not saying I did, but I might've used my badge to convince the super the contents of your mailbox were a matter of grave police business."

Why did that make her smile? "You're not above that sort of thing, I see, using your badge to your advantage?"

"Not at all," he said, taking out a rectangular envelope. "But I thought you might want to see this." It was a letter from New York State.

She actually laughed though soundlessly. "It came! Did you open it?"

"Of course not. It's a federal offense to open other people's mail."

Her eyes twinkled at him a little bit. "Oh, but not to go through their mailboxes? Could you open it now?"

He opened it, handed it to her. She seemed happy to hold it, to look at it, to read aloud the amount. "$7,348,200! Look at these numbers, Spencer."

"I see them clearly, even from here, but I can't count that high."

After sitting for a while and chatting idly, she put the check on her lap and cleared her throat. "Spencer, I hate to ask. I don't know if you can help me . . ."

"If I can, I will."

"I can't leave here, Dr. D says, until I hire a 24/7 nurse for my apartment. He won't let me leave. Can you believe him? He says neither my grandmother nor my sister will do. He seems wary of Anne, I can't quite figure it out, but he keeps repeating that she is not up to the job, and about Grandma he says that I'll end up taking care of her instead of the other way around. Naturally Grandma has completely stopped speaking to him."

"If she keeps that up, soon there won't be anyone left."

"Anne left her job though, you see, so she could help me and in return I could pay her mortgage. How can I tell her no?"

He breathed through the mask. "DiAngelo is right—you need a professional, not a sister. I'll be glad to inform her of this."

"If you speak one word to her she'll get an injunction against you."

"Yes, and I'm the one who'll have to enforce that injunction. Oh fine, I'll have DiAngelo tell her as per his strict instructions you already hired someone."

"You don't think she'll know I'm lying since I can't even stand up on my own?"

He was thinking about what she wanted from him, what she needed from him. "Do you want me to help you find someone?"

"Yes," she said quietly. "God, yes, please."

"Why don't you just ask me? If there's something you need, don't make me guess, just ask me. If I can, I'll take care of it. My father had a nurse for a while when he was sick. Heart attack, he's fine now. It cost him seven-fifty a week, but it was money well spent. I'll call the agencies. I'll get you someone."

"Sounds good. Please could you put in a request for a tall, dark, Hawaiian, good-looking, easy-going solitary man who answers to the name of Keanu. Nursing experience a plus but not a must."

Spencer laughed. "I'll take care of it."

She looked grateful and relieved. "When I get out, I'll take you to lunch somewhere nice, if you want."

"That'll be some lunch, Lily, for seven million bucks."

She held the check in her hands. "Mary can come too. I don't want to exclude her. We can go for Sunday brunch at the Palm Court, and dress up like we belong on the Upper East Side."

"What a good memory you have. Can't remember my beeper number, but remember fine the name of my girlfriend."

She twinged.

"Look," said Spencer, "DiAngelo is coming to throw me out any minute, and believe me, I know you're not up to this, but I have to ask . . ."

Her gaze cooled dramatically. "Quid pro quo, huh, detective?"

He went on. "Why didn't you tell me after you came back from Hawaii that Amy worked at a homeless shelter? I mean you don't think it would have been helpful to know if she was in her regular life that Friday morning?"

"It slipped my mind. I wasn't thinking. I still don't see the big deal." She paused. "Did she go that Friday morning?"

"She did."

"Did she leave the soup kitchen?"

"Well," said Spencer, "she's not still there."

"No, of course not." Lily was pensive.

Both Spencer and Lily watched each other, warily, sickly, thinking, formulating, trying to put into words what they couldn't articulate, couldn't figure out.

Lily was not in any shape to be made upset. He didn't want to tell her that in the bottom of one of the couture bags, folded neatly at the bottom of Amy's closet, he had found a small receipt, though from the rest of the bags the receipts had been thoroughly removed. A receipt for a Ferragamo belt, bought on one Friday afternoon last March, for a hundred-and-ninety-five dollars, paid for in cash. Two hundred dollars for a *belt*, paid for in *cash*. Did Lily really think Amy had been jogging all those hours?

Bags from Prada, from Louis Vuitton and Versace. Small bags from Tiffany's. And where was that jewelry or crystal? It certainly wasn't in her room. Where were the belts, the purses? All the things he suspected Andrew Quinn of buying for her?

If Andrew Quinn, a man making a government salary, with a wife and family to support, was so generous with Amy McFadden, did that sound like he was mired in a shallow fling? And yet the only things Amy had kept were the empty shopping bags.

"Why did Amy go to the soup kitchen?" Spencer asked.

Lily was thoughtful before she replied. "I think once she had been hungry herself."

"Have you ever heard the name Milo?"

"Who?"

He told her about Milo.

Lily said nothing because there was nothing to say.

231

"Could Milo be one of the people she had gone traveling with, one of the other people who went missing?"

Her mouth agape, she said meatlessly, "Could be. So what?"

"Maybe this Milo knows where she is. Wouldn't you like to help me find him if he can help clear your brother?"

She mutely and dumbly nodded.

DiAngelo burst through the door. "That's it," he said. "Wrap it up."

Standing from his chair, Spencer wished he could touch her hand before he left. She looked as if she desperately needed it.

Marcie and DiAngelo had been taking blood from her every two days to see how she was responding to the chemo. She could see the results of her blood counts by the looks on their poker faces. They didn't have to tell her anything, but she asked anyway, and they hemmed and hawed, and they brought in another nurse, who gave her a transfusion of red and white (and blue, ta-dah!), of plasma, of platelets. Her Hickman became infected; they gave her antibiotics, and forbid visitors for two days until the infection went away, and DiAngelo didn't think she was strong enough for a continuous drip of cytarabine, so they waited, a day, another day. But her body wasn't recovering, so they went ahead and gave her the drug anyway and counted her blood, the platelets were at 48, 45, 42 when they should have been inching up to a 100.

She didn't want to ask because she didn't want to know but finally she said something like, "Is that forty-two platelets in my *whole* body?"

And the doctor smiled and shook his head. "It's short form. Add three zeros, then you've got something."

And she smiled in return, so hopeful, so encouraged. "Forty-two thousand is a colossal amount!"

"Sure, Lil. Compared to what? To normal? Normal on the low side is two hundred thousand."

"Oh."

"Exactly."

Third day with no visitors. The hospital staff wore masks around her, and in the night when she had the strength to wake up and retch, Lily thought she saw angels with wings in her room, and the angels were all wearing masks too.

"This is the worst of it," DiAngelo said. "It's intense, no doubt about it. It gets better, and you get better. Just buck up, Lil, you're doing great. You really are, I'm proud of you. Just keep going."

She kept going. "How much longer?"

And the doctor paused and then said portentously, "How much longer for what?"

And she said, "Before the pizza comes."

"Just one more day. Then you'll rest, a quick biopsy and you go home. Just one more day, Lil."

But one more day was more than she could take. She couldn't breathe on her own. They took her off the drug and put her on an oxygen machine instead, and she wanted to ask if the oxygen could just go into her little port, like everything else, but she didn't have enough breath to say it.

And so she lay and imagined dying.

She stared at the dark ceiling and imagined herself getting sicker and sicker, imagined the black mass amassing at the corners and the borders of her body, moving in, marching through all her organs on their way to her heart. What was it like to sleep and not to wake, to fall into the blackness and never come back?

She wouldn't like being alone at the moment of her death. No, she would die in the hospital with her family around her, holding her hands, stroking her face, her head, crying over her, and then she would slip away and still hear them, but fainter, hear them cry and see them bend over her, but dimmer.

There was no pain anymore, no cancer.

And they would sing for her, sing in a beautiful church, and her mother, bent with grief, would stand at the altar of her daughter and sing "Panis Angelicus," and the church would echo with her lovely voice, and she would make everyone cry even more—

Wait right there.

233

Hold on right there to those colorful horses.

Even the dream was having a hard time believing itself. Her mother at the church?

Her mother wouldn't be at the church! Her mother would still be in Hawaii, and she would call Grandma and say, *I want to come, really I do, but I can't, I'm very sick, I can't even move off the bed. I don't have the strength to go to the bathroom. George is doing everything for me, bless him. That's why he can't come either.*

Ugh. Suddenly breathing on her own, Lily struggled up from the bed. Unbelievable. Her mother ruined death for her even in fantasies. Even in fantasies, Lily's death couldn't be about Lily, it was all about Lily's mother. She couldn't even die the way she wanted to.

The next morning, feeling better and off the oxygen, Lily asked Anne to go to the art store for her and buy her some pastel-colored pencils, which when wet turned into pastel watercolors. She spent the afternoon drawing. When Spencer came to see her later that day, Lily was sitting propped up in her bed, and he said, "What in heaven's name are you painting on your mouth?"

She picked up a small make-up mirror. Around her chin, her tongue, her lips were lavenders and lilacs and pinks. She smiled and showed him her small painting of . . . "Spring," she said. "I'm redecorating."

"Yourself?"

"Yes, I'm redecorating myself. Here, do you want it for your apartment? You haven't got a blessed thing on your walls."

From then on, Lily no longer fantasized about the hour of her death.

DiAngelo wrote out the discharge papers, telling her she would have a week at home, and then would come back on the first Monday in October to start thirteen weeks of consolidation. She would have chemo drips Monday and Tuesday, and then recuperate at home Wednesday through Sunday. She would be done by New Year. Just in time for the new millennium.

Was the cancer all gone?

"No, but I told you not to expect it to be all gone after induction. We just expected to kill the existing cancer cells."

"Did we?"

"Most of them."

"Most of them? Does *almost* even count in a cancer treatment?"

DiAngelo laughed. "That's the new adage, *almost* doesn't count in hand grenades, pregnancy, or cancer."

Lily said nothing, stuck on the word *pregnancy*. DiAngelo quickly stopped laughing and went on. "It does look like we have slowed down the production of new cancer cells. That's extremely significant."

"Slowed down?"

"Oh, look, Lil. This is not the end. This is not even the beginning of the end. This is just the end of the beginning."

"This is all I need, my oncologist quoting Churchill."

September 22 came and went. Lily cancelled her twenty-fifth birthday.

29

Spencer Stuck Twice

Complicating matters of intuition for Spencer, a subpoena of registration records from the Four Seasons Hotel did not yield Andrew Quinn's name. Certainly it didn't produce Amy's. Yet the 57/57 matchbook remained. Perhaps the four-star diamond hotel was too rich for Andrew, and he took his young lover to the Sheraton on Seventh. There were three thousand hotels in mid-town New York City. What a fruitless search it would be.

He was stuck on the Four Seasons Hotel because the full essence of it matched Amy's empty shopping bags. One did not bring Prada purses home from 57th and Frederick Fekkai mousse home, also from 57th, and Mont Blanc pens, also from 57th, and then traipse to Seventh and 51st to stay at the Sheraton.

And he was stuck on May 14, because Amy told her mother she would be home that Friday night. She told her mother she would be coming, she never came, never called, and there were no phone calls made from her apartment after Thursday, May 13. She had been at the soup kitchen on the morning of May 14. It seemed highly probable that this was the day Amy had disappeared.

And now there was Milo.

Police went to every homeless shelter in New York City to look for an average size man in rags with freaky eyes and possible facial tattoos who answered to the name of Milo.

He had Harkman call Riker's, Sing-Sing, Attica, asking if there was a man named Milo released from prison recently. He had no luck.

Spencer didn't know what this Milo was up to on Friday, May 14, and so he concentrated his efforts on what Andrew Quinn was up to on Friday, May 14. Andrew was easier to track.

Andrew's schedule told Spencer that Andrew was in D.C. on Thursday, to which five hundred or more people could testify, and came back to New York City on the early train on Friday, to which sixty-three people who were on the train with him could testify. He was home by 8:30 that evening, according to his wife. A little late for a Friday night? Not at all, she said. He usually came home around then.

Was he upset, preoccupied, normal, odd when he came home? Miera over the phone icily said she did not remember.

Before he came home, Andrew stopped at the bank and at his Port Jeff office. He took out money for the weekend from an ATM in Port Jeff Main Street branch of Chase Bank at 7:22 p.m., and carried a receipt to prove it. Was that odd? Carrying on his person a receipt from four months ago for an insignificant ATM transaction? Spencer didn't keep ATM receipts from a hundred minutes ago.

Andrew's bank statements showed that indeed he took out five hundred dollars at 7:22, but also showed that he took out two thousand dollars at Penn Station at eleven in the morning on the same day. That was a lot of cash to carry in his pocket. Why the two ATM trips?

A look through Andrew's bank statements going back to the beginning of 1999 showed Spencer that on a regular basis, on a Thursday and Friday, vast amounts of cash moved out of Andrew's account and into Andrew's hands, explaining perhaps some of the Prada shopping bags. Did he pay for the Four Seasons in cash? Even so, he would still have to register as a hotel guest.

The staff at the Four Seasons could not corroborate one way or another if Andrew Quinn had used their concierge or bellman services. Perhaps they had seen the congressman, but they couldn't be sure. Perhaps they had seen Amy, but they couldn't be sure of that either.

Andrew's train from D.C. arrived at Penn Station in New York at 10:45 a.m., yet he didn't alight in Port Jeff until seven that evening.

Train from Penn Station to Port Jefferson took about eighty minutes. Where was Andrew in the intervening six and a half hours?

Andrew's office manager in Port Jeff confirmed that he came into the office just after seven, as she was about to go home, signed a few documents, dictated a letter that she was able to show Spencer, regarding new parking regulations on Main Street, and checked on his schedule for the following week.

With this kind of scrutiny, how did the congressman manage to have an affair at all? Still, there were six-and-a-half unaccounted hours. He couldn't take money out of the ATM without someone checking the time on the receipt. Didn't anyone notice Andrew Quinn with a young attractive redhead on his arm? How did Amy escape such scrutiny? Andrew had said he and Amy had ended their relationship mid April, yet here it was the middle of May and he was missing on a Friday afternoon.

The alibi hours were narrowing. It was time to talk to Andrew Quinn one more time. But apparently, in an attempt to save his marriage, Andrew and Miera Quinn were spending two weeks in Oahu, Hawaii, even though Congress was still in session. Andrew had asked for a leave of absence.

30

Advanced Chemotherapy

Joy appeared at Lily's doorstep, courtesy of Spencer, in the form
of a thin, cranky fifty-year-old woman, who looked inside, took
a sniff, and said, "You live here? Your . . ." She waved off in the
direction of down the stairs, where Spencer was supposedly and
invisibly lurking. " . . . The man who hired me, he said you had
money."

Taken aback, Lily said, "I do, I do have money, but what does
. . . excuse me, what does that have to do with anything?"

"Nothing. Just thought you'd live better, that's all." She smiled.
"I was expecting a Park Avenue-type apartment."

"On Avenue C?"

"You're right, wasn't thinking." She stepped in.

Lily had gotten home three days earlier, and in a week had to
go back to the hospital for her first round of outpatient chemo
treatment. Was there going to be gentleness, compassion from
Joy? And is that what she needed? Truth was, she didn't know
what she needed.

Her apartment was a foreign space to her. Five weeks gone
was five centuries gone. It seemed odd to Lily that the president
was the same, the year was the same, the deli was still selling
peaches, the pizza place around the corner was still having a two-
for-one special on Tuesday nights. Her grandmother and her

sisters with her four nieces brought her home. Very soon it got too loud with the little ones.

Before they left, Amanda said "Paint something, Lil. You'll feel better."

Lily didn't know what to make of that. Paint something and you'll feel better? Did Amanda mean physically? All she had to do was paint and the cancer would go? Then why did it come in the first place? Did it come because Lily liked to sleep, was not dedicated enough in her painting? Or did Amanda mean feel better psychologically? Paint something, and you'll feel better inside. Feel better that you have cancer at twenty-four. Twenty-five now.

Lily stood in front of the full-length mirror in Amy's room. She stood for mere moments, divided into smaller moments where her memories flashed, of wearing Friday night club clothes, school clothes, naked bodies with tan lines from bathing suits. Amy's body in front of that mirror in her matching bra and panties, and Amy saying, I got to lose me some weight, sister, if I'm going to have a prayer of getting a man, but as she was remembering Amy saying it, the memory of that moment was tinged with the disingenuousness of it all—Amy was already seeing Andrew then, already had a man, already had Lily's brother.

Anne grumbled about it but did as Lily asked. She removed the mirrors from the apartment, all three of them, dragging them out on the landing. The bathroom mirror was attached to a bathroom cabinet and would not be removed, but Lily covered it with masking tape and paper and then painted the paper black. Perfect in its lack of reflection and therefore thought.

The Mickey Mouse sweatshirt Amanda had bought her hid the emaciation of her body but couldn't hide what had happened to Lily's face in the five weeks of lying on her back or bent over the toilet bowl, the sunken-in cheeks, the skin stretched over bone, the gray, turned down, slightly shaking lips, the bald head.

She took a bandana and tied it below her jaw like a babushka and suddenly she looked sixty, seventy and felt it, suddenly she looked older than Grandma and felt it. Now in a juxtaposition of souls, Grandma had left her house, was taking cabs and subways to get herself to the hospital to look after Lily. Lily's cancer made Grandma young again! Free again! Lily is diseased and Grandma, cured of agoraphobia, is taking subways. Yippee. Meanwhile Lily is under strict orders not to venture from the house. Marcie and Dr. D don't trust her bones not to break from brittleness, for her skin not to tear, for someone not to sneeze on her.

Her first three days went by in a glacial blur. One thing she did do was pick up the phone. She knew her apartment would be like Penn Station at rush hour if she didn't answer. So she picked it up to remain alone. Yes, I'm fine, feeling pretty good, yes, eating, yes, drinking fluids, yes, showering, even reading, and yes, watching TV, everything is good, thanks for calling.

And then Joy came. Joy had straight brown hair, a hippie bag thrown on her shoulder, a long, loose hippie skirt, and a large shirt, as if Joy were hiding herself. But the face was smart, the nose was smart. Joy kept her face, her hair, her clothes in such a way that she wouldn't have to think about primping, or make-up, or fashion. Her skin looked as if it had been casually tanned many times, and her brown eyes had traces of old make-up. Days-old make up.

Joy wanted to know where she would sleep and was pleased with the presence of a second bedroom. Lily wanted to say that she didn't expect Joy to be staying overnight, but then remembered Joy was hired as a round-the-clock nurse. Uncomfortable with Joy staying in Amy's room, Lily could not explain it, not even when the woman asked where her roommate was. "She's been gone a while," said Lily and to the question of when the roommate would be coming back, Lily replied, "Don't know, and can we talk about something else?"

Amy's bedroom was much larger than Lily's, and Joy offered gladly to switch, but Lily declined, so Joy said she would sleep in the room until Amy came back and then she would take the futon. Lily asked how long Joy expected to stay. After all, she wanted to say, *I'm not going to be sick forever.*

"I will stay until you're not sick anymore, how's that. But anytime, if I'm not working out for you, you say one word and I'm outta here. I will need Sundays off, though. It'll be your easiest day anyway. Can you swing that? And who's paying me, you or your . . ." She waved again.

"Me."

"Um, who is he anyway?"

"He's the one who takes care of things."

Lily felt better having Joy sleep in Amy's room when she realized that most of Amy's personal things had been confiscated by Spencer as evidence. Amy's pictures, her clothes, her books, bags, knick-knacks all made exhibits A through ZZZ in the small evidence room at the precinct.

Lily gave Joy three hundred dollars and asked her to go get new sheets and new towels, and as soon as she was left alone she called Spencer and asked him if he thought Joy was a good choice. "She is just what you need," he said. "You'll see, and trust me."

Why should I trust you? she thought. You want to put my brother in prison.

Unfortunately Spencer was right about Joy. The woman never stopped moving, cleaning, cooking, shopping. She called Amanda and Anne and Grandma and told them all to stay home on Monday and Tuesday, as she would be taking Lily to the hospital for her chemo sessions. Somehow Lily's being in protective, capable hands made everyone feel better, including Lily. And Dr. D seemed exceedingly pleased with Joy as a choice of nurse. Turned out he knew of her. A doctor-friend of his treated Joy's husband for lymphoma. Joy still had a wedding band on her finger, but when Lily casually asked her how her husband let her stay with someone 24/7, Joy replied that her husband had died a year ago in August after a bone-marrow transplant left him with a raging pneumonia.

Lily didn't know how to respond. She wanted to say, don't

they have antibiotics for that, but before she could speak, Joy added, "So don't worry, I've seen plenty sicker than you." And to that Lily did respond.

"I don't want to hear that other people have also suffered," she said. "I don't want to hear that other people had it worse than me, were sicker, felt terrible. That's why I'm not rushing to any support groups. I'm sorry about your husband, but knowing about him only makes me feel worse because I can't imagine anything worse than this. What makes me feel better is to think that I'm unique, that I'm unbelievably sick, and yet unbelievably strong too, like my brother, a mighty Quinn. I don't want to hear about other people. I don't want to read about other people. I don't want to read their cancer stories. I'm living my own, thank you. Can you understand that?"

"Yes," said Joy. "You're surprisingly verbal for someone so weak." They'd just returned home after Lily's first chemo.

"Actually I don't feel too bad." Just two plastic bags, one of VePesid, one of cytarabine dripped for two hours into her right atrium.

She shouldn't have spoken so quickly because after Tuesday's two bags, she quickly deteriorated. Days went by without food. She didn't want to eat. Joy insisted. Her grandmother with her chicken soup insisted. Amanda, as ever a mother, with her brownies insisted. Anne with her take-out Thai, paid for by Lily, insisted. Spencer with pizza insisted, and Lily had a piece of what he was offering before she went to the bathroom to throw it up. In front of the bathroom stood Joy. "You can't throw up the only bite of food you've had all day." She did not move from the door. Lily had no choice but to lean forward and throw up at Joy's feet onto the wide plank wood floor as Spencer turned his head. After that Joy no longer blocked the bathroom, but tried to find and make food that Lily would keep. Harder realized than imagined. After the second week, Lily couldn't keep anything down at all Mondays and Tuesdays. By Wednesday she would have some chicken soup. Spencer brought the soup from

Odessa. "Lily, you have to eat. You understand. You can't not eat."

"I'm not hungry."

"I don't care what you are. It's not about the hunger, it's about the food. Your strength comes from food."

"I'm not hungry."

"I don't care. Eat."

"Talk to me. Any news?"

"I won't tell you unless you eat."

So Lily, because she was curious, would have some liquid, some crackers, and then listen to Spencer, all the while fighting with herself not to retch. If she lay very quietly on the futon and did not speak or nod her head, she felt in balance.

What can I do to make you feel better? What can I do to help?

Rachel. Paul. Dennis, Rick the manager, Grandma, Amanda, Anne, Spencer all in unison now, WHAT CAN I DO TO HELP?

Stop talking to me about Andrew. Stop. I can't hear another word of it. I'm sick, can't you see? But sometimes, she had to turn away from the cancer, too.

Where to turn to?

31

Advanced Interrogation

A week after Andrew got home, Spencer drove out to Port Jefferson to talk to him. Harkman came with him, but extremely reluctantly, mumbling about other cases, other leads, other investigations, things piling up on his desk, and about not feeling well. Spencer started to argue, then stopped. There was no point. Something had to be done about Harkman. Spencer needed a new partner. He needed his friend Gabe McGill from homicide. They drove to Port Jefferson in stony silence.

Spencer knew he might have to bring Andrew in for questioning, and to do that, Andrew would have to be formally detained and then formally charged.

"Have you no decency?" said Andrew. "I can't believe you're still coming around. I told you last time, I know nothing about Amy's disappearance, and nothing's changed since then. Have you any idea what this is doing to my wife?"

"Would you like to come with us then and speak privately at the station?"

"Why are you here?" He swung open the door.

"Because I have new information. Believe me, if I had nothing new to ask you, I wouldn't be here."

"You've got something against me," Andrew said. "You've had

245

it from the start. You sit on your bar stool and you moralize about me—"

Spencer's eyes darkened. "Whoa," he said. "This has nothing to do with me. No matter how flattering it is to talk about myself with a United States Congressman, we are going to talk about you. Here or at the station? Your pick."

"Here, but I'm telling you, detective, for the last time."

Spencer took a step toward a bigger, bulkier Andrew. "I'm telling you, congressman," he said, nearly cornering him into the hall. "I will talk to you as many times as I need to, and when you stop talking to me, I will book you for obstructing justice, is that clear? I don't give a damn how many friends you have on the police force."

Andrew didn't respond. They followed him into his office. He slammed the door and bounded to his desk. "What?" he said loudly. "What is it now?"

Harkman was standing next to Spencer with an expression almost as sour and angry as Andrew's.

"Did you buy Amy a $195 belt from Ferragamo on 5th Avenue back in March?" Spencer asked.

Andrew laughed. "Are you honestly asking me if I remember buying a belt six months ago?"

"No. I'm asking you if you remember paying cash for a $200 belt six months ago."

"Detective, I can honestly say, I don't recall."

"Is that *honestly* to contrast with all the other times you said you didn't recall?"

Andrew's face swiftly grew colder. "Have you got anything else besides the belt?"

"Yes. Tiffany's, Prada, Guess, Gucci, Versace, Mont Blanc, Louis Vuitton. All gifts from you?"

"I don't know. Some possibly. Not all. I don't think so."

"My point is, you treated her rather well, didn't you?"

"Detective, what in the world does this have to do with your business?"

246

"I'm going to try to explain. Now, I don't mean to be indelicate, and I'm going to ask this as politely as I can, but surely you and Amy didn't just go shopping when you got together?"

Andrew said nothing.

"Your train from D.C. drops you off, you two meet, you have lunch, and then? Where did you go when you weren't having drinks at 57/57, or buying pens at Mont Blanc?"

"I don't know what you're asking me."

"I'm going to have to be *more* blunt? Where did you go when you—"

"Here, there. A hotel."

"The Sheraton? The Grand Hyatt? The Marriott? The Hilton? The Holiday Inn?" Spencer said that disparagingly.

"I can't remember."

"You don't remember where you stayed?"

"No," Andrew said defiantly.

Such intransigence. Spencer had to take a chance here. But Andrew was being as evasive as possible, leaving Spencer no choice. "Hmm. I see. Well, Amy has quite a stash of little shampoo and lotion bottles from a certain hotel. Would looking at them perhaps help you remember?"

Andrew heaved out a breath. "The Four Seasons, if you must know."

Aha. So the congressman answered truthfully only when his back was pressed to the wall. "The Four Seasons." Spencer whistled. "I didn't know the Four Seasons was the kind of establishment that rented rooms by the hour."

"Oh enough already!"

They were all standing. Andrew stood with his arms crossed. Harkman was sweating. It was difficult for him to stand so long: his legs became swollen and numb. His sour smell filled Andrew's office.

Spencer glared at Andrew. "You obviously knew where you used to stay. Why not just say so?" he said quietly. "What you're doing is the definition of obstructing justice. You're giving me ample reason to believe that you are hiding a great deal more than I'm asking you."

"Detective, you're being remarkably obtuse for an investigator. I've got a wife whom I have not taken to the Four Seasons! I feel extremely uncomfortable talking to you about this, *now* do you understand why perhaps I'm not being as forthcoming as I might be if we were talking about sports or politics?"

"Indeed, you treated Amy McFadden extremely well." Spencer was studying him. There seemed to be plenty of reason for Andrew not to be honest. $600 a day hotel rooms with his wife's old Hartford money.

"Under what name did you register at the Four Seasons?"

"You know what?" said Andrew. "I refuse to answer that question. I simply refuse."

"Why?"

"Detective!" Andrew exhaled. "Can't you see how this is going to look? I've already ended my senatorial bid. I'm desperately trying to hold on to my job and my marriage. Your questions are not going to help you find Amy, but they *are* going to cost my wife and me a great deal."

Spencer noted the absence of an answer. "Under what name?" he repeated.

"Under my wife's maiden name," Andrew said through his teeth. "Happy now?"

"Not happy, no. But I understand things just a little bit better. Congressman, what did you do on Friday, May 14? You took your customary train that dropped you at Penn at 10:45 in the morning. But you weren't at your Port Jeff office until seven o'clock. What happened to you between the hours of eleven, when you took two thousand dollars out of an ATM machine at Penn Station, and five-thirty, when you took the ride to Port Jeff?"

"What happened to me between the hours of eleven and five-thirty?"

"Why do you keep repeating my questions, congressman?"

"Because I don't understand what you're asking me. What hours?"

"The afternoon hours of Friday, May 14, 1999. The hours you usually spent at the Four Seasons, but you have told us yourself you and Amy had ended your relationship in April."

"That's right."

"Well, then, where were you, congressman, on May 14?"

Andrew nearly stammered. "Frankly, I don't remember. I don't understand what the afternoon of May 14 has to do with anything."

"Six hours in the middle of the last Friday that anyone has seen Amy alive, that's what it has to do with."

"I don't think you're listening to me, detective."

"I hear you loud and clear. If you weren't with her, where were you?"

"I was—nowhere. I don't know what you're talking about. I thought you had no idea when she disappeared?"

"We know when she was last seen alive. You got off the train at eleven, took out two thousand dollars and didn't show up in Port Jefferson until seven. Where were you?"

"I was nowhere, I tell you. I may have gone shopping."

"Where you used to go shopping with Amy?"

"Around there."

"This time did you go shopping with her?"

"Is English your second language? I told you a thousand times, I didn't see her that Friday!"

"So what did you buy?"

"What did I buy?" He was incredulous. "I don't remember."

"You must have bought something."

"I must have, but it was four months ago. I don't remember."

"Do you have receipts for your purchases? You kept an ATM receipt from that day when you took money out in Port Jeff. Did you keep receipts for what you bought that Friday? Perhaps next to the ATM receipt?"

"I don't have receipts for the things you're asking. I can't remember what stores I went to."

Harkman and Spencer shook their heads. Harkman spoke his first words of the interview. "Congressman, I have never met a man who remembered so little about so much. I don't think you're fit to make laws for our country."

"Come on, give me a fucking break."

"Will us booking you on suspicion of a capital crime help you remember?"

"How many times will I have to repeat myself? I hadn't seen her since April when she—when she and I ended it! I didn't see her that Friday, I tell you!"

"Then why did you take two grand from an ATM at Penn Station?"

"I have no idea! That's the money I probably spent shopping."

"Shopping you don't remember, buying things you can't recall, in stores you can't name?"

"Detective, I'm calling my lawyer and your captain because this constitutes nothing but blatant harassment!"

"And you know what else?" said Spencer. "I don't believe that a man who buys his lover at least four lots of jewelry from Tiffany's and takes her to the Four Seasons is the same man who can't remember the first time he met her, the first time they got together, how long the affair lasted, what he bought her and how often he saw her. Either one is true, or the other, but both cannot be true, they don't make sense. Do you get what I'm saying?"

"I get nothing you're saying. I've stopped listening."

Harkman struggled up. "Spencer, let's go," he said. "Let's just go."

"One more thing," said Spencer. He asked if Andrew knew that Amy volunteered at the shelter.

"Vaguely. Superficially. So what? I'm pretty sure there are a number of things about her I did not know." Ice was in his voice when he spoke.

"Do you know who Milo is?"

The congressman blinked before he answered. "No."

250

"Never heard of him?" Spencer didn't blink so as not to miss a single thing.

"I can't recall. I don't think so. Who is he?"

"That's what we're trying to find out." Did Andrew know who Milo was and wasn't saying? Spencer didn't understand *anything*.

"Congressman, if you know who this Milo is and we can find him, perhaps he knows where Amy is, and if that's the case, we don't come here to bother you again. I'm sure this is something you'd like, no? But as things look now, I'm coming back, congressman," said Spencer. "I'm coming back with a warrant for your arrest."

And in the car, an exhausted Harkman, his eyes closed, said to Spencer, "I don't remember any empty shampoo bottles from the Four Seasons Hotel in the evidence room."

"Ah," said Spencer. "That's because there weren't any."

Harkman's whole body shook in disbelief. "Man, you got some fucking balls."

Next day's headlines were full of the congresssman, and the rest.

32

Andrew's Alibi

Colin Whittaker called Spencer into his office and asked him to close the door. "O'Malley, are you nucking futs?"

Spencer could see Harkman through the glass windows, sitting sweating with a satisfied smirk on his fat face. "What's going on, chief?"

Whittaker was tall, rumpled, gray-haired, carrying two weapons strapped to him, not wearing a jacket, already perspiring even though it was early morning and cold. "Our honorable congressman is fit to be tied."

"Yes, tied up in jail."

"He said you came into his home and completely overstepped your bounds. He says you harassed him. He is ready to sue the NYPD."

"How? I didn't harass him. I asked him some routine questions, which he was slow in answering, by the way. Cagey, stalling for time, stammering, evasive, quick to anger, repeating my questions back to me. *Slow*. Hiding something. Lying, chief."

"Did you get him to cough up information based on evidence you didn't have?"

"I got him to tell me the truth about one fucking thing, yes." Harkman was such a bastard. Some partner.

252

Whittaker pressed his hands together and when he spoke he used a placating, deliberate, through-the-teeth tone one uses with wayward children. "Spencer, I have been so good to you. I never second guess you, I let you do what you want, I watch your back, I stick up for you, sometimes I cover for you. You've been worth it. But I'm afraid I have to put my foot down on this one. Do you know who Bill Bryant is?"

"No."

"He is a retired New York City councilman, turned businessman, philanthropist, charitable contributor to historical landmarks in New York City and also a very generous contributor to the NYPD. Most of the new Kevlar vests we have, including yours, are because of his generosity."

"Bully for him. What does he have to do with anything?"

"He has an office in the Carnegie Hall Tower. On 57th Street."

"All right . . ." Spencer drew out.

"Bryant called his good friend the police commissioner late last night—the police commissioner!—and said that Andrew Quinn came to see him on the afternoon of May 14, around one or two p.m. They spent two or three hours together, went out for a drink at the 57/57 bar, and then Quinn went to Penn Station to catch a train home. Our councilman, who's been in public life for fifty years and is a revered member of the community, is willing to swear an oath to this. This morning he sent us the original copy of his private planner, where Andrew Quinn's name in Bryant's own handwriting is penciled in from the hours of one to four in the afternoon."

"Really?"

"Really."

"Why didn't Quinn remember this yesterday when I spoke to him?"

"I don't know why. I'm not privy to everything that goes on in his sleazoid, adulterous brain. However, if he needed an alibi for that Friday afternoon because of some cockamamie theory you dreamed up, he's got one."

"Conveniently he got one the day after I came to speak to him when he didn't have one."

"He didn't remember. He said he was flustered, there was a social gathering at his house, he was feeling extremely stressed and harassed by you."

"Oh, bullshit."

"Spencer, you know what, how about if you and I make a little deal? Until you find the body, parts of the body, bloodied clothing, or photographs of the deceased in the congressman's wallet, you don't bother the congressman, the councilman, the senators, the governor, or the frigging president. You simply leave all politicians out of it until you have a scintilla of evidence of wrongdoing. How would that be for you?"

"Chief, come on. Quinn has a lot at stake. How do you know he didn't kill her because she was going to go public with the affair? Perhaps she was pregnant. He's going to run for the Senate again, you'll see. He's completely shameless. And you know he is, look, he used his wife's name to register in a hotel so he could pop his mistress! I mean, this is the kind of man we're dealing with."

"I hope you're using pop in the one sense and not in the other, O'Malley. Yes, he is a son of a bitch to his wife. That's what divorce is for. The rest of what you're telling me is nothing but conjecture, supposition, assumption, guesswork. It's not police-work. Speculative motive yes, but no evidence, not even circumstantial evidence! And he's got an alibi now."

"Well, then perhaps she wasn't killed that Friday. Perhaps she was killed on Saturday, or the following Monday when the congressman was heading back to DC."

Whittaker banged his head several times on his desk before he spoke again.

"Spencer, I'm serious. This isn't homicide. It's missing persons. You're making half of New York law enforcement furious and you don't even know if a crime has been committed. Leave the congressman the fuck alone. Do you hear?"

"Let's arrest him and have the courts sort it out."

"Arrest him for what? Shopping? He's got a provable alibi! Oh, and by the way, something else, because you keep forgetting it—we got no fucking body!"

"Yes, we also don't have *her*! And we know she was supposed to go to her mother's and never showed up."

"Oh yes, that's right." Whittaker coughed and sat up straight, assuming a proper mock-legal air. "Mrs. McFadden, tell us, how often did you talk to your daughter? Oh, twice a month you say. Sometimes even less. Was Amy reliable? No you say? What? There were many times in the past when she said she'd be coming up for the weekend and then never showed up and never called to explain? Why, that simply can't be, Mrs. McFadden! We have built our entire case on Amy's reliability. She simply could not have not shown up and then not called! Why, it is our only incontrovertible proof of murder!"

Spencer stared blinklessly at his commander. "Whenever you're done, chief."

"We got nothing, Spence. You got nothing. We don't have a body, we don't have physical distress in the apartment, we don't have a letter from her, a journal entry implicating Quinn, a suspicious phone call. We don't have a ransom note from her kidnapper, we don't have blood on the congressman's suit. We have no witnesses, no fluids, no evidence, no *body*! We got nuffin'! Time to move on, my friend. Time to move on. You've got eighteen MP cases open on your desk and Harkman is getting testy."

"Fuck Harkman."

"You don't want me to promote him over you just to shut him up, do you?"

Spencer wanted to spit as he left the office.

From that day on, Colin Whittaker began the daily meeting of all the station detectives and patrolmen like this: "Good morning, ladies and gentlemen, I'd like to start our meeting reiterating the following point regarding Detective O'Malley's

McFadden case. As of this morning, have we found a body?"

In unison the officers would say, "No."

"Detective O'Malley, did you hear that? There is no body. Therefore, is it a homicide or a missing persons investigation? Detective O'Malley, I didn't hear your answer."

"Missing persons." Through his teeth.

"Good. Now that that's settled, let's move on to the next item on our agenda for today."

33

The Laugh Track

By the beginning of only her *third* week, Lily said to DiAngelo,
I can't do this anymore. She thought the words must have come
out whispered, because he said, "What?"

"This. I can't do it."

"Stop it. You're doing great, this is nothing."

"I'm serious. I just . . ." She wanted to say, I'm too sad, I can't
get over how low I'm feeling, and I can't shake it. The sadness
never leaves. And it was pervasive; the sorrows that afflicted her
were assailing her from all sides.

For example:

She and Spencer were sitting on the stoop outside her building. It was an Indian summer day, and by promising to carry her
back up five flights of stairs if he had to, he somehow got her to
come downstairs and sit for a few minutes in the October afternoon warmth. Both were wearing jeans, jean jackets, both were
pale and drawn. He had a buzz cut. She had no more hair on
her head. They were sitting lazily, chatting about nothing when
his cell phone rang. Before he flipped it open, he showed her
the caller ID. J. McFadden, it said. Lily waited quietly while
Spencer had a five-minute stilted conversation with her. She
seemed upset. When he hung up, Lily said, "She calls you even
on Sundays?"

"Lily, she calls me every God-given day."

Suddenly she didn't want to be sitting on the stoop anymore. She knew that something ticked over in him when Mrs. McFadden called, and he was no longer thinking about his nephews or her nieces, which is what they were chatting about before the phone rang. As if to confirm that, he said, "Jan McFadden was drawing my attention to page eleven of *The New York Post*. Did you see it?"

"No."

"I saw it. A girl, sixteen years old, was found floating in the Atlantic ocean, weighed down by chains that were tied around her feet."

Lily closed her eyes. "Do I have to hear this?" Why does Jan McFadden continue to read the papers?

It was as if she hadn't spoken. "The girl was bound, gagged, and strangled in a Delaware motel room, then dropped with chains and cinder blocks from an airplane that one of her killers chartered. She'd been missing for two months."

Lily was quiet, trying to stave off nausea, trying to decipher meaning.

"Two young punks killed her. Do you know why?"

"I don't want to know why."

"One of the killers was dating the girl's foster stepsister, who didn't like her. She didn't like her, and wanted her out of the way. So they killed her."

Lily gave a theatrical sigh, replete with vocalization. "And this is pertinent why? Because most killings are done by people we know? By people who are close to us? Or is it that you think you should check out some Delaware motel rooms?"

"No, no, and no. But I'm glad you asked. The two suspects were apprehended long before the girl's body was found. *Eventually* they confessed and were charged with first degree murder. So it is pertinent because it shows you that you can have a homicide investigation without the body. All you need is a potential confession."

"Tell that to your boss, not me." She struggled up to her feet. "I'm not feeling good," she said, using her cancer to turn away from Amy. "My throat hurts. And I know what you think. And you know what I think. I can't hear about this anymore, Detective O'Malley."

Other times she tried to turn away from the cancer to sift through her brother's outrageous inflicted miseries, but turning to him meant instantly having to turn away from Spencer; leaning toward her brother meant by necessity turning away from Amy and all good feelings for her, turning away from caring about Amy's vanishing, from Amy's happy life in their apartment, from two years of their intimate friendship; turning to Andrew meant invariably turning to a hostility for Spencer, such a naked hostility that after the stoop talk Lily asked Joy to ask him not to come for a little while until she got her head together. She was so pathetic, she couldn't even tell him herself.

There was just one little problem. Vague thoughts of feebly defending a secretive and invisible Andrew weren't going to replace for Lily Spencer's very real and solemn taking of responsibility for things that weren't even his. And what remained, even without Spencer and his crazy Delaware parallels was this: Andrew, her brother, lied and deceived and betrayed Lily and his whole family by being with Amy. Nothing Spencer did or said could change that.

But there was no avoiding the detective in Spencer. He brought the detective with him even when he brought the chicken soup and the blue eyes.

She didn't know of a way to see him and not think of Andrew and Amy. Spencer made it so impossible for her to be in denial about so many things in her life and all at once, that she frequently found herself thrashing from side to side, unable to find comfort in any cranny of her mind. She was sick but the person who helped her feel a little bit better thought her brother had something to do with the disappearance of her best friend. There was no way to get around that elephant in her head. So this was why she did the only thing she could to remain half-sane. She asked Joy to withdraw her from Spencer. Joy refused. Lily said it was an order not a request, to which Joy replied, "You're getting rid of him, now you're threatening to get rid of me, too? Who are you going to be left with, Lily? You want him not to come? Tell him yourself."

She left him a pained message on his beeper. Without even calling her back, he stopped coming around, stopped calling, and now Lily couldn't face her life.

Without saying any of this to the doctor, this is what she was saying to the doctor: I can't do this anymore.

And what did the good doctor suggest by way of solution out of the quagmire?

"You should watch Jay Leno at night. Watch Comedy Central. Old re-runs of Saturday Night."

"Completely devoid of humor, by the way."

"Just using them as an example. Rent comedies. Buy yourself a DVD player, a new TV, a new couch. Rent movies, only funny ones, I'm going to tell Joy, nothing outside the comedy section."

"I don't think Joy would understand. She doesn't have a humerus bone in her body."

"Funny. Comedies only, Lily."

She tried DiAngelo's approach. With Joy's help she bought Best Buy's most absurdly expensive television—a fifty-inch plasma TV. The TV was good. She hung it on her wall like a painting. This pleased her. The DVD player was good. The $300 chenille blanket heavy like a sheepskin rug was good. The Pottery Barn couch was goooood. Soft. Mushy, with big pillows. The whole thing barely fit into her living room.

"If I didn't need all of my money for cancer, I would buy myself that Park Avenue apartment you were talking about, Joy," she said. The bill for September had recently come. With the hospital fees, the anesthesiologist, DiAngelo, the X-rays, the blood, the medicines, the drugs (she couldn't believe she had to pay to put those into her body!) and Anne's mortgage and bills, September cost Lily four hundred thousand dollars. At this rate, she better die or get better by spring, because there was going to be nothing left of either her or her money.

"Money well spent," said Joy. "You'll be broke, but you'll have your life."

"Mmm, what joy to be alive and broke," said Lily.

"You'd rather be dead and rich?"

Covered by a heavy blanket, Lily sat through the rest of week three watching *Tootsie*, *Airplane*, *Animal House*, *Bachelor Party*, *Porky's Revenge*, and *Bill and Ted's Excellent Adventure*, the stupider the better. Joy sat with Lily on the couch once or twice, but watched as if the movies were *I, Claudius*, not *Bachelor Party*—not a facial muscle moved on Joy in response to the antics on the screen. By the beginning of week four, when the VePesid was being piped in, she said to DiAngelo, the movies aren't helping.

"Have you tried Conan O'Brien? He's very good."

"Doc, you're not listening." She didn't think that was it.

"You're not eating. Lily, you have to eat."

She didn't think that was it.

"What would you like, a week off? We'll have to start from scratch. We'll have to do continuous cytarabine again. Is that what you want?"

"No, but I don't want this either."

"Only nine more weeks to go."

By week four all the hair had gone from her body. Only the eyelashes remained. What were they made of if not protein? "Don't worry," said Joy, who was helping her out of the bath. "It'll all grow back."

"Like I care. I'll never have to shave or wax again."

Week four, *Some Like it Hot*, *Annie Hall*, *The Great Dictator*, *My Fair Lady*, not technically a comedy, but one of her favorites. *The Graduate*, *Blazing Saddles*, *Ghostbusters*. She rediscovered Bill Murray, and watched *Caddyshack*, *Stripes*, *Ghostbusters* again, *Ghostbusters II* and *Groundhog Day*. She got stuck on *Groundhog*

261

Day. Something in it stuck in her. She watched it three times on Friday, three on Saturday. And then on Sunday, when Joy had her day off, she called Spencer and nearly stammering into the phone asked if he wanted to come and take a look at her new plasma TV.

He came—bringing Coke and ginger ale. His hair had gotten a little longer. He was so sullen, he was like Sinead O'Connor's "Gloomy Sunday" song right on her new couch.

But then they watched *Groundhog Day* and he laughed. After it was finished, she asked if they could see it again. "If you want," he said.

There was a line in the movie spoken by Bill Murray to one of the regulars in a bowling alley bar: "*What would you do if you were stuck in one place and every day was exactly the same and nothing you did mattered?*" Bill Murray looked at the guy with his deadpan face, and the regular responded, "*That about sums it up for me.*" Spencer looked at Lily with his deadpan face, and then reached over and took the remote off her lap, and pressed STOP saying, "Okey-dokey, I think that's enough *Groundhog Day* for this evening."

They sat on the couch, she at one end, he at the other. He said he had to be going, and she agreed that was best.

On Fridays when she felt like she could move, she put on Amy's skicap and with Joy's help walked to HMV on Broadway or Best Buy on 6th and bought movies. No renting and returning business with Blockbuster. She would buy dozens at a time. One day at Best Buy, she offered to buy a refrigerator for Joy, who declined. "I'd wait for your October hospital bill before I started buying refrigerators."

The October bill was only a hundred thousand dollars. Lily was so excited, she bought Joy a refrigerator *and* an oven. She gave ten thousand dollars to Anne for her November mortgage and extras, and another five thousand to Amanda for the girls' birthdays. She bought another $300 chenille blanket for the couch, in case Spencer needed one.

She bought every comedy in the comedy section, even *A Life Less Ordinary* that didn't look remotely funny. Sometimes she slept through them. Sometimes she watched them with one eye. She put the same movies on again and again until she saw them whole. Sometimes she even laughed.

During week five Steve Martin said, speaking from the TV as if straight to Lily, "You don't watch enough movies. All of life's riddles are answered in the movies." So Lily watched *The Out of Towners, Dead Men Don't Wear Plaid, Planes, Trains and Automobiles, All of Me, Man with Two Brains, My Blue Heaven,* and *Lonely Guy* to get Steve Martin to answer her life's riddle.

"He answered it in *Dead Men Don't Wear Plaid*," Spencer told her. "Remember? He said, 'All dames are alike: they reach down your throat and they grab your heart, pull it out, and they throw it on the floor, step on it with their high heels, spit on it, shove it in the oven and cook the shit out of it. Then they slice it into little pieces, slam it on a hunk of toast and serve it to you, and then expect you to say, thanks, honey, it was delicious.'"

Spencer could be funnier than any comedy, especially *A Life Less Ordinary*. Laughing inside Lily said, "I can't imagine you really believe that."

And he said no, he didn't, he just thought it was funny. "I think the answer to the riddle of life is more from *Bill and Ted's Excellent Adventure* than from Steve Martin. Bill says, 'The only true wisdom consists of knowing you know nothing.'"

And Lily, as Ted, said, "That's us, dude. That's us."

34

Lily's Stations

She feels that her body has left her spirit, not the other way around, and only the spirit remains on the bed or the couch. She lies in bed and imagines riding a bike through Central Park or rollerblading through New York City rush hour. She imagines roller coasters, and loop the loops, and haunted houses, and river rapids and log flumes. She imagines jet-skiing even though she has never jet-skied, she imagines snorkeling, her legs moving, her arms moving, her lungs filling up with air from a tube, she imagines jumping off a high rock into the sea, into a freshwater lake, as if she were still a child, swinging like Tarzan on a rope over a river, a slow-flowing wide river. She imagines swinging—a bat during softball, playing badminton, and table tennis, running, out of breath doing ten 440-meter sprints with only two minutes' rest in between.

When she can hold a charcoal, she draws, but the things she draws she hates, and so she throws them out instantly. They're so black and bleak. When she can hold a pen to paper she writes, doodling all around the words; she pens small poems, even attempts haikus.

> *Death stared at me*
> *I stared back undaunted*
> *Just false bravado*

Though life beckons me
I am too busy sleeping
Sleeping not dying.

He stands in his suit
Holds out candy and Coke
I wish he would sit.

Her intestinal tract hurts all the time. Hurts in twisting shards, as if she's being poisoned.

Spencer brings soup, the fattiest chicken soup he can get the Odessa chef to make. He makes her eat every last drop. He knows she is being poisoned by the chicken soup, but he doesn't care. "Eat," he says. She eats. When he leaves, as inevitably he must, she goes and throws up, as inevitably she must. When she comes out, Joy stands by the door holding out a disapproving towel in her hands.

Spencer brings her vanilla shakes, strawberry shakes. She drinks and keeps them down! Hurrah. Joy must have told Spencer this, because suddenly he comes every day times five with the strawberry and vanilla shakes. He comes so often and at all hours and then the intercom breaks and the super is on vacation and Joy has to traipse down five flights each day to let him in. That gets old fast, and Lily asks Joy to give him a key to her apartment. Joy has now become an intermediary to Spencer.

When Spencer can't come, he sends the delivery boy from Odessa, Pedro, who brings her stuffed cabbage, red cabbage and schnitzel, Greek salad and Manhattan clam chowder. He brings bread pudding and cheesecake. Joy sits and watches her not eat. When is her next day off? When can Lily be alone again?

"You'll be alone when you're dead," says Joy as if hearing her. "Eat." Spencer was right about her. Lily can't do without her.

Amanda calls every day. Anne comes once a week and regales her with stories of her financial woes. Lily listens and listens, and then writes Anne a check. She wonders if she should just send

Anne a check at the beginning of each month to circumvent the continual blather but is afraid Anne won't come anymore if she does.

Her grandmother comes once a week—like Lily used to come and see her once a week. Comes and sits by her bed and reads her the newspapers and regales her with stories of great suffering, of Death Marches, of burning ovens, of dread, and starvation and fear, of depravity and malice Lily cannot fathom. Listening to Grandma, Lily feels a little better. As long as it's not about cancer, she can hear it. Her grandmother asks if she wants to hear about Love, but Lily doesn't. She doesn't want to hear about Love. She's soured on it.

Not me, fellas, not me, girlfriends. I'd give up love forever if only I could have my one life. If only I could have my minutes back, the minutes that I lost pining, regretting, crying, the minutes I spent wallowing over boyfriends who betrayed me, over friends who ditched me, over my mother who stopped being a mother to me, over my father who forgot to talk to me on the telephone, over my beloved brother, God! my brother, who is hiding from me, I don't want to know, don't want to believe. I just want LIFE!

I want to be that girl with a red scarf and flowing brown hair, all alone in Times Square, standing by the wall as she looks upon the enamored and the entwined, the coupled and homeless, wishing for a bit of what they have—LIFE. Except that now the girl stands and doesn't even look at them, but stands, eyes closed, slightly smiling, grateful only for her small insignificant but vivid SELF in Times Square one late wet winter evening.

Is Spencer looking thinner, paler, or is she just projecting? She can't tell anything anymore.

No, that's not true. She doesn't care. She doesn't care about the news, about movies, about politics. She doesn't care about Amy or Andrew, or her mother. She doesn't care about anybody. She feels only for herself. Week six she gets on the scale—eighty-six pounds bald. Week six she notices lesions on her face, on her body. The leaves are falling, she loves the fall, but she can't go outside, she can't let anyone see her like this.

On Friday night Rachel and Paul come uninvited. The shock in their eyes in unmistakable. They try to hide it but can't. She hears Rachel on the landing crying as they descend the stairs.

She is not a very good patient, a good aunt, a good sister, a good friend, a good anything. She is barely a Lily.

On Sunday, Amanda asks her to come and spend the day; Lily wishes she could bring Spencer. She calls to tell him not to come in the afternoon, taking a hired car to Bedford. She thinks the visit might be good for her, but the girls running around, shouting, jumping on her, despite their mother's strong protestations and Lily's feeble ones, exhaust her after an hour. She is not up to going to the playground, not up to crawling on the floor, not up to board games, or helping with dinner. She is not even up to talking. She goes and sleeps in the guest room, and then takes a car back home, where she calls Spencer who comes over at night for another installment of couch and *Groundhog Day*. "I know this stupid movie by heart," he says.

"That's funny, because I could watch it again and again and again."

"Funny, Harlequin."

He called her Harlequin. "Okay, now *that's* funny."

Just eight more treatments. Just eight more treatments, just eight more treatments.

And then somebody coughs.

"Somebody's cough is your coffin," DiAngelo had said to her.

The shell casing of a body depleted of all antibodies gets sick. It catches bacteria that travel from the tongue to the throat to the stomach to the intestine, to the blood to the lungs.

In the lungs the infection becomes pneumonia.

Lily, feverish and bleeding from her gums and teeth, is flown via helicopter to Mount Sinai. They hook her up with some antibiotic, some glucose, some morphine through her Port-a-Death. But

267

all her vital signs are down. She has almost no blood pressure, she barely has a pulse.

She doesn't know how long she is out, it seems like one long sleep, but when she opens her eyes she finds a priest by her side. She looks at him, he looks at her and says, *You're closer to God now, my child,* and she shuts her eyes and thinks *That's unmistakable but I don't want to be this close just yet* and doesn't open them again until he is gone. Three, four days later? Three, four years later? Twenty years later?

Instead of the priest in the chair next to her bed sits her grandmother, and next to her stand Amanda, and Andrew, and Anne.

Andrew!

Her gaze stops on him, she watches him, wants to say something to him, but can't open her mouth to speak, a breathing tube is inside her throat. That lung machine again keeping her breathing. She holds out her hand to him, and he comes, and she grasps him, and tears run down into her ears. He looks away from her even at this moment.

Andrew, why are you here? she wants to cry. Why are you here, you who betrayed me, who have hid from me all these months. She's vanished and you have vanished too. Both of you have gone away from me, and I don't know why and I don't know how to fix it. How to fix anything. *Come all without, come all within . . .*

Spencer is not here.

Looking into the eyes of her grandmother and seeing something peculiar and disturbing there, too—though markedly different from Andrew's expression—she asks for a pen and paper, and writes, "You think I'm going to die, don't you?"

Her grandmother doesn't reply at first, then looks away. "No, darling, I don't think so. I think you're going to be just fine."

Lily looks at Andrew again. That's why he is here! He thinks I'm going to die. My whole family thinks so. But there is something else in Andrew's eyes, other than that tacit acknowledgement. Almost as if he hopes I will.

She doesn't know what to say. She thinks of writing nothing. But she can't not write anything.

"Where is my mother?" writes Lily.

35

Lily's Mother is Here

George came back from the beach by eight, and as soon as he walked in, he saw Allison on the floor near the kitchen, struggling to get up. He had just come back from an hour-long walk, a swim. He hadn't had a cigarette, or a coffee, and there she was already on the floor. Through the double glass doors, in the darkness of the morning apartment, with the curtains drawn, on the floor, struggling to get up. He put down his sunglasses and went to help her up. But she couldn't stand. She reeked of alcohol. "Oh, for God's sake," George said, letting go of her. She couldn't talk, she was incoherently mumbling. Drool was coming out of her mouth, her eyes were rolling in their white sockets.

This morning George felt anger at her and striking pity for himself. Hawaii, he decided, was not for him, a sixty-six-year-old man. Hawaii was for young people. For snorkeling, deep-sea-diving, jet-skiing, volcano-climbing, uphill-bike-riding young people. For Lily perhaps. The things that gave him most pleasure—fishing from a rowboat, a vegetable garden, he couldn't have in Hawaii. And his other passion—sports—was rendered meaningless by an hour-long tape delay. No live sports coverage in Maui. He couldn't get a satellite system because he was not allowed to install it on the roof of the condo. So he entertained his love of cooking. But Allison wouldn't eat his food. What she ate, she threw up. Cooking for just himself was meaningless. Like singing for just himself. He liked to be praised for his gifts.

She threw up right on the carpet. George couldn't even get into his kitchen to make himself his morning coffee. He cursed and walked past her to the shower. He spent a long time shaving, washing. When he came out, the vomit was barely cleaned up and Allison was nowhere to be seen. She must have made it to her room. He went to check on her, to ask her if she wanted coffee. She was unconscious on the floor and he couldn't pick her up to put her on the bed. He left her there.

He didn't have many days like this, but there were some, he had some days like this, where he lay down on his bed in the middle of a God-like day, put his arm over his face, and thought, I can't believe this is my life.

Today she must have drunk more than usual, quicker than usual. When he went to check on her again, she was lying in her own vomit, and moaning.

"Allison," he said, "I'm going to go to New York and visit Lily. All right? I'm going to leave tomorrow. Do you hear me?"

"I'm dying," she moaned. "I'm not going to do this again, but please . . . right now . . . I'm dying. Call for help."

He stayed, called for help. Somehow she managed to recover.

Allison had showers every three days now. Maybe not that frequently. It was hard to tell, she spent so many of her days in a haze. She couldn't go swimming, go for a walk: her unshaven legs embarrassed her. But why didn't she shave them?

Because she couldn't bend down without falling over. And she couldn't put one leg on the edge of the tub without losing balance and falling over. Falling over seemed to be what she did best these days, and so she refrained from shaving her legs not by choice but by necessity, because one time she slipped and fell over, and really hurt her rib. There was a good chance she had broken it. But after six weeks, the rib didn't hurt as much anymore.

271

Her hands shook. They began shaking in the morning and didn't stop all day. When she raised her glass to her lips, her hands shook, and the cigarette shook in between her unpainted nails. She could no longer write letters to her friends, and she could not sign her name to her checks. She did it anyway because she had to, and she didn't care how sloppy her name looked on the signature line. It was illegible. But she couldn't write illegible letters anymore. She could barely dial the phone. There was only one thing that stopped her hands from shaking. Where was that one thing now?

36

Lily's Stations, Continued

Lily regains consciousness, and pulses again and breathes on her own and even puts food into her mouth. Of course! They've had to forgo the chemo while they were getting her blood pressure back up. She had had a blood transfusion, and was sitting up when DiAngelo came to see her. "You're doing great, Lily. I'm telling you, you're going to lick this thing."

"Hmm," she said. "I'm going especially great when I don't have chemo. Look, I'm having Jell-O. I used to love Jell-O. What do you think? Should we just forget the whole thing? Let me go home and eat and buy that Prada purse my sister has been telling me I absolutely must have if I'm to have a life at all, even a short one?"

He smiled. "Eight more weeks of chemo, Lil. Almost halfway done. Then you can sleep in an extra large Prada purse. By the size of you, you won't even need that big a one. But this is what I wanted to tell you—I'm restricting your visitors. For just a little while."

"Until when?"

"Until you're discharged."

"Oh, come on! Who are you trying to keep from me, Doctor D?" She lowers her voice. "Are you like Grandma and are keeping the detective away?"

"He's the only one who can come," says DiAngelo. "And only for ten minutes."

He doesn't come at all, but the next day, Lily wakes to see Anne by her side, clearing her throat for five minutes.

Finally she speaks. "As your older sister, Liliput, I hate to be the one to advise you on these matters, but it's my responsibility. Please understand. Have you thought—even briefly—about getting your affairs in order? You don't know how sick you've been."

"I don't know? What are you talking about?"

"Lily, must I spell it out for you?"

"Yes, you must. If you want me to understand, you must."

"Have you thought about a will? Funeral arrangements? Have you thought about even a living will?"

"A what?"

In hushed conspiratorial tones Anne asks Lily if she will consider signing a DNR form statement for the hospital.

"What's DNR?"

"Most hospitals require you to sign a release statement because normally they will try to keep you alive at all costs."

"I like that."

"Stop being funny."

"Who is funny? Really. I like that."

"Listen, when all your faculties are gone," Anne says, "and you've slipped into a coma, and there is no chance of coming out of it, a Do Not Resuscitate clause, a DNR, will save you and your family a lot of grief. It's more decent, more humane. After the kind of toll that cancer's taken on you, a DNR means comfort for your family."

"Annie, I'd like the hospital to keep me alive at all costs, if it's all the same to you."

"Even if your body has been ravaged beyond all healing? They keep you alive artificially."

"Any which way they keep me alive is fine with me."

"Suit yourself. I just want you to know your options. Some of them are a little kinder on your family."

"I'm assuming my family would like me to survive, no?"

"Well, of course, but if there is no hope . . ."

"Mrs. Ramen!" DiAngelo walks in officiously. "No visitors before six in the evening, I was very specific."

"But it's visiting hours," Anne says.

"Cancer doesn't know about visiting hours," says DiAngelo. "Cancer is here for Lily twenty-four-seven, and she needs her rest. No, not even family during the day, no one. It's for Lily's protection. And you must wear a mask, I told you that time and time again. Come back in the evening if you wish. Actually, this evening she'll be getting a CT scan. Perhaps you should come back tomorrow."

By tomorrow, having skipped a week of cancer for pneumonia thus prolonging her agony to fourteen weeks, Lily is discharged and sent home.

Lily makes herself get out of bed. She forces herself. She makes herself make the bed every day even if she then gets on top of it and sleeps until after lunch. But every morning, on her hands and knees, she crawls around her bed tucking in the edges.

Week eight she can't get up except for the bed-making. Mondays and Tuesdays are gone. Wednesdays are non-existent, Thursdays are foggy. Fridays she makes the bed. Saturdays she used to go out for a walk down the block with Joy. She eats a little. Sundays she reads, bathes, sleeps until Spencer comes. Sundays are her best days, but then Monday comes again.

Amanda is doing Thanksgiving this year and she wants Lily to celebrate with them, but there is no way Lily can. She'd ruin everybody's time. She gives Joy a day off, and tells Spencer she is going to Amanda's, but she is alone on Thanksgiving. He has gone to Long Island to be with his family. Rachel, Paul are with their families. Jan McFadden calls early to wish Lily a happy holiday, crying. "People say such awful things to me today. They say, well, consider yourself lucky, be *thankful* they say that you still have two other children."

"They just don't know what to say, Mrs. McFadden."

"They show their true colors. They say, everything happens for a reason."

"I hate that one the most, I know." Lily knows.

"Oh, Lil, you'll be all right, you just have to be strong."

Is that *all* she has to do? Or just *one* of the things? Mrs. McFadden too falls into the trap of not knowing what to say. "You too, Mrs. McFadden, you too."

Spencer never says anything, except I'm sorry and eat. Why can't the rest of the world be like him.

She has lost track of time in these last months and to help herself stay sane she has put clocks on every wall in the house— chiming clocks, Mickey Mouse clocks, digital clocks, second-hand clocks, Mexican clocks and Chinese clocks to tell her what her mind cannot. Such as how long she spent bleeding from her nose into the toilet on Thanksgiving afternoon, when she couldn't stand up long enough over the sink. Sixty-five minutes, she thinks. She can never remember the hour anything starts. She can't remember anything. She has to keep Spencer's beeper number by the phone.

Week nine all the leaves are gone and the weather gets cold. But she can't put her coat on and go for a walk because she can't get out of the house, can't walk down the stairs, doesn't have the strength to move her legs down the steps. Joy force-feeds her reluctant mouth some home-made chicken soup her grandmother has brought. Lily fights to keep it in. Rachel comes to visit and goes on and on about how she always gains weight in the winter and how there is no diet good enough to stay on permanently. Lily jokes that a permanent diet is probably a misnomer and Rachel laughs too, and says, am I an idiot for talking to you about this? And Lily says, what else are you going to talk to me about?

Rachel asks what she and Spencer talk about.

"Nothing," replies Lily. "Seriously," she adds when she sees Rachel's skeptical face. "Nothing. He sits, we watch TV, we laugh sometimes if the comedy is funny, he goes home. The other day we were watching *Something About Mary*, and you know how obscenely raunchy that movie is, I couldn't even look at him, I was so embarrassed, but he was laughing so hard, he nearly cried."

"That's all?"

"That's all."

"He doesn't ask you how you're feeling?"

"He knows."

Lily can't come to the phone. She records a message to tell callers how she's feeling, which is not good, not feeling good. But when she plays back the messages sometimes the patient grows agitated. "Lily, it's your mother. I don't understand. You're never home . . . Or maybe you are home and are just not picking up. Lily? LILY?" That is guaranteed to upset Lily. Thereafter, contrary to Lily's express wishes, Joy answers the phone. In a machine-like voice she gives out some clinical information and informs the caller that Lily is sleeping. She offers to take a message. She almost beeps the tone. So Lily gets her messages through the mediation of calm and dedication to the cause—getting Lily well again. What would Lily do without this nurse machine?

Joy doesn't say Lily is in the bathroom retching. Or unconscious. That Lily can't watch TV, cannot concentrate on the newspaper. Cannot sit up long enough to draw. Sometimes she sketches with charcoal while lying on her side, and falls asleep, her face on the paper, and when she awakens, her cheeks are black from coal.

Her skin suddenly has patches on it she has never seen. All over, strips of reddish brown. Her skin's coming off. It's the chemo, Dr. DiAngelo tells her, burning her from the inside out. She thinks her brain's burning up as well.

Joy finds her crying in the bath, pink bathwater from the blood that trickles from her nose.

She tells Joy how grateful she is that she and Joshua broke up before he could see her like this, this sick, her body this destroyed. That is something she is truly thankful for—that he didn't have

277

an opportunity to break up with her *after* he had seen her go through her greatest distress.

Joy wipes her face, helps her stand up, gives her a towel, dries her. "Spencer's outside," she says quietly. "He brought you Jell-O."

She is losing her power of speech. Not just of speech, but of sight too. Certainly of smell, she can't smell anything. And could she be wrong? Have the trees stopped rustling in the wind, or can she just not hear them anymore? New York is getting quieter, no fire engines, no police cars, no women screaming drunkenly at their boyfriends early on Sunday mornings instead of quietly going to church. Even the women are mute. She turns up the TV, sits closer.

Nearly four months shut off from the world. Four months.

Soon it will be over.

That is the light at the end of the tunnel. Not life, but death.

37

A Too Beautiful Mother

Today was Sunday. Spencer was coming over soon. Before the phone rang, she had been sprawled out on her bed, crucifixion-style. She thought that death might be a day like this, cool wind, the golden, yellow, reflected light off the bare oaks, the gray maples, soft sounds of Sunday cars, Sunday strollers, the cat sunning on a window across the yard, the old lady down below in her garden sitting in her coat having her coffee and reading the paper. There would be no pain after death, no bleeding, no vomiting, no weakness. Just happiness, and lightness of heart—

And that's when the phone rang.

In heaven there would be no phone. No one would ever interrupt you. You'd never feel annoyed or frustrated. Death would be an eternal Sunday.

And now, I submit to you that no matter how bad you thought you were feeling on Sunday, it wasn't as bad as you thought.

Maybe it was her father. There was always that possibility.

"Hello?" she said, expectantly.

"Finally! She picks up the phone!"

It wasn't her father. She struggled with the next line. "Hi, Mom." How was that?

"That's a fine hello. What's the matter?"

"Nothing. Why?"

Her mother didn't sound drunk, her speech wasn't slurred, wasn't slow, it was just a little sharp.

"So how *are* you?"

"I'm good, thanks," said Lily. She thought of asking her mother how she was, but she didn't care and couldn't fake it.

"Aren't you going to ask me how I am?"

Big breath in. "How are you, Mother?"

"I'm fine now. Don't worry. The tumor was benign."

Lily closed her eyes. "What . . . tumor?"

"What, your father didn't tell you? He's too busy telling you lies about me, not actual information about my health. So what's the matter with *you*? Are you still taking that *chemo*, or whatever?"

"Yes. Four more treatments."

"And then you're all better?"

"I don't know."

"So what's the matter *now*? You sound like you swallowed a can of worms."

"No, no, I'm fine." She didn't say anything else.

Allison said slowly, "I've been meaning to call you, but I've been really sick, Lil, your father hadn't told you . . . I had to go to the hospital. They took X-rays of my lungs. They think I might have a spot on one of them. God!"

"Surprising," Lily said. "He didn't tell me."

"You know you could pick up the phone once in a while and call your mother. Your arm wouldn't fall off."

"I've been busy, Mom."

"Doing what?"

"I've been busy dying."

"Oh, stop it, stop being *so* melodramatic. You're just like your father. You should hear the stories he tells about Andrew to his former co-workers. He's always on the phone with them. He's got Andrew practically in the White House already, after that whole missing girl fiasco was cleared up. How *is* your brother?"

"I have no idea."

"Hmm. You don't call him either. Well, that's surprising. You know the doctor told me I was depressed. He said I was *clinically* depressed. He put me on Prozac, but it didn't agree with me. I kept throwing it up."

Lily, the phone slightly away from her ear, turned sideways on the bed so she could look out the window and smell the air. She breathed in and out to teach herself detachment. She was quiet. "Mom, I have to go."

"Go? I just called you. We haven't spoken for months! Why is that? Do I not call you? Do I not leave messages?"

"I don't know, do you?" Did her mother think she had left messages with a machine? She said, "Sometimes when you call, I can't understand a word you're saying."

"I don't know why, I'm speaking perfect English. Well, I'm calling you now. Tell me how you are."

"I'm just great."

"Grandma says you're hanging in there. Amanda too. Annie is really concerned for you, she is being a very good sister."

"Mom . . . do you know, I've been sick since August, and this is the first time you and I have spoken?"

"You never pick up your phone! What's the matter with you? You always sound like you don't want to talk to me. No matter when I call you sound like this."

"I don't think that's true."

"You sound almost as depressed as I am, Lil."

Lily made an exasperated sound. If she had any hair left on her body, it would have all stood on end. "Got. To. Go. Mom," she said through a closed mouth. A perfectly good Sunday ruined. She couldn't press the TALK button sharply enough. So dissatisfying. She threw the phone across the bedroom at the opening door and hit Spencer in the shin as he was walking in.

He raised his hands in surrender. "Ouch," he said. She turned away to the window.

* * *

281

They watched *LA Story* because Lily was convinced the answer to the riddle was there.

She didn't find it there.

So they watched *Parenthood*. Maybe it was there. Spencer said, "Tell the truth, are you watching it for the answer to life's riddle, or are you watching it for Keanu?"

"Am I that transparent?" she said.

The movie was mostly about fathers and sons, but Lily couldn't help thinking about mothers and daughters. When Spencer asked why she was not laughing, she PAUSED the movie and turned to him. "Do you know what the problem with my mother is?"

He turned to her. "Well, you've told me. She's got some issues."

"She is too beautiful," said Lily. "And worse—she's always thought so. Not just beautiful, but more beautiful than anyone else. You've seen pictures of my mother in Maui."

"Yes," said Spencer but noncommittally.

"What? She's still beautiful. Older now."

"That's not it."

Lily knew it wasn't. "I know, she's not looking as well as she used to. But I'm telling you, something happens to beautiful people. They think that something extra is owed to them by life, by God, by all the people around them. They think their life has to be better, more dramatic, happier—in color, not in black and white."

"Everyone wishes their life were happier."

Lily shook her head. "No. Not like beautiful people. They walk on the earth, their chin up to the rest of us, and think that great happiness, great love, great joy is their right and their prerogative. Passion as the entitlement of the beautiful, the way power is the entitlement of the rich." Lily paused. "Especially when it comes to love. Beauty and love become somehow synonymous. How can plain people have great love? They can't, that's how. They can have average love, mediocre love, but their hearts can't soar. Only beautiful hearts can soar."

"I think you've hit on the nail right there," said Spencer. "Beautiful people don't necessarily have beautiful hearts."

"But it doesn't matter, don't you see? You don't fall in love with a heart. You fall in love with a woman's face, with her body, with her hair, with her smell. That's first, everything else is secondary. My mother's beauty when she was young was so extreme that she didn't understand how every man who met her didn't love her *in extremis*."

"Did your father?"

"He did. Another problem—after nearly forty-three years of marriage, she still wants him to."

Spencer didn't say anything for a while, and Lily thought he was thinking about what she just told him, but the next thing that came out of Spencer's mouth was, "Was Amy beautiful?"

"Oh for God's sake, Spencer!" She turned to the TV and pressed PLAY on the remote, cranking up the volume. Leaning over, he took the remote out of her hands and pressed PAUSE.

"Why do you always do that?" she said, not looking at him. "Why do you always, *always* turn the conversation back to that?"

"Because that is what I do, and you're not answering me."

"Yes, she was beautiful, yes, yes, yes, but I don't want to talk about her right now, I don't want to talk about her or him, or about them. I don't want to *think* about them, can't you understand?"

She fell quiet, he fell quiet. The movie remained on PAUSE. Finally he said, "Tell me, was your father handsome?"

She sighed. "Very. He was very popular with the girls, my grandmother tells me. But he didn't think much of his face except as a way to get girls. He thought much more of his brain. He was too smart to give too much credence to his external features."

"But your mother . . ."

"She was also smart, but she didn't care a whit about that.

283

When she looked in the mirror she saw Botticelli. And all the men around her saw it, too. So when she fell in love— with someone before my father—she thought it was going to be forever, because her beauty seemed eternal. So when he ended it after only a few months, she was shocked, she couldn't believe it."

"Why did he end it?"

"I don't know. She never said. I don't think she's ever told anyone why, even my father. But we know one thing—she burned two cigarette butts into her wrists by way of dealing with this unfathomable rejection."

Spencer raised his eyebrows. Lily smiled. "Told you. Cuckoo as a bird."

"So tell me, who is Andrew like?"

"Spencer!"

"All right, all right." He took a breath. "You know, you've turned out surprisingly well."

"Hmm, no, I don't think so."

He was quiet. "Do *you* think love belongs only to the beautiful?"

She pondered. *There are things about you I could never love.* "Yes," she said at last. "I don't want to admit it, but I guess I do. Believe me, I don't want to think that Joshua would have left me anyway, but I can't help feeling that he would not have left if I had been more beautiful."

"I don't see how that's possible," said Spencer. "And didn't that boy leave your mother despite her beauty?"

"Yes, but that just confirmed to my mother that inside her was a black hole that her beauty hid from the rest of the world but not so well from her lovers." She fell silent. Did he just say, *I don't see how that's possible?* She stared at him from across the couch but he had turned back to the TV. "Andrew is nothing like my mother," she said, pressing PLAY. "To answer your stupid question."

He smiled. "Liliput," he said, "stop denying your rightful place in the universe. You don't want your mother's extreme beauty, nor her black hole. Look where it leads."

The doorbell rang. Not the downstairs bell. The apartment door bell. Lily pressed PAUSE. It was six in the evening.

"Are you expecting someone?" He got up.

"No," she said. "Maybe it's Rachel. Go see."

Spencer went to the door to go see. Slowly he turned to Lily. "I don't know how to say this. It's your family."

She put her hand over her face. "Oh, no! Which ones?"

"All of them."

"Oh, no! Oh, no!" The doorbell rang again, but Lily's confusion was so great, she couldn't even get up.

"I have to open the door, Lily."

"Spencer, they're going—" He let them in.

To have a cow, she thought, knowing even before she saw, the looks on their faces when they walked in, Amanda, Anne, Grandma, holding trays of pasta, of brownies, pitchers of Kool-Aid, bags of potato chips and found Spencer, extremely casual, comfortable, worn-in jeans, a sweatshirt, his off-duty weapon on the coffee table, his boots by the door, letting them into a tiny apartment where there was only him and Lily.

No one, not even he, had any idea what to say.

It was Lily who spoke first. "Grandma, Annie, Mand, you remember Detective O'Malley."

They said nothing, still holding the food out.

He took his gun, his jacket, put his boots on. "I'll see you, Lily."

"See ya."

After he closed the door behind him, they whirled on her, and she fell back on the couch. They stared at her so accusingly demanding an answer, an explanation, but she didn't know what to say. Did he come on police business, harassing a girl in her tenth week of chemo? Or did he come to sit with her awhile? And which was worse?

"I don't know what you want me to say. He gives Joy Sundays off."

285

"Of all the people in New York City, you let THAT man into your house?"

It was a short, stifled visit. Twenty minutes later they were all out the door and Lily was alone.

38

Cancer Shmancer

Lily's family stopped speaking to her, except for Anne, who was remarkably still calling and asking Lily if she needed anything, and Lily tiredly would say, "I need nothing. Do *you* need anything?" Amanda had stopped calling. Grandma regressed back into her house, citing Joy and her returned agoraphobia as the reasons she no longer *had* to come and see Lily. Her father didn't call.

But it was her mother who made things clear for her—oh, why does she *ever* pick up that damn phone! Her mother who said to her one fine cold day, "Everyone's furious with you, you know, for taking up with that scalawag."

"What scalawag?"

"You know very well who I'm talking about. Aside from the fact that he's old enough to be your father, have you got absolutely no shame? He wants to put your brother behind bars for something he didn't do. Your brother!"

"I haven't taken up with him, what are you talking about?"

"Oh, come now! Stop playing games. Yes, there's a generation between you two, but you're a twenty-five-year-old woman, not a child. He has set out to destroy your family and you're letting him in your house? He is sent by the devil. He is the enemy. There is something wrong with you, Lily, if you can't see that. Really, you simply have no soul and no conscience."

287

"Mom, what are you talking about? I have cancer. He brings me food . . ."

"Oh, cancer shmancer. Don't use your cancer as an excuse, Lil, as a weapon against the rest of us. You still have to make good decisions, smart decisions. Why can't you tell him your brother is innocent?"

"I do, and I don't want to talk about this, I have to go."

"Amanda tells me your quality of life is terrible. She says you're not doing anything to help yourself, you're not going out, you're not exercising, or reading, or painting. No wonder you've taken up with him. You're bored, Lil, but you need to get yourself together."

"I'm together, Mom. Are you together?"

"Why do you think your brother doesn't want to speak with you anymore—"

Lily hung up on her mother.

How could she say this, how could she say this, how—could—she—say—this.

Groaning, groaning, she lay on her bed, trying to drown out the words that were pounding like drums in her entrails. Mothers . . . so much power, so many knives . . . so many ways to stick it to you.

Oh, why in the name of all that was holy did she pick up the cursed phone . . .

Dare she think it? She would prefer her mother bitterly drunk and unavailable than her mother blind sober.

The cumulative effects of four months of chemo were destroying her. There was no joy in knowing it would soon be over, because every single day she felt as if it would all be over. As in, oh, would that it would all be over.

Just two more treatments. One was right before Christmas.

For Christmas, Lily reluctantly went with Spencer—who would not take no for an answer—to his mother's house in Farmingville. She didn't want to go and said she was going to

Andrew's, but Spencer said, "You told me that lie at Thanksgiving and then I found out you were here by yourself. You are not going to be by yourself on Christmas, Lily, that's all there is to it."

So she went.

In the car she said, "How are you going to explain me?"

"I'm a big boy. Why do I have to explain anything?"

His family was an army division without the discipline. He introduced her as "Lily." As in, "This is Lily." And that was all. Two of the sisters—she couldn't remember anyone's name—did a slow double take, from him to her and back to him for a lingering look, and that was all. The family shouted, they drank, the music was loud, the children were louder, the adults tried to outshout both. Lily's bald head, unprotected by an acoustic curtain of hair had every sound emission echo and bounce off it until the head became a large red ball of viral nerve endings, one more whisper and she would be spun into a spectacular neural overload. Still, the kids didn't care about her head, they all wanted to touch it, despite the shouts from the adults, including "Uncle Spence," to "leave the girl alone!"

"Uncle Spence already has a girlfriend," said Sam, Spencer's eight-year old nephew who was turning forty-seven next month. "She is in Chicago with her family. Mommy says he only brought you because you have cancer."

"Sammy!" The mother was redder than Lily's overloaded head.

Lily smiled. She didn't glance at Spencer, next to her at the dinner table.

"Lily, I didn't say that, please forgive him," said the mother, throwing livid looks toward a son she had once apparently loved.

"Don't worry." Lily was amused. "Really. And Sammy, your mommy is right, your uncle did only bring me because I have cancer."

A terrible silence followed at the dinner table before every one laid in to the turkey and yams. Lily ate cheerfully, and asked for seconds, and thirds, and then threw up everything in

289

Spencer's seventy-seven-year-old mother's white and clean bathroom.

"He's just a child," Spencer said after they'd been on mute in the car, driving home. "And it's not true."

"Oh, like I care about that."

"What then?"

"Nothing."

"Come on, it's Christmas."

"Yes, I know, you've told me. Thank you for your Christmas charity, Detective O'Malley."

"Ah. So you do care about that."

"Not even slightly. But it *is* true."

"Lil, what's the matter? Something is the matter, what?"

She didn't reply.

"What?"

"You know, I would've gone to Andrew's today, where my whole family is. You know why I didn't? Because they didn't invite me. In fact, what Amanda said, was, 'Lil, in light of the circumstances it's really better that you not come. You understand. Have this all die down a bit.'"

"I'm sorry. It's my fault."

Yes, she wanted to say. It *is* your fault. And my fault. When Spencer didn't speak for a while, she said, "They're so upset with me."

"I know."

"You don't know. You don't understand anything."

"No?"

"Of course not! They think I'm selling them out."

"To who?" He looked at her so sharply he nearly drove off the road. "To me? You've got to be kidding me. Have you told them that you are the most reluctant sell-out, you are a failure as a sell-out, you are the worst witness, you have the worst memory, you remember nothing, and what you do remember you keep from me anyway. You tell me nothing, have you told them that?"

"They don't care and they don't believe me."

"How is that your fault?"

"Oh, Spencer. It's not about them." She fell quiet. It's about *you*. She thought they were right. Her mother was right. On Christmas Day, Lily felt unholy for being in the company of an Irish Catholic who wanted to put her brother away. How did this happen? How did her brother turn the family upside down and it was Lily who was on the guilt rack?

"I don't know why they're getting their panties in a twist," said Spencer. "I haven't talked to him in a month. I have not called, I've done nothing. I'm wrapped up in a dozen other things. Christmas is the worst time for the missing. Too many of them, and their families all want them back." He paused. "Most families want their loved ones with them on Christmas."

"Oh, stop it. Stop judging my family. Look, you want me to tell you something about my brother? Is that what you want?"

"No! What I want you to do is make peace with your family. Make peace with yourself."

"You want to hear it or not? It won't help you, but here it is." Her voice was shaking and low. "Years ago when he was in college, every other weekend, he would come home from Cornell and on the Sunday before he went back he would take me to New York City. He was twenty and I was three. He took me to the Museum of Natural History and to the Met and to the Guggenheim. He took me to the movies, for ice cream sodas at Serendipity's, to the Cloisters, to Battery Park, to the Empire State Building, and to the Twin Towers. I learned to love New York City because he showed it to me for four years of Sundays, holding my hand on the subway and on the way back home to our apartment he carried me. He was in law school and I was seven the last time we went out and he carried me. Then he got married, and got busy, and I saw him less frequently, but still he took me to lunch, to the movies, to dinner. He called me; we spoke. It's never been like this—this complete shutout of me."

291

She saw his hands tense around the wheel. He was staring grimly at the road.

"Can't you understand that I worshiped him? Amy being involved with him, it's like incest. She may as well have been my sister having an affair with my father. And Andrew knows it's a brutal betrayal. He can't face me. *That* is why he hasn't been to see me, and not because of the vicious things my mother says, and not because of your stupid and completely wrong suppositions!" Her whole body was trembling now. Her nose started bleeding.

He raised the palm of his hand out at her. "Okay, Lily."

"Okay, what?" she yelled.

His palm was still up. "You are sick, you are sick with cancer, and I am not, simply *not* going to have this out with you. It's impossible. That's what I mean by okay, Lily. So calm down."

And what did Lily say to him when she calmed down and cleaned herself up? "Oh, cancer, shmancer."

They drove the rest of the way in silence, and when he tried to help her up the stairs, she said she was going to be fine and didn't need his help anymore. But he took her by the shoulders. "You know what, after I get you upstairs you might be fine, but there is no way you're getting up there without me, so just stop the nonsense."

She shut up. She couldn't get up to her fifth floor walk-up without him. She let him help. He had to carry her the last flight of stairs.

When they were inside the apartment, he asked if she wanted him to stay.

"No!" she said.

"Merry Christmas," said Spencer and walked out.

A penultimate chemo five days before the New Year. Joy had time off for the millennium. A relenting Grandma invited Lily to come to Brooklyn and stay over, but Lily declined: she was too sick, her nose was constantly bleeding, and besides she couldn't stand one more word about Spencer, who himself was not available on the Saturday the millennium ended. She didn't know where he was, he didn't offer, and she didn't ask. On New Year's Eve, Rachel and Paul came over with champagne, begging her to come with them to a blowout party at the Palladium, but she couldn't get up off her made bed. They stayed for an hour and at ten went without her, leaving her with a glass of champagne by the bedside.

Lily slept through midnight 2000, though she left her windows open to hear through black dreams the cork-popping joy from other windows, other rooms.

39

Larry DiAngelo as Imhotep

"Detective O'Malley, I need your advice," said DiAngelo.

"What's going on? How was her biopsy?" It was the first week of the New Year, and Lily had just finished her last round.

"Biopsy was fine. Excellent. Her bone marrow's clean. Her blood is clean. Her blood counts are still low, but I'm not too worried about that. She did great, she really did."

The doctor should have looked happier telling Spencer this. "So why the long face?"

"There's this . . ." DiAngelo coughed. "She tested positive for a protein marker on her malignant myeloid cells called the CD56 antigen."

"What does that mean? Testing positive for this, is it good, bad?"

"Well, this genetic marker causes a resistance to the chemo drugs by working extra hard to build up an immunity to them. A quarter of all myeloid leukemia patients test positive for this protein."

"It builds up immunity to the chemo?"

"Yes. Though the cancer cells have been eradicated, the presence of CD56 signals likely problems with remission."

"What kind of problems?"

"A short remission, a prolonged relapse, a worsening prognosis."

Spencer stood silently in the hall, looking at the doctor's face. "You just learned this?"

"I knew it for a little while, a month. No point in saying anything when the last weeks were so difficult."

"So what advice do you want from me?" Spencer said.

"Should I tell her? I've been so frank with her about her treatment. She expects nothing less, but she's been through so much."

Spencer interrupted. "Under no circumstances tell her. You go in there, walk toward her with a big smile on your face, and you send her home and treat her in all ways as if she is going to live forever."

DiAngelo stretched his lips over his teeth. "Got it," he said.

Lily had been chatting with Marcie when DiAngelo came in with a big smile on his face. "Well, Lilianne Quinn, you've done it. Look." He showed her something on her chart. She tried to draw importance from what he was showing her. She was seeing double—that always made life infinitely more interesting. Double numbers. They were even more impressive double. Platelets 74 he was saying. Double that was 148—much better.

"What's left of me?"

"Surprisingly little," he said cheerfully. "But turns out just enough. Platelets at 74, up from 48 last week. It's very good. You're all clean."

"I passed the biopsy?"

"You passed the biopsy. Spencer is waiting to take you home. Marcie will help you get dressed."

Marcie kissed her head. "You see, Spunky. I told you, you were gonna do just great."

"I go home and then what?"

"Good question. Then you come back every Tuesday for blood work."

"For how long?"

"How long what?"

"How long do I have to come back for?"

295

"Five years."

She did a double take to see if he was kidding.

"Once a week for five years?"

"No, once a week for the next six months. Then once every two weeks. In a year, once a month. In three years, once every three months. Got it?"

She didn't know if she got it.

"Any questions?"

"Why Tuesday? Why not Monday?"

DiAngelo grinned. "In case you live it up too much on the weekends. I want your body to recover from revelry before we test your blood."

Marcie pinched her. "I've seen that Rachel friend of yours. You two are definitely going to be getting up to no good."

"When am I going to feel better?" Lily wanted to know.

"That's not the question you should be asking," DiAngelo said.

"No?"

"No."

"Why do I feel like shit, pardon my language?"

"You're cleaned of all the bad stuff, but cleaned of all the good stuff, too. Don't worry. Give yourself a few weeks, a month. You'll grow yourself a whole new Lily. In the meantime, be careful of public places. They carry germs."

"Will I grow some new cancer too?"

"That's not the question you should be asking yourself," he said quickly.

"I can't guess what I should be asking myself."

"Well, let me illustrate by answering the question for you."

"I don't know what the question is."

"Bear with me," he said. "Did I tell you that I had a quintuple bypass last year? No? Well, I did. No one can believe I've gone back to practicing medicine. My doctors didn't think I'd ever walk again."

"But you're always coming in from the running track!"

"Yes, I'm busy proving them wrong."

"I don't know . . ."

"Prove *me* wrong," DiAngelo said. "Prove the statistics wrong. Do the unthinkable. Even now, you're lying in bed because you can't move. You can't imagine moving. Move, Lily. Prove yourself wrong."

"I would except I can't move."

"I have to move slower these days myself. Can't take on as many patients. Can't be as involved as I once was." He tapped on his chest. "The old ticker just can't take it any more."

"An oncology doctor with a bad heart?" Lily found that humorous. She smiled.

"Laugh all you want but tell me something about yourself. Do you like jogging?"

She stiffened, recalling Amy. "No. Is *that* the question?"

"No."

"Doctor, you're perplexing me."

"You want me to tell you something about myself?"

"If you like."

"I write in my own candidates at every general election. In the last one I voted for George Burns. How was I supposed to know he'd been dead nine months? What else? Wife number three thought I was too sensitive. Wife number four thinks I'm a heartless bastard, right, Marcie?"

"Right, Doctor."

"Wife number one . . . ah. She was something. Her legs were too long. I married her thinking I'd be lucky to keep her through the honeymoon, and I was right. She met someone at the health club while we were in St. Croix."

"What about wife number two?"

"Who?"

"I see," said Lily. "If you're so rotten why did your current wife marry you?"

"I don't think she herself knows. She's divorcing me for my money."

"Oh. You're getting divorced?"

"For the past two years. Even the divorce is not working out."
Lily laughed.

"My time was up last year," he said. "It's my bonus round. And this is yours. Here are your two questions. The ancient Egyptians asked themselves this to determine what kind of an afterlife they would have."

She couldn't take *one* more question. "*Afterlife?*"

"The first question was, 'Did you bring joy?' And the second question was, 'Did you find joy?'"

Lily stared at him. "You've got to be kidding me."

"I came into philosophy quite late," he said. "Until now my only other hobby was fishing. Transcendental in itself, by the way, but never mind." Getting to his feet he zipped up his track-suit and held his Yankees cap in his hands along with her chart. "Get up off the bed, Lily. You're going home. I don't care how sick you are. Get up and go live your bonus life. Go find some joy. Go bring some joy."

PART III
THE END GAME

And therefore it seems (though rarely) that love can find entrance not only into an open heart, but also into a heart well fortified, if watch be not well kept.

FRANCIS BACON

The effort by which each thing endeavors to persevere in its own being is nothing but the actual essence of the thing itself.

BENJAMIN SPINOZA

40

Lily as an Ancient Egyptian

Joy left. She had found Joy, but now that Joy was no longer needed she packed her few things, took her paycheck, hugged Lily's shrunken body, and left. Lily was alone in her apartment, alone with her little bag from the hospital and her little charcoals. No more chemo on Monday, no more chemo on Tuesday. No more missing days of the week.

No more comedies with Spencer? After Christmas, things have been tense all around. They didn't speak about things that made them tense; much better that way.

It was two in the afternoon. Was she hungry? Was she thirsty? Was she sleepy? Did she need a shower, a movie, a coat? It was January and freezing.

What now?

What now?

What now?

She lay on her bed, but that wasn't satisfying. She went and lay on Amy's bed, but it had turned into Joy's bed. Lily went back to her own bed, opened the windows for some cold air, and looked to see the couple she used to sketch, the couple that got up to coupling with the shades up.

The shades were drawn, the cat was gone.

She went and made herself a cup of tea, the first cup of tea she had made for herself in four months, sat down on the couch, turned on the TV and aimlessly flicked through the daytime channels. There was nothing on except news and low-minded but spirited melodrama.

She got involved in the story of a married woman pregnant with another man's child. Should she tell her husband? Apparently he was usually very understanding—but she didn't know if he'd be understanding about this sort of thing. Before Lily learned how it turned out she fell asleep. On the couch, sitting up, with the empty cup of tea on her lap.

When she awoke it was dark, the TV was still on but low and Spencer was sitting by her. "Spencer?" she whispered. "Joy left."

"I know. She's been hired part time by someone else."

They sat. He had taken the tea cup from her hands, had covered her with a blanket.

"Is your family going to help you, Lil?"

"I don't need them to help me anymore. I'm going to be fine."

"I don't want them to be angry with you on my account. I am completely not worth it."

"I know. I keep telling them."

"Funny, Harlequin. But tell them I've stopped coming around. Tell them it was just because you were sick, but now you're all better, and you're fine on your own."

If that was true, why did she feel herself so utterly and completely dependent on him and on Joy?

He was sitting on the couch, quietly watching John Goodman on an old Saturday Night Live rerun, and she was drifting in and out of sleep.

"Spencer?"

"Yes?" He lowered the TV. "What can I get you?"

"I'm fine, I don't need anything. I just wanted to ask you something. Do you think you've found joy?"

"What?"

Lily told Spencer about DiAngelo the philosopher.

Spencer was quietly contemplating. "Well, look. The answer is a measured yes. I'm in the wrong line of work for joy. Like your Egyptian doctor. He sees too much."

"Like you?"

"Hmm."

"But still?"

"Well, yes. Still. At the baptisms of my godchildren. I'm godfather to six of my thirty nieces and nephews. I used to have a good time at the weddings of my sisters, my brothers." He paused before continuing. "When playing tackle football on the lawn of our house in Farmingville with my older brothers and getting clobbered by them. Playing soccer every Saturday for the Hanover Police League. I guess I feel all right when I'm home for the holidays and my mother fusses and frets and my father and I sit and watch a football game, and the kids are climbing all over me, and there is noise. Happy noise. My apartment is so quiet all the time that sometimes I like a little good noise. I like the summer. I hate winter. I'd like to live somewhere where it's summer all year round. Let's see, when else? I don't entirely hate bachelor parties." He grinned. "And I've been to some, how shall I say, joyous ones. Police bowling tournaments. They're hilarious, too. The guys get trashed and then bowl. You really have to see it to believe it."

Lily was listening.

"Did I answer your question?"

"Hmm."

"What about you?"

But she was falling asleep. When she woke up next, it was morning and he was gone.

It was Thursday, January 6, 2000. It was the first day of the rest of her life. Lily would have to learn how to live again.

All right.

So what now?

What now? That chant became interspersed with I'm not broke, which was a bit of a revelation in the unquiet healing mind, in the quiet unhealed body. I'm not broke, so what now? What now that I'm not broke? I'm alive and not broke, so what now?

I'm alive.

Grandma called and said, "Well, it's Thursday, aren't you coming?"

Lily said maybe she would come next week.

On Tuesday she had to go back to the hospital for blood work. Joy, though now belonging to someone else, came to take her. When Lily protested and said she didn't have to come anymore, Joy said, "I want to come. I do it for you as a friend, like Spencer. You don't have to pay me."

DiAngelo took her blood himself. That's a hands-on doctor, thought Lily. Usually nurses take blood from patients. Where was that Marcie? But Dr. D. is so thorough, so involved.

And then she saw the nice new skirt that Joy was wearing, and the traces of new make-up on her face, and the slight breathlessness in DiAngelo that betrayed his unclogged heart. The blood test came back clean—though waiting for the results was the least pleasant thing Lily had to do in the first week of her new life. And Joy smiled, all flushed, and DiAngelo smiled, but not at Lily, and Marcie came in and gave Lily a hug, while Lily looked incredulously at all three of them.

The nausea persisted and there was no appetite, but there was no more retching so that was something. Her abdomen still hurt.

Tuesdays were the worst days for Lily—she held her breath in her stiff fingers—but the first week, the second week, the tests came back clean, and her platelets and red blood cells were rising and her white cells were remaining healthily low, her neutrophils were small yet growing, and Joy's skirts were getting shorter, and Joy was getting thinner, and DiAngelo stopped wearing his tracksuits, and the blood tests were still clean, and Joy was smiling, and it was still the dead of winter, and cold, yet some spirited melodrama was going on in the middle of Lily's blood-testy January afternoons.

304

Spencer called on Tuesday to ask about the blood work. She asked if he could meet her for lunch.

"Spencer, you will not believe when I tell you this, but I think DiAngelo has a thing for Joy," said Lily. They were having pretend lunch at the Odessa. Spencer was certainly eating. Lily was playing with her soup.

"Stop swirling your spoon, Lil. Eat. I can't sit here all day. I still have to walk you back and then I've got to go to the shooting range."

"Did you hear what I said?"

"Yes."

"Well?"

He raised his eyes to her. "Do me a favor, don't go into detective work. Where have you been? DiAngelo's had it for her since she first came in with you."

"He has?" She said that a bit too loudly. Even the short-order cook came out of the kitchen.

"Shh. Yes."

"Stop!"

"Would I lie to you about something like this?"

"I think you would, yes."

"Since the first day, Lily."

"I can't believe it! I'm usually very good at spotting things like that."

Spencer steadily stared at her, and she became keenly self-conscious until he said, "Lily, I find that very difficult to believe considering how blind you were to things going on in your own apartment."

"Once again this." She struggled up, pulling her hat over her ears. "I'm done not eating. Let's go."

They walked back, slowly. She still had little strength in her legs. He offered her his arm.

"No, I'm fine, I'm fine," she replied quickly—just false bravado. But she was done with his charity.

* * *

She found an old sketch in one of her books that afternoon, decided to re-sketch it and then fill it in watercolor on an eight by eight cold press board, and when he came to see her the following Tuesday after the blood work, he looked at it for a long time, and then said, "Lily, what's this?"

"Oh, do you like it? I did it last week."

She could see he didn't know what to say. "I am very confused by this picture," he said finally. "When did you do it?"

"Last week, I just told you."

It was a picture of Spencer with Mary clinging to his arm, in front of a row of flowers at Dagostino's.

"Remember I ran into you last summer?"

"I remember," he said slowly. "I can see how you might have been able to drum up my likeness, but what I want to know is how did you drum up Mary's? You did only see her for those two seconds, no?"

"Yes, I did only see her for those two seconds," said Lily, smiling. "I re-sketched an old drawing."

"Hmm. Maybe you should do a little more of this re-sketching." He didn't take the picture.

"You don't want it?"

"You know—I'm going to have a fine time explaining it, so no," said Spencer. "Because I hate explaining anything."

41

Shopping as Healing

Whoever said that money did not bring happiness obviously had none. She was feeling a little better, a little stronger, eating a little. For the two weeks that Lily went out every single day and came back with stacks of stuff, it brought her great happiness. She would go out in her new cashmere suit, in her new black wool coat, her cashmere tracksuit, her new boots, a new bag, a new spiffy red hat to cover the fuzz growing out of her head. She bought new earrings and new books, and more DVDs, addicted to comedies. She bought Joy a cashmere coat. She bought Amanda a new car—to drive the girls around in. She bought Anne another month in her apartment. She paid the property taxes on Grandma's Brooklyn brownstone for five years up front. After two weeks of Gucci and Guess? and Prada three-quarter length red rainslickers (the coolest raincoat *ever*), she was done. She bought a digital camera, a digital video recorder, she bought a new stereo and a new kitchen faucet because hers was leaking. She bought an iMac. She bought a new plush down quilt for the bed, new comfy pillows, a throw rug, a vase. Two weeks of shopping and she was done.

And now what?

She called him. "Spencer, can I buy you something?"

"I told you no. Not a thing."

"Come on. Don't be such a stickler for propriety. This isn't about a detective and his witness."

"What is it about then?"

Good question. "When is your birthday?"

"Don't have one."

"How about an Armani suit for your birthday?"

"If you want me to lose my job, go right ahead."

He was so stubborn. "I think I want to move," said Lily with a sigh.

"Good idea. Move where?"

"I don't know. Central Park West? Central Park East? SoHo? Chelsea? Where do you think?"

"Anywhere but that apartment would be good."

Just for fun she decided to go look at some apartments that were available. She asked him to come with her because she didn't want to appear to be the gullible sap she actually was. But though Spencer agreed to come, she didn't hear from him that Saturday, and even when she beeped him, he didn't call her back. She didn't see him Sunday, which was odd. On Tuesday after her blood work when he did call, he said he would go with her the following weekend, but the following weekend came and she couldn't get hold of him again.

"Spencer, where were you?" she asked, almost plaintively. She didn't want to sound upset, he certainly wasn't obligated to come with her, but if he said he would, why didn't he? Was he not as good as his word? Lily hadn't expected that from Spencer.

He didn't answer, and when she pressed him teasingly, he got a funny cold look in his eyes that told her that she was over-stepping her bounds, even kidding around. So she quickly let it go and didn't ask him to come with her again and he didn't offer.

She went with Paul and Rachel, even though Paul said, "Lil, I don't want you to leave your apartment. What happens when Amy comes back and finds you all moved out and gone?"

"This is just for fun, Paulie," she said, squeezing him.

The real-estate woman, Marilyn Alterbrando, asked, "Will you be selling your apartment?" and Lily replied that no, she was only renting at the moment. The realtor's face soured. "Will you be needing a mortgage?"

"No," said Lily, "I'm paying cash."

"The apartments we're seeing today, they're a bit pricey."

"I know."

"Oh."

Okay, that felt good.

They saw a loft in Greenwich Village, a studio on the West Side, a one-bedroom in Hell's Kitchen, a tiny two-room on the Upper East Side, all for a million dollars. "If you have two million, I can show you some really nice places. Maybe you can get a mortgage for the other million."

"Won't need to." Okay, that also felt *very* good.

After two weekends of going around Manhattan, Lily found her dream life: a 5000-square-foot, brand-new floor-through on 64th Street overlooking Central Park, which was going for $9,000,000 without all the options or $11,000,000 with extra crown molding.

"That's a lot of fucking crown molding," said Spencer when he heard.

She liked the apartment so much she arranged for a Sunday morning second viewing and dragged a reluctant but curious Spencer to see it, afterward taking him to the long-promised, long-undelivered brunch at the Plaza. They sat at a little table in Palm Court. She was monochromally red—beret, rainslicker, galoshes. He was monochromally gray—chinos, shirt, tie. His hair was growing out. Her bald head was under cover.

"So what did you think?"

"Lily, why do you want to live on the Upper East Side? You're not an Upper East Side kind of gal."

"That's where you're wrong, Mr. Know-It-All. I want to be that kind of gal." The waiter came and asked if they wanted mimosas—champagne and orange juice. Lily said yes.

Just orange juice and black coffee for Spencer. "You need one bedroom and an art studio. What do you need with five bedrooms, formals and a library?"

"My art needs to go somewhere."

"Your art can fit into your closet. You're not going to be storing your future art, are you? You plan to be selling it, right? Because you can store your non-existent art for a lot less than eleven million bucks."

"I want an elevator that goes right up to my apartment. I want park views. I want crown molding."

"Why do you want five bathrooms? You'll have to clean them all."

"Well, I don't plan to use them all. I'll use just one."

"So what do you need five for?"

"Oh, Spencer! Didn't you like it?"

"You don't need a 5000-square-foot apartment." They were having this conversation with waffles on their plates while waiting for their custom-made omelettes, while the violinist and the pan-flutist played a *pas de deux* of Brahms's Hungarian Dance No. 1.

"I didn't say I needed it. I said I wanted it."

"You don't have eleven million dollars."

That was true. Her money just was not going far enough in New York City. Yet New York was all she knew. That was the conundrum. She remained where she was, but one thing was becoming abundantly clear. She couldn't remain where she was. Amy's ghost was living with her in the apartment. It started to feel crowded. Now that Lily was healthier, the ghost got healthier too.

She started to get the ill feeling she was being watched. She started closing all her windows, drawing her shades, like the couple across the yard. Turned out they weren't drawing the shades, they were no longer together. Two women lived in the apartment now.

Was it crazy, the slight paranoia? Or was it just a rationalization for wanting to move to eleven-million-dollar digs on Fifth?

She asked Spencer if he ever found anything about Milo. When he said he had not, Lily became tightfisted. She sold her second Prada bag on eBay, and her second pair of Stuart Weitzman shoes, and her only Tiffany bracelet. She started renting her DVDs, and buying clips for all the snack bags so they wouldn't go stale. Suddenly life loomed large in front of her again, and it was no point throwing away her money—after all, there might come a day when she would need it.

But though she had sold all her baubles and beads, she still felt she was being watched, almost as if the two had nothing to do with each other.

"Everybody has their own karma. Can I help it that I think mine is to die young?" Amy said to her once. Forgotten words that would have stayed forgotten, if only, if only Amy had not been missing for nine months. For nine months, every single night as Lily turned out the lights in the apartment and walked past Amy's closed door to her own bedroom, the words sounded out with her every step—but only in the darkest hours when she felt ghostly eyes on her. Because during sunlight and during morning, during occasional lunch with Spencer and sketching and shopping, Lily, like Amy's childhood friend Paul, continued to cry over homemade margaritas as they hoped that Amy was safe somewhere.

Alive somewhere.

42

The Financial and Eating Woes of a Lottery Winner and a Cancer Survivor

In early February, after a fifth clean blood test and a celebratory removal of her Hickman catheter, and after realizing she could not afford an eleven-million-dollar change of life, Lily decided to seek the services of a financial consultant.

She was still giving cash to Anne. And Amanda's husband had called, hemming and hawing, to ask for a "small loan" to jump-start his own body shop in Bedford. There was a really nice space becoming available in a really good location, but the banks were proving very difficult, and could she make him a small loan of two-hundred-and-fifty thousand dollars, to change her sister and nieces' lives for the better? Lily gave him the money so that her sister Amanda would love her again, and call her again. The car for the girls just didn't seem to do it.

It worked. She got some sisterly phone calls. It was worth it, but now she had to think about her future. After all, she had a family to support.

She picked a name out of the phone book at random. She figured the lottery came to her at random, she might as well pick at random the man who was going to take care of that money.

The man turned out to be a forty-year-old woman named Katherine, a vice president at Smith Barney. She was intimidating and tall, and had perfect bone structure that didn't come from her bodyfat being eaten away by chemo drugs. She said, looking Lily over carefully, "Please, call me Katie," but did not become less intimidating. She looked at Lily full on and said the sort of right things that a compassionate stranger might say. Not an awkward moment in Katie's office, the walls of which were covered in books but no art.

Katie and Lily established that if she continued to live in her rat-hole of an apartment on 9th Street, with her current food, utility, entertainment and art supply needs, her yearly expenses would come to $50,000, and that included Christmas and birthday shopping, and an occasional backpack or boots but not both. A safe six-percent return on her remaining six million dollars would yield Lily $360,000 a year. "You can get a mortgage on a great apartment," Katie said, drumming on her desk with a pencil, "buy boots and bags, go on vacation, give money to charitable causes to offset the capital gains tax, family gifts are not considered charitable contributions by the way, and still have a hundred thousand a year left over for knick knacks."

Lily chewed her lip. Clearing her throat, she timidly asked, "A mortgage, huh? How much would a mortgage be on, say . . . just for the sake of argument . . . an eleven-million-dollar apartment?"

That made Katie stop drumming on her desk with a pencil.

"About a hundred thousand dollars," she said. "A month. Over a million a year." She raised her eyebrows. "I don't think we're investing for that."

"Perhaps then we should invest a little bit more aggressively," said Lily with an ahem. "Perhaps slightly less safe—but more rewarding?"

After another hour of looking over various mutual fund plans, and Lily wishing only for her charcoal so she could draw this room and this computer and this woman sitting across from her in a suit and talking about money, they had agreed on a fund that would—provided nothing catastrophic happened in the world—yield Lily between fifteen and twenty-six percent a year

313

in income. That was some serious cash, some meaningful return on investment. Since she would need only fifty grand of that to live on, she could reinvest her dividends annually, and her capital would double every three to four years. In other words, at the five-year cancer survival benchmark, Lily, if she lived frugally—and lived—could buy the eleven-million-dollar apartment for cash and still have money left over for food.

Now that was a plan she liked. She signed the papers, filled out the forms, got new check cards, new checkbooks. By the time she got out of there, having left all of her money behind with Katie, she thought she would have paid double not to have been in one stuffy office for the whole afternoon. Is this what working is like, she thought? Is this what I'm going to have to do when I take my college course and finally get a degree and have to look through *The New York Times* employment section every Sunday looking for a job just like this one?

That thought was enough to send Lily for the next three days into a tizzy, spending practically her entire annual allowance on art supplies. She asked Spencer to help her clear Amy's room of all of Amy's things, putting them into a small storage facility for a few bucks a month. Spencer was glad to help. She bought three rolls of canvas, wood planks, a staple gun, turpentine, gesso canvas primer, four easels, paintbrushes, and paints! She bought oil paints, and oil pastel crayons, watercolors and acrylics, and color pencils and color markers, and charcoal and black pencils that were so beautiful, she immediately sat down on her bed and from memory on a 12-by-16 sheet drew Katie the stockbroker in black pencil sitting behind her desk with books all around her, and her window open, and spring trees far down below and the Hudson river far down below too, and Katie in her sharp suit behind her desk, looking out at her next client while at her fingertips lay *The World According to Garp* and the *67-Pound Marriage* and *Hotel New Hampshire*. In two days when Lily went back to see Katie, she brought the picture, in full color. Katie looked at it for a long time, and then asked how much Lily wanted for it.

Lily was surprised. "Nothing. Why would I want your money? I give *you* money, not vice versa. How much have I made, by the way, in two days?"

"Twenty-one cents," said Katie, but before Lily left, she added, looking at the portrait of herself, "I wouldn't worry about that floor-through on Fifth, Lilianne. I've got a feeling it will come sooner than you think." Lily wasn't quite sure what Katie had meant by that, but the next day Katie called asking her if she would, "for money only", paint The Children. Lily agreed, and painted in acrylic the two small Katies, one male, one female, sitting together close and wistful in a park in Brooklyn, with an orange ball between them that looked like a pumpkin.

Katie gave her a $500 check that Lily took and had framed on her wall, as the first ever money she made from her art.

She spent the week sketching new things in her book—refrigerators, lamps, trees outside, cats across the way on windowsills, sleeping women on beds through windows. Then she rendered them in her new art studio, Amy's bedroom, with the great southern exposure and wide plank wood floors on which paint splattered. She watercolored some, she colored-penciled others. She used acrylic paints, which dried in hours, and she even did two small oils on canvas that took all of Thursday and Friday, one of a cat sitting watching the trees while his mistress slept on a bed behind him, and one of Spencer draped over a couch watching TV with a sulky look on his face.

"I don't look like that," he said sulkily.

She laughed. "No?"

"What is that *smell*?"

"Turpentine!" she said. "I need it for the oils. Is it terrible?"

"It's not an alluring smell, no."

"Well, I'm not in the alluring business," she declared to him happily. "I'm in the painting business." Besides her sense of smell had not fully returned. She painted with the windows open. "I'm selling it on 8th Street on Saturday morning."

He walked around the studio, inspecting her work. "Well, what do you think?" she asked.

"I don't think you'll be able to give me away for free," he replied.

On Saturday morning, Lily took a cab with her twenty pieces of artwork, a folding table and a folding chair, to 8th Street, the art thoroughfare in Greenwich Village, and with three tiered standing easels and the table, set up her twenty pieces of artwork by nine.

By noon Lily had come back home. At one on Saturday Spencer came to her door. She was very surprised to see him. "What happened?" he said. "I went to 8th to find you and you'd disappeared. That's not much staying power."

"Hmm."

"Why did you leave? You have to have patience. It's like fishing. They'll bite eventually. The weather has to be right."

"Hmm. The weather must have been real good, because I sold everything."

"You what?"

She jumped up. "Yup! I sold everything. Every last painting. Including you, Mr. Grumpy. For the last two, there was nearly a dust-up. I had four customers in an auction type situation. It was pretty heated. Eventually the two paintings went for a hundred bucks each."

"A hundred bucks? Whew!"

She looked at him askance. "Are you being sarcastic?"

"*Frames* cost more than that! Why don't you just give your art away? How much did you make altogether?"

"Enough to buy you lunch. Let's go."

"I can buy my own sandwich. How much?"

"A thousand bucks."

Spencer whistled. "Well, that's nearly a living."

"Yes. I'm trying to save up eleven million dollars."

And Spencer laughed with all his white teeth and blue eyes, and Lily laughed, and on a cold February Saturday, they sat for three hours in Odessa. And then he said, "*Scream 3* is playing at Union Square."

Lily spent half the movie buried in her knees. She hated horror movies, and she didn't know what Spencer found more enjoyable, the movie, which was so-so, or her being scrunched up, eyes closed, too scared to look at the screen. They got separate popcorns and separate drinks.

But when she painted next week, she painted one medium bag of yellow popcorn and one of his hands and one of hers in it together.

She painted popcorn hands, and smiles, and tufts of hair; she painted black-rimmed eyes, and tears, and cats. She painted empty beds, and wet showers, and Tompkins Square Park, all its bare trees and benches, its stone fountains and iron fences. She painted Spencer's hands in the shape of a teepee. She couldn't wait for spring when she could spend more time outside. She spent all day every day in Amy's room where she was not just outside, but everywhere at once—in stores and parks and galleries and on the water. All in one room. And on Saturday mornings she set up her table and easels on 8th Street, and no matter how much or what she drew, she went home with nothing but a wad of cash.

Her appetite came back—slowly. Eighty pounds, then eighty-two, then a big jump—eighty-six. Must have been all those Double Chocolate Milanos. When she told Grandma this, the next day a case of Milanos came from the supermarket. In two weeks the case was gone and Lily was ninety pounds. Jelly donuts from Dunkin' Donuts. Vanilla shakes. Protein shakes, morning, noon and night. Then solid food other than cookies and heavenly eclairs from Veniero's—the best bakery on the planet. She spent breakfast and dinner at the Odessa and at Veselka, the Ukrainian restaurant on Second Avenue near Spencer's precinct. Omelettes, corned-beef hash, bacon, sausage, home fries, stuffed cabbage, pierogi. On Thursdays when she visited her grandmother, she baked brownies in her kitchen.

317

"That *man* is not coming around any more, is he, Lily? Because you're all better now, and your brother is moving on."

"I don't want to talk about it, Grandma."

"Lily."

"Grandma."

If my brother is moving on, she wanted to say, then how come he hasn't called me? And how come I can't call him? And where is Amy?

A hundred and two pounds. She looked almost just frightfully underweight, not Dachau-outbound. The blood work was still clean. The hair, little by little, was growing back. Painfully slow and blotchy. It grew in ugly clumpy tufts, making her so self-conscious that she kept asking Spencer to cut it, to even it out. She continued to ask him, and didn't let Paul do it, because Spencer held her head with his left hand to steady her, as he sheared her with his right. It was the only time he ever touched her.

Rachel told Lily that as soon as she grew her hair she had a guy for her that would knock her panties off. That's what Rachel said. "Would knock your panties off."

"And this is something I want?" Lily felt that the chemo didn't just remove the cancer from her, it removed the sex organs from her also.

"Just grow your hair, will you?"

43

A Little Thing about Spencer

Sometimes he was completely withdrawn into himself. When she was sick, she had barely noticed. She just wanted a human being to sit by her side. But since she had finished treatment, she noticed it.

He was better during the week, she couldn't figure it out. He was much less moody during the week than he was on Sundays. She decided to press PAUSE on *Roxanne*.

"Why are you so quiet? It's funny, no?"

"It is."

She raised her eyebrows.

"What? It's funny. I'm laughing on the inside."

"Yes, but why on the inside?"

"Just am, that's all."

"But you're not just quiet, you're . . . morose."

"Hmm."

"What's wrong?"

"Nothing."

"Do you want to talk about it?"

"No."

"So there is something to talk about then?"

Slowly he turned his head in her direction. She became flustered when confronted with his detective stare. "Lily-ANNE," he said, "don't use my methods of interrogation on me. They won't work."

She faltered for a moment, then regained her speech. "Spencer, I can't help noticing that sometimes you're just not yourself."

"Wrong, Lily. This is myself. It's the other me that's not me. This is the actual me. Sullen, quiet. Morose."

"When I was sick, I didn't see it."

"You were sick. You hardly saw anything." He wasn't looking at her, he was looking at his stemmed and knuckled hands.

"I don't believe this is really you."

"Believe it."

"I don't. I think this is you being upset about something."

"I'm not in the least upset."

"Is it trouble at work?"

Spencer smiled. "No, it's not trouble at work." He turned to her. "Look, I appreciate it, you taking an interest. But please— don't worry about me. Let's just watch our movie."

But Lily wasn't going to give up. He wasn't angry yet, she had a little rope. Light cajoling wasn't working. She was going to try self-pity. "You don't have to be here, Spencer, you know, if you don't want to. I'm fine now. It's not like before. I'm okay to be alone, I can take care of things, take care of myself. You don't have to come if you don't want to."

Spencer rubbed his face. "What's this about? Did I just mention your brother and not realize it?"

"No, no, really. You don't have to pretend. If you want to be somewhere else, you don't have to sit here with me. I mean, what's the point, really."

"We like our comedies."

"When we laugh, yes!"

"Lily, you spent four months watching comedies and not laughing. You'll understand, I know you will, if I don't laugh for just one Sunday."

"It's not that. It's . . ." But she didn't know what it was. "What's

320

bothering you? Come on, tell me. You helped me so much, please tell me."

"Nothing to tell."

"Do you want to be alone?"

"That's the last thing I want."

When in the world did it happen? She told herself that it was inevitable that after days and weeks and months of him calling her, sitting with her alone, shopping with her and for her, eating with her, it was inevitable; there would be something seriously wrong with her, in fact, if she didn't start to feel a slight anticipation ahead of hearing his voice or seeing his face, he was like a habit now, a good friend, like Paul. And she cared so much for Paul, how could she not care at least as much for Spencer, who spent all that time with her when she was sick? It's gratitude, that's what it was.

Except . . . she didn't feel a quickening somewhere in her cancer-addled capillaries when Paul called or didn't call, and she didn't slightly hold her breath so she could hear Paul better, and she didn't study Paul's face for new feelings, and she never tried to make Paul laugh and feel dissipated when he didn't.

Oh my God, she thought. What's happening to me? I'm barely a survivor yet. My Hickman chest scar hasn't healed yet. I barely have tufts of hair on my head. It's the chemicals. VePesid has affected my brain. I've gone partially deaf in one ear, fuzzy in one eye, and I can't smell anything. The shapes of the mystery that form in my head are the product of drugs, the shapes that form these completely inappropriate unrequited idiotic sensations of Spencer are just a product of the kindness that he has shown me, of the care that he has given me, and of fear that when I'm truly better, he will leave and not come back.

I'm sick in the head. Maybe I need that cancer survivor group after all. Where is Joy? Where is Marcie? Where is Dr. D?

She wanted to call Spencer, so he could set her straight. What's

321

happening to me, she wanted to ask him, and have him look at her calmly like always and say, "Lily-Anne, I have no earthly idea what you're going on about."

But she knew there was something terribly wrong with her when she could no longer bring herself to call his beeper just to say hello, just to ask if he was going to be in the neighborhood to have lunch, or what movie he wanted her to rent. She realized there was something terribly wrong when she wanted to go see *The Whole Nine Yards* at Union Square, and could not call and casually ask Spencer to go with her.

She called Rachel instead. Rachel Ortiz, the advisor to the habit-forming.

When Paul and Rachel came over, they got drunk on margaritas in Lily's apartment, and listened to Tori Amos, or Enya, or something else equally lugubrious and bleak, and kept crying to *her*, instead of the other way around. Paul just broke up with Ray, and Rachel was having a hard time with TO-nee. Oh, they kept saying, licking the words around their salt-rimmed lime-filled glasses, we want love, we want love, we want love. Love!

"Not me," Lily said. "I don't need love. I have Spencer."

And Rachel laughed, and Paul laughed, and they punched her on the arm and made more margaritas and told her she was so funny, and that her apartment smelled awfully of turpentine and gesso, and she didn't want to talk about it with them anymore, but she didn't see what was so funny, what was so worthy of laughter.

Spencer was impenetrable. There was not a single thing he did or said that could be interpreted in any way other than the proper, courteous, appropriate Spencer way, which was—I am here, to talk, to watch a movie, to eat. If you want to walk, let's go. If you want soup, I'll get it for you. Central Park? Sure. Palm Court, absolutely. You want me to move beds out of rooms, or help you stretch your canvas, I'll do that too. You want me to call you after your blood work? Sit on the couch with you on Sundays? Here I am. She studied him with her artist's eye so intensely, trying to decipher other meanings, other expressions, other thoughts, that one time, she must not have been paying attention to what he was saying, because he put his finger under her chin.

"What in the world are you thinking?" he said.

She came out of it. "What?"

"You're not even answering my question."

"What am I thinking?"

"You're stalling for time."

"No, no. Oh, nothing, nothing at all."

"Ah, now you're evasive." He grinned. "Must have been something pretty bad, Lil. Was it about Keanu?"

This is what she meant—in his G-rated world, she was a cancer patient. Somebody's sibling. A witness in an investigation. She could be a man calling him about a horse.

Not one-hundred-percent impenetrable. Maybe a *little* penetrable. One Sunday evening, they had just finished watching *A Fish Called Wanda*, and Spencer got up to get a drink while she stretched and remained on her stomach on the couch. He stood in the archway between the kitchen and the living room, a Coke in his hand. She caught his face in the reflection in the fifty-inch plasma TV, when he didn't think she was looking at him. He was looking at her, but not just at her, but particularly at her hips as she lay on her stomach, in her black leggings, legs slightly apart, splayed head-down on the couch. Her heart hammered in her chest, as she lay there longer than necessary, trying to see the contours of his expression, and then he said, "Did you want something before I go?"

She sat up. "No, no. I'm fine."

Was she mistaken? Was it too vague for the dark reflection of the intention of his gaze at midnight on Sunday?

The following Sunday he came to watch *It Happened One Night*.

Lily was in her studio. He knocked on Amy's door.

"Hey," she said. "Come on in. I'm just finishing up." She was painting the ice rain on the windowsill. She was wearing her low-rise black leggings, and a cropped yellow tank top. Her stomach was exposed. She had on no bra.

He came in. "What's going on around here? It's *freezing*."

"I have to keep the windows open. It's that turpentine," she said innocently, taking a drink from a can of Coke. "Would you like a sip?"

"Of turpentine?"

Ha. Lily was very cold indeed in her little tank top. She might not have had big breasts, but she knew her nipples were plenty big.

Spencer noticed.

She knew he noticed because as he took the can of Coke from her hands that were near her breasts, he didn't say anything, he just raised his eyes to hers, and that's when she knew, and her breath stopped in her chest when she saw his eyes. Carefully he said, "You might want to close the windows. It's quite cold in here."

She went to close the windows, trying to suppress her ear to ear delight. After putting on a cardigan, she settled into her side of the couch, like always, and he into his, but watching a simple movie was less simple and was somehow greatly improved by its newly acquired lack of simplicity. Something about him looking at her breasts hit her right in the stomach with its delicious pleasure. He had always put up such a stoic, sexless front. But this Spencer might just be a man!

She knew what it was. She knew exactly what it was. It was the new weight. It was the Milanos and Krispy Kremes, where they had settled between her skin and her bones, in her shoulders, on her chest, it was vanilla ice cream on her breasts, Chunky Monkey ice cream on her thighs, on her hips, all round, all around.

Soo Min, Hannah, Dana were right. Perhaps even Spencer

324

was not immune to creme custard sways of hips, roundness of buttocks, softness of thighs, stretched-out calves, eager nipples pushing out through thin cotton, bring it on, baby, bring it on, where is the cheesecake, where's the butter and the marmalade? Maybe when I get enormous he won't be able to keep not just his eyes off me. And so she ate and ate voraciously, and when she went shopping she didn't just buy fleece sweatshirts from the Gap like before, but velour H. Starlet snug sexy sweats from Bloomingdales for $120, that were sooo low rise with silk stitching—kind of like how she would describe herself. When she put them on, the top triangle of her black thong showed, the very tops of her newly returned round buttocks showed. Yes, she shopped thoroughly at Victoria's Secret, at LaPerla, at Sak's lingerie department. She needed a new apartment for all the g-strings, all the lacy, see-through bras she was buying.

She put mousse in her hair to spike it up, and balm and gloss on her lips, and lots of it, as if she were a thirteen-year-old at a roller skating rink, hoping to catch the eye of the sixteen-year-old, standing in the corner with his teenage buddies. She put lotion on her body, to make it softer, to make it smell nice so when he sat on the couch he could smell her. She found a pair of jeans to die for in Bergdoff's. When Spencer schlepped in one Thursday at eight, changed from work into his Levi's and his Yankees baseball jersey and his Yankees cap, and saw her with her new high-heeled boots and her new jeans, with her reddest lips, her blackest mascara, and newly gelled clumpy hair, he stood looking at her as if he were in the wrong apartment. "Where are we going?" he said after a moment.

"Odessa," she said, flustered.

"Oh, okay. I thought for a sec I'd forgotten something. Are you going clubbing after I leave here, Lil?" he said, smiling. "Did that good old Rachel finally fix you up?"

Her low-slung spirits just slung lower, Lily mumbled something incoherent in return, and dinner was a silent affair, after which he dropped her back home and without a note in his voice said cheerfully, "Have a really good time tonight. You deserve to have some fun."

Just great, just friggin' great.

44

The Muse

She started, ever so slowly, to get a following. The same people came every Saturday to see if she had anything new. She started to think about her week—Sundays, she was in the studio, painting before Spencer came. Mondays and Wednesdays she traveled the breadth of Manhattan, sketching possible subjects and objects into her book. Tuesdays after the hospital, she had lunch with Spencer, and then painted at home. Thursdays she sketched Brooklyn, because she was with grandma. Fridays and Saturdays, she rendered the sketches into acrylics or watercolors, or oil pastels. Very rarely did she do an oil on canvas, though she loved them best. They just took most of the day, and never dried, but they did always go first, giving her the idea that she simply wasn't charging enough for them—but here was the thing, no matter how much she charged, they always went, and they went first.

Would she consider painting live nudes on oil on canvas? Would she consider painting the Serengeti plain for a baby's nursery? What about a woman naked and very pregnant? A wife and a husband making love on their tenth wedding anniversary?

On oil on canvas from memory she painted his face. From memory his whole person. His hands first, knotty and tense, she noticed them right after the eyes for expression and the lips for movement. He was standing next to his desk and the phone was to his ear. He was looking right at Lily, not smiling. He was not a smiler. He had strong white teeth. He had a great smile. He just didn't smile much.

He was standing wearing gray slacks, a black belt, a white shirt open at the collar, a thin black tie loosely on. His clothes were loose too, he was slim; Spencer, who looked as if he ran twice around the cursed reservoir three times a week. She painted him with compact deltoids under his white shirt, and biceps and pecs. He was all in shades of black and white except for his lips and eyes, for which she procured blues and reds, and gave dye to his eyes and mouth. The artist in her appreciated the esthetics of both—his mouth was from an artist's perspective a perfect human mouth, a sharp line of the plump seagull on top, sitting on a plump bowl at the bottom, a Cupid mouth like a wrapped gift from God. With slight shame she realized how well she knew his mouth, how etched it was in the place in her heart from which she painted. His eyes deep-set, open wide, day blue, but relentless, a bloodhound's eyes, framed by his thin black rimmed glasses. She gave him thick wavy hair, because his long hair meant no sickness in her. She gave his face stubble and cheekbones and a set square jaw and an exposed, large forehead. She was embarrassed at the care she took in painting him.

"This is not me," he said to her when he saw it. "I've never looked this good. Where are the bloodshot eyes, the bags under them, the pale face, the coffee stains on the tie – and my shirt is pressed, come on! This is definitely art, not life."

"Who is going to want to buy you if I draw you the way you are?" she said jokingly. "I'm trying to make a living here."

On the street on Saturday, she refused to sell it, even though she was offered a thousand dollars for it(!).

Spencer came by, looked at the picture of himself standing inclined on an easel. "I told you no one wants to buy me."

"That's because you're not for sale," she replied.

Just then another woman walked by looking at her paintings.

"How much is that doggie in the window?" she asked, pointing at Spencer.

"Sorry, display only, not for sale."

The woman shrugged at Spencer, then did a double take, first at the painting, then back at him. Spencer shrugged himself. "Picture's better, right?"

"She is obviously very talented," said the woman, walking away.

"Nice," said Spencer, turning back to Lily.

It doesn't do you justice, Lily wanted to say, busying herself with counting her money.

45

A Master's Course in Chemo

Mid-March, another Tuesday, another blood test.

She usually waited about an hour. This time it was closer to two. When DiAngelo came back he said nothing at first. He was quiet, and Joy, though all gussied up, was quiet, and she wasn't smiling, and he wasn't looking at her. "Did I ever mention Alkeran to you?" he asked.

"No, what is that?"

"Just a little pill. You take it three times a week. Important not to skip."

"What's it for?"

"Just to keep you all nice and clean inside."

Lily said in a low voice, "What are you talking about?"

"Nothing. Remember I told you this is a process? Well, some-times the process takes one tiny step back. We've taken gigan-tic leaps forward. But your white blood cells are increasing again . . ."

She shook her head.

"And your reds are not producing as well as I've been hoping. You're still on the low end for the counts on those. So a little maintenance therapy . . ."

She kept shaking her head.

"Don't worry, this is why we check you every week."

"That's impossible!"

"I know, I'm sorry. But Alkeran is easy and very effective, you can take it by mouth with a little prednisone, it's only for a few weeks, and I think it'll fix you right up."

"Please. It's impossible."

"Compared to what you've been through, it's nothing."

"Please, no. No, no, no."

"Lily."

She couldn't take it.

DiAngelo and Joy sat around her bed, saying nothing.

Alkeran would make her nauseated again, and it had an unfortunate side effect of destroying the very bone marrow it was trying to save. It would reduce her ability to withstand infection—she'd be the girl in the plastic bubble tent again, afraid of a Kleenex in someone else's hands. A white thin soft tissue scarier than *Scream 3*. No more public places, no more movie theatres, lunches, parades. Possibly no more art sales on Saturday mornings.

Maintenance therapy! Maintenance therapy, as if she's an old car in need of an oil change, a tune-up, possibly new belts and hoses all around.

She stayed in the hospital through the morning for another aspiration biopsy, for a quick red cell transfusion. The biopsy showed that the marrow was once again producing blastocytes. Her sister Anne showed up, in an Armani suit paid for by the lottery money, and threw up her wool-jacketed arms. "I told you," she hissed to the doctor out in the hall when she was outside of Lily's hearing, or when she thought she was outside of Lily's hearing, because Lily could hear. "I told you this three months ago. How long are you going to torture her? You gave her false hope, you kept her artificially healthy, and now look. Have you any idea how excited she was, thinking it was never going to come back?"

"I know she's disappointed, but this is very normal, this is nothing to worry about yet."

"Maybe not for you."

"Mrs. Ramen, she's got cancer. This is what cancer does. So we treat it again. And again if we have to. She's entering a small relapse, we want to stop it, she understands that."

"She's only pretending to understand that! I don't understand it."

"Anne!"

Anne continued talking.

"Anne!" Lily called again. She walked out into the hall, dragging her IV stand with her. "Anne, can I see you at my bed, please?"

And inside the hospital room she said, "Stop it, this isn't helping."

"He told us it would be all gone!"

"And it was all gone. All except one little cell that the January biopsy couldn't detect. And that one little cell is now two million. We have to do what we have to do."

"Oh my God, oh my God." Anne grabbed her hair as if it were she who was about to have more chemo. "When is this going to end? When is this going to be over? How long are you going to have to suffer like this?"

Lily turned away. Her guess was, until the end.

After she was dressed and released, she said no to being accompanied home, and slowly walked down Fifth Avenue by herself, pulling closed her red Prada rainslicker, and pulling her beret tighter over her head. She opened her huge red umbrella. It was raining.

She came inside the nearly empty St. Patrick's Cathedral on 51st and Fifth and sat in the front pew, took off her beret for respect, and cried because she thought the burning incense made her cry, and a priest in robes came by and sat next to her. It must have been her tears and her clumpy thin hair that drew him to her, he must have seen the things she could not express except through painting. "Are you a Catholic?" he asked.

"I'm a New York Catholic," replied Lily. When he raised his eyebrows in a question, she said, "Means I haven't been to church since my confirmation."

"Ah, yes. Most of the people who come to me are just like you."

"So they do come, eventually?"

"They do. Looking for answers."

He was an older priest, very kind, and gray, and soothing. "I saw you crying. And I wanted to tell you that in some of our churches during mass, the babies would cry, cry so loud that we couldn't go on with the service, and so we would have a room for them where their mothers could take them, and they would spend mass there. It was called the crying room."

And Lily said, "I wish I had a mother who could take me to the crying room." For a few moments she said nothing else.

At last she spoke. "Trouble is, I think my mother went in there once herself and never left."

"Many people who come to me are similarly afflicted," said the priest. "The Bishop of Rome also goes into the crying room. Did you know that? Right before he puts on his papal robes. The mightiest, the mystics, they all go in."

Lily listened, nodded, tried to understand.

"My advice is, whatever you can do to give yourself comfort, do. Whatever you can do—Isn't there anything that brings you joy?"

Oh, God, why was she always eking out a long hour of comfort when what she desperately needed was an eternal moment of extreme distress? Well, she had her distress now, didn't she? She glanced at him through the veil of her own emotions. Saw something familiar around his eyes, something Claudia Vail carried, a knowing weariness. "Do you know my grandmother?"

He smiled. "She is from the war generation then? Where we've seen things we can't forget and these things enable us to find comfort in the smallest things?"

"Well, if only the rest of us could've been starved and tortured. We'd all be better off," said Lily without rancor.

"What's your name?"

333

"Lily."

"What a wonderful name. Lily, you're upset about the things you don't have? What about all the things you do have? What about all the things you don't have that you don't want?"

"I don't know about any of that. I have too many things that I don't want. I have cancer."

"I'm sorry."

"My best friend has disappeared without a trace. I don't want that either. No one can find her, no one knows where she is."

"How awful for her parents."

"Yes. But explain to me my mother. She's suffered greatly, yet can't find comfort anywhere."

"Ah, no. Your mother must find comfort in her suffering."

Lily struggled up. "I think she must. So where's this crying room, Father? Take me there."

He made the sign of the cross on her. "You carry it with you wherever you go, my child. That's the mark of the afflicted. We all go inside. The question is, do we leave there? Do we remain there? Who do we drag in there with us?"

She came home and didn't go into her studio, didn't go into her bedroom. She took off her shoes, and went into the kitchen to get a drink, and was weighed down, pulled down by the anchors of her life, and suddenly she found herself on the floor, against the wall. She couldn't get up.

The phone rang. Lily picked it up without looking at the caller ID. She must have thought it was Spencer.

But it was Jan McFadden calling to invite her and Paul and Rachel to an eighth birthday party for her two children. "With Amy not here, I think it'll be better for all of us to see you kids. Will you promise you'll come?"

Lily wanted to tell her about herself, but Mrs. McFadden sounded like she herself was down on the tiles of her kitchen floor. "We'll be there," Lily said. "Of course we will."

She heard the knock, and then the key in the door. She heard his voice. "Lil?" He dropped the keys on the table, looked for her in the studio, came into the kitchen. She was on the floor and didn't look up. He stood silently in the archway, and then came in, and sat on the floor by her side. "Hey," he said.

"You must've heard," she said dully.

"Yes, when I didn't hear from you the whole day, I called DiAngelo. But what are you so glum about? So you take a little pill. I take twenty Advil a day, do you see me on the floor?"

She turned to him, her face wet.

"Come on," he said, jumping up and putting his hands under her arms to lift her. "I'll take you to Odessa, sparing no expense, and then *Wonder Boys* with Michael Douglas is playing at Union Square."

He helped her down the stairs. He was wearing his suit, a dark raincoat. He opened the large red umbrella for her, he held it over their heads. He gave her his arm, and this time she took hold of him as they walked to Odessa in the March rain. She told him about the priest and the crying room. Pensively he rubbed his chin, saying nothing but seeming to agree. At the movies he bought them just one popcorn, but ate most of it himself while her hands remained on her sad lap.

Walking back home, Spencer, who knew quite a bit about music from before her time, sang the Bob Dylan song from the movie, "Things Have Changed." "*I've been trying/to get away as far from myself as I can . . .*" he sang.

She had dozens of requests for paintings of children, nurseries, dogs, cats, some fish and an anaconda. Lily turned most of them down. How to tell them all that she was taking Alkeran every other day now, and any day Dr. D. was going to tell her she needed to go back into the hospital for an infusion of VePesid. She made self-portraits, of herself sick, losing her hair, bald, with a Hickman in her chest, and then just the scar, and then just eyes on a page with black anguish around them. Spencer took that one. And gave her some advice. He said she was under-charging for her work, which was why she was drowning in requests. The next Saturday she started charging more and the requests died down a bit.

46

The Mighty Quinn

Lily, Paul, and Rachel took the train to Port Jefferson at the end of March to go to Amy's siblings' birthday party. Lily, who had stopped eating like she used to, and whose hair had stopped growing out at the same uneven but flagrant rate, was holding up. Her good blood was being killed by the Alkeran, but her bad blood was being killed by it too—so somehow it was all working out. The party was on a Saturday. When she saw Spencer two days earlier, she didn't tell him she was going. She didn't know why she didn't tell him. Perhaps it was because she was entertaining thoughts of calling her brother's house, which was just a few miles away from Amy's. Maybe it was because she hadn't seen the detective in his blue eyes for a while and didn't want to.

She found Mrs. McFadden to be in a particularly ill humor despite the fact that it was her young children's birthday party. The house was decorated, there were balloons floating about the living room, and the Carvel Cake was on the counter defrosting. The candles were on the kitchen table, the presents were wrapped, there was a Disney tablecloth on in the dining room and the potato chips were out. On the surface everything looked like it would in any other house where young children, a twin boy and girl, were turning eight and the grownups were throwing them a party.

Yet in this house, the father of the children was sitting in front of the TV, barely glancing up when they walked in, and the mother was in the kitchen. When Lily, Rachel and Paul walked through, she put a drink down on the counter. Her face had no make-up on and she looked as if she was still wearing a house-coat.

They said their hellos, Jan even remembered to ask them if they wanted something to drink. They held glasses of Coke in their hands and stood awkwardly. Paul hated awkward situations, and so immediately started talking about the kids, the yapping dogs, the hair salon where he and Rachel worked, anything rather than just stand there.

"How are you, Lil?" said Jan McFadden. "You're looking . . . much better. I haven't seen you in so long. I'm sorry I haven't been to visit."

"You've had a lot on your mind, Mrs. McFadden."

"Yes, yes. But you're holding up?"

Lily nodded. "I'm holding up."

"She's still doing chemo, Mrs. McFadden," said Rachel. "She was doing a lot better a few weeks ago."

"Yes, Paul said you're still struggling."

"A little bit," said Lily. "But spring is here, I'm optimistic."

Jan turned her face to the sink, as she ran the cold water to make fruit punch.

"At least you're living, Lily. My Amy, she had not lived."

But she had, Lily wanted to interject. Amy *had* lived. Amy lived big, and danced every weekend, Amy wrote essays and painted though she could not paint and sang though she could not sing. Amy colored her hair a different color every two months, courtesy of Paul. Amy went to a number of upscale, ritzy restaurants, and wore upscale ritzy clothes.

Amy skied and rollerbladed, and sat in the passenger seat of a single-engine plane over the Long Island Sound. Amy water-skied and jet-skied, and ran the New York Marathon and played tennis. Amy studied hard, and partied harder. She drank, she smoked pot. Once she did stand-up comedy.

Amy loved. Amy loved when she was in high school and when she was older.

And more important, Amy was loved back. Amy, throwing her hair about in Central Park, adjusting her sneakers while she was trying to steal second base in a Sunday game of softball; Amy, running three times around the reservoir in full makeup and brightest lipstick, was loved. She was loved! She had lived.

Lily didn't say anything to Mrs. McFadden's back.

Paul, who didn't like this kind of moroseness on a day of celebration, pulled Lily's hair, slapped her behind, and said, "Let's not talk about Amy today, this is supposed to be a happy day. And our Lily here has no choice but to come out of this whole mess flying, whole, and perfect, and do you know why?"

"Paul, stop it," Lily said, trying not to laugh.

"I know why," said Rachel, tickling her ribs. "Because she's the mighty Quinn."

"That's right," Paul said, starting to sing *"And you ain't seen nothin'/ like the Mighty Quinn!"*

Jan McFadden turned from the sink, crying. "Amy used to sing that song," she said, a wooden mixing spoon in her hands.

"We *know*," said Paul, rolling his eyes. "I'm singing it now."

"I remember it as if she's standing in this kitchen right now— even though it was the kids' birthday three years ago. She'd been away for months and came just for their birthday. She's standing here with cherry blossoms in her hair, singing that Mighty Quinn song . . ." She sobbed and put her head in her hands. "I can't do this," she said. "I can't do any of it, I can't do my life. I can't get up every morning."

The ice cream cake melted into the counter. The twins were in the living room with the TV with dad, blowing party favor blowers, smacking each other with paddle balls, flying wooden planes, popping balloons, yelling. The TV was on—loud. Jan

339

McFadden was crying. Rachel was sitting down, looking down into her hands. Paul was standing next to Jan. And Lily was sinking into the round table, looking dumbly at Jan, opening her mouth, trying to say, *Mrs. McFadden, what are you talking about? Amy didn't know me three years ago.*

But nothing came out of her mouth when she tried.

Her distress was obvious though, even to Paul from across the kitchen. Rachel said, "What's the matter, mama, you not feeling good? Sit."

"Lil, what's up?"

Amy didn't know me in the spring three years ago. We met in our fall art class, two and a half years ago. I know that for a fact.

"Lil?"

She said the only thing she could say. "You have cherry blossoms here?"

"No, no. Amy had brought them from DC that weekend."

Two years ago, they had gone down to DC at the end of March to visit her brother, and Amy and Lily both put the cherry blossoms in their hair while strolling around the Tidal Basin of the Jefferson Memorial. They had walked the length of the long Mall to the Capitol Building. By the time they saw Andrew they were flushed and panting. How happy he was to see them.

Oh my God.

"Maybe you mean two years ago," Lily said, holding on to the Formica table. "Two years ago, right? A year before she disappeared?"

Jan McFadden was crying. "The twins had turned five. That's why she came. It was a big deal. She came from DC with blossoms in her hair for their fifth birthday. She didn't come two years ago. She didn't come last year. It was the last time she was here for their birthday."

Now Lily sat down. Fell down in the chair.

"What's wrong, Lil?" said Paul.

"What's wrong, Lil?" said Rachel.

Nothing was making any sense. How did Lily continue to sit, to say nothing, pretend to stretch her mouth into a pasty smile. Thank goodness for Cancer. She blamed it for the whiteness of her face, the numbness of her mouth and the loss of her speech.

Jim came in, Jan's husband. He took one look at his wife, one look at Rachel, Paul, and Lily, and gritting his teeth and gripping the kitchen counter, said, "Your *other* children are waiting for you in the other room to throw them a fucking birthday party. Now are you going to do this, or are you just going to stand here like you do every other fucking day of your life?"

For the next two hours, there was some running around, some singing, some musical chairs, pin the tail on the donkey, some cake. Lily barely spoke at all, but right before they left, she asked Mrs. McFadden if she could make a local call, and went upstairs into the master.

Lily called Andrew.

Miera picked up the phone.

"Hi, it's Lily," she said. "Can I talk to Andrew?"

"He doesn't want to speak to you," Miera said and hung up.

Shaking, Lily called again. "Miera, please don't hang up," she said. "Please. I just want to say hello to him."

"He doesn't want to say hello to you. He doesn't want to speak to you."

"Why?"

"Oh, stop it. Just stop it. Look, you can keep calling back all you want, but I'm not putting him on the phone."

"I'm in Port Jeff," Lily said, her voice unsteady. "I wanted to see if I could come visit for five minutes."

Miera laughed. "Are you kidding me? You're not coming into this house, Lil. Not after everything."

The other line was picked up. No one was speaking on it.

"Andrew?" said Lily. "Is that you?"

Only a heavy breath from the other line.

341

"Andrew it's me, it's your sister, it's Lily. Let me come and see you."

"No, Lily," he said. "Stay away from me. Stay sharp, and for your own good, stay away."

"Andrew! Miera, can I talk to my brother in private?"

"No." That was Andrew. "Anything you want to say to me, you can say to me in the hearing of my wife."

Not even bothering to wipe the tears from her face, Lily said, "Andrew, tell me, is it true?"

"Is what true?"

"You and Amy, were you having an affair *before* she and I ever met?" How did she get those words out? Miera and/or Andrew slammed down the phone.

Lily sat in Jan's bedroom and continued to cry until Paul and Rachel came to get her. "Oh, what is going *on* around here?" said Paul. "Boy, this Port Jeff. It really knows how to throw a kids' party." They left Jan's house, went to have dinner at Paul's mother's house, and took a late train back. Paul and Rachel stayed with her until four in the morning, plying her with margaritas trying to make her feel better about being inconsolable.

She didn't go to sleep until dawn.

When Spencer came on Sunday, she was still asleep. He knocked on her bedroom door, and came in, and she was still in her bed. Parts of her may have been uncovered, legs, shoulders, back, perhaps. She couldn't even remember if she had taken her clothes off. She did, yes. She half-heartedly pulled the quilt up as he came into the room.

"Are you okay?"

"I don't know," she said staring at him.

"What's the matter?"

"What time is it?"

"One in the afternoon."

"Oh."

"Were you out late last night?" he smiled.

"No. Well, yes. Paul and Rachel were over."

He stared into her sleepy face. "Why have you been crying?"

"Not crying, sleeping," she lied. She didn't like lying to him. It felt unnatural.

"No, crying. Your lids are all puffy from the salt. And your cheeks, too."

"Nothing gets past you, Detective," she said. "Well, let me get dressed, go grab a quick shower. Are you hungry?"

Lily had no defenses against his inquisitive stare, against his questions, against his persistence. When she was so clearly distraught there was no hiding it from him. And there was no telling him either. Obviously. The knowledge would be used against her brother. She was in the shower forever, thrashing from side to side, figuring out the impossibilities of her Sunday, and when she came out, Spencer was sitting on the couch reading the newspaper, which he put down, grimly looked her up and down in her robe and said, "You have been in there for forty-five minutes. Something is so wrong you can't even come out and face me."

"No, no, it has nothing to do with you, honestly." But she couldn't even speak these words without looking down at his feet.

He got up, and went to get his jacket. "Lily, you know what, I make it so easy for you, so easy. Any time you don't want to see me—"

"Spencer, I do."

"—Any time you don't want me to come, you just call and leave me a message. Write me a letter, beep me, tell me through Joy. I can't make it any simpler for you. But don't stand here and pretend you're not lying to me now when you can't even look into my face."

She tried to apologize, tell him she was just hung over, not feeling well, nauseated, sleepy, she told him lies upon lies, all of them into his chest because she couldn't look at him without spilling the thing she absolutely could not say. It was screaming

343

so loud in her chest, how could he not hear? Ah, that was because he was already down five flights of stairs and in the street.

AMY KNEW ANDREW BEFORE SHE MET LILY!

How could this be?

The credit cards, the cash, the ID, all lying on her dresser, of course, from the very beginning. Lily didn't attach the memories to the years, but of course! From the moment Amy moved in, she would leave her life behind, and disappear for days, or go off on Fridays, and hum, hum that merciless song, from the very beginning, and Lily, so swollen with Amy's affection, thought Amy had been singing it for her! Oh, the hubris, the childish idiocy! The Mighty Quinn indeed.

Amy knew Andrew *before* she met Lily. Amy was involved with Andrew, wore blossoms in her hair for him.

What then? Why then? How then?

How did she meet him? How would she know him?

And if she did, and met him somehow, and got together with him, why, *why* would she transfer out of Hunter into City College, enroll in Lily's class.

Hi, is this desk taken? I don't know how I'm going to do in this class, everybody else is so talented, my goodness, look at how well you draw, you must have a gift, so this desk is not taken then?

That Sunday night she tried again, she called Andrew once more. Miera hung up on her, but not before she said, "If you ever call here again, I'll have a restraining order put on you."

Even worse than Amy. Andrew. He had kept it all secret. Lily could tell it was true from its weight on her. He and Amy knew each other before Lily introduced them. They both practiced deception around her, kept up a false front, so that she never suspected. And that wasn't even the worst of it. The worst was that Andrew was still perpetuating that falsehood for Detective Spencer O'Malley, that Andrew felt the need to lie and *carry* on lying. If it was just a simple thing, a nothing thing, that Andrew and Amy were involved before Lily, why continue to lie?

Lily couldn't paint that week.

Lily couldn't do anything that week, except throw up before she even took the Alkeran. Throw up the alkaloid indelible taste of betrayal and deception in her mouth.

47

Harkman

"O'Malley. How was your weekend? Mine was fine, thanks." That was Gabe McGill.

"Good morning. Why are you scowling at me like that?"

"O'Malley, you bastard, this better not be subterfuge on your part. Whittaker wants to see us both in his office."

And Whittaker stood behind his desk and said, "What did you do, O'Malley? Did you push pins inside your little Harkman voodoo doll?"

"Would somebody please tell me what the fuck is going on?"

"Harkman's in the hospital."

"Oh. What's wrong with him?"

"Heart attack." Both Whittaker and McGill crossed their arms.

Spencer laughed. "What's wrong with both of *you*? What, did *I* put him in the hospital?"

"It's his fourth heart attack, and his doctor said no more for him. No more work. He might not make it as it is."

"What, you think I made his job too stressful for him? He hasn't left the office in months! I've been going alone everywhere. I let him sit behind the desk and never move, I made Sanchez his personal bitch, ask Sanchez how he feels about it. Everything I could do to stave off the inevitable for him, I did. He always complained. Then I sat him behind a desk, and he never moved, and again it's my fault?"

Whittaker and McGill were not persuaded by Spencer's apparent innocence in perpetrating a heart attack upon Chris Harkman.

"We're not going to make light of this. The man might not recover, and he's been on the force longer than you, O'Malley. So show some respect. He was a good cop. Never found a single MP, but he was a good cop."

"Not true," said Spencer. "He closed custody cases, found some runaways."

"He didn't find them! They came home." Whittaker waved his hand. "Oh, look, he's gone, and we've got a situation here. How clear is your desk?"

"Clear? I never stop, I'm working until nine at night every night, picking up Harkman's slack. What's going to happen now, I don't know."

"Now you need a temporary partner until we find you a permanent assignment."

Spencer glanced at McGill, who rolled his eyes.

Harkman was gone! The man who for years made his working life so difficult with his apathy and inertia and hostility was gone. Spencer felt such relief.

Gabe McGill was a young Irish bruiser of a detective, straight from the "don't fuck with me" academy. He was completely wrong for detective work. He would have been much better as a uniform, patrolling Tompkins Square Park and the rest of the East Village. He looked unruly, like any moment he was going to explode. His brown-reddish auburn curly hair was in constant need of cutting, his stubble was in constant need of shaving, his clothes of ironing. No one looked more alien in an ill-fitting suit. The shirts were always too small for his massive arms and neck, they were always unbuttoned and untucked somewhere. Spencer compared with Gabe was a model of grace for Brooks Brothers. Why Spencer liked him so much, he didn't know.

Whittaker said, "I'm making McGill your temporary assignment, O'Malley."

"O'Malley," Gabe said. "Heed those words. This is a temporary gig. This isn't a fucking marriage. This is simply for convenience. I remain in homicide, and I help you out when you need me to. Got it? Chief, explain it to him."

"McGill, you stay in homicide, but until we figure out a permanent solution, you're O'Malley's bitch."

"Chief, no!"

Spencer smiled.

"McGill, we've got eight homicide detectives besides you and Orkney, but in MP, there's only him. Sanchez and Smith were pulled out of MP into robbery last week, and your friend over here needs your help."

Spencer was thrilled. "Gabe, I'm a different man."

"Just because I'm here?" They walked into the common room.

"Yes. Can't you just hear it? I am Detective O'Malley, and this is Detective McGill from *homicide*." He laughed with satisfaction.

"You think title-dropping is going to help you find the McFadden girl?"

"Something better. Soon it'll be a year and I won't be able to keep her on my desk without new evidence. She'll have to go into the inactives and then I'm even more shit out of luck."

Spencer didn't want to have Amy's file, alongside dozens of others, put in the cabinet labeled "*UNSOLVED*", left for the next shift, the next detective, the next generation. Every ten years, the department re-opened all the files, sorted through them, and then, if there had been no new information, placed them in a whole different category: "*UNSOLVED TEN YEARS AND OLDER*." That's where the missing persons files went to die. Teenage children of desperate mothers, of divorced fathers, addicts unable to find their way home, disappearing without a trace, and the families went on, and the police force went on. Spencer knew—Jan McFadden would not go on. She was a woman who was stuck in that moment on Friday, May 14, 1999,

348

and from that day her life did not move—and could not move. She held out a crazy hope that her child was alive, would come back. At the very least she wanted a scrap of information, not to live in purgatory for the rest of her life. One way or another Spencer would get her that information.

Gabe and Spencer walked out of the precinct and went up to Second Avenue to McCluskey's for lunch.

"So you think we should go visit Harkman in the hospital?" Gabe asked.

Spencer thought about it for two seconds. "Fuck Harkman."

They just turned the corner on Second when Spencer heard a voice calling for him. "Spencer!" He turned around and there was Lily, with sketchbooks in her hands, walking up to them and smiling. She had put her choppy hair into a dozen pastel pony tail holders and her head radiated with lilac and pink and blue and yellow rubber bands. It was a glorious early April day. She was wearing all pink today, pink denim skirt, pink denim jacket, pink boots, pink sheer blouse, pink bra. Her legs were bare.

She came up to them, and her smile was so well-known, he took half a step *back*, so familiar she was looking to him, and at him.

"Hello, Detective O'Malley," she said, pretending to be professional.

"Hello, Lily," said Spencer, trying to be serious. "This is Detective McGill."

Gabe was grinning at Lily. "Well, *hello* there," he said, taking her hand, shaking it, holding it. "Hello, Lily, you can call me Gabe."

"Detective McGill will do just fine," said Spencer.

"So you're the famous Detective McGill," Lily said. "Spencer talks so much about you."

"Every single thing he's said to you is a vicious lie."

Spencer told her what had happened this morning with Harkman and Gabe.

"I'm sorry to hear about Detective Harkman," she said. "He

must be quite sick. But Detective O'Malley must be happy to have you working with him." Her eyes were twinkling.

"Well, I don't know if you know this about Detective O'Malley, Miss—

"Quinn."

"Miss Quinn, but he is a miserable bastard. I don't know if anything can make him happy, and personally, I'm not going to kill myself trying."

"All right, you two," said Spencer, nodding to Lily. "We have to go."

"Would you like to join us?" asked Gabe. "For some lunch?"

Lily glanced at Spencer, who kept his lip bit. "No, thank you, perhaps another time. I've got to sketch in Astor Place while the weather is still good. Nice to meet you, Detective McGill. See you, Detective O'Malley." She smiled up at him, her face flushed.

Gabe frowned for a moment. "Did you say your name was Lily Quinn? You aren't related to—"

"Gabe, let's go! I'm not going to stand on the street all day."

He turned around once to glance back at her, but she had disappeared.

"O'Malley, I can't help feeling that you were trying to pull me away from that colorful adorable creature," Gabe said when they were inside the bar.

"For reasons more numerous than I have time to enumerate."

"Name me one, aside from the most obvious."

"One, oh, all right. Let's see—your wife and two small children maybe?"

"I don't see your main squeeze stopping you from befriending girls half your age. What was with the hair?"

"Cancer."

Gabe looked at Spencer, at Spencer's own buzz head. "Still?"

"Touch and go."

"Is she related to Amy McFadden's main squeeze?"

"Gabe, I can't *tell* you how much I don't want to talk about it."

48

The Yellow Ribbons

Yellow ribbons were tied to the poles next to Amy's pictures, and the yellow ribbons grew old and faded with time.

With Paul and Rachel by her side, Lily was putting new ribbons and new posters on the poles when she *felt* someone watching her from across the street. She couldn't speak, couldn't move even though it was broad daylight. From the periphery of her eye, across the street, she thought she saw a shape standing staring at her, at them, just three young kids on a Wednesday morning before lunch at Veselka on Second Avenue, tying yellow ribbons to poles, and . . .

She felt afraid. She was afraid to lift her eyes as she continued to go through the motions of tying the ribbons, but her hands started shaking. Paul asked what was the matter. With him talking to her, Lily felt a little braver, and she lifted her eyes. There were several people across Second, and no one was staring: there was a man buying flowers in a deli, another man talking to a shopkeeper on the street, a couple standing looking at a restaurant's menu. And then the brown back of a man in rags, shuffling down the street, but far from her. He started running, not like a man in rags, but like someone who had running in his blood: his legs moved strong, he was fast, his arms swung, his body did not look degenerate. Perhaps she had made up the rags, perhaps he was wearing a long brown coat.

Lily had to wonder . . . as she with shaking hands went back to slowly tying the ribbons under the poles. She had thought she imagined it. It was just paranoia, just an irrational suspicion, the kind that made her draw the shades in her apartment because she felt someone was watching her. She had thought it was Amy's ghost. But here, on a Wednesday morning in the East Village, on Second Avenue, what was it, really?

49

Baseball as a Metaphor for Everything

On Saturday afternoon Spencer found her in the very early April cool, just two bottomless eyes and an unbuttoned coat, sitting on a bench in Tompkins Square Park. She had already sold all her paintings that morning. Around her was a crowd of ten or twelve men. She was giving out twenty-dollar bills to them. They would extend their shaking filthy hands and into them she would put crack money. "Get yourself something nice with it," she was saying to them, and they muttered, "I will, honey, I will, sugar, thanks so much, darling, don't you worry, and God bless you."

Spencer pulled her from the bench as she handed him a C-note. "What are you doing?"

"Passing the time," she said, almost brightly. "Answering life's riddles."

"Oh, for Mary's sake. What are you giving them money for?"

"I'm hoping to find Amy."

"Very good. Are you asking them about Amy? I didn't see you asking them anything."

"I'm hoping one of them will look familiar."

"Have you met a lot of familiar homeless men?"

"He'll come, you'll see. That Milo. I'm looking for him."

"Yes, you and me both."

353

"He'll hear about me through the grapevine, giving out money. He'll come, I know it."

"You're baiting him with your money? You're fishing? Very, very good, Lily. But you might want to raise the bait a little. I mean, twenty bucks is not enough to buy a bag of scag."

"He will seek me out. The way she sought me out."

"What?"

"Nothing," she said quickly, her gaze clouding. "Are you hungry? You want to go have lunch?"

"No." Pausing, he cleared his throat. She frowned at him confused. "But the Yankees are playing the Angels."

"They are?" Lily held her breath. *Maybe he'll ask me to go to a game with him. Spend a rare Saturday afternoon with him. Away from cancer, away from Amy, a day with him, just me and him—and fifty-five thousand strangers.*

"Yes. When was the last time you went to a ball game?"

"When I was sixteen." *Hold breath, hold breath, bite lip, act cool.*

"So you're a veteran." He paused. "Want to go?"

"Sure." She smiled with a shrug, oh so casually. *Sure, yeah, I'll go, whatever. I was going to go home and be alone and stretch some canvas, but yeah, I'll go to a game with you.* She wanted to jump in place. But she remained so restrained, so collected. "Let me run home quick. Put something on my head." *She wanted to put make-up on her face. She wanted to put on a different shirt, her nice jeans, some perfume. She wanted to paint her nails, and maybe even toe nails, take a shower, clean up a little.*

She wanted to put on lipstick to go to a baseball game with him.

"Let's just go. Or we'll never make the first inning. I'll buy you a Yankees cap to put on your head."

"Cool." *What could she do?* "Do you have tickets?"

"I might have some tickets. Is that all the painting money you made today that you just gave away to crack addicts?"

"Finding Milo is not coming cheap, Spencer."

354

Ten good things about losing your hair:
10. You can use the men's room or the ladies room.
9. You don't have to rinse and repeat.
8. No one ever says to you with a fake smile, "Where do you get your hair done?"
7. Cooties, lice, ticks, dust mites don't stick around.
6. Shower now takes ten minutes instead of forty five.
5. No hair in the bathtub.
4. With the sun reflecting brightly off your scalp, you provide lighting services to the permanent patrons of Tompkins Park.
3. You get a thousand sympathetic stares a day.
2. When people say, "Oh, you got a haircut," you say, "No, I got them all cut."

And the number one good thing about cancer hair . . .
1. When Spencer Patrick O'Malley buys you a Yankees cap, you don't get hat hair.

Lily, her head covered by the baseball cap, went to a game with Spencer between the Yankees and the California Angels. That funny Spencer. Through his Benevolent Patrolmen's Association contacts, he had gotten great seats, right behind the first base dugout. So he must have gotten them in advance, knowing he was going to ask her to go. Why didn't he just ask her yesterday or the day before, so she could have time to prepare?

It was April but cold and windy, and though Lily wore three layers of clothes, she was still shivering. Spencer bought them two hot dogs and two Cokes. "No beer?" she asked.

"If you want one, I'll buy you one."

She didn't want one. She was just cold, and when he saw, he gave her his policeman's jacket that said NYPD on it. It was such a fantastic jacket that the cursing and spitting guy behind them had tapped Spencer hard on the shoulder and said, "Hey man, great jacket, where'd you get that?" and Spencer taking out his badge and showing it to the spitting curser said, "From the New York Police Department." And Lily laughed, and Spencer laughed too when he turned around. Spencer laughed! He showed his teeth!

Lily was shivering, even with Spencer's great NYPD jacket.

"Are you still cold?" he said, and when she nodded, he put his arm around her.

He. Put. His. Arm. Around. Her.

Carefully she sidled into him. The score in the game was close too but not as close as Spencer was to her.

Lily jumped up and cheered, and the arm came off, and she did the wave and the seventh inning stretch and sang "Take Me Out to the Ballgame" and "We Will Rock You." The squalling April wind kept taking her breath away. It was the squalling April wind, right?

The Yankees tied the game at the bottom of the ninth, and everyone jumped up, including Lily, including Spencer, and when she beaming and clapping turned to him, he was staring at her, and she looking up at him said, "What?" And he bent to her and kissed her, just like that, during the shouting, the applause, the revelry. Spencer, with the warmest lips, the softest, fullest lips; Spencer Patrick O'Malley, lead investigator, detective lieutenant, a police officer, with a Glock-26, his off-duty weapon, fastened in his holster, Spencer, forty-three years old, leaned his head in and kissed her with teenage lips, with teenage ardor, and Lily, who had not been kissed in nearly a year (how twisted was that?) raised her face to him, pressed her body to him, lifted her hand to hold his head, to rest on his chest, and then she could barely look at him, and didn't care anymore whether the Yankees won or lost, but when they won, in the overtime eleventh, all she wanted was Spencer to kiss her again—and he did. And joy drummed on her dimmed-by-cancer heart, and coursed through her weakened-by-chemo veins. *We will/we will rock you* kept pounding inside her all the way home on the D train.

She didn't know how to ask him to stay. She felt sexless. Unsexed. Undesired, under-used, sick. Sickness was so unsexy. Sickness was the opposite of youth, the opposite of beauty, the opposite of sexy, the opposite of sex. Once she had been a little more sure of herself, but now she was sure only of her old age, her ugliness. Perhaps she and he were just caught up by the tied ballgame in the bottom of the ninth, who wouldn't kiss during that? Or in overtime when they won—even if the kiss was breath-less and open and exquisitely long.

Shockingly—and despite her crushing fear and evident self-hatred—he came in. No formalities between them. No buzzing in. He kept her key, he used her key. Tonight, there was no, would you like to come up. He just came up like always.

He sat by her. "You must be so tired. It's been a long day."

She said nothing.

He waited. "I don't want to go—"

"I don't want you to go."

He kissed her on the couch, cupping, holding her face, after a while scooping her into his arms and bringing her into the bedroom. Sitting on the edge of the bed, he stood her between his legs and unbuttoned her blouse. It came off, her jeans came off. She was left in her black see-through bra, her black g-string. With one hand, he unhooked her bra and took it off her, dropping it on the floor, and she stood like that in front of him in her thong, topless, her breasts, her aching nipples level with his face, while his hands caressed her up and down her arms, her ribs, her hips, her thighs. He was breathing so hard, she was breathing so shallow, and she moved just a little bit forward, just a little bit, oh my God, she thought, I'm being touched by someone other than myself. I'm being touched. "Spencer . . ." she whispered, desperately wanting his mouth on her.

"Wait."

He undressed to his boxer briefs that looked—because she hadn't seen a man in so long—like the hottest boxer briefs she had *ever* seen, he lay her down on the bed, and straddled her, keeping his weight off her, supporting himself on his knees and his arms, he softly kissed her neck and her throat, and very lightly rubbed his chest against her palpitating breasts, and she, in a stiffening spasm arched into him, trying to pull him down on top of her. He kissed her and whispered, "I'm afraid, Lily, afraid to hurt you," and she whispered back in a moan, "God, don't be afraid of anything, of nothing, I want . . . I want some sugar in my bowl, Spencer. Come on, anything, everything, leave me nothing but my skin and bones . . . just please . . . put some sugar in my bowl."

On the radio Nina Simone continued to wail for some of that sugar, the Pointer Sisters were ridin' in your car, on fire, Bruce was also on fire, Johnny Cash was walking the line, Peter Paul and Mary's kisses were sweeter than wine, and then she didn't hear any more music. Spencer made love to her as strenuously as her fragility would allow, but love-making could be gentle before—and was—and after—and was—but rarely during, and so he reaffirmed the motion of life with her, beat back death from her—from her, from Amy, for that one driving instant, for that hour in time, and then held her quivering body under the blankets, until he gave her another remarkable hour, and then held her perspired racked body without the blankets, and then! gave her some miraculous more with no gentleness and no fragility, and fell asleep soundly, and as Lily lay in Spencer's arms, utterly sleepless, her bowl overflowing with sugar, barely even skin and bones left on her, she thought that if today were the last day of her life, she would have no regrets.

She lived today. She ate comfort food, and drank Coca-Cola, the drink of the Americans, she breathed fresh, crisp air, and rejoiced in someone else's triumph, she was with her cheering fellow men, she had good conversation, she jumped up, screamed for joy, laughed.

358

She was kissed. She was *loved*. By Spencer. She loved back. She loved Spencer back. The air smelled like spring trees and new grass. She was whispered to. "Lily, you are beautiful . . ." Her body was devoured by a *man*. And then she felt beautiful, felt like a young *woman* again. It was a perfect day.

Spencer, *you're* beautiful, she wanted to say to him, but he was blessedly, exhaustedly asleep. You have a perfect face, you have a perfect scarred heart. You have arms that raise you above me, raising me. You have strength—for everything—you have legs for the long run, you've got it all in spades, and I can't believe you gave it all to me tonight.

She could write that essay now. There wasn't a spot on her heart this chilly Saturday in April. No shadowlands, no darkness, no penumbras on her soul, no shadows on the flawed yet flawless man who changed her life. Despite her supreme reluctance, he had cleaved her heart, and poured himself in, brought down by force her forcefield, by virtue of nothing but himself. He had given her the one day in her life she wanted to have before she died.

50

April Fools

Lily could not believe the dizzying waves of happiness washing over her. She was having sex again! She was having SEX. She wanted to shout it from the rooftops, wanted to tell about it to strangers on the street. She wanted to have it with the windows open with the shades up. She wanted to do it in public places, in corridors, on the bus, on the subway. To Paul, to whom she ran for hair color on Monday, the first thing she said was, "I'm having sex!"

"You are? Congratulations! Maria, come here!" he yelled across the beauty salon. "Did you hear? Our Lily is having sex!"

"Having sex, you? With who?" Across the salon!

"Like that's important," scoffed Paul. "Nobody cares, Maria. She's having SEX, didn't you hear?"

"I hear, I hear."

They were so loud, so fantastic.

Rachel came in to work, and Lily didn't even have time to open her mouth, Paul was already volunteering information. Rachel said skeptically, "Sex with a man in his forties? Is that even possible?"

"Well, obviously."

She remained unconvinced. "Is he any good?"

"Oh my God! He's awesome, why?"

"I don't know. I hear men in their forties stop being any good in bed."

"Where did you hear such nonsense?"

"I read it in Cosmo," Rachel said, flipping her hair back, forward, sideways. "Their sex-drive disappears. Can they even get it up at that age?"

"Lil's brother somehow managed it," said Paul, and was instantly slapped on his bleached head by Lily, who said, "Why, why do you have to ruin absolutely *everything?*"

"Well don't just give us the bare bones, tell us everything," said Rachel, grinning. "What does he do?"

"What doesn't he do?"

"I don't know how you did it. How did you do it—snag him?"

"You should try getting mortally sick, I think that's what did it," said Lily, running out, full manicure, pedicure, thoroughly waxed, her tufted patchy head full of copper highlights.

He had stayed overnight, woke up in her bed, a naked Spencer woke up in her bed, stayed with her all day Sunday. They ordered Chinese in, ate in bed, crawled out to watch a movie, she already couldn't remember what it was. On Sunday night he went home because he had to work the next day, and here it was the next day. She walked past his precinct wondering if she should go in, say hi, beep him maybe. She decided not to. She rushed home instead, to see if there were any messages for her. Since when was she eagerly checking her messages? Since she was having SEX again!

And there was a message from him. Even his voice didn't sound the same anymore, it sounded deep and husky, it was a voice that was having sex—with her. "Hey," he said in the message. Lily loved the familiarity. Not even an "It's me." Just "Hey." "Hey. Where are you? Pick up. I'm out all day in Jersey, and then uptown in Washington Heights. I'll call you later. Try to be home."

She never moved from the phone the rest of the day. She didn't even have music on, just in case some tympanic drum

361

would mask the sound of the phone ringing. She made sure it was charged and plugged in, and all the lights were invitingly green.

When it rang she was in the bathroom—of course!—and she lunged for it and said, the most expectant "Hello?" of her life.

"This is your grandmother. How are you feeling?"

She was on the phone for ten minutes. She hoped the caller ID was working. She waited until seven in the evening for him to call, and he didn't. She painted, she drew. Unfortunately all she saw in her mind to draw was naked bodies, naked male bodies, lean muscles, lean waists, the space between the navel and the pubis—and then some. The wide spread out hands, the fingers, all the digits, his and hers, in the moment of their greatest tension. Two large masculine hands tightly gripping two female calves. The man's lips from heaven, ready for more, wet, slightly parted. She couldn't sell these pictures on a Saturday afternoon on a family street. They were nearly pornographic.

Nearly?

At seven o'clock, she was finishing up a drawing of a man's thigh, and heard a strong knock on the door. She jumped up, ran to the door, then slowed down to open it, trying to appear calm, but she was out of breath when she opened it, and there he was, standing in the hall, smiling at her. Spencer smiling. He must be having SEX too!

"Hi," she said, stepping out of the way for him to come in.

"Hey."

How to ask? "You said you were going to call." Like that, she guessed.

He turned around to glance at her bemusedly. "I was with Gabe all day, I could hardly call you with him right next to me." He stood in his suit. She stood in her H. Starlet sweats, in her little tank top with no bra.

"Did you forget your key?"

He shook his head. "Perhaps you've never heard me knock before. I always knock before I barge right in."

"Oh."

"So are you hungry?"

"Starving."

"Me too."

They had SEX on their couch, he was wearing his lead investigator, detective-lieutenant suit. He did show the presence of mind to pull down his trousers, whispering that his other suit was at the cleaners and he couldn't get this one all messy. And then, too soon, he was lying on top of her, his silk tie rubbing against her bare shoulder, and whispering, "Liliput, is that the sexiest thing or what, you under me all naked while I'm wearing my work clothes . . ."

She laughed, holding him to her. "You say work clothes, but it's not like you're in the construction business, or lumberjacking. You're wearing a suit. You could be an accountant, for God's sake."

"Yes, but I'm not an accountant, and you know how you can tell? Put your hands a little lower down and feel my Glock."

She laughed until she became aroused again.

They ordered Odessa in (it was worth it just to see Pedro's expression when he delivered the food to a barely clad Spencer), but he went home at midnight. "I have to be at work at seven, Lil, I can't be doing this all night long. I'm an old man."

The next day he called when she was in the shower to say he was in court and then in Jersey until late tonight and he would call her later, but later came and he didn't call. At midnight when she was already in bed, she heard the key in the door and then his footsteps walking through the dark living room to her bedroom. The door opened, he came in, kneeled by her head. She opened her arms to him. He went home at three.

On Wednesday he called first thing in the morning and asked if she wanted to go out to dinner.

"Spencer, are you asking me out on a date?"

"No. I'm asking if you want to go out or dine in."

She laughed.

When he knocked on her door, she said "Come iiiin," and he used his key and came in saying, "Where's the gatekeeper?" From *Ghostbusters!* But the gatekeeper in the form of Lily was sitting nude on the couch, her legs parted and drawn up.

"I'm here," said the gatekeeper. "Where's the keymaster?"

Spencer dropped the keys on the floor, barely shutting the door behind him and kneeled in front of Lily. Did they go out to dinner that night? Lily didn't know. She didn't know anything anymore.

She had been with only boys before, clumsy fumbling boys, eager, ever at the ready, but without any idea of what to do or not do to enhance and gladden Lily. But Spencer was a man, and there was nothing clumsy or fumbling about him. He did this thing that had never been done to her, this *enslaving* thing that made her burn in her whole body when she even thought of thinking about it, that made her unable to look him in the face when she even thought of thinking about it. He spread her open with the palms of his hands, opening her, holding her tightly before he put his soft mouth on her. It felt like she was coming before his lips ever reached her. And then—he wouldn't stop holding her open, stop anything, not even when she begged him up and down the octaves to cease and desist.

"I'm not sure, but I think," she breathed out, clutching to him in bed, "that you're muddling my brain. I forgot to take my pill on Monday, forgot to go for my blood work yesterday."

"Oh no."

"I didn't even know it until they called."

"So what are you going to do?"

"I'm going to double-up tomorrow." She grinned. But she had no intention of taking it tomorrow. She was skipping cancer this week.

"What were you doing Monday that you forgot?"

What *was* she doing Monday? "Getting my nails done."

"Ah. Vital, yes."

"Getting highlights."

"Essential."

"Getting a Brazilian wax."

"Well, now you're talking." He was on top of her.

"I thought you didn't notice. You didn't even mention it."

"Lily, ahem, I can hardly help but notice. I thought my being here every night kneeling at the altar would speak for itself."

And it did, it did.

On Thursday she went to visit her grandmother, like always, because she didn't want anyone to get worried about her. She stayed for dinner because Grandma seemed lonely and wanted her to stay. Spencer called her at her grandmother's. "How do you know this number?" she said, flattered pink to be tracked down.

"I'm paid to track people down. That is what I do."

Very quietly she said, "Why does that sound so damn hot?"

Very quietly he said, "I'll come pick you up."

"Wait, wait."

He waited. Grandma would go through the roof if she saw Lily getting into his car. He must know that.

"In an hour."

"No, Spencer, wait."

Grandma called from the other room. "Lily, are you coming?"

Spencer waited.

"I'll never hear the end of it."

"Either from them or from me, Lil," he said and hung up.

Oh, dear Mary, mother of God, the next day, the next day.

"Lily! Are you completely out of your mind? What in the world do you think you're doing?"

Who was that? Grandma? Anne? Amanda? Her mother? All of them? Grandma in the space of one morning managed to tell everybody, and Lily meant *everybody*, because even the Korean Soo Min called to wag a finger at her. Grandma said, "How do you think your brother is going to feel knowing you've taken up with Inspector Javert?"

"First of all, you're being melodramatic." And tiresome, she wanted to add.

"I don't think so."

"And second of all," Lily calmly continued, finally speaking up good and proper, "My brother is in no position to pass judgment on anybody, don't you think?"

Grandma had asked her not to come Thursdays. She said it was shameful what she was doing, shameful and immoral.

"I know, I know. I've heard this a thousand times. I'm the shameful one, the immoral one. The rest of you are saints. You know what, Grandma, I think you're right. It's best I don't come for a little while."

"And have you even called your mother?"

"No, but that's all right, because she's been calling me. The other day before she hung up on me, she cursed me to the devil, telling me some parable about a mother who put a curse on her daughter who then died."

"Why are you talking about your mother that way?" Grandma said quietly. "You don't know what she's been through."

They were wrong about Spencer—he was worth it. The night he had picked her up in Brooklyn, he parked his car by the Greenpoint docks, and with Manhattan Island twinkling across the East River, they had fumbling, cramped, orgiastic teenage sex in the backseat of his Buick while Bruce Springsteen's "Ramrod" rocked on the radio.

Friday night Spencer was in Pennsylvania: there was a custody abduction and he went to retrieve the twelve-year-old twins from their father and bring them back to their mother. He called to say he would go back to his place to sleep but then come to her art sale on Saturday. By the time he made it, Lily had already sold every one of her erotic drawings (in record time, she was embarrassed to say), and she was sitting at the empty table sketching herself sitting at an empty table. A woman in a mini-skirt walked by, bought the unfinished drawing, asked Lily to draw

366

her, and that's what Lily was doing when Spencer ambled by, in scuffed jeans and a worn T-shirt. "I'm forced to take in extra work while waiting for you," she said mock-plaintively, but he stepped over to her chair, threw her head back and kissed her so deeply that the hot pocket exploding in her belly made her drop her pencil. She gave the woman the drawing for free. And next week drew ten versions of the man in jeans leaning down to kiss the girl in the white shirt sitting in the chair with her face raised to the heavens. They sold in minutes.

Saturday night they went out to dinner. They got dressed up and went out to Union Square Café, where they had calamari and pot roast and apple hot cake, where the waiter said, "would you like a cocktail", and Lily nodded and Spencer shook his head, ordering two more Cosmos for her so that she was very tipsy by the time they blew off the movie and rushed home where the SEX they had was so extreme she thought she had gone deaf and blind.

And on Sunday night, during their movie night he took off her clothes and made her watch *Moonstruck* completely naked, while he sat close to her in jeans and played with her for half the movie before he made love to her. She did not hear a word of Nicolas Cage or Cher. She did hear Spencer though, and all the things he whispered to her. She made a mental note to watch that movie again when she became sane and stopped moaning aloud at the barest thought of him.

He went home on Sunday night, and on Monday she got up and dragged herself to Mount Sinai where she was reminded of what she had forgotten during an intoxicating seven days that her neutrophils and platelets and red cells and white cells were being slowly destroyed by Alkeran that was in turn keeping her from dying. They gave her VePesid by IV and an anti-emetic to help her nausea, and told her not to forget her Alkeran any more, but the VePesid made her so tired that when she got home, she lay down and went to sleep and didn't wake up until Tuesday, when she felt like she was rotting from the inside. And worse, sexless again. Sexless once again. How short-lived that was, she thought weakly, retching in the toilet. How joyous and yet fleeting. And how joyless this is, and yet how much there is of it.

She stopped taking the Alkeran. Stopped cold. It was doing nothing for her counts and it was affecting her SEX Life. It was either cancer or SEX. Lily chose to have both.

Then, a miracle! The following week the platelets were up to *150*, without any drugs! The white cells were not elevated! The red was almost normal. DiAngelo was very impressed with her platelets and the flush to her cheeks, he said her blood looked good and clean. He shook her hand and sent her home.

Lily skipped from the hospital on 66th down Fifth Avenue, past St. Patrick's Cathedral, past the pews and the priests and the crying rooms. She couldn't wait to get home before she called him, so she beeped him from the noisy street near the Empire State Building. When he didn't call back in five minutes, she beeped him again.

"Guess what?" she burst when he finally called. "I'm clean!"

"Is that so?"

"No . . . I mean I'm *clean.*"

"That's great. Thanks for letting me know."

"My counts are all up. No more chemo, Spencer. Do you understand? No more Alkeran. No more tiredness, throwing up, feeling horrible, looking horrible."

"I understand."

"Where are you?"

"In the car."

"Your police car?"

"Yes."

"Are you alone?"

"No."

"Hmm." She was still out of breath, but so giddy, so happy, and feeling a little mischievous. "But *sometimes* you're alone in your police car," she drawled, lowering her voice to bedroom.

"Yes."

"Mmm. Say you're alone drivin' in your car, and you find me in the street, like now, say, being rowdy, disobedient, suspect me perhaps of being . . . indecently exposed, would you, mmm, pull me over?"

"Yes."

"Maybe turn me around, pin my hands behind my back, splay my front against the hood of your car, my back to you . . ."

". . . Yes."

"Put the cuffs on me . . ."

"All right then, thanks for calling."

"And search me between my legs . . ."

"Right, yes, that was very helpful. Call me if you have any more info."

"Because, Detective O'Malley, I'll confess right now, under my short short denim skirt, I've got a completely bare p—"

"Thanks, you have a great day yourself." He hung up as Lily laughed with joy.

Gabe was driving and he looked over at Spencer, who sat staring straight ahead. "Nice charade there, O'Malley. You think your terse little yeses and nos are going to fool a homicide detective?"

"Oh, nothing can get past you, McGill," said Spencer, trying in vain to calm the fire in his loins.

At lunch they walked up 5th Street to Second Avenue. Gabe pointed to a public phone booth on the corner, where stood Lily, her back to them. Spencer took her in, Gabe said isn't that your friend, and then Spencer's beeper went off. Gabe raised his eye brows. Spencer glanced at the display. *Harlequin* it said.

He motioned to Gabe to keep quiet, moved his gun a little to the back so it wouldn't accidentally hurt her and came up behind her, gripping her just above her hips and saying into her ear, "Very very naughty."

He knew she would get scared, and she did, she squealed and whirled around, his hands remaining on her hips, and then saw Spencer and Gabe, and relaxed and punched him lightly in the chest as he stepped away from her and laughed. "Detective O'Malley, isn't it against the law to frighten young civilian women?" she said. "Hello, Detective McGill."

"Hello, Lily. Nice to see you again."

The three of them stood. "You boys are going to McCluskey's for lunch?"

"Yes, would you like to join us? You just paged Detective O'Malley, is everything all right?"

"Yes, yes." She squinted at Spencer, he squinted back. "No, you go ahead, I'm sure you don't have much time."

"We don't. Let's go, O'Malley."

Spencer's eyes were only on Lily. "Gabe, can you give me a minute? I'll meet you inside."

Gabe slapped Spencer's back. "You know what, how about if I just meet you back upstairs at two. We need to be in Trenton by three-thirty, so don't be late."

As soon as Gabe turned his back, she moved closer to him, so close, and looked up smiling so happily, and he moved closer to her, sliding his hand around her waist. When Gabe at the doors of McCluskey's glanced back at them, Lily in a jean skirt and a cropped pastel shirt, with spring ponytailed hair, was completely encircled by Spencer in a suit and tie, in a crowd on Second Avenue, being kissed by him as if the war was over.

Saturdays she hired a Lincoln Towncar to come pick up her and her work and take them to her spot on 8th, where half a dozen people might be waiting. Waiting! For her to show them what she drew that week.

Her art was full of Spencer and herself. She painted them eating waffles in bed, and in Odessa, painted them walking

370

through Tompkins, having ice cream on the corner of 9th and Avenue C, sitting having hot dogs in the well of the Twin Towers.

The kissing pictures always went first. Lily started drawing more of them. No matter how many she drew—and one week she drew twenty-seven—they always went first and to the last one.

"I'm glad you're immortalizing me," said Spencer, "but are you keeping any for yourself, or am I going to find myself one day hanging in Wal Mart next to the stationery and party supplies?"

"Next to the hardware, maybe."

Spencer kissing her neck from behind, near his police car, with the lights flashing. Spencer kissing her hands across the Odessa diner booth, Spencer and Lily kissing in front of the April tulips on the streets of New York. Lily on Spencer's lap on a bench in Central Park, her arms around his neck, her lips on him.

"All right, saucy, you're not drawing me naked, are you? I draw a line at that."

She showed him that she did draw him naked, standing in front of her, while she was sitting on the bed. The artist's eye was on him, fully frontal, while she was seen from behind, her bare back exposed, just her eyes turned up to him, her breasts turned up to him. The picture was so sexy that Lily had to hide it behind eight others, but even then the voluptuous span of it was overwhelming her studio in Amy's room. Spencer breathed out when he saw it. "This is what you do when I'm at work? You do this from memory? It's unnerving. I thought artists needed models to draw? I thought that was mortal man's only protection?"

"You're not safe from me." She grinned. "I see you fully at all times."

"Do you have to see me so fully naked?" But his delight and hunger were apparent on his face.

In Lily's exquisite April, joy was wildly brought and wildly given.

* * *

371

They were lying in her bed. She was staring at him, circling his lips, his face with her gossamer fingers. "Spencer?"

"Hmm. Talk to me but don't stop doing that."

"Tell me about Mary."

"Oh no. All right, stop doing that. What about her?"

"I don't know. I never asked before, it wasn't my place."

"Is it your place now?"

"I don't know. Is it?

"What do you want to know, Liliput?"

"Are you . . . still seeing her?" She couldn't believe she got those words out. Was she going to be the other woman? Is that what she had been? It hurt her a little bit to think it, drawing parallels that led her to demon rooms within. But she couldn't not ask. She didn't even know what she was going to do with the wrong answer.

"No."

She only realized she was holding her breath after she let it out in relief. He laughed and kissed her face. "You're a funny one. Lily, I can only handle one woman at a time. My life simply won't allow for your brother's personal complexities."

"Oh. That's good. When did you stop seeing her?"

"Early March."

"You were seeing her until March?" Why was that so sharply, unpleasantly surprising?

"Yes, on and off." He gathered her into his arms. "She was my insurance against the complexities of Lily."

"What does that mean?"

"I didn't want to be accidentally swayed by your ice hard nipples that you were so gamely parading for me, trying to lure me into your bed." His fingers, his mouth, went around them.

"Spencer!"

"What? Lily, for a long time you were extremely vulnerable, then sick, then vulnerable again. Sometimes it hurt for me to even *think* of coming to see you, much less actually sitting on your couch. Such susceptibility to a man screams have sex with me, have sex with me now. The flesh is weak. I didn't want a base appetite akin to hunger to cloud my judgment. It's clouded enough as it is."

"You kept sleeping with Mary so that your judgment would not be clouded by your wanting to sleep with me?"

"Now you got it."

"So what changed?"

"I really really wanted to sleep with you, Lily."

She wanted to draw sustenance from him. She wanted him every day, and realized that every day was not enough. She wanted his hands around her, she wanted from him his humor, his Irish blood, his lips, his heart, his whole person, his soul. She wanted to say so much and couldn't find the words. She drew him obsessively and hoped that spoke to him louder than her words ever could.

She hadn't meant to do it. Falling this crashingly in love with Spencer didn't take Lily by accident. It took her by storm.

51

At Internal Affairs Once More

They were asking for him upstairs. He just couldn't under–
stand it. He hadn't pursued any new information on the
McFadden case in months and Harkman was permanently out
of commission. So why was he being called into the lion's den
again?

He sat with his arms crossed, his legs crossed. He hadn't even
nodded when he walked into the room, did not speak a hello.

"We are not the enemy, Detective O'Malley," said Liz Monroe,
reacting to his quite visible hostility.

"I have a job to do," said Spencer. "Twenty-five separate special
investigations into missing persons, all open, all pressing."

"We also have a job to do," she said. "We investigate allegations of corruption and serious misconduct by our fellow
officers."

"I know what you do, Ms. Monroe. Do you have new witnesses?
Have you collected and analyzed some new records and evidence
you would like to share with me?"

"Yes."

"Shoot."

"Detective, a Pontiac Firebird that fits your car's description
was spotted very late at night at the Old Greenwich train station.
Some coincidence, wouldn't you say? What looks like your car

is parked two miles away from Nathan Sinclair's house and then he turns up dead?"

"Ms. Monroe, you cannot be serious. You can't. What you're saying . . ." He shook his head, then laughed lightly. "Come with me to the Old Greenwich train station now, I will show you fifteen Firebirds."

"The parking lot was empty then. It was night."

"The Long Island parking lots are not empty even at night, but whatever, I don't know anything about the Greenwich station. Perhaps it wasn't empty. But I'm sure if you talk to enough people, you will find that there was a quote unquote dark blue Firebird parked at the local gas station, at a local diner, at a Dunkin' Donuts down the street, and at the empty shopping mall. Come on now, Ms. Monroe. I've got work to do."

"The person who gave us this information didn't know you drive a Firebird, detective. He happens to be an owner of a local body shop, so he knows his cars. He simply described what he saw in the parking lot that night."

"All right, Ms. Monroe. It doesn't change any of the things I just said. Because you see, no matter what car your body shop owner saw at the train station, my Firebird was on its way back to Long Island at midnight. Perhaps your witness saw a dark Firebird passing on Interstate 95, also two miles away from Nathan's house, around midnight. Now *that* could have been me." He almost snickered but didn't want to make her more hostile, though he didn't see how that could be possible. "Where is all this information coming from?"

She didn't answer, writing things furiously in her notes, finally letting him go "for the time being," but Spencer knew this wasn't over. Now that they were seriously looking, they wouldn't stop until they found something.

52

Failing Test Number One

It was May. It was moving toward May 14. It was May 14. It was a difficult day. She wasn't feeling well anyway, and on top of it, it was May 14, and the mind could not escape from it. It was a Sunday, and he was with her. He had been with her the day before, too, even though Saturdays for one reason or another were not great days for him. Their baseball game day was great, but other Saturdays were much less successful. He brooded. This Saturday she brooded too. She had her morning in the Village. She'd painted Amy all last week, sold Amy this week, sold a beautiful oil on canvas of Amy for seven hundred dollars, but even the person who bought it said, "No love this week?"

Yes, love. Love of Amy she wanted to say.

She went to lunch with Paul, with Rachel. She couldn't call Jan McFadden.

And on Sunday night, in bed with him she cried, and he held her.

"Spencer," she said, "Tell me honestly—"

"Please, Lily, don't ask me in that tone to tell you anything honestly."

"Please, tell me what you tell Mrs. McFadden when she asks you? When she asks if you think Amy is alive or dead."

"She never asks me."

"Never?"

"Never."

"Well, I'm asking you."

"Please don't."

"Tell me. Tell *me*."

"I think she's dead. I think she's been dead since May 14 of last year."

"Oh, Spencer." How upset Lily was, how sad. He held her, kissed her.

"I think in her heart, Mrs. McFadden must fear that, too," she said. "I think she must. I've never seen anyone less able to deal with her life. I mean, last month, she couldn't even put together a proper birthday party for her kids because Amy wasn't there. She just stood and cried into the sink. We didn't know what to do. Her husband was so upset with her, you know?"

Spencer for many minutes didn't say anything. He didn't know what to say. She was lying in the crook of his arm, and she couldn't see his face, and wasn't that interested in it anyway, she wasn't looking for his reactions, she was trying to understand her own. So the silent minutes dripped by unnoticed by her, and if his body had stiffened, if his arm around her became more tense, she didn't notice it either.

Lily saw Jan McFadden and didn't tell him!

Spencer breathed in and out, in and out. He remembered Lily's distress that one particular Sunday. She hadn't wanted to face him, a familiarly Andrew-related reaction. At the time he couldn't figure it out.

But now—

Finally: "Yes, yes, Jim is upset with her. When she called me a few days ago, she sounded positively distraught. She said she didn't know how she could hang on to her marriage."

"Yes," said Lily. "I saw that. Yes."

So she went to Jan McFadden's house for her children's birthday party. That's an innocent thing, so simple. Why would she not tell him this?

What happened at Jan McFadden's house that was Andrew-related that Lily could not tell him and was so upset by, that she couldn't face him?

Quietly he lay in bed with her. What to do? He too had trouble speaking when things were weighing heavily on his mind, especially things like this—where to draw the line, what was acceptable, what wasn't, what he could use, what he couldn't. She told him about seeing Jan McFadden by accident, she told him this naked in bed with him, betrayed by her own feelings of closeness to him, after he had just made love to her, after she felt safe with him, secure, in his arms, kissed. He was just Spencer when she accidentally inadvertently slipped and told him that she had been keeping her visit with Jan a secret from Detective O'Malley for six weeks.

To say that the conflicted beast raged in Spencer would have been to understate matters.

He got up out of bed, went to get a drink, stood over the sink for a few minutes, his head bent, trying to figure the unfigurable out. She came out, and watched him for a moment. "What's the matter?"

"Nothing." He finished pouring the glass of water.

He glanced at her and looked away, and then, because he knew she wanted him to, he went back into her bed and lay down beside her.

"Spence?"

"Yes?" He was very quiet.

She was curled up on her side and he was spooning her.

She thought they were lying together in warmth. "What happens to you on the weekends I don't hear from you? Where do you go?"

Such warmth. That was then. Now such cold. Now Spencer moved away, now he caught his breath, now she could feel him grinding his teeth. Why did she have to go and ruin it?

"Why do you do that? Honestly, you can't have five minutes of nice without blowing it," Spencer said.

She turned to him and sat up because she didn't want to be having this conversation lying comfortably down. "Why are you keeping secrets from me? I mean, how do you think it seems from my point of view?"

"I don't know, Lily. Why do you keep secrets from me?"

She became upset under his intent cool gaze.

Then he was up, he was getting dressed. He didn't answer her. His getting dressed was her answer. What to do? "Are you leaving?"

"I'm going home."

"Why? Why do you run out when I ask you anything?"

"Not anything, Lil. This. Why can't you just accept that I don't want to talk about it? You have things you don't want to talk about."

"Like what?"

"I don't know. You tell me."

Her heart was a sledgehammer in her chest. "I don't know. Like what?"

"Just forget it."

"You mean about Andrew? That's completely different. It has nothing to do with us. This does."

"No, it doesn't."

"Tell me, I won't be upset. Are you married?"

"You've been to my apartment. Was I hiding a wife in that apartment? What a stud I am – you, Mary, a wife. I'm surprised I can keep a job."

"Why are you angry with me?"

His jeans on, his sweatshirt on, his boots on, God, his jacket already on! he sat at the edge of her bed. "Listen to me," he said. "I don't want to have this discussion again. I don't want to talk about this with you. Just like there are things you don't want to talk about with me. But believe me—*this* has nothing whatsoever to do with you."

"That's what I'm afraid of," she said.

"Nothing to do with you! Why would you be afraid of that?"

"So if it's got nothing to do with me, why won't you tell me?"

"Why can't you let it go? Why are we lying in your bed on a Sunday night, happy, or so I think, and all the while you're stewing, figuring out when is a good time to ask me things that you already know I don't want to discuss. I'll give you a hint when— how about not after I've just made love to you, how about that? How about a different time?"

"Okay," she said in a quiet voice.

"It's not okay." He got up. "It's not okay. I'm not ready to tell you. I don't want to tell you. It's none of your business. Nothing we do here entitles you either to ask me, or to have an answer. Nothing."

"What about when you ask me things about my brother?" she flared up. "Anything we do here entitle you to that?"

She stopped speaking as soon as she said it, and he stopped listening as soon as she said it. He stepped away, she fell back on the pillow. "What, I hadn't asked you about your brother before we started this?" he said at last, but his back was to her. "You are really something." He walked out, closing the door, on a Sunday night, at one in the morning.

53

A Cop First

Spencer had three choices. He could go back and persist and get Lily to tell him what she knew. It wouldn't even take that long. Lily was extremely persuadable. But then he'd have to live with himself. Or he could go to see Jan McFadden, and pretend Lily never told him anything. He would still have to live with himself—but easier.

Or he could do nothing at all. Pretend he hadn't heard, pretend he didn't care. And still—it was the living with himself.

He went to see Jan McFadden. She was in bad shape. She said Jim was miserable, was threatening to leave, take the kids from her. He sat at her kitchen table beating around this bush and that. Paul, Rachel, Lily, yes, doesn't Lily look fine, and she's feeling good too, was all well when she came to visit? What did you do? What happened?

Sifting through someone else's life: you became afraid you would find something too personal from which you desperately wished you could turn away, like walking in on someone masturbating, and that's how Spencer poked and prodded—one eye on the door, with the word *excuse me* constantly at his lips.

It was morning when he came to see her, she was still in her housecoat. She must have felt something, seen something in him, something comforting, something non-judgmental, because she took out two glasses and set them on the kitchen table. "Detective," she said, "I could make us coffee. But I don't feel like coffee in the morning any more. When the kids are at school, when Jim's at work, I walk around my house, I can't function." She took out a bottle of Chivas.

"Can I pour you a glass, too? Just for company?"

Spencer swallowed dry. "I have to drive back, Jan," he said. "But you go right ahead."

"Just a little bit? So I don't drink alone?"

"Just a little bit, then," said Spencer. "So you don't drink alone."

And when they had sat and commiserated with each other about the child that once was here and now was not, after they had clinked and drank and sat, Jan told him about her daughter Amy and the cherry blossoms and the Mighty Quinn three years earlier.

When Spencer got back to the city, he went straight for his own round table, his own glass, his own bottle, trying to figure out what in the world to do.

It might have seemed to someone observing him wholly from without that he had choices. Instead of doing something he could do nothing, he could leave her brother alone, he could put the file into inactive, he could leave a woman who had lost her whole life to continue to lose it and not know, and not grieve properly and be unable to feel love for the things she still had. But it was clear to Spencer—who knew himself better than anyone—that he had no choice at all, only the struggle beforehand.

He spent a sleepless night getting sober, chewing pencils and erasers and cardboard backs of legal pads, he didn't answer Lily's page when she called, and the next morning, at eight, he and Gabe McGill were fifty-five miles east in Port Jefferson pushing past the Treasury agents at the honorable congressman's door.

"Good morning," said Spencer. "Congressman, this is Detective Gabe McGill from *homicide*. May we come in?"

Just as Spencer suspected, the word worked like a charm.

Andrew opened the door for them, even shook hands with Gabe. "I haven't seen you in months, detective," he said to Spencer. "What can I do for you?"

Spencer walked in and headed straight for the office without any niceties with either Andrew or Miera, who was in the kitchen making coffee. Andrew and Gabe followed.

"What do I owe this visit to, detective? I thought we were all square."

"Tell me where Amy is and then we'll be square."

"If I could, I would," said Andrew. "Now what do you want to know? How can I be of help? I can feel your desperation." He smiled affably at Gabe who stood with his arms belligerently crossed right in front of Andrew's desk.

"Until yesterday," Spencer said, "I had not considered the possibility that you and Amy knew each other before Amy went to City College and got to be friends with your sister. You are on record as saying the affair had been going on for just a few months. Yesterday, Amy's mother gave me reason to believe that your involvement with Amy goes back three years, at least. Your first meeting in front of your sister was a charade because you and Amy already were involved. So now, once again how long had you known Amy?"

Andrew faltered. "I don't know—"

"Congressman," said Gabe, "just answer the damn question. Did you know Amy three years ago?"

"I don't—I don't understand what you're trying to get at. I told you I didn't remember. It could have been longer than a few months, I guess. I don't know."

"Congressman!" Unbelievably, that was Gabe yelling. Spencer wanted to slap him on the back. No good cop, bad cop this morning, just bad cop, bad cop. "Stop it with the I-don't-know, we won't stand for it. The girl has been missing over a year. No more trying to pull the wool over our eyes. You know everything, and you're not telling."

"I made an honest mistake with the dates, that's all."

"In the middle of your honest mistake, your lover transferred colleges and moved in with your sister!"

Andrew's face was flummoxed, confounded. "Detectives, Detectives . . ." He put his hands up as if to calm them down. "Come on, now," he said in a conciliatory tone. "The charade was because of the relationship, that's all. Obviously we were trying to keep it secret. From Lily. That's why we pretended not to know each other. I got confused with the dates. Where is the deliberate malice here?"

"Who said anything about deliberate malice?" Gabe asked with narrowed eyes.

"And it's not what we're asking you," said Spencer. "I'm interested in understanding why you would push Amy to change colleges from Hunter to City."

"What are you talking about? I did no such thing."

"Without you, how would Amy know about your sister at City College, taking art classes?"

"Obviously, we talked about my life." Andrew's face was deeply contorted. "We were involved. She knew quite a lot about my life, Detective O'Malley. That is what happens. You are with someone, you tell them things. And then, sometimes, they use this information against you or against the people close to you. You know how that can be, detective?"

Paling, Spencer took a step back from the congressman and fell mute. For a minute he couldn't speak. For a minute he almost wanted to say himself, I don't know what you're talking about. Then it occurred to him the congressman was talking about himself—but the bitter look in Andrew's eyes didn't go away, not when he spoke to Spencer, not when he spoke about Amy.

"Did you feel that Amy used the things you told her against you?" Spencer asked slowly.

"Perhaps that's a little strong." But Andrew's voice remained strong. "I was very surprised that she transferred colleges, made friends with my sister. When I found out, I told her I felt it was inappropriate. That it would make things harder for us. But by the time I found out, they had not only been friends for months, but had moved in together."

"You never asked Amy why she would do this?"

"Of course I asked Amy why she would do this. She said that she wanted to be closer to me. She said that being friendly with Lily would give us more opportunity to meet. Make things more proper, instead of less proper. With my busy life sometimes it was hard for us to get together. Through Lily we were able to see each other more often, and still maintain an air of propriety. Family functions, lunches with the three of us, the campaigning for me. All of it so we could be together more." All the words that Andrew spoke were spoken through his teeth.

Spencer exchanged glances with Gabe. He just could not tell what was the truth and what wasn't. He said finally, "But the deception there—it's staggering. For years to constantly try to cover up in front of your sister the intimacy between you."

"It was easier than you think. Lily can be quite oblivious to what's going on around her." He stared coldly at Spencer.

Spencer's gaze darkened. "That's enough," he said in a low voice. Deflated, pensive, he stood before Andrew with Gabe tugging on his arm.

Gabe asked, "If you didn't meet through Lily, how did you meet?"

Andrew looked at them in turn, said nothing, until Gabe had drawn Spencer to one side and Andrew found himself with only Gabe to look at.

"I don't remember. I think she came to my Port Jeff office, asking for some pamphlets."

Spencer stopped in his motionless tracks. "*She* came to your office?"

Andrew took a deep breath. "Yes."

"Amy McFadden came into *your* office?"

"Yes. She kept stopping by and stopping by."

Spencer, staring at Gabe, was rendered temporarily without questions. This went against *all* his assumptions.

385

"When was this?"

"I told you, I don't know and can't recall. Winter break possibly. Winter break 1996."

For a long time Spencer stood in front of Andrew absorbing what he had just heard.

"You're telling me," he said at last, "that you had known Amy for almost two years before your sister introduced you?"

"I can't recall exactly."

"Do you recall exactly if Amy helped you with your campaign back in 1992? Your first campaign for congressman? Did she help you then?"

"I can recall *that* exactly," said Andrew. "Amy did not help me with my 1992 campaign." He stopped speaking. "I did not know of her then."

And then the question came. Spencer could not have asked this before, when he himself had been oblivious to the truth of things. "Congressman Quinn, were you . . . in love with her?"

Andrew blinked. "Well, as you say, it was just an affair, a fling. She was a young girl, half my age. We were at two completely different places in life. I was for a little while swept up in something, I admit. Do you know how that might be, detective? Knowing that something is so wrong and yet being swept up in it?"

And now Spencer blinked.

Gabe just looked from one man to the other. "No one is asking the question that's on my mind, frankly," he said. "The only thing that I am swept up in—and that is, Congressman Quinn, do you know where Amy is?"

"No."

"Has your memory improved on this Milo character we are investigating and his ties to Amy?"

Andrew blinked. "No." Gabe and Spencer saw the blink, exchanged a look.

"Is he perhaps someone she had been involved with?"

"I don't know."

"Did Amy mention anything unusual about high school, perhaps in her travels with her friends before she met you?"

"No." He paused. "She did tell me that during her time away she was experimenting with different religions, she even tried some American Indian church to see if they had the answers."

"What American Indian church?"

"I don't know . . ."

"Native American Church, perhaps?"

"I guess."

All these were asked by Gabe. Spencer was not speaking until he said, "Did she end it?"

"What?"

"Oh, come on! These games you play to give yourself a little bit of time. Is that a difficult question? She sought you out, she sought your sister out, she moved in with Lily without your knowledge, presented you with the situation as a *fait accompli*. It seems like she was in the driver's seat. And then she ended it. I can sense that is right. Why?"

"It was time for the relationship to come to an end. That is all." Andrew lowered his gaze to his desk.

"This Milo character came back into Amy's life at the shelter right around the time that she broke it off with you. Did it have anything to do with him?"

"I don't know what you're talking about. God! I don't know! Enough already. You just asked me this. I told you this in October, I'm telling you now, I don't know anything about this Milo."

Spencer stepped up to the desk. "If you know who Milo is, why won't you tell us? If it will help you, why won't you tell us?"

"Who says it will help me?" said Andrew, stopping Spencer in his tracks.

"I am trying to get some answers for Amy's mother," he said, "so that her life can move forward. And for your sister, too . . ."

"Don't you dare," Andrew said with gritted teeth, "you of all people, talk to me about my sister. You think I don't know what you're doing? That I don't understand you? Taking advantage of her sickness. She doesn't know anything. You aren't going to get any answers from her."

Spencer's fists clenched. "You don't understand me at all, congressman. Because this isn't about me. And this is not about your sister. This is about you and the girl you were involved with for over three years who has been missing for one. That's what it's about. You keep forgetting that."

Andrew's grim face squared off against Spencer's grim face.

"You're picking the wrong man to go after, detective," said Andrew. There was something menacing in his tone. "Understand?"

Spencer started for Andrew around the desk, and was stopped by Gabe, grabbing him, restraining him. "No, man, no. Not worth it," Gabe said quietly. "Not worth it."

Andrew said, "Come on now. I'm waiting for this. You'll spend five to fifteen in jail for assault, you'll be thrown off the force, you son of a bitch. Come on now, show me your true colors."

Spencer pulled himself from Gabe and stepped away to the door. "I don't have the time, you're so busy showing me yours." He struggled to get hold of himself. "You just don't get it. *You're* picking the wrong man to lie to. You think your threats with the IA, your entreaties to my supervisors will quiet me down? You won't get me off your back until your signed confession is on the desk of my captain. You understand?"

On the way back, Gabe started to speak, and Spencer cut him off, saying, "Gabe, not a word. I don't want to talk about anything right now. Not a single thing, all right? We'll write it all up when we get back. I just need to think."

54

Infernal Affairs

Next day he was summoned upstairs again.

Whittaker looked at him with sympathy. "Spence, what the hell are you doing out there that they're pulling you in every five minutes?"

"What can I tell you, they don't have anything better to do." He shrugged casually. That fucking Andrew. "Chief, I've been asking around, but no one seems to know. Have you ever heard of the Native American Church?"

"I've heard of it."

"What's their deal?"

"I don't know much about them. All I know is that they're the only ones in the United States who are allowed legally to use peyote in their religious practices."

"*Peyote?*"

"Mescaline. They claim the hallucinogen brings them closer to their god. That's all I know about them. You better go. Ms. Monroe is waiting for you." And Whittaker made a snapping towel movement against Spencer's groin.

Once again he sat opposite a brusque and business-like Liz Monroe and two of her minions.

"Detective, I'm not going to beat around the bush, we have a new witness."

A new witness, just like that, a day after his visit to the congressman.

Monroe continued. "Ms. Edith Stanley lives in a house diagonally across the street from Nathan Sinclair's house. I have a statement from Ms. Stanley here. She says"—she paused to put on her glasses while Spencer waited—"that that night she saw a shadow . . ."

The details in Ms. Stanley's statement were so vague it was astonishing to Spencer that he was being asked questions based on an assumption of usefulness.

Spencer interrupted her, "Let's put me in front of her, and see if she thinks I'm the man she saw as a shadow across her lawn after midnight one evening. She still lives there? I'll call her myself, if you like. We can get her to the station in a few hours."

"You will do no such thing, detective," Monroe said, her voice rising. "For one, she is no longer living on Sound Beach Avenue."

"Oh? Where is she now?" Spencer inquired innocently.

"She is in a care facility in Greenwich."

"A nursing home? But how did you hear about this woman now? What made you seek her out?"

"We get information in all sorts of ways, detective, as you well know."

"I know. I'm asking how you got this particular piece of information."

"We have people who . . . have been talking to most of the residents of Sound Beach Avenue."

"You have people." Spencer rubbed his forehead. "But you just said Ms. Stanley no longer lives there."

"That's right."

"So did you interview her in person?"

"I didn't personally, no. We have . . ."

"People for that. I know. Did anyone speak to the director of the home?"

"I don't have that in my notes. I don't see how it is relevant."

"Well, if you'll excuse me for inquiring after such an indelicate matter, how old is Ms. Stanley?"

"Detective O'Malley . . ."

"How old? Is her date of birth in your notes?"

Reluctantly: "She was born in 1907."

Spencer kept his voice even. It was difficult. "So let me understand," he said slowly. "You have an affidavit in front of you from a 93-year-old woman who says that four or five years ago on some unspecified evening, she saw a *shadow?*"

"Ms. Stanley says she saw a man in dark clothes walking very briskly away from the Sinclair house late at night . . ."

"I'm sorry, excuse me for interrupting again," interrupted Spencer again. "But I'm still confused. What night?"

"The night in question . . ."

"What date does she give in her statement for this *night in question?*"

The anxious movement of her manicured fingers told Spencer Ms. Monroe could not find that precise information just then. He added, "And someone should talk with the director of the care home, don't you think? To see what health crisis brought Ms. Stanley into their care?"

"I don't see how it is relevant."

Spencer nodded. "I will show you. Just one moment, Ms. Monroe." He flipped open his cellphone. "Do you have the number for me, or should I just dial information?"

She grudgingly gave it to him, and while she waited, Spencer spent two minutes on the phone with Mr. Cerone, the director of the facility, asking him two or three questions and nodding.

When he hung up he said, "You see, it's always helpful to have all the details. You might want to call Mr. Cerone yourself, for your records. Mr. Cerone will confirm for you that Edith Stanley has been in his care for nearly three years, since just after her ninetieth birthday, when the glaucoma and cataracts she had been *battling for years* made her functionally blind and she could no longer live independently."

Liz Monroe sat like a stone statue; the men who flanked her fidgeted cruelly.

"Will that be all, Detective O'Malley?"

Spencer stood from the table and gave her a humorless smile. "That'll be all, Ms. Monroe."

55

Failing Test Number Two

She read in the papers of the new allegations about Andrew and
Amy. Certainly she didn't hear them from Spencer. She didn't
hear from him for two days. She couldn't take it for two minutes.
When she absolutely couldn't take it anymore, she called him,
and as she was listening to the beeper ring, it occurred to Lily
with stunning clarity that if something were to happen to her,
Spencer's life without her would go on just as before, while hers
without him would stop completely—as proven. She had no life
without him. From morning till night, every day, he filled the
minutes for her, thinking about him, waiting to hear from him,
talking to him, seeing him, worrying about him, painting him.
She could give herself a foxy do with her growing out hair, she
could put on make-up for him and buy a negligee to wear for
him, but despite all that, it remained what it remained: without
her Spencer would be exactly the same, whereas without him,
she would be nothing. That was too pathetic even for Cancer
Girl. So when he returned her call, she didn't pick up the phone.
When he called back again, she tried not to pick up the phone.
   "Lil? Come on. Pick up."
   Breaking down, she picked up the phone.
   "Hi."
   "Hi."

Her larynx wasn't working. She said nothing. He said nothing.

"I'll come tonight after work, late. Okay?" he said, but there was heaviness in his voice.

She was in the studio when she heard his keys in her door. She loved that he could come and go whenever he pleased. That he could do in her life whatever he pleased.

She came out, stood in the living room. He looked so good, so serious, so grown up, and for some reason so haunted.

She wanted to tell him how much he meant to her, what she felt for him, but by the way she cried and clasped his head and neck and whispered, *Spencer . . .* when he was on top of her, his arms supporting his weight off her, staying that way, not tiring, by the way she cried afterward, buried under him, hanging on to him, shuddering in her limbs, in her shoulders, in her abdomen, she guessed that he already knew.

They were lying in bed, and it was all wrong. Lily felt it. They may have made love, but whatever tension it released it did not this time resolve the tension of their conflict.

She was afraid to ask him what was the matter, she wasn't making that mistake again. She wasn't going to ruin their making up with her senseless idiocy.

Suddenly it was he who spoke. He told her things. Quietly he told her he had been for the past eight months investigated by IA. She took hold of his hand in mute sympathy, while thinking hard of the next considerate thing to say. She didn't quite know how to get to the next question. Her stomach fluttered.

"I don't understand. What exactly are they accusing you of?"

"They think I had something to do with Nathan Sinclair's death."

Lily fought the impulse to let go of his hand.

Why did she think he was fighting the impulse to let go of hers?

She mustered the courage in her chemo-ridden entrails to say, "Why don't you tell them you didn't do it?"

"I told them."

"And?"

"Obviously they don't believe me or they wouldn't still be talking to me."

Spencer wasn't more forthcoming about this, as if he had something more to say but didn't want to say it to her. It felt as if he had more to say about all manner of things and didn't want to say them.

And interestingly—she didn't want to hear them. She suddenly did not want to press. An awful heaviness was descending on her from feeling Spencer's grim and determined body around her.

"I've been so involved with myself," she said quietly, "and all the while, you needed me, too, I knew you were going through something." She turned to him.

Spencer shook his head. "I'm not going through anything. You on the other hand do need my help. I'm fine. This whole thing with the IA, it will blow over. Or it won't. In either case, I'm ready for the consequences."

He said it. She thought about it. "What consequences?"

"Lily, mine is not an existential universe. It is not meaningless. Like you I believe in a universe in which actions don't happen in a vacuum. Where all actions, minuscule and enormous, have resonating effects. I believe that Nathan Sinclair took actions that eventually resulted in consequences that he did not intend or foresee. Like many people."

It was his bitter tone that she could not fathom but felt was somehow related to her, it was hurting her, prickling her skin. Lily felt her skin get cold and transmit anxiety through her body, she could not stop the involuntary gasp, could not stop the moving away. She put her hands over her eyes, and as Spencer was bending over her, Lily was thinking that indeed this was something that affected not just Spencer. It exploded inside her:

This IA thing with him was about her too! Her. And Amy. And Andrew.

"This isn't just about Nathan Sinclair, is it, Spencer?"

He let go of her and moved away on the bed. "No, Lily. It never is just about one thing."

"Okay, let's have it. What does your IA investigation have to do with my brother?"

"The same thing that you going to Jan McFadden's and not telling me has to do with your brother."

Her heart fell. "There was nothing to tell," she said in an unsteady voice.

"We're in bed. Stop lying. I know the truth now. And your brother is out to quiet me, there is no question. He's got private detectives looking into every cranny of my life, to get me off the case, to shut me up. It is not a coincidence that every time I go and see him with new evidence, not a day goes by before my ass is hauled up to IA again on some new bogus charge or new suspicion. He's got *people* hard at work on this. If I've ever taken a bribe, used excessive force, drugs while at work, fired my weapon indiscriminately, been involved in any corruption. But the only thing he's got is the death of Nathan Sinclair, and he wields him like the sword of Damocles."

Lily moved away from him. "Spencer," she uttered, "who are you? Why are you so paranoid? This is my brother we're talking about. This isn't some organized crime boss. My clean, even-tempered congressman of a brother. You are being completely unreasonable."

"Lily, your friend Amy was with your clean, married, even-tempered congressman brother for three years while he lied to your face, she lied to your face . . ."

She jumped off the bed. Where did she find the strength? "Maybe. Yes, you're right, he's a liar, and a bastard, he didn't do the right thing, you're right, yes, but he didn't kill her!" she yelled. "He didn't do it. You don't know him like I know him. This isn't your Nathan Sinclair, this is different, this life is different!"

He also got up, sat up. "Calm down."

"People get kidnapped all the time," Lily said, panting. "I hear it on TV. Girls, young girls, taken, abducted by strangers or bare acquaintances."

"Lily, you're talking to a missing persons investigator. I know. I get hundreds of those cases a year. *Young* people is the key. Not twenty-four-year-old college students. Amy went out one morning and never came back. She left all her money and credit cards behind. Unlike the time when she went traveling with her friends having actually tied up her life, this time she left one Friday morning for the afternoon and evaporated off the earth. And by the way, don't think I haven't noticed that she disappeared as soon as you left."

"What are you talking about?" Lily was aghast. "What does *that* have to do with anything?"

"Nothing? Everything? I'm merely saying, it's been noted, Lily, you being out of the way."

"Out of the way for *what*?" she gasped. And then she remembered Amy saying to her, *oh, yes, Lily, by all means, do go to Maui, you definitely should,* and Andrew saying to her, *are you sitting down, Liliput, definitely go to Maui, go as soon as you can, soothe our mother,* and she stared at Spencer even more bewildered.

"So what happened to her?" said Spencer. "Where is her custody battle? Who is fighting over Amy? Where is her ransom note? Who wants money for her?"

"Not my brother." Her voice was shaky.

"What do you know about your brother?"

"I know that he couldn't kill her."

"No?"

"No." She got her bearings back full throttle. "Because aside from running for public office, aside from wanting to be president of the United States, he has never felt passionately about anything in his whole life! Never, about anything in his whole life! No extremes for him, just right down the middle, just one speed, one steady, rock-solid speed, a gentle up-slope, that's my brother!"

"Just like you, huh, Lil?" He said that ironically because she wasn't down the middle at the moment, standing in the dark, shrieking.

"People like that," she went on, hyperventilating, "don't kill other people. They barely even break up with them. One day they just stop calling, and hope that no one cared enough about them to notice." She lowered her eyes. "Kind of the way you treat the women in your life, Spencer."

He lowered his eyes too, for only a moment. "Lily, I repeat, you don't know anything about your brother. You don't know anything about Amy. You don't know anything about Milo. You barely know about yourself. She transferred to your university, took your classes, sought you out, moved in with you, was involved with your brother under your very nose, in this tiny apartment, and you didn't know! And Jan McFadden is still waiting for her. I mean, are you on my side, or what?"

"No! I am *not* on your side," she whispered fiercely, suddenly giving such clarity to the unspeakable. "I'm not on Amy's side." She lowered her head this time for good because the intensity of her feelings overwhelmed her. "I'm on my brother's side."

Spencer got up out of bed, naked still, eyes glaring, his own intensity apparent in the stiffness of his body. "Well, it took you long enough to say it."

"I will never, ever do anything to help you hurt him, not for Jan McFadden, not for Amy, not for you, ever, you understand?"

"Perfectly."

"So what are you going to do now, Spencer?" said Lily. "Are you going to kill him, too?"

Spencer sucked in his breath, and his head tilted sideways, as if he had been struck. "Ah. If only I had known a little earlier you harbored this much malice toward me," he said. "That you would use what I tell you against me the first chance you get."

"What about you using what I told you the first chance you get? You knew I didn't want to tell you about Jan McFadden, you

398

knew I didn't mean to tell you, you got me at my weakest moment, and then you went to try to wreck my brother's life a little bit more. What do you call that?"

"You lied to me, you tried to keep it from me, even though you yourself thought something was wrong with him hiding it!"

"No, I just knew you would turn it around and use it against him, like you use every single thing I ever tell you against him!"

He was still standing naked in front of her. "You shouldn't have hidden your true self for so long, Lily, shouldn't have let me waste my time with you."

"What about me wasting my time with you?" she cried. "I've got less time to waste than you."

He started getting dressed on one side of the bed. She was crying on the other.

"We are all each minute closer to death," said Spencer, straightening up. "With every fight, every harsh word, every evil deed, one step closer to our eternity. Not just you."

"Please leave my brother alone," she said through her tears, her voice breaking. "For me."

He was fixing the straps that harnessed his on-duty Glock-20 to his body, not looking at her.

"Please. And I promise he will leave you alone."

"I will not leave your brother alone," he said, grabbing the last of his things off her bureau—his wallet, his keys, his beeper. "But I will leave you alone."

What was he doing, what was he doing, what was he doing? He thought this every night he walked home. The question was never why. The question was and remained: What now?

He decided to go home via Michael's Pub. He knew Gabe might still be there—and he was. They ordered drinks, clinked them together. Spencer barely put his to his mouth. Oh how good he was at pretending! How good he was tonight at sitting straight up on the bar stool as he pretended to sip his whisky and didn't even lick his lips or ask for a double or another round. He just sat, and clinked, and put the empty glass down and continued talking, as if it was all nothing, just a normal late night at a bar downtown. It wasn't a Friday or a Saturday but Spencer simply didn't know how to get out of what he was feeling without the drink.

"What's the matter, O'Malley? Hard stuff on the McFadden girl?"

"Stuff, no stuff, I don't know." He sighed. "Got myself into a bind, McGill. Into a real bind. Don't know what to do."

"This ain't over a goil, is it?"

"'Tis, McGill. 'Tis."

Spencer motioned Ted for two more drinks, and when Gabe wasn't looking, opened out his thumb and forefinger for Ted, who quietly brought Spencer a fat double. They drank.

And on the way home, Spencer knew that he could no longer have it both ways, all ways. A call needed to be made by him on what to do about Lily Quinn. A choice. To have her, or to have justice. To have her or to have Glenlivet instead of blood in his veins. Tonight it was Glenlivet. What a relief not to think of her, not to talk, not to feel.

Lily couldn't sleep.

The weekend passed with no word from him. Tuesday came and she had to go to the hospital for blood work which was neither good nor bad, no bad news, but no good news either. But she could tell DiAngelo was keeping to himself. He gave her Alkeran again. She spent Tuesday night on her back, and then on her hands and knees. When she could finally sit up she painted, sketched, stapled down the drying canvas, crying. Screaming black mouths again, black buildings, black trees. No one would want her damn paintings of existential despair.

She wanted Spencer back, but she wanted her brother left alone also.

On Wednesday, the day from the rings of hell, she was lying

on the sofa, not picking up the phone, not getting up, not eating, not drinking, not reading, not watching TV, or listening to the radio, certainly not painting, just watching the clocks tick by the slow beat of her life, when there was a knock on her door.

She wanted to get up, but found she had no strength. Please let it be him, she prayed as she pulled herself up. But she prayed to him. Spencer, please let it be you.

Outside her door he stood.

He was mute as he watched her, and she knew she must have looked like quite a sight, because he said, "What in the world are you doing to yourself?"

"Nothing," she replied and swayed. "Why didn't you just use your key, like always?"

Without replying, he came in, came in as familiar and true as he was, he put his arms around her, brought her to him, they sat on the couch. She wanted to ask him if they should go to bed but was afraid. This is your life, Lily, someone inside her shouted, the only life you're ever going to have, the only life you want. Aren't you going to fight for it?

With a lowered head he said nothing for a while as they sat in the quiet, hearing only the ticking of the clocks.

"I'm sorry, Spencer."

"You have nothing to be sorry for."

"I do. I do. You've been so good to me, and I—" she became choked up. "And I let you down."

"You didn't let me down."

"I did. You confided in me, told me about your trouble, and I took your confidence into my angry fist and punched you in the face."

"No, you didn't."

"I said such awful things. I'm very very sorry. I failed the test."

He shook his head. "There was no test, Lily."

"I have been tested and have been found wanting. I backed away from you, I was deliberately cruel to you. Despite how I feel about you, I treated you like shit. What does that say about me?"

401

"You didn't treat me like shit. You just forgot about me."

"You were right to leave. You should have left sooner."

He didn't protest that one. He said, "I should have never taken advantage of a sick girl."

"I'm not sick, I'm better."

"I'm not the pure one here. I've been torturing you with things you can't possibly deal with—and shouldn't have to. I should know better."

"I can, I can. Believe in me. Please. Please believe I can get better, and be a help to you and be supportive of you. I can be someone you turn to, someone you need."

He took her hands into his. She got up off the couch and knelt in front of him, knelt between his legs, looking at him beseechingly. "I can, Spencer, please forgive me," she whispered. She didn't know how she was getting the words out, they were so painful. "I will do better. Please give me a chance to show you, to prove it."

He let go of her, and got up, stepping away from the couch, away from her.

"Lily, you know I will not stop helping you. But . . ."

Oh no, no, no, no, please, no but.

"I can't do this anymore."

"No."

He pulled her up, sat her down on the couch, but himself remained standing and away from her. "I can't. We shouldn't have started, though I suppose it was inevitable. I don't know what I was thinking. You are on a rebound from tragedy and I took advantage of your weakness. It's my fault."

"No. I will be different, Spencer. I promise. I didn't mean those things I said. I was just upset."

"Lily, I don't care about what you said. I don't want you to change into something you're not. He is your *brother*! It can be no other way. I would be no other way if I were in your shoes. But you do recognize that we remain in terrible conflict, you and I."

402

"No."

"*Terrible* conflict. You know it. I know it. Your grandmother knows it. Your brother knows it. We pretended for a little while it wasn't so, but we can't pretend any more, and it remains."

"I want my mother!" she cried. "I wish I had one. But I don't want you to be my mother, Spencer. My mother or my father. I want us to be together as equals. I want to help you, too."

"Lily . . ."

"Forget about everything else, everything. I will get better, I promise. I want to walk by your side, that's where I want to be. Please."

He didn't even touch her when he said, "Lily, you don't understand anything. Finding what happened to Amy is what I think about day and night. That's what I do. That's what I want. If I had one wish . . ." he stopped. "You want to talk about wrong?" he said coldly. "Well, here. If I had one wish, I would wish not for money, not even for you to get completely better, but to find out what happened to Amy. And when I'm with you, I have to confess that I am not pure of heart, I am not free of ulterior motive. Amy, your brother, they are always in the back of my mind, sometimes in the front of my mind. They were from the very beginning, they will be till the end." He took a breath before saying, "I'm still canvassing."

"Spencer, *no*."

"Yes, Lily. It's not easy for me to say that, but it's the truth. You have the right to remain silent, because everything you say can and will be held against you. And we can't continue like that. *I* can't continue. I have to live with myself too. For a little while, we cannot even continue as we were, as friends. I have to get my head together. You'll have to bring Joy back to help you if you need help. I'm losing my edge since I've been with you. I'm getting soft. I am getting fuzzy around the eyeballs, all these comedies we've been watching, all this focus on your illness."

She couldn't believe what he was saying.

403

"It's too much for me," he continued. "My judgment has been clouded by you, my senses are dulling. I spend the night with you and the next morning I can't think straight. I'm thinking crazy things and my work is slipping, the missing teenagers are turning into prostitutes, the missing in the projects are being overrun by drugs, the kidnapped are remaining napped. Jan McFadden is losing her marriage. Plus, there is this damn IA thing hanging over me and I have to protect myself, and think on my feet, I have to make sure I don't end up in prison just because I was blithely daydreaming of your body."

She thought she heard him say I'm sorry after that, but she couldn't be sure.

When he left, he took her key off his ring and set it on the table by the door. Lily never got up from the couch.

I love you so much . . . I'd die for you . . . and all they can say is . . . he's not your kind . . .

And they were right.

On the way home past the traffic lights, Spencer was thinking about his black lies to her, and about how falsely liberating it was to be free of her, to concentrate on the areas of his life where he could still exist and remain hidden. With her there was no hiding. And Spencer knew that if he had only one wish, it would not be to find Amy. It would not even be to have Lily get permanently better.

It would be to stop drinking.

So he could give Lily a whole man, instead of the fragment fraud he had become.

56

Unraveling at Home and Overseas

Maui on the caller ID was one constant distress call. Either from a desperate, at-the-end-of-his-rope father, or from her ranting railing slurring mother.

Her mother said she was divorcing him, she didn't care what it would cost, because he was a liar and he promised her hundreds of things he had reneged on.

Papi opened his own bank account and transferred $30,000 of their money into it.

Mother was screaming so loud into the phone with Lily about the withdrawn funds that the neighbors came (this was eleven in the morning Maui time) and said she is screaming so loud, if you don't call the police, we will.

So Lily hung up.

Later her father called her back and said the police came and, "Your mother lifted up her skirt to the officers and said he beats me, look at my bruises."

It was the *Titanic* sending out distress flares to the *Carpathia*— the ship that thought the *Titanic* was setting off fireworks. Lily didn't think Maui was setting off fireworks. Lily was certain Maui was sinking and by this time in the metaphorical tomorrow would be immersed and unraveled and possibly rent in half. And perhaps she might have noticed more, cared more, paid more attention, if only her own unraveling at home and rending in half were not as complete.

But the unraveling at home was complete.

She didn't know what to do with the minutes of her life. She didn't know what to do, what to make of her evenings or her growing hair. What to do with Sundays without him. The habit formation of passion felt surgically removed from her, it felt as if limbs were missing and the days without limbs lasted years.

"Oh, thank the *Lord* you're not with that awful man anymore," said Grandma when Lily told her. "The good Lord looks after you, Lily, and there is just one more proof of that."

Lily didn't want to talk about it.

Thank God for Paul, for Rachel. Amy vanished, and Lily had inherited them, they were hers, and she loved them. It was like Amy knew she was going and had bequeathed to Lily a way to make her life a little bit easier. It was better to have friends, even passed down friends, than to go without. It was better to have sisters, even ones like Anne and Amanda, than to go without. It was better to have a brother than to go without. It was better to have agoraphobic grandmothers. Drunk mothers. Now that Lily was plumbing the sewer of despair, it was better to have them all.

She spent the days in her studio, lying down in the paint, pressing her face onto the floor that once supported Amy's bed, and now had paint on it that dripped from the oils and the acrylics and the watercolors she had painted Spencer with. That was all that was left of him now, just the remains of the vivid paint from his lips, from his eyes.

It was as if he had died.

It was as if she had died.

She called Jan McFadden. How are you holding up, Mrs. McFadden, she asked. Not too good, Lily. I know. Me neither. And Jan cried and Lily cried, both having lost the irreplaceable.

What if Amy was never coming back.

What if Spencer was never coming back.

It was better to have Spencer, on any terms, any terms at all, any terms he laid down, than to go on like this—without.

On Saturday they stood around her tables, they quietly gave her money, they took the paintings from her hands.

"No love this week, Lily?"

"No love this week."

Her paintings that week: not many, all watercolors. The two windows with the tied blue curtains, beyond them sunshine and spring, and in front of them, the empty bed.

"How could he give up on me so easily?" she said to her friends one Friday evening. They were strolling to St. Mark's Comics to buy a present for one of Rachel's nephews. "He spent practically every day with me, how could he just not call me, not ask after me like this? How could he just turn off like this?"

Paul didn't say anything, but Lily felt he had something to say, just wasn't saying it. "What? Tell me, what?"

"Lil, it's like parents. How can they live without us when we go away to school? They take care of us for eighteen years, suddenly we're not sleeping in their home, eating their food, we're not there. How do they manage so well without us? How come they start to travel, and join groups, and take classes, and learn a foreign language, and when we come back for the weekends we find them thriving not pining. How come?"

"I don't know. Are you asking me? Or are you being rhetorical? What does it have to do with Spencer?"

"I'll tell you what it has to do with Spencer," said Paul. "You won't want to hear it. But it's hard to take care of another person. It's a lot of responsibility."

"What about being with me? It wasn't all about my cancer," said Lily. "I tried to make my cancer fun for him. We cut hair together, and we did laundry together, and had Chinese together, and I took him out for Sunday brunch, and painted him, and taught him medical terms he probably wouldn't have learned in his lifetime." And I did other things with him that I can't believe

407

he surrendered so quickly, so easily. Her heartbreak dripped from her eyes in big wet balls onto the New York City sidewalk, her shoulders shook.

"Well, I'm not saying that wasn't fun for him, darling," said Paul, hugging her. "Come on, buck up." Rachel, taking Lily's other arm, nodded her head wisely, as if she knew what Paul was talking about. "But still the relationship wasn't equal. He had to take care of you."

"Not anymore. I was getting better. I'm a survivor now."

"Well, sure," said Rachel, and then in an astonishing feat of philosophical fervor, pitched in with, "but he doesn't know the future. He only knows the past."

Lily fell quiet. But she suspected that the straw that broke Spencer was not him taking care of her, for he did that too willingly, but her failing him in his test of her. He wanted from her what she did not give him, perhaps could not give him.

When Joshua left, she barely felt it, she realized only now. Being with her friends was good, it helped pass those anguished eternal minutes without limbs—but nothing was what being with him was, with him whom her heart loved and needed.

After getting the new Batman toys from St. Mark's, they were standing on the corner of Astor and Mark's debating whether to go for Ukrainian, Indian, or Diner-American, when a male voice said, "Lil?"

And before Lily turned around, in that one second, she prayed, prayed, PRAYED pleasepleaseplease let it be Spencer, and she turned around, her eager face to the voice, and it was Joshua.

Her face must have shown her disappointment, because he said, "Don't look so happy to see me." He looked *surprisingly* happy to see her. There were awkward handshakes all around. He asked how she had been. Oh great. He asked how she was feeling. Oh, great. "Really?" he said. "I'm not surprised. Because you look *great*."

He called later that Friday, but Lily was out dancing with

Rachel, and he left a message, but when she came home she was too exhausted to listen. The next morning she listened. "Lil, can I come over? I want to talk to you."

It was Saturday, she was selling her lousy paintings today. She called to tell him she was busy. He asked to come over for just a little while in the evening. He really needed to talk to her. They agreed on a time, and he showed up half an hour early, wanting to take her out.

She had nothing to do and was sick of herself so she went out with Joshua to dinner and a movie. They saw *Bowfinger* with Steve Martin. Joshua wanted to see a drama but Lily said she didn't do dramas anymore. "*It was a beautiful dream,*" she said to him afterward in Republic, a Thai place on Union Square, but he didn't pay attention, and all they talked about was him and his thoughts, and feelings, and jobs, which was just fine with Lily who pretended to listen, until she finally said in a tired voice, "*Think of this as an errand. Your errand is to run across the freeway until I yell 'cut.'*" And he caught on at last and asked if she was quoting *Bowfinger* to him, and she said yes, and if she was yelling *cut*, and she smiled, as in *finally he gets it*, and he said, so you want go back to your place?

When they got back and were on her couch ("nice couch!"), Joshua said, "Lily, honestly you look great. Your hair is so sexy short and red, and your body looks amazing."

"Thank you," she said. "Cancer agrees with me."

He coughed, choked, spluttered.

"I'm just kidding."

"But seriously, though, you're all better?"

"Who knows these things?" She wished she could check her messages surreptitiously. What if Spencer called? From the couch she could see the machine blinking, but she couldn't read the number of new messages. He *could* have called.

Joshua was touching her hair. It was late, they'd had a couple of glasses of wine, the lights weren't on except in the kitchen.

"So where's Shona tonight?"

"We didn't work out. She wasn't you, Lily."

"I'm not me either, Joshua," she said, getting up. "Wait, I have to . . ." She went to the blinking message machine. "It could be my grandmother, something could be wrong." She pressed NEW. Please please, please Spencer.

But there was no message from him. Just from her grandmother. Lily couldn't go back and sit on the couch with Joshua.

"It's getting late, you better go."

"Go? Why? I just got here."

"I know, but I have to go out."

"It's after midnight, where could you be going?"

She was quiet. He was quiet. Then she said, "Josh, there was once a time when I would have given anything to have you touch me nicely, to have you say nice things to me, to have you back. You left, Amy left, and I was so alone. But that time has passed. We had something once, but now that I know the difference, I can't even say it was a beautiful dream. Please can you go?"

"Lily, I know it's been hard for you, and I'm sorry—"

"You have no idea what anything has been for me. The Lily you knew—she is gone, Joshua. Gone. The way Amy is gone. You don't know me at all anymore. I'm a stranger to you."

He didn't understand, he thought it was about the way he had left her. But she suddenly grew so tired, so tired of standing, of talking to him, of his presence in her apartment. She didn't want to be explaining anything, and didn't.

"You really want me to go?"

"More than anything."

He left abruptly. And Lily herself left soon thereafter. She ran to Spencer's apartment, long avenue blocks, from C all the way to Broadway. He wasn't there. No one was answering and his light was not on. She waited, she called him, she beeped him, she waited by the apartment door, she went to Dagostino's across the street, bought a pound of cherries, stood at the awning in the night and watched the door. Two o'clock in the morning, there was still no movement at his place.

410

Where was *he* at two o'clock in the morning on a Saturday night?

There were other things she could do with her life than stand in the middle of downtown Broadway waiting for Spencer.

She could go to an art exhibit in Dumbo in Brooklyn.

A rock concert on top of a roof.

Comedy improv at Caroline's.

Webster Hall, Mondays ladies night, dancing.

Rachel said she could fix her up with a guy named Martin from the club. Martin was young and very built and very interested. They had shaken hands last night, flirted a little. He said maybe they could go to a movie next week. *Me, Myself, and Irene* had opened at Union Square. Yes, yes, a movie. And perhaps while they were waiting in line for the tickets, they would run into Spencer, who lived only a few blocks away, with a girl on his arm, and they would smile awkwardly and introduce their dates, and he'd ask, *how've you been, Lily? Fine, fine, and you?* And stand for a few seconds and look at the pavement. And then he would say, *well, we'll see you,* and walk on, and Martin would ask, *who was that,* and Lily would say, *oh no one.*

He was just someone I once knew.

The forcefield went up around what was left of Lily.

Wrapping her arms around herself, slowly she crossed Broadway and walked back home.

411

57

An Encounter at Tompkins Square

Spencer and Lily had been walking home one night from Odessa, and a stringy guy accosted them. "I'm not going to bullshit you," the guy said, a Michael Jackson lookalike, tall, skeletal, barely standing. "I need a dollar to score some scag. Can you give me a dollar?"

Spencer took out his badge and stuck it in the guy's face. "You'll spend the rest of your life in jail if you don't clean up. Get away."

"What are you shoving in my face, man?" the guy said, as if he were blind. "That's not a dollar."

"NYPD. Get the fuck away, I said." Spencer put his arm around Lily to cover her, to prod her forward.

They continued walking. "Lily, don't ever walk through Tompkins Square at night alone, all right?"

"Like I would."

That was then. This was now. With the gateway to hell behind her, this time at two in the morning she walked through Tompkins Square and sat on the bench and watched wasted people shuffle through the paths, talking to themselves or to each other, rummaging in their ripped pockets, adjusting their rags, looking for a lost bill, or a bit of old powder that they could eat or snort. People smelling like nothing else on earth, human bodies, caked with sweat and feces, unwashed for months, decaying, and still they shuffled and begged to score some H for a dollar from an NYPD cop. She didn't sit for long there, just long enough to wish to be home, to be in bed, to forget this day, this sixteenth day of her deadened life.

Leaving through the iron gates of the park, she was suddenly shoved from behind by a man also heading out of the park, so close as if he had been walking right behind her. He was moving fast, nearly running, he bumped into her with more force than her startled body could handle and then grabbed her elbow and did not let go. Lily screamed. But not because she had been nearly knocked down. It was this man, his face from a nightmare, from a horror movie Lily had never seen. He smelled like a bum, preter-naturally foul, unforgivably filthy, but somehow he had found money to wear regular clothes, jeans, a black jacket, to cut his hair completely off—he was bald, with words tattooed above his eyebrows. She couldn't read the words because she was being overcome by a blinding terror. His eyes were slit and bloodshot, and were a color of crystal blue like slivers of polished-by-ocean glass. They were almost transparent. Under them he had blood welts and black and blues. One eye had been partially closed after a beating, and one of his front teeth had been knocked out; his nose was badly broken once, twice; he looked menacing and strung out, he looked starved and heartless. Lily gaped at a wide black bruise on his neck, but realized it was another tattoo, a faded hammer and sickle covering his Adam's apple. Her mouth fell open, she was paralyzed and breathless while he stared at her closely, panting. *And he wasn't letting go.* His mouth stretched into a grimace, exposing his decaying teeth and a raspy grating whisper came out of him. He whispered—or she thought he whis-pered—"*Lily.*"

Someone rushed up to her in the nighttime street, a young guy. "Hey! what's going on here?" and the man released her, and ran, and she, out of her mind with fear, ran too without looking back, ran down the block and across Avenue C, ran terrified that he

413

was right behind her. Once inside her building, she flew up the stairs and fumbled for her key, her heart beating so furiously she was sure heart attacks started with less, her heart felt fully ready to explode and burst out of her chest.

After locking the door and chaining the door, and barricading the door with the phone desk and a single dining room chair she owned, she called, she paged him, and then she went into the bathroom and threw up the pound of cherries she had just eaten. At three in the morning the phone rang, and having barely cleaned herself up she ripped the receiver off the base. "God, Spencer! You have no idea what just happened to me."

"Lily, it's Papi."

"Oh my God. Papi, do you have any idea what time it is?" She was panting, she could barely get the words out. Was that call waiting? She couldn't get the deafening whisper out of her ears.

"Lily, it's only nine in the evening here in Maui. But something's happened. Your mother called the police an hour ago and told them I beat her."

"Oh, Papi. Is she drunk?"

"What do you think? Can't you hear her in the background?"

Lily could barely hear him in the *fore*ground.

"Did you . . . beat her?"

"Lily!"

"All right. So when they come tell them that."

"Is this a good time?"

"It's never a good time." Holding on to the phone table, she closed her eyes.

"I think she's hurt herself. There's blood in her bathtub. And I don't know, she can't walk anymore. I think she fell while getting out of the tub."

Lily stayed on the phone. He smoked. "They're here. The doorbell just rang. I'm on the lanai, my back is to them." He continued to smoke. "Sit with me on the phone, Lily," he said. "Be close to me on the phone."

They came onto the lanai, and he said, "You want to talk to my daughter? She can tell you everything."

A man's voice said, "She is not involved."

Papi said, "No, she is very much involved, she knows everything."

A man said, "You have the right to remain silent. Everything you say can and will be held against you. You have the right to an attorney. Do you understand these rights as they have been explained to you?"

Lily's father said yes.

The police officer came on the phone. "Please," Lily said, "you cannot arrest him, he is an innocent person, all his life all he's been trying to do is help her."

The police wouldn't have any of it. "Your mother is very intoxicated. We see that. She has quite a bad laceration on the back of her head, but she refuses to go to the hospital and she is having trouble walking. But if she says your father did this to her we have to take him in. If he cannot post a thousand dollars bail he will spend the night at the precinct and tomorrow go before a judge and enter a plea. He'll have to be arraigned and appear in court."

Lily said dully, "Let me speak to my mother."

Allison came on the phone and said, "I cannot talk to you right now," and hung up.

Lily called back four times. Allison said I'm busy right now, I cannot get your father, I'm too busy to get him. She said, "Don't call and waste your money, give it to your older sister."

When Lily called back, the police officer said to her, "It is obvious you have to come, he cannot handle this situation on his own. Does he have any friends here who can help him?"

Her father came on the phone. "When I come back from jail tomorrow I'm packing my stuff and leaving. I can't take this anymore."

"Papi!" shouted Lily. "Tell them you didn't do it, tell them you never touched her."

415

"I can't. They won't listen. They're saying if there is an accusation of spousal abuse, they have to arrest me." His voice trembled. Her father had never been arrested for anything in his life.

"This is ridiculous. She is so clearly drunk!"

"They don't care. Lil, can you talk to them? I need your help, daughter. I don't know what to do. Please can you talk to them? Is your detective friend there? Maybe he can talk to them. I don't judge him, you know. I know he is just doing his job."

Lily's own voice nearly broke when she said, "He's not here, Papi, but let *me* talk to them."

He put a Hawaiian-sounding polite man on the phone, who listened to her, who was courteous, who understood, "but my hands are tied. It's the law here in Maui. If a spouse calls in an abuse on her spouse, we have to arrest the accused. Don't worry. He will just go to the police station and make bail, and then he can go. But he cannot show up at your mother's for twenty-four hours. You have to explain the situation to him, Miss Quinn. He doesn't seem to understand it's the law."

"Oh, he understands," said Lily. "He just doesn't believe it."

Her father came on the phone. "Lily, what am I going to do? How am I going to get out of this?"

She told him not to worry, that he would be all right.

"I need help," he said. "I cannot deal with your mother anymore. This is just the last straw in what she has put me through the last year, ever since I proposed that we sell the condo and move back east. You have no idea what my life has been like."

I have some idea, Lily wanted to say to him. "Papi, I'm not the best person for this. I'm the worst of all your children for helping my mother. I don't know what you're thinking."

"Please, Lily, they're arresting me, don't you understand, and your mother cannot be left alone, you don't understand what state she is in. Don't you see? You have to come."

"Papi, how can I come?"

416

"I'll pay for it, if that's what you're worried about. I have some money of my own. I have my own account now. Your mother has not completely emasculated me."

"I'm not worried about that . . ."

"So come then. Talking to your mother, trying to help her, putting yourself on the line, even when you know she doesn't want it, giving her what she needs because you know she needs it, that's what love is. Fly first class if you have to. I'll pay. I have to go now. I have to go and be booked and fingerprinted like a common criminal. Now I understand what Andrew was afraid of."

Lily felt the rebuke even if there wasn't any.

My father beats against the wall. I am my father's daughter, and I beat against the wall.

Before the police took him away, Papi said, "Lily, I love you."

In the night her mother called her.

"What have you done?" Lily said. "Papi is in jail, Mom, jail! What have you done?"

She said, "He beats me."

"Mom, the police will find out you're lying and they'll arrest *you!*"

"I don't need you to get hysterical on me, shut up shut up shut up." And hung up.

Lily called back six or seven times and Allison hung up all of them.

The last time she said, "Soon I'll be dead and you'll all be happy."

"You cannot go to God this way, Mother," said Lily. "I'd ask Him for help if I were you."

Allison hung up.

Lily barely slept, kept awake by the anxiety of the terrible face in the park, of his hands on her, was she mistaken? Were they *on her?* Holding *her?* Did he follow her, stand near Broadway,

417

watching her waiting for Spencer? It was inconceivable and terrifying. The next morning she was on the plane to Maui. She barely even packed. She brought a couple of summer outfits, a bathing suit, her sketchbooks and an empty suitcase, in case her father wanted to come home with her, come back with her. She brought it to save him.

Spencer didn't call before she left.

She didn't even know what flight she was taking. She just asked the driver to take her to JFK, and once there, she opted for Delta, who had the first flight out. She bought a first class ticket, and was in the air in two hours.

Unraveled at home and abroad, unraveled at sea and in the air.

Unraveled—to begin to fail, or to come to an end.

58

Eight Days in Maui

At LAX the airport is so uncosy, and there is fog in LA, you can't see the sky, but Lily bet the air smelled nice, and it looked like it was warm. "They put handcuffs on me," George had told her just before she got on the plane. "They hurt. No one talked to me. I couldn't call you earlier because I was in jail." And he laughed!

But he wasn't in jail. He bailed himself out immediately. Wasn't that story good enough? He was arrested on false charges, wasn't that enough drama? No, he had to say he was in jail, though clearly he was in a police station for the shortest possible time.

And George was now pretending Lily was coming for a visit. "What would you like to eat? I'll make you dinner. Would you like shrimp? I can make very delicious shrimp with celery." Lily answered dumbly, sure, though she hated celery.

What was he doing at the house? Lily thought he was supposed to keep away for twenty-four hours? Whatever, since he was there, why wasn't he packing his stuff? Didn't he tell her he was getting his stuff and leaving? Yet he was right back there, making dinner, smoking, saying he would meet Lily at the airport and she must not rent a car because he had the Mercedes and it was at her disposal. Didn't he know she had never learned to drive a car?

She had sat in the driver's seat of Spencer's car. The engine was on. Her back was against the wheel, her legs and arms were wrapped around Spencer.

Did that count as driving?

I'm ridin' in your car/you turn on the radio . . .

On the flight Lily read most of the *Understanding the Alcoholic* book, but what she really wanted to do was not think about her mother, which was ironic considering her mission. She succeeded because most of the way she thought about Spencer.

Her father was waiting for her at the airport. She hadn't seen him in so long. He was salt-haired, full-haired, heavy now. They hugged.

"Lily, you have to be prepared for how you're going to find your mother. She is in a terrible state."

"I understand."

He shook his head. "I don't think you do. You've never seen her this way. She is really banged up and . . ." he paused here. "I think there is something wrong with her toe. You'll have to take a look at it and tell me."

"What's wrong with it?"

"I don't know. I'm not a doctor."

"Am I a doctor?"

"No, but . . . you've been sick. You know about such things. By the way, how are you feeling?"

He didn't wait for her answer. They talked about nothing else but Allison all the way through the volcanic hills of Maui, from Wailuku, and no matter how she tried, she could not remember the name of the airport they had just left. Lakuhui? Walakui? Somethinglui?

In the apartment, clothes hanging everywhere, towels that had been left damp too long, sinks full of toothpaste and soap residue, hair on the floor, carpets all askew, stuff everywhere, unfresh odors.

Before she went in to see her mother in her bedroom, George insisted Lily eat some dinner. Tuna sashimi on the lanai. He told her he walked home about twelve miles from the police station. "Do you know what it's like to walk that long and think about your life? It's very mind-cleansing."

"Papi, I thought you were going to leave."

He shook his head. "Lily, you just don't understand. Your mother can't be left alone. She has to be seen to be believed."

"I'm going to go and see her then. Thanks for the sushi."

Her mother was sleeping on her high bed, and she did not stir until Lily finally woke her. Allison said, "What, came here to comfort your father?" She could barely speak. She did let Lily touch her and look at her toe. Oh my God, thought Lily, the toe. It was a compound fracture, with the white bone sticking out, the back of the toe nearly completely sliced off, and the toe itself all twisted back. For some reason the foot around the toes was looking unwell, blistery and swollen, but it could have been the bad lighting. Lily tried to turn on the light to get a better look—she was scared by the bone sticking out—but Allison wouldn't allow it. "Mom, when did this happen?"

"How do I know?" she said slowly. "I think when I fell in the bathtub, or when I was trying to get out. It's my head that's much worse. I have a crack in my head. Want to see?" She turned herself sideways and parted her hair in the back. Blood had caked around the injury and dried in the hair. It was difficult to see the actual wound.

"We have to take you to the hospital."

"No!" Allison said adamantly. "No hospital. Absolutely not."

"What are you talking about? You have to go to the hospital."

"I have to do no such thing. We don't all love hospitals like you do, Lily. We're not all so comfortable in them. I don't need the hospital. The head is feeling better, and the foot will heal. I think I may have had a concussion, you know."

Lily called the only hospital in Maui, the Maui Memorial, and said the words *compound fracture*. A nurse directed her to call Urgent Care in Maui on South Kihei Road, which she did. The receptionist there didn't know what a compound fracture was. "So is the toe broken or not?" This was said in between gum chewing. Lily asked to speak to the doctor and wouldn't take no for an answer. But the doctor at Maui Urgent Care, Dr. Tavakoli, said, "If it's a compound fracture, I don't know why they would tell you to call here. You *must* go to the hospital. A compound fracture can get infected very quickly, especially in the extremities where the oxygen supply is low."

Allison said she wasn't going to the hospital. It was too late. It was nine o'clock in the evening. George, having spent all day, all long day, filling out paperwork at the public defender's office, cooking, taking care of his sick wife, did not want to go either. He said, we'll go tomorrow.

In daylight, there was no hiding from *the toe*. Distinctly there were bubbles under the skin around it, bubbles at the top of her foot. It was a funny brownish color, and it smelled. Lily recoiled from the foulness and said, "That's it, we're going to the hospital."

"I'm not going anywhere," said Allison.

"Leave her alone, Lil," said George. "She'll be fine. Leave her be, the toe will heal."

"The foot is going brown," Lily told 911.

They came in five minutes. The paramedics walked in wearily, as if they had been down this road before, in this house before. In seconds, they had her on a stretcher and inside the ambulance. They were speeding away before Papi could say, "We'll be right behind you."

The stressed, overworked, impatient triage nurse looked at her dismissively until she saw Allison's oozing toe, and bubbling brown foot. Then she was straight away calling for the attending physician. Once inside Trauma One, Allison began crying and saying this was the end of her miserable life, but young tall thin unsmiling Dr. Aillard was focused on her foot.

He said to Lily, drawing her away from the bed where Allison was acting delirious, "Do you know what moist gangrene is? Gas gangrene?"

She shook her head.

"It's worse than dry gangrene as we call it, when there is uniform tissue death. Now what's happening is her still-living cells are leaking fluids making the surrounding areas moist. Bacteria flourishes, hence the term moist gangrene. Well, your mother's gangrene has taken an even worse turn. The bacteria in the dying cells have begun to produce a deadly gas, and this gas thrives in low-oxygen areas like her broken toe. Brown pus, gas bubbles." Aillard stopped looking at her. "This poison spreads rapidly, causing high fever."

"Well, that's why she's in the hospital!" Lily exclaimed. "Fix her."

"It's good that you brought her," he said simply. "This saved her life, but . . . we cannot save her foot."

Lily had to sit down.

"We're going to put her on antibiotics. But the foot will have to be removed surgically. Tell me, what is going on with your Mom—is she drinking?"

Lily looked at him, words failing.

"Is she an alcoholic?" the doctor persisted.

Lily found herself nodding, yes.

"Is she sober enough for me to explain all this to her?"

"I don't think *I* will ever be sober enough for you to explain this to her," Lily said.

The whole thing took no more than thirty minutes. Papi remained outside, smoking. When he came back in, it was over.

"Well," he said. "Well, well." He couldn't say any more. "We should go home. You must be tired. You should call your brother, your sisters. Tell them what happened to their mother."

"And Grandma."

"And Grandma," he said, almost as an afterthought. "Where do you get that energy from? You've been up a long time."

Lily had had three hours sleep in forty-eight. She had missed

423

her blood work, had not spoken with Spencer. She wanted to call him but she only had one phone call in her. She called Grandma. No news could spread any faster than news told to her.

At home when they searched Allison's closet and found a big, nearly full bottle of gin, Papi first said, yes, we have to take it away, then he said, but if we take it she is never going to give the statement to the DA to get me free.

But he took it and hid it in the trunk of the Mercedes. He didn't pour it out because, he said, "It's a sin to pour out perfectly good liquor."

Lily didn't recognize any of the morning smells in Maui. George wanted to go to the beach, seemingly not remembering any of the anguish he felt the night he begged Lily to come to Maui.

"Papi, we have to take care of the police thing before we start gallivanting around beaches, and we need to go and see Mom."

He sighed. "Your mother does not get the pleasures that other people might get from getting old. You'll never find a bumper sticker on her car that says, 'Happiness is being a grandparent'."

"What about you, Papi, will I find that bumper sticker on your car?"

George did not reply.

He moved on Maui time—he was six hours behind the rest of the world. It took him a while to get ready and get out.

Lily was thinking of calling Spencer. What time was it in New York?

In the supermarket the torture began. "Why are you buying that?" George said when Lily took some cooked shrimp. "I already bought her smoked salmon."

Lily replied that she knew that, but her mother sometimes liked cooked shrimp.

"Why are you buying iced tea? She doesn't drink iced tea."

"No, but I do, and maybe she would like some."

"We don't need soap. We have plenty of soap."

424

"If we have plenty, then why did I find only a tiny little piece this morning?"

"You should have asked. We have plenty."

"It's only two bars of soap. I tell you what, I'll take one with me, and the other you can throw out."

"That's the problem," he said angrily. "We buy a lot of crap we don't need and then end up throwing it all out."

Traffic crawled along the coast. Driving north through the mountains to the hospital, Lily saw a beautiful tree with glorious bright red rhododendron-like flowers. She thought, I have to find out what it is before we go. I could paint that. She saw Maui in its grand drama, its youthfulness, grand majestic beauty fresh from the fiery earth, and the tree stood like a symbol of its creation.

Unlike the tree, there was no dignity in Allison's ordeal. Her speech was garbled and spoken through gritted teeth, as if she were still drunk.

Dr. Aillard, with the splendid bedside manner, came into the room and out of nowhere without so much as a hello, said to her, "You have to stop drinking, missy. And you have to start now. It's time to face the music."

Brilliant, thought Lily. Yes. Why didn't my mother think of that?

Allison was looking at her bandaged and raised stump with disbelief. Lily too felt disbelief, like Grandma, last night, who had kept repeating, it can't be, it can't be, how could that happen, why amputation, wasn't there something else they could do?

"It's too late now, Grandma, to think of alternatives. She had poison gas inside her."

"I know all about poison gas," said Claudia. "Your mother avoided it narrowly when she was very young. Why did it have to be inevitable that it would catch up with her later in life, in America? It doesn't seem fair."

With the jaded doctor they couldn't talk about *the foot*. Allison was staring numbly at where it was not. So they started to talk about the drinking. It wasn't much easier.

425

She didn't touch the food they brought her.

Another doctor, Dr. Matthews, came to say he would be taking care of Allison from now on, but Papi kept trying to tell him his whole life story, long, detailed explanations of Washington and *The Post*, and how there was an arm-breaking incident with my mother when he had been sleeping . . . Papi was tired, and didn't know what to say. He couldn't keep to the matter at hand, because the matter at hand was so large, and footless, he just didn't know where to begin.

Matthews said Allison was going to go through DTs and he said he would keep an eye on it. He said morphine would help and that made Allison happy. Morphine!

Matthews said she would be in the hospital for ten days, until "the stump" was more or less healed. He made all of them cringe and didn't even notice. He said he would corroborate that Allison's injuries were inconsistent with physical abuse and try to get the DA to drop their charges. Lily nearly missed the meaning of his words because of the cringing. Then with relief she escaped from "the stump" to the telephone. Now her mother only had to retract her statement and her father would be off the hook.

Eventually, a police officer came in response to Lily's calls to the prosecutor's office and Allison said, "It was completely my fault, and I'm very sorry."

Lily couldn't believe those words. It had taken many calls to get the policeman to come and take a further statement from Allison and it was amazing to Lily that her efforts were rewarded. She had had to argue with the police officer— Spencer would have been proud of her. Making Spencer proud of her was her goal in life. She wanted to call him but everything from that life, him—her sickness—suddenly seemed so far away when she was on the other side of the world. All she knew about was police statements and mandatory arrests. And gas gangrene. Perhaps if she stayed here, bought a house here, painted here, mangoes and sushi and palm trees, she would

426

forget Spencer, forget she was ever sick. She had money now, she could live anywhere she wanted, even by the ocean near the palm trees, away from him and from Amy and Andrew in their bed.

When the patrolman left, she told her mother that was a very brave thing you did Mom, you used brave words.

Allison turned away from Lily. "Brave words are forgotten *instantly*. But I lost my foot," she said. "I lost my foot *forever*."

Despite Allison's brave words to the patrolman, despite Matthews's offer to clear George from charges of abuse, in the evening her father acted like a big tired pessimist. "No, Lily, we will never cure her. She will never get better. I see that now."

"So why are we trying so hard then?"

He said, because the most important thing is not the goal, it's the movement, it's the struggle.

Where did Lily hear that before?

On the way to the beach the bushes are red, creating a striking contrast against the sea and the sky. It's all breathtaking. Lily wondered why she was noticing it much more this trip than last year.

And the palm trees, the palm trees. How they bend like violin bows, bending to the volcanic ash and to the setting sun.

The sun was not red, it was yellow all the way to the bottom of the ocean, and how relentlessly it squeezed itself into the horizon, between the island of Lanai and the Maui volcano on this side of Lahaina.

She found a rock on the beach and sat and watched the sunset, and then went into the water. The healing water. It burned her eyes that were like sandpaper and burned her lips that had raw spots on them from the stress and made her face all sandy. It was lovely. She wasn't numb, she *felt*.

The water was warm, and the air was warm. Lily swam, and for some reason got a haunted sense that she was seeing Maui's colors so vividly, and feeling the water so calmingly because she was seeing them for the last time. A premonition passed through her that she would never see Maui again after she left here.

She didn't like that premonition. She tried not to look at the indigo mulberry sky again as she walked back in twilight.

George had made shrimp with mushrooms and onions and delicious sauce, and rice, and Lily had two helpings and then some ice cream and called her mother at the hospital. The orthopedic surgeon had not come yet and she said her stump was all pus. The dressings needed to be changed. Lily said it was healing – the body, broken as it was, was trying to heal it. Allison didn't want to hear it.

The Maui prosecutor's office called George.

"They said they got the police report and a Kim Fallone, who is the assistant DA, can see us next Monday," George told her. "They want to know, can your mother come?"

"Can my mother come? I don't know if my mother can come. Will she be able to use a wheelchair by then? Maybe she'll even be discharged from the hospital, be dried out by then? I know nothing," said Lily. "Besides I'm supposed to be leaving on Saturday."

George asked her to stay until Monday. Extremely reluctantly she agreed.

Maui at night has stars that pepper the sky; it almost looks fake, there are so many stars and they are so bright. But the most amazing thing, right below the orange crescent moon hanging above the ocean, is the bright, lucid, large and round Jupiter. She has never seen anything like it in all her life and wonders if Spencer would like to see it someday, because he has probably never seen anything like it in his life either.

Thursday. How much more of this could she take? Her father continued to be a downer. This is all going to fail and we're going to have to stay in Maui forever, and we're going to have to go

428

to court, and I'll be prosecuted and you'll be prosecuted, and I don't know what to do. It's all hopeless.

Five feet away from entering Allison's room, he said, Liliput, let's make a deal, we will feed her, stay for about an hour, but then we'll go, okay? He wanted to go to North Beach. He wanted a little therapy himself.

They sit there and listen to Allison rail and rant and rave and tell her lies to the doctor, even to Papi, as if he doesn't know the truth, but from the dull-eyed look of him, who knows if he does? In front of her, he is just a different person, Lily thinks. He walks around, he doesn't know what to say, he doesn't know what to do, and then he wants to leave.

Her mother is telling Dr. Matthews how the drinking has only really been a problem for the last four months because her husband is so bad, because he wants to leave this beautiful place, and because when she is stressed and frustrated she drinks to help her relax. "A glass of wine does relax me a little bit," she says to him with a little smile. The doctor nods, and says this and that.

"Doctor, can I see you outside, please?"

In the corridor Lily tells him that her mother's drinking has been out of control for many years, a decade, and it's gotten worse in Maui, but it did not begin in Maui and it didn't get out of control in Maui.

"Have you seen my mother's bruises, have you seen her amputated foot? She lost a foot, for God's sake, you think she could escalate to that level of drinking in four months?"

Back inside, the doctor says, "Mrs. Quinn, your daughter tells me that you haven't been telling me the truth. She says you are drinking much more heavily than you say."

The look her mother shoots her makes Lily recall those moments of her life when she felt like a non-human: like when her mother told her last year that Andrew was not talking to her because she had taken up with Spencer; like when Spencer left her.

To the doctor, Allison says, "Well, my daughter's never seen me drink. *He* tells her that," and she points to George. "She is not telling the truth, and he is not telling the truth."

"Mrs. Quinn, why would they be lying to me?"

"Ask them," she says.

"Mr. Quinn, you've been by your wife's side all along. Is the drinking as bad as your daughter says?"

Papi hems and haws and then says, "I love my wife very much. I want to stay and take care of her. No matter how sick she is. I won't go. Leaving her is tantamount to leaving a paralyzed person in the middle of the woods in the dark. I cannot do it. But it's not as bad as my daughter says. It's much worse than that. It's an unimaginable nightmare." He starts to cry and walks out of the room.

Allison is crying too, and her expression reads, if only you didn't butt in, Lily, none of this would be happening. A look which tells Lily that her mother is not exactly wishing for sobriety despite the lack of right-footedness.

She is now crying for morphine, saying she's in incredible pain. She says to Lily, leave here, leave and don't come back.

Dr. Matthews says, "What do you want, Mrs. Quinn?"

She says, "I just want to be left alone. That's all."

"You want to be left alone so you can drink?"

"Well, no."

"You want your husband to leave you? You want him to pack his bags and leave you? What do you mean?"

She doesn't answer. She cannot look at him because she is so angry with Lily.

Dr. Matthews says, "And by the way, Mrs. Quinn, I don't agree with your husband's analogy. The difference between you and a paralyzed person in the woods is that you can help yourself. A paralyzed man cannot get up."

"Look at me, I can't get up either."

"You can, you can choose to get help and get sober. But I understand you cannot do it on your own. There are treatment centers here in Maui. There is a very good place, Aloha House."

Allison shakes her head. "No, I can't go to Aloha House."

"Why?"

"I love my home, I want to go there."

"So you can drink?" he asks.

"No."

The doctor says before he leaves, "I'm going to recommend that you be placed in Aloha House when you're discharged from here."

"Why, *why*, do you have to open your big mouth?" Allison says to Lily.

Papi and Lily sit around her and try to talk to her. Papi says his silly things. Papi likes to talk, loves to talk, but Lily sees it all now—when it comes to Allison's drinking, he prefers to just go to the beach.

She knows they have done nothing to quell the beast inside Allison. She will say anything to get herself back home.

Papi, who is half-happy that Allison is sober, a state he has not seen her in some time, says, Mom is right. She doesn't have to go to Aloha House. He says, there is no liquor in our house anymore, and your mother is going to promise she won't drink. Allison says bravely, coolly, no, no, I won't drink. I've learned my lesson good and proper now.

Papi says, "I believe her."

"Are you even kidding me? Are you *kidding* me?" Lily exclaims.

"No," he says, shaking his head. "Lily, I know about these things. I'm older, wiser than you. I understand."

This is what they mean when they say alcoholism is a family disease.

The same man, who not four days ago told the police he could not handle her, who begged Lily to come because she was a danger to herself and to him, who could not control her, could not help her, that same man suddenly thinks it's a good idea for his wife to come home!

Lily tells him, "This is the same woman who two days after

431

a foot amputation asked us to wheel her to a garden on the second floor so she could have four cigarettes in a row. When she returns to her bed, she'll have some morphine. The woman who was not able to control herself at any time in the past is *suddenly* going to stop herself from drinking?"

And then a light goes on in Lily's head. Her mother is right! George *is* the reason she continues to drink! Of course the addiction is hers and hers alone, but every time she gets sober for a day, for a minute, like now, she is not the only one who gets cocky—he gets cocky too. And he says, I think this time it's going to be okay. He says, Mommy is never going to admit she needs help but this is a big step. I can help her get sober, I can do it.

George says in a determined voice, "We will make her sign a statement that she will not touch liquor, otherwise I will take her to the hospital myself."

Lily stops herself from saying *Oh sign a statement, that's good, that'll do it*, but barely.

How she wishes she could talk to Spencer about this, ask his advice. She can just imagine what he will say. He has no patience for this kind of nonsense.

Dr. Matthews tells Lily that her mother will not be leaving the hospital unless she is discharged into Aloha House and that they can keep her in the hospital until there is room for her there.

Happily Lily informs her parents that mom won't be able to leave the hospital.

Allison says, "That's why, that's *why* I didn't want to come to the hospital. I knew this would happen. That's why I didn't want you to open your big mouth and say so much. You say too much, Lily. Your father, now he says little but just right, you say way too much and that's why we're in this mess right now."

"Mom, are we in this mess because *I* have an amputated foot? Are we in this mess because *I* slipped and fell and hit my head on the bathtub, are we in this mess because *I* have bruises all over my body because *I* am drunk?"

"That's what I mean," Allison said, beginning to cry. "No one needs me. I just want to die."

I needed you, mother, Lily thinks, turning away. I need you. Where are you?

Now Lily knows.

On the way home from the hospital George is upset with Lily. He says she just doesn't understand anything.

No sooner do they get home than Allison calls and says that Dr. Matthews has explained to her about not releasing her from the hospital until there is a place for her in Aloha House . . . but then she can leave Aloha House any time she wants!

Lily is listening.

Allison says, "So as soon as there's a place for me at Aloha House I go there and immediately get discharged so I can be home the same day."

"Wait, so you mean to say you'll go to Aloha House to *fool* the doctors?"

"Just find me the number of Aloha House."

Silence from Lily.

"Find my Yellow Pages on the floor. You found my bottle in the closet, find my Yellow Pages on the floor."

"Mom, we cannot have you leave Aloha House, the whole point is that you want to get better."

Allison said, "Then why should I leave the hospital? Here they are giving me morphine, they are giving me sleeping pills."

Lily understood. "So you are trading one addiction for another? Why are you taking the morphine if you're not in pain?"

She said, "I'm in terrible pain. Have you seen I have no foot?"

"We sat with you for five hours today and you never moaned or complained once."

Allison the stoic said, "So I should complain every time I have a pain?"

Then she hung up.

433

Morphine. One addiction for another. Morphine dulls her desire for drink though it doesn't dull her desire to lie.

The lies just never stop, never. To the doctors, lies, to the police, to me, to her husband, even to herself.

Every word she utters about her drinking is a complete lie, and the lie is the sign, if there is one sure sign of an alcoholic it's the lie, how much you drink, and the alibi—it's his fault—and the denial—it's not so bad—and Lily's mother is the queen of them all. And the crown on the queen? "I can stop any time I want to. Any time. I just don't want to. Why put myself through such an arbitrary test? What, just to satisfy you?"

She lies about her drinking to everybody who will listen and if you don't catch her in the lie, she continues to lie, asks you to lie for her, and if you do catch her, she gets upset you are knocking her house of cards over.

But every word she utters is a lie.

The water, the palm trees, the complete absence of wind, the transparent lapping water, the Pacific. For millions of years it has surged up Wailea Beach, bringing its animal life, plant life, news of wars and death. Tsunamis and coral reefs, all washed into the same salt now rinsing over Lily's face. She becomes afraid of her own shadow in the water, thinking it's a shark.

Volcanoes rising out of the water. The gentle Pacific carrying with it the souls of the universe, washing Lily's face with Jurassic spirit and WWII spirit, and the ghost of every whale who's ever died, all of it into her face—eternity, and that's exactly what it feels like.

She has broken out in a hivy rash all over her lips and chin. She is not feeling great. Right after she and Papi got back from their walk, she fainted on the lanai. Papi found her on the floor.

George does not want to spend time in the hospital with his wife. Visiting Allison, he mills, he smokes, he sits for two seconds. It chafes him, he wants to be done, so done. Her father, Lily

434

realizes, oh he is so brave, getting on with his life, talking to his daughter while he smokes his cigarettes. But sitting beside his sick wife isn't a smoking talking situation, there's only the stump, the morphine-quiet. He wants to go home, get a beer and talk about her.

He is not going to think about how she is going to get around when she gets home. How is she going to go up and down that step? Get herself into the bathroom, into the tub? When her stump heals completely she can, if she wants to, get a prosthesis, but in the meantime what?

Lily wants to go home. She has been sketching Maui into her book, but now she wants to paint it in her studio, feel the New York breeze on her face, walk down Second Avenue, get Chicken Tikka Masala from Baluchi's. She paints here instead. She's brought some oil pastels with her, some watercolor pencils. With the oil pastels, though they're very messy, she paints a small picture of the beach and the water, and Jupiter in the sky.

George paints in his own way—he cooks. He cooks asparagus and brings it to the hospital with mustard sauce, papaya, and mango and pineapple. When she tastes the asparagus, Allison says, oh, no, he put too much salt in it. He knows I can't have a lot of salt.

"Mom," Lily says, "what are you talking about? He sees how much salt you pour on your cucumbers."

"Well," she says, "that's special salt."

"You know what? When someone cooks for you, you have to say thank you very much and eat what they bring you."

Allison says there are more important things in life than just to stuff your face.

Lily gives her mother the picture she had painted. Allison looks at it for a few moments. "Do you see what I mean? Sun every day. What could be more depressing?" She lets the picture fall on the blanket. Lily takes it, rips it into little pieces and throws it in the garbage.

"What's the matter with *you?*" says Allison.

The subject of Aloha House has been dropped. Dr. Matthews tells her that when she is discharged in two weeks' time, she will have to go to AA meetings every single day, no ifs, ands or buts. Allison is nodding, but Lily knows what she's thinking: I'll say anything to leave the hospital.

Back at the condo, Lily empties the gin bottle that was hidden in the trunk of the Mercedes and fills it with water. How funny is that going to be?

Allison told Lily that when she was home she would sleep during the day and wake up and sleep again, and wake up at five in the morning when Papi was sleeping and there was nothing for her to do, so she would drink.

At five in the morning she drank! Papi didn't know that and it shocked him, the depth of her drinking, even though he had lived it every day, letting her continue, watching her kill herself, powerless to help. He would make her breakfast, and he would make her sashimi for lunch and he would make her soup for dinner, and he would bring the food to his drunk wife on the lanai, and would serve her, and would give her utensils and a napkin and she would eat half-heartedly, her mouth barely moving, barely opening, and she would tell him it was too salty, and then she would scream that she wished he would die like a dog, and then she would crawl back to her room again, and have some more gin.

George is bitter now not about Allison, but about Maui. He loves it as a man could love anything that has brought him such complete despair. Its drama, its beauty, its very grace, its whole Godliness and primevalness reminds him only of its utter and dismal and complete failure to please Allison. The most beautiful place he had ever seen brought his wife to depths of hell he had never seen, and it sickens him now, all of it, together, sickens him with its colorful Maui birds of paradise flowers and its resplendent morning glory.

He says all he'll remember about his two-hour morning walks—when everything in the universe seemed not only possible but attainable—was that during those divine, Resurrection-mass mornings his wife was already drunk since five, was already on the floor, broken, slurring, incoherent. He doesn't seem to know how to cope with that—and doesn't. He goes out for a smoke, and stays out.

An AA sponsor named Shelly came in the afternoon and talked to Allison.

"Such a mess I've made," Allison said to Shelly. Accent on the *I*.

Perhaps there is hope? Has the amputated foot given her a new perspective?

But after two hours the AA sponsor left, and Allison said to Lily, "I have a disease, Lily. I'm *sick*!"

No, Lily wanted to say to her mother. *I* have a disease. *I'm* sick. She said nothing.

"I'm sick. Shelly told me. She told me not to feel bad, not to blame myself too much."

"Do you do a lot of that, Mom?" Lily asked casually. "Blame yourself too much?"

"Shelly thought so. She said all I talked about was how it was my fault. She told me to stop being so hard on myself."

"Mom, why do you say these things to Shelly when you know they're not true?"

"They are true, I have a disease!"

"That's not what I mean. You spend your entire life blaming Papi for all your troubles, and I mean *all* your troubles, why do you pretend to Shelly it's otherwise? How is that going to help you?" Lily was disgusted.

"This is counter-productive, Lily," said her mother philosophically. "We need to look forward."

"Okay. I agree."

"I have a disease, daughter! A sickness!"

437

"It can be cured." Why were these words so hard for her? She was trying not to draw parallels.

Allison shook her head vigorously. "That's just the thing. There is nothing anyone can do. Do you know what Shelly told me? Once an alcoholic, always an alcoholic. She has people in her AA meetings who have not drunk for fifty years and they still call themselves alcoholics. It's incurable. Until their dying days all they want is a drink."

Lily listened to her mother. "What is your point?" she asked slowly.

"This is all hopeless," Allison said with a breezy air. "I can never be cured."

"Mom, how many limbs will you have to lose before you stop drinking? You only have three left."

Her mother said haughtily, "Shelly said that once an alcoholic, always an alcoholic."

"The responsibility is still yours. Shelly was not telling you you couldn't control it, was she?"

"No . . . But I'm always going to want a drink. And Shelly said we slip, we are not expected to be perfect."

Why was Lily starting to hate this Shelly? Could she have been more unhelpful? It's almost as if she provided Allison with absolution—I'm sick! I have a disease! It's out of my hands! I'm not in control!

How many more days till she could go home?

" Is this your crying room, Mom?" said Lily.

"What?"

She told her mother about the kindly priest in St. Patrick's and about the Bishop of Rome.

And Allison turned away from Lily and said the most incomprehensible words of the entire week. "No, my child," she said. "This is not my crying room. This is only the wolf at its door."

On the beach. Sunday morning. Sunday morning in Maui, not a flutter in the sky, so peaceful. She sketched, and sketched, palms and hammocks, and cliffs and volcanoes and flame trees, and valleys between mountains.

Lily thought about herself and her mother. Thinking that most of us aren't at peace because we don't know what we have to be at peace with. Most of us aren't happy because we're not living the life we want and we don't know how to deal with that. We don't know how to cope with that. And so we flutter onward, with apologies to Ralph Nader, wretched at any speed.

We should all be so lucky as to get cancer.

She thought, and I don't mean that flippantly.

I mean—to get cancer and be lucky enough to survive.

Cancer—such a clarifying experience.

Alcoholism—less clarifying.

But without alcohol, what does her mother have left? Nothing, Lily thinks.

She perceives her life as wasted, she perceives herself as old. She's gone to therapy, she's been on psychiatric drugs—Zoloft, Prozac. She hates her life—sobriety only points that up. She hates herself when she's drunk, but she hates herself sober more. At least when she's drunk, blackout time passes quickly.

Time passeth until death.

And with every blackout, death is closer—not a bad thing. Why doesn't she kill herself. She's a coward. Afraid of God. Why would she risk eternal damnation? If she's wasted enough and drives the car into a ditch, she can pretend to God her death was accidental. She thinks she can fool God with her little charades. And our father sitting on the phone for years trying to scare us with the possibilities of Mommy's death—can't he see it's precisely what she wants? All the things that make up this life, she's discarded, thrown away, turned her blind back on. All things like shopping by catalog, make-up, travel, reading books, writing, Communion with God, with friends, with her six grand-children! All the things that make life pleasurable she does not want, except the gin burn in the throat, and the oblivion that soon follows. She is the walking dead. Dead to us, dead to herself.

"I can stop any time I want to. I just don't want to."

Papi closes his eyes to have a quiet life, and she is so pleased with that.

She says, your father will live so well without me. And Lily thinks she is right.

He will fish, he will go online, he will watch his sports, he will cook. His days will continue to be full. Only cooking will be hard because it's better to cook for someone. Only watching the movies at night will be hard, because it's better to watch movies with someone. Lily knows this to be true. She will not cry on this Maui beach, she won't. She draws Spencer's eyes, watching adored *Groundhog Day* with her; laughing, adored. She will not cry.

Her mother's disease is not alcoholism. That's just the symptom. Her disease is the black hole inside her that the drink helps to close up. And she needed to drink quite a bit before the drink closed it.

In the hospital Lily sits with her. Papi is elsewhere.

Lily tries the soft approach. "Do you want to talk to me?"

"I'm all talked out."

She doesn't know what else to say. She tries again. "Do you want to tell me? Tell me about your . . . crying room?"

Allison just waves her off. "God, where's that cigarette."

"Can't smoke in here, Mom. Oxygen tanks everywhere."

"Oh, all these rules, rules. I can't stand it. I just want to be in my own house again. Be in charge of my own life again."

"Is that what you were," said Lily, "before? In charge of your own life?" Seems to her that life was in charge of her mother.

Silence. She looks at Lily. "Aren't you fresh. How am I supposed to tell you anything when you talk to me like that?"

"I'm sorry. Please tell me."

"Forget it now. Ask your grandmother about me, if you want. Tell her to tell you. She knows more than me. I'm surprised she hasn't said anything to you already, the way she never stops yapping about her past."

"Tell me what?"

"Let me ask you, don't deny it. You sometimes wish I wasn't your mother, don't you? That you could have a different mother?"

Lily is silent.

"I know you do. I know you do. The way you treat me, the way you're always on your father's side, on your brother's side. Against all sense and reason."

"Mom . . ."

"You better be good to me, Lily," whispers her mother, pointing a finger at her, and then tapping herself on the chest. "Because I'm the only one you've got."

Am I leaving tomorrow? Next minute won't be soon enough.

Monday morning the hospital will allow the invalid mother special dispensation to go to the prosecutor's office and talk to Kim Fallone. If Fallone dismisses the charges, all will be well.

On Monday morning Allison in a wheelchair is with Kim Fallone for an hour. Before that she was trying to convince Lily that all her injuries were sustained in one fall in the bathtub, her toe, her head and *all* her leg and arm bruises. As if. Allison sober is completely unable to understand that she, as a conscious human being, could ever have inflicted such terrible injuries on herself. She was presumably trying to explain this single catastrophic fall to Ms. Fallone.

Lily and George wait and pace. Lily discovers from a book she had brought with her that the red glowing tree is called the Poinciana, or the Flame Tree. Love that. Want to buy that.

Love that tree.

Will paint that tree a thousand different ways when I get back home. Will paint Maui, the ocean, the volcanoes when I get home.

Papi said, "You know your mother's bottle of gin? I threw it out."

Eyes behind sunglasses, Lily said, "That's good."

He said, "Yes, but an unexplainable thing. I tasted it, and, I don't know how, it's mysterious to me, but it seemed to be mostly water."

Lily said, "That is surprising."

He said, "You did it?"

She nodded, trying not to smile.

He shook his head. "What are you, crazy? It's not me you have to keep a check on."

Lily said, "I was afraid after I left you would give it back to her. Would you give her one of your beers if she asked for it? Just a little beer? Just one, because she says she can handle it?"

He left to buy himself an iced tea. He had really taken a shine to the Snapple iced teas he had railed at her for buying six days ago.

When he came back, he said that if someone had told him ten years ago that he would be the kind of man who could not keep vodka in the house, could not keep cognac in the house, could not keep gin in the house, could not drink a beer in front of the TV in his own house! he would have said the hell with you and this life, I want no part of it. "Yet look at me, I curse my life, I curse that I cannot do the things I love because your mother has no self-control, yet I live it."

Lily didn't say anything. There was nothing to say.

"You know why?"

"Because you love her."

"Yes." said George. "But what is she going to do when she comes back home? She'll be hobbled yes, but she doesn't know how to do anything else besides drink."

"I think that's one of the problems," Lily said.

"She says to me, what am I supposed to do now? How can I as an adult answer that question for another adult?" George was indignant. "She has no interests, suddenly it's my fault? It's my fault that she needs constant attention?"

"It's not going to be easy. Maybe she can take up knitting?" But Lily is thinking of something else. She is thinking of her mother. Of the sadness inside her that she simply can't shake. Lily knows a man just like that.

Kim Fallone recommended to move to dismiss the case

442

without prejudice. Which means they can reopen the file if there is another similar complaint within a year. Lily's mother was wiping her eyes, looking so relieved. Was God looking out for Allison? Did God show his presence in Maui? That 49, 45, 39, 24, 18, 1 presence? She is footless, but not dead. And if not her, who was God looking out for?

Lily said, "Well, that's all folkssss. Not that it hasn't been fun. But I have to be going now. I've got a plane to catch."

59

And Now—About Spencer

When Lily got back to New York, her message box was FULL. There were ten messages from DiAngelo telling her she needed to come in and see him. "Lily, blood work once every two weeks, and I haven't seen you for three. Call me." Out of 27 messages, there was a short one from Spencer. From the *new* Spencer. "Hello, it's Spencer." As if she wouldn't know. The formality is just for distance. She understands. "You called last Saturday, late, just making sure you're all right. If you still need something, call me at the station at—" He leaves his number! Who *is* he, who is *she*?

There was one more. "Hi, it's, um, Spencer again. I'm assuming you're all right, since I didn't hear from you."

Okay, fine. Just *fine*. Two can play that game.

She got casually dressed up, her hair was growing out. She had been feeling so tired. Ever since she got to Maui. The damn jet lag. The mother didn't help. But her hair looked dark red and short and choppy and thicker, and she wore summer strappy sandals, and a little Hawaiian-print silk sheath of a dress she had picked up at the *Kahului* (!) airport. She put on make-up, earrings and walked to the precinct.

She informed Carl, the reception officer, that she wanted to file a police report on the man who accosted her in the street.

Carl knew her, said hello, asked, already picking up the phone, if she wanted Detective O'Malley paged. She glanced up, trying to look through three floors to where he was at that moment. "No, that's okay," she said seriously. "Isn't Detective Sanchez your vagrancy detective?"

"Yes . . . but—"

"He'll do fine. Could you page *him* please? Tell him that Lily Quinn would like to file a report."

Upstairs on the third floor, it went like this: Sanchez got the phone call, listened carefully, glanced over at Spencer, in Whittaker's office, having his morning coffee. Hung up the phone, got up, went and knocked on the door, asked if he could see Spencer a moment, and lowering his voice, said, "Carl downstairs just called me because someone wants to file a vagrancy report."

Spencer slapped him on the back. "Detective Sanchez, thank you for bringing the particulars of your job description to my attention. Well done. Go to it."

Sanchez hemmed and said, "The young woman says she is Lily Quinn. Specifically asked for me, Carl says."

Spencer didn't slap him on the back this time. He stared at Carl and then said, "All right, smart-ass, go back to your desk."

"That's what I thought," said Sanchez.

She stood very calmly with her hands on the visitors desk as he came down the main stairs. Her heart was beating wildly, and if her hands hadn't been clutching each other, she knew they'd be shaking, but outwardly she managed to remain composed. He looked . . . well, he was Spencer. He was in a sharp suit, white shirt, silk blue tie. His hair was waving, longer. However, he was drawn, and somber, and extremely pale, and the circles under his eyes were darker than she remembered. He came up to her.

"Hello, Lily."

"Oh hello," she said nonchalantly. "I thought Detective Sanchez was on vagrancy detail."

"Would you like me to get Detective Sanchez for you?" said Spencer.

"No, no."

"Okay, then."

They stood for a moment, saying nothing. "So what's going on?" he finally said, and Lily had to look away from him, because his voice was unsteady. Suddenly this didn't seem like such a good idea anymore, in front of Carl, who wasn't taking his eyes off them.

"Lily," Carl said, "you haven't been selling your paintings on Saturdays. My wife went down to see what you had and you weren't there. You should have seen how many people stood waiting for you last week."

"Yes. I'll be there this Saturday, Carl."

"Have nice new things, Lil?"

"Have some surprising things."

Spencer said, "Come upstairs."

They walked up three flights of stairs. She was more winded than she liked by the time they got to the third floor and had to hold on to the railing the whole way.

He opened the door for her into the Special Investigations room. Gabe McGill came over. "Hello, Lily." He glanced at Spencer, then back to Lily. "You're looking well. Very tanned."

"Yes, I had a couple of days away."

"Did you have a good time?"

"Yes, very good."

All this said in front of an expressionless Spencer.

Gabe sat down at his desk, which was right next to Spencer's. Whittaker was looking at them through the glass. Sanchez, Smith, Orkney, they were all staring. I mean, was there anyone here who didn't know they had been together?

Pulling out a chair for her next to his desk, he sat down himself behind it. "So what's going on?" he said quietly. "How've you been? How are you feeling?"

"Fine, fine," she said off handedly and loudly. "Great, everything's great." She hoped he didn't see her fingers twisted on her lap. "I just came because I wanted to file a report on a man who I think may have accosted me in Tompkins Square."

He sighed and flipped open his notebook. "All righty then. When was this?"

"A week ago Saturday."

"What time?"

She coughed uncomfortably. "About two-thirty in the morning."

Spencer, who was writing this down, stopped, lifting his eyes to her.

"You were in Tompkins Square at two-thirty in the morning?"

"It may have been closer to three, I'm not exactly sure. I did not look at my watch."

"Reasonable precaution for your own safety is a requirement," he said.

"I know."

"What were you doing out at two-thirty in the morning?"

She couldn't tell him. Couldn't even look at him. She said, "I was going home," but suddenly the memory of the pound of cherries in her leaden stomach and standing across the street from his darkened windows wondering where *he* was at two in the morning on a Saturday night, filled her throat with such misery, remembering her pathetic self, that she got up, and said, "I'm sorry, I have to go now. Do you have enough?"

He looked down at his notebook. "I have nothing. What man? What did he do? Can you describe him?"

"I think he may have been . . . M—" But she was already faltering. "I think he might have been following me. I have to go, detective," she said. "I just remembered, I've got to run. I can't believe what time it is."

"What time is it?"

447

"It's going time."

He got up too, but she was already walking away from him, desperately trying to hold herself together long enough to get out of the police station. He didn't follow her. Which was best, because he wouldn't have liked to see the calm, even-tempered Lily that he knew bawling like a baby, while her mascara ran in raccoon streaks down her face as she tottered to Second Avenue to catch a cab to go see Paul and Rachel.

She spent the rest of the day out—with them, having lunch, going to the bookstore, getting Grandma her magazines. After they finished work, they all went out for Indian, and then went back home to her place, where they had some margaritas, like always, and talked about love, and Amy—like always. Her jetlagged eyes were sandpaper, too sore now even for tears.

And Milo—he was a new subject to talk about.

At eleven, the intercom rang.

Ah. First her heart felt it.

"Who could *that* be, I wonder?" said Rachel.

Lily pressed the button. "Who is it?"

"It's me."

Lily turned around to say to Paul and Rachel, you better go, but they were already getting up.

She threw the door open. On her landing stood a disheveled and panting Spencer.

She said, idiotically, "You remember Rachel, Paul."

He nodded to them, but said nothing. He was still standing out in the beige corridor.

"You want to come in?"

He was eyeing them, and didn't.

"We were just leaving," said Paul. "Rach, come on, hurry up. How long does it take to put on a pair of shoes?"

Spencer didn't come in until they said goodbye to Lily, and were on their way down the stairs. Then he came in. He came in and slammed shut the door, glancing puzzled at the barricades—the chairs and the tables—but his hands were already in her hair, and his face was in her face, and his lips were on her lips. He smelled of alcohol. Lily noticed because she had never smelled alcohol on him before, but tonight his breath was strong with it. He was gripping her so tightly that as she was whimpering under his mouth, she raised her hands in surrender.

He pulled her down on the couch and knelt in front of her, and held her to him as if he had been at the front.

"Where've you been?" he said hoarsely.

"Me? Where've *you* been?"

"Here. Coming every day to your place, ringing your bell."

"Spencer . . ."

"Oh, Lily, don't cry . . ."

"Oh, God, Spencer . . ."

They made love on their couch with the TV on silent, with *Lonely Guy* frozen on the screen.

"How much sugar, Lil . . ."

"More, Spencer . . . more."

"How much more . . ."

"Empty, empty, empty." She was clutching him, her hands on his bare back, her mouth on his neck, she was kissing him and not so silently, not so gently weeping.

"Shh, Lily, Shh."

"Now I understand," she said. "I understand it only now, what you were saying to me then. It wasn't Steve Martin, it was you saying it. To me. *And he stubs his boots on your heart and then boils it and cuts it up into little pieces and feeds it to you and afterwards asks you if it was delicious and you say, oh yes, thank you, it was delicious.*"

"Lily, come on, no."

"Yes, Spencer."

He picked her up and carried her into the bedroom. "You've lost weight," he said.

"Good, bad, or indifferent?"

"Indifferent. I take you any which way." He got them water,

and came to bed, and kissed her and caressed her, a little gentler now, and went down on her with his maddening whisky-breath mouth, holding her open with his maddening whisky hands, indeed driving her mad, making her come until she nearly fainted, and then making love to her every which way until she was limp, but there was something going on with him, he wasn't done, he remained impossibly hard, and though she had nothing left—and gave it to him anyway—he still was not done. "Spencer?" she whispered, saturated in perspiration, the windows open, her moans carrying out into the summer yard where the cats were listening, "Spencer, what be up with you?"

"Nothin'," he said. "Just whisky. Can't come with whisky."

"Well, last call, mister, because I can't take it anymore."

"You're going to have to take some more," he whispered.

The cats caterwauled in the courtyard.

"Spencer . . . have mercy on me . . . I don't have this much time . . ."

And finally he had mercy on her.

And eventually stopped moving.

He held her so close to him, and she cried again.

"I'm sorry, Lily."

"Don't be sorry. You have nothing to be sorry for. Nothing."

"I do."

"Nothing!" she repeated. "I was wrong and selfish. It was all about me, about Andrew, about Amy, me, me, me. There was never anything left for you. I was a terrible friend to you, a terrible everything." She pulled herself back from him a little to look into his face. They were pressed like papers against each other, shivering.

She kissed him softly. "Spencer," she whispered. "I'm sorry."

He stared at her, barely forming an acknowledgement she heard. She kissed him again. "Did you hear me?"

"I heard you." He wasn't smiling. "Where've you been? I missed you."

"I went to Maui."

He didn't say anything.

She made a fist and hit him on the back and started to cry. "How could you not have called me for so long? How could you have just forgotten me, don't you have any idea about me?"

"God knows I do."

"How could you not have called?" She was sobbing. "Don't you have any idea what I feel for you?"

"I do," he said, his palms fanning her back. "That's why I didn't call you. I don't deserve you."

She held him in her naked embrace. He asked if she wanted to talk, and she said, no, yes, whatever you want, talk, don't talk. I don't care. I never really cared. I just want you near.

"Lily, please . . ." he said, turning away. They were quiet, for minutes? For hours? Then she talked.

She told him as much about Maui as he could stand. Suddenly he closed his eyes, put his arm over his face, couldn't hear any more. He moved away from her, he said, don't tell me any more.

She didn't know what was the matter.

"Don't tell me any more about your mother," he said at last. "It's too hard for me to hear. I know all about her."

"What are you talking about?"

He said something, quietly, into his hands.

She thought she misheard him. "Drink?" She sat up in bed. "What are you talking about? *You* don't."

"Oh, I do."

"Spencer, I never see you drink."

"Nevertheless."

She shook her head. "Stop."

He said nothing, but sat up in bed, drawing his knees up, looking down.

"Spencer." She laughed nervously. "What are you talking about?"

His mouth tightened.

"You don't drink, Spencer. Whatever it is you do, you don't drink. My mother drinks. I know what drinking is. I've just come back from her drinking. You haven't seen her sitting with the bone in her foot sticking out for days, her very foot bubbling off her body because she was too drunk to know the difference between a stubbed toe and a gangrened toe; and her not wanting to go to the hospital because she didn't want to sober up, even if that meant losing her foot in the process. Now that's drinking. You hold a job, you have a life, and you have *all* your limbs—"

He interrupted her with a shake of his head. "I have no life. I have work, that's true. I have work Monday through Friday, and then I have drink. That's my life. Until you came along, that was my life."

"You drink on the weekends?"

"That's *all* I do."

He was silent.

She was silent. "It can't be true, it can't."

The June breeze blew in from the open window, and the cats were wailing.

"Oh my God," she said at last. She tried to figure it out, she tried to wrap her brain around it. "I don't understand," she said. "It's not my mother's drinking. You work, you have a job, stress, responsibility. You function, it just sounds like . . ."

"You're right," he said. "You don't understand."

She thought back to all the weekends he had spent with her. His absences, his lapses, his silences, his broodiness, moodiness, his soul on mute and she saw but didn't see.

"But you stop for five days a week."

"Yes."

"And sometimes when you're here, longer."

"Yes."

"I've never smelled drink on your breath before," she said, catching with embarrassment the pang of desire in her groin. He was telling her of his darkest demons and she found herself

452

craving him. This is what she meant by failing him. Did men do this? You pour out your soul to them and all they want is to get into your pants?

"I never drank and came to see you before."

"Why did you drink tonight, a Tuesday night? For nerves?"

He smiled slightly. "I'm not in the least frightened of you, Liliput. Just that, since I stopped seeing you . . . the drink has unraveled me."

It has? She stared at him as she would at something she was about to render—consumingly.

"Spencer, this drinking, is it something serious?"

"What's serious?"

"As in, something you can't stop?" She said it but she didn't mean it even when the words came out. It was just words to say.

And Spencer said, "This is something I can't stop."

"I don't believe you."

"Believe me, Lily."

"But you stop every time you go to work, when you come to see me!"

"I stop because I know my reward is waiting for me. I stop and as a reward for stopping I drink to oblivion. I drink until I can't stand up, until either all the whisky is gone or I pass out, whichever comes first."

She was astonished. "That is how you drink?"

"That is how I drink."

Vehemently she shook her head. "No. That can't be true. It can't be true, because that is how my mother drinks. She drinks until she passes out."

"Yes."

"But, Spencer, my mother is an alcoholic."

For a moment there was only the cats crying outside. "Lily," he said, "I am also an alcoholic. I am the textbook definition of an alcoholic. I cannot not drink. And when I drink I can't stop. I hide my drinking from other people because they would be shocked if they knew how much I drink. You say you cannot

453

imagine your life without me. Well, I cannot imagine my life
without the drink. I have not been able to be in a relationship
with one woman for any length of time because of the drink.
They all run their course in about a year. As soon as they think
they can change me, I'm gone."

Lily was watching him. "It can't be," she said.

"Friday night I drink. Saturday the whole day and night, I
drink. Sunday I spend sobering up. Sunday is the hardest day I
live all week. Which is why when I spend it with you, it's easier."
He smiled a little then. "A true Harlequin, like a jester with your
comedies and your cancer, you keep me forgetting about the
drink. Monday I go to work."

"Every Monday you go to work?"

"Every Monday I go to work."

"Never skipped a Monday?"

"Never skipped a Monday." He opened his hands. "What can
I tell you? Appearances are everything. The appearance of seeming normal, of behaving normally is essential to continuing to
drink. Because if you're seen to be losing it, you will be asked to
stop—by your family, your friends, your women, your employer. So
you do everything to hide yourself, so that you're never asked to."

She was thinking, alert, she sat up straighter, her body was
hyper. He saw it; reaching for her, he carefully brought her down
on top of him. He lay her down on top of him, and cupping her
head kissed her face gently, kissed her lips, her cheeks, her eyes,
her forehead. "Liliput, you are adorable, you want to help me?
You want to help me overcome? I'm not saying you're not
admirable. You're a rock. I used to be a normal drinker but now
I'm hopeless. I've been drinking since my late teens. Whereas a
few years back, when I thought I hit bottom, I needed one bottle
of whisky a weekend, now I need two, maybe three, sometimes
four, depending on how strong the Scotch is. I spent two fifty a
week, twelve thousand a year on drink. I spend on drink nearly
what I spend on my rent. I can't afford a life even if I wanted
one."

454

"You can afford me," she said. "I won't cost you a penny."

"You indeed are a powerful drug yourself," he said, lowering his hands to her hips, squeezing her, opening her, not letting go, holding her.

She couldn't concentrate on his words. "You've stood up admirably for me. You've always shown up. Nothing thin-lipped about you."

He kissed her. "Yes. I've shown up. Because I know it's temporary. I'm always going back to my place. The drink is the forever thing."

"Is that why you haven't lived with anyone?"

"Yes. Can't have anyone see me when I'm like that."

She was mulling. "Have you tried that twelve-step approach? My mother is trying it."

"Your mother is lying to you."

He said it so swiftly, so brutally. How did he know that? "No, no," Lily protested, wanting to give him hope, even though she knew he was right. "She was very earnest. She saw her life flash before her. She lost a foot, Spencer. She wants to do everything she can to stop."

"No, she doesn't."

"You're not my mother, you're much stronger."

"No, Lily. I'm just as weak. It's just that I drink differently than she does, because I have responsibilities, because I have a job. But tell me, if I didn't have anything to do, like your mother, how long do you think the sober Sunday night would last? How many sober Mondays would there be?"

"Spencer, don't say that. You're not like my mother."

"I am, Lily. I know you don't want to believe it."

"Because it's not true."

"It is true. Believe it."

"Well, my mother is going to AA."

"Then she is stronger than me."

That was the most absurd thing she had heard all evening. Her mother was so weak. She turned her face from him, tried to get herself together, but she was shaking uncontrollably now. Get it together, Lil, get yourself together. This is what it means to fail him. This is the definition of failing him. You pretend you love him? For God's sake, raise your eyes to him and stop your nonsense. It's not about you. This isn't about you.

"What if you try the AA?" she got out, getting herself halfway together.

"How do you think I'm able to lie here and tell you how much I drink? I tried. But I can't go to AA. They demand total abstinence, and I abstain totally for four days. After several months they see through me. They know I'm a fake."

Still on top of him, her whole body continued to shake and he said, "Don't cry for me, Lily", and she wanted to say, "I'm not crying just for you, I'm crying for my mother, too" and he was quiet, and then she felt him getting hard, unquietly, and suddenly many things were forgotten, and anguished bliss severed the air again, and glued their hearts, and her breasts to him, and her hips and lips to him, and their ailing bodies. "Spencer Patrick O'Malley, you're not a fake. You're the realest thing I know," she whispered.

"I am disfigured," he whispered to her. "Why can't you see it?"

"I see it. I see right through you. I know your crying room."

They lay side by side, face to face, panting in the sweltering night.

"So what are we going to do?"

Who said that? Him? Her?

"Look, is this ideal?" she said. "No. Would I prefer it if it weren't so? Yes. Would I prefer that my roommate and best friend hadn't been involved with my only brother? Would I prefer she weren't missing? Would you prefer I hadn't been sick? But yet here it all is. I didn't know how to live my life, and suddenly I was thrust into it and had no choice but to live it."

His hands on her hips, on her stomach, he observed her. "Have you been to see DiAngelo?" He was so quiet.

456

"No. I have to go, I know," she said just as quietly. We are thrust into our life, kicking, screaming, and we have no choice but to live it out to the bloody end.

60

John Doe

Wednesday *mid-morning*, he was—spectacularly!—still in bed with her. He called in to work, said he was working in the field and would be coming in late.

"Working in the field? Is that what you call it now?"

Pulling her to him, he said, "I do call it that. Because you're going to tell me about your accosting vagabond. Or did you make him up just to come in your little slip of a dress and make me crazy?"

"Well, I'm not saying that was not a desired side benefit," she said with delight. "But I didn't make him up."

She told him what happened. She told him about how silly she had felt about the slight anxiety that she was being watched, about the weekday morning hanging up yellow ribbons. "But that night, Spencer, his arm was around my elbow. He wasn't helping me up. He wasn't letting go. I know the difference. And he did whisper, *Lily*. I mean, did I imagine that? If that guy hadn't interfered, I don't know what would have happened."

"You're unbelievable," he said, "walking through that place at night, despite all my admonitions."

"Well, maybe if you had answered your doorbell, I wouldn't have had to walk through Tompkins Square."

"Yes, perhaps if I was a different man, none of this would be happening at all. But let's just deal with realities, shall we? Can you remember what he looks like?"

"I can. Unfortunately he is etched in my memory. I can draw him for you, if you like."

It took her an hour. She had to get out of bed to do it, because seeing his face, even with Spencer by her side, frightened her and she didn't want her white and light fluffy comfy bed associated with such ominous portents. She drew him in her studio while Spencer showered and got ready for work.

He looked at the face for a briefest instant, "Oh, fuck."

"What, you've seen him?"

"Somewhere I've seen him."

"You think it could be Milo?"

"I'll check with Clive." He took the drawing from her hands. "When I saw him, he didn't quite look like this. The memory of it is so vague. But I never forget. Let me see what I can find out. You go see your grandmother, go see DiAngelo, and I'll take care of this."

"But Spencer . . . what could this person possibly have to do with Amy? You know what I mean?"

"We'll find out, won't we?"

"Oh!" she exclaimed. "Wouldn't it be so great to finally learn something, to finally know something." The unspoken remained unspoken—to finally learn something that would push a missing Amy away from my brother.

"Yes. In the meantime, do me and yourself a favor, promise me that under *no* circumstances will you walk out of your apartment in the evening."

"I promise," she said. "But, what about that week*day* at Second Avenue?"

"That could have just been your anxiety talking. This is real."

It could've been. For some reason she didn't think so.

As he was strapping on his weapon, she asked him timidly what they were going to do about the other thing that drove them apart—the essence of him and the essence of her clashing

459

against each other, her brother, his work. Spencer took her into his arms. "I will advise you as I advise everyone who finds themselves in a similar situation. *You have the right to remain silent.*" He kissed her. "I suggest you avail yourself of it. I intend to avail myself of it."

Spencer spent the rest of the morning looking through mugshots for the years 2000, 1999, 1998. He buried himself in the evidence room, unreachable, as he pored over every face that had been photographed by the New York police after bookings. He found nothing. He wasn't getting discouraged yet. Because he *knew* the face that Lily drew. He knew it. He had been going through mug shots daily for five years. And if he had seen it, that meant that he would find it again. What did Clive tell him at the homeless shelter? He said when he first started running it, there was no Amy or Milo. They came after him, then Milo disappeared for two years. So 1997.

In February of 1997 photos, Spencer found him. It was a mugshot from one of the Bronx precincts. There were no bruises on the face, no tattoos, no goatee, the face was covered with hair, and his scalp was not clean shaven, as per Lily's drawing, but the eyes were the same, the dead expression in them was the same. Before he called the station that had booked him, he allowed himself a small swelling of astonishment that the girl had this gift in her—distilling on paper the very essence of what was true of life. Yet it had lain dormant until cancer woke it.

He dragged Gabe to the South Bronx.

Spencer asked for the original documents of the perp in question, and found out that this man was arrested in a drug bust of a crack den off Cortland Avenue, in February, 1997, in a house that was full of addicts who were trying to stay warm. The man violently resisted arrest, and had to be physically subdued. After he was booked and fingerprinted he refused to speak. Clearheaded or not, addicted or not, he did not open his mouth, he did not tell them his name, he did not volunteer who he was,

460

not even after he had been very roughly interrogated. He simply never spoke, as if he knew no English. They had tried a Spanish interpreter, and German, and Greek, but there was no response.

Spencer read on. Did he use his one phone call? He did not. Did he make bail? He did not. When he was arraigned he did not give his name, nor did he enter a plea. The Bronx Public Defender's office entered one for him. Not guilty they said. He was charged with resisting arrest, assaulting a police officer, possession, and illegal use of controlled substances.

He refused to speak even to his public defender. He was detained for months, a psychiatrist was brought in, got no results, and even the threat of going to prison for ten years did not force him to say who he was. He was put in the Bronx House of Detention while the District Attorney's office and the courts tried to figure out what to do with him. A judge finally allowed for him to be institutionalized pending a disposition of his case. The public defender's office cried foul, the Bronx office being famous for vigorously defending those who could not defend themselves. Involuntary institutionalization was against the law. He was released and sent back to the Bronx House of Detention, where he kept to himself, ate little, bothered no one, and preferred solitary confinement to sharing a cell.

They tried to threaten him with the loss of his few privileges, of books, of work in the cafeteria, if he didn't give what they wanted in return for what he wanted—but not only did he refuse, but stopped eating too. They went on like this for a little while, and then had to feed him intravenously. The public defender got an injunction against any unauthorized medical treatment or examination, saying it was an invasion of his privacy and a violation of his human rights. He was not allowed to be medicated, treated, examined, or tested. They were working on getting him released on the grounds of the Seventh Amendment clause against cruel and unusual punishment and the Fourteenth Amendment for due process. The Bronx ADA argued that giving due process to a man who refused to tell the courts even his name

461

was impossible. Human beings had to participate at least super-ficially in their own rights of habeas corpus. "Monkeys don't tell you their name. Dolphins don't tell you their name. Human beings tell you their name!" In March of 1999, as he was being transferred from the Bronx House of Detention for men where he had spent most of the previous two years to the Vernon Bain Center, a more secure barge prison facility, he escaped, jumping into the East River, but not before he bashed one of the guards transporting him with a lead pipe. Miraculously he did not kill him.

His name was John Doe.

61

Something about Olenka Pevny

She went to Brooklyn to see her grandmother, as promised, to bring her some macadamia nuts, some Kona coffee beans, and some pictures of Allison without a foot.

"Lil, how could you have gone to Maui only to come back so pale?" was the first thing her grandmother said to her.

"I'm not pale, Grandma, I'm tanned."

"You're pale. But also you're smiling. Oh, no. You're not back with that man again, are you?"

"I am, Grandma." She was smiling.

Her grandmother snorted. "I don't know why you're not looking any better then. Are you feeling well?"

"I feel all right," Lily said. But that was a lie. She did not feel all right.

"Sit."

They sat on the Mylar couch with their cups of tea. They talked about Maui, and about Andrew, and about Grandma, and about Allison. There was only one thing Lily wanted to ask her grandmother: to tell her about her mother's crying room. Lily explained about the crying room and saw her grandmother's cup tremble slightly, and Lily's cup, at seeing that, trembled too.

Lily pressed and pressed. Oh, Claudia said, don't you have to be somewhere?

"Why are your hands shaking? Please tell me."

"Lily, what are you worrying your head for about these silly things? Don't you have enough on your plate?"

"Yes. No. I want to know. Tell me. Tell me about my mother."

Claudia was silent.

"Grandma, please!"

"Don't yell at me, I'm your grandmother." She sighed deeply. "Are you sure you're ready to hear this?"

"Frankly, with the kinds of things I've heard in the last seven days, I can't imagine how much worse it can get. Let's have it."

Claudia finally spoke after a pause of several protracted minutes. "Well, you know Tomas and I got married in June 1939, and I became pregnant right away. My baby was due in March, exactly nine months and a day after our wedding. But then the war began in September, and Tomas and his three brothers went to the front. His mother and father were left behind, waiting for news of their sons. And I was next door with my family, waiting for news of Tomas. I was young, still working around the house, carrying heavy things, taking care of the goats, the cows, the chickens. I had a lot of anxiety about him. There were no letters from him, you see. I lost the baby that October, after there had been no news of him for five weeks."

"You lost what baby that October?" Lily said dumbly.

"Lily. Listen. Do you want me to tell you or not?"

"I'm thinking of reconsidering, Grandma."

Claudia continued. "The baby I lost that fall was Tomas's baby, darling. Your mother wasn't even born yet."

"Grandma . . ." whispered Lily. "You're confusing me."

"Tomas's mother was an exquisitely beautiful woman, in her early forties, and unbelievably as I watched her at the gate while we were both waiting for the postman, for our news, I saw that though she was painfully thin, she did have a belly on her. Tomas, his brothers were 18, 19, 20, 22, and suddenly their mother is pregnant again! Oh, what a scandal. No woman even in her thirties got pregnant, much less in her forties.

464

"The Germans came to Skalka in December 1939. Our soldiers fought very bravely, but we had horses and the Germans had tanks. Imagine the stupidity of standing in front of a tank on a horse. We fought, we weren't going to go down without a fight, but after three days, Danzig fell and our village of Skalka with it. The Germans came into the huts, took our china, our dishes, demanded food from us. They kicked several families out of their homes and quartered there. Not ours. Because we weren't Jewish. But they did kick out Tomas's mother and father, because they were."

"Your Tomas was Jewish?"

"He was. And the Jews all went to fight for Poland. Tomas's father said he wasn't leaving his home. The Germans beat him to death in it."

"Oh God." She never heard this part of Grandma's story before.

"Tomas's pregnant mother, because she had nowhere else to go came to live with us. The Germans made her wear a yellow armband to distinguish her from the non-Jews." Claudia coughed. "Because she was a Jew she never got any food even though she was pregnant. We shared our food with her."

"Grandma, how come you never told me any of this? I'm twenty-five years old."

"You're a young twenty-five."

"Do my sisters know this, my brother?"

"They know."

Lily couldn't believe it.

"What can I tell you, Liliput. Sometimes people close to you, even people who love you, keep secrets."

"No kidding."

"Some things are just too painful to tell."

"Are you going to tell me the rest of it? Because I have to go to the hospital soon."

"So why don't you go?"

"No, no. Go ahead. Continue. So she lived with you through the whole war?"

465

"She stayed with us for as long as she could. She was a very sick woman, alone, depressed, and to boot a desperate, irredeemable drinker."

Lily groaned.

"We didn't think she'd make it to the birth of the baby. She used to disappear for days even when pregnant, go to Danzig. Beg for vodka on the streets. Offer herself on the streets for some vodka. But, somehow, in January 1940 she had the baby. And Lily, that baby is your mother."

Lily dropped her cup of tea. She didn't even bend down to clean it up.

"What did you say?"

She couldn't have been sunk farther down into the back of that couch, slunk down, stooped, lowered, debased. "My mother is your husband's youngest sister?"

"That's right."

"Grandma . . ." Lily couldn't take the hands away from her mouth. Her grandmother, who raised her, who adored her, who took care of her, who was the family's only matriarch, was not her mother's mother!

After five minutes of a trance-like silence, her grandmother continued in a lowered voice. "I wish I could tell you that Tomas's father was your mother's father, but I'm afraid no one thought so, not even the father himself. Hence all those rumors about his wife. Everybody suspected she became pregnant on one of her excursions to Danzig while begging for the drink.

"The baby was born in the dead of winter, in Danzig during one of her trips. When my father and mother found them, both were nearly frozen, the naked baby was wrapped in her coat and skirts.

"Believe it or not, as if in a miracle, after the baby was born, she sobered up. All the cows were long eaten, all the goats were eaten, there was no milk, and no one else was having babies. Not even me. There were no wet nurses. Someone had to feed the child or she would die."

Numbly, dumbly, mutely, Lily stared at her grandmother. "Grandma . . . her mother's name . . . was Anya, or something like that? Anna? Anika? . . . *Anne?*"

"That's right," Grandma said, frowning. "How do you know?"

"I don't know," Lily said inaudibly. That remarkable Spencer. Saw even then at the very beginning, something, everything. Saw without knowing, simply saw a shape of *Anne* with his own damaged heart.

"Your mother must have acquired a taste for that vodka in the womb and later while being nursed. You think I don't know, but I know everything, Lily. The way your mother is and has been, I don't think it was milk pouring from Anya's teat into her baby's mouth."

"Grandma, please . . ."

"The sobriety lasted exactly until weaning. Then Anya would take Olenka and disappear to Danzig, using her to beg for vodka. Interestingly she had enough sense to not get drunk in the city, like before. She would come back to Skalka, leave Olenka with me and go off into the woods with her bottle, like a bear." Grandma collected her thoughts. Lily was curled up in a ball on the couch. "Once or twice my own mother and I had to go to Danzig to bring them back. We'd find Anya cold on the ground, in the alley and Olenka would be sitting by her, not moving, every once in a while saying *Mama, Mama.*"

"Grandma, I can't, I can't. I just can't." Lily put her hands over her ears. Grandma was right. At twenty-five, she was just a child.

"I'm sorry. That's why we didn't tell you for so long."

"I would have happily lived out what's left of my life without ever knowing," breathed out Lily. "Had I known, I never would have asked, never. So my mother is Jewish? I am Jewish?"

"Well, no."

"No?"

"You know you are christened Catholic. And we christened your mother. We *had* to christen her."

467

"Why had to?"

"Because at the end of 1942 all the Jews in the village were moved to the Warsaw Ghetto."

"So my mother and her mother were taken to the ghetto?"

"No. Oh, Lily."

"Don't 'Oh Lily' me now, Grandma. You're so far down into the precipice, there's no way back."

"In December 1942 the Germans came to our house, and said all Jews had to leave immediately for the train to Warsaw. The woman with the yellow band and her child had to go. At that moment Anya laughed very loud, shoved Olenka away from herself, and said, 'My child? She's not my child. I wouldn't have a child, I have four grown sons, I'm forty-five years old, do I look to you like I'm capable of having a child?' She grabbed the girl and thrust her in my arms, and said, 'I can't take care of it for you anymore, Klavdia, do you hear? No more!' She turned to the Germans and said, 'It's her child, look! It looks exactly like her. I've been helping her a little bit because she is so young and doesn't know anything about children, and I've been using the girl to help me get the vodka I need. I'm a drunk, you see, I've been stealing her from them to beg for vodka. Isn't that true? Tell them, Klavdia,' and I didn't know what to say. I said, 'That's right.' The Germans looked at me and said, 'This is your baby?'

"I was light-haired then, and so was your mother, she was very light blonde, while Anya was dark-haired and dark-eyed. The hair saved Olenka because aside from the blonde–dark contrast, she was really a carbon copy of her mother. They had the same face, the same features. The Germans believed her and took Anya with them, and left Olenka with me." Grandma began to cry. Lily had never seen her grandmother cry, it frightened her. "When they took her mother, the child in my arms ripped herself free, and shouted, '*Mama!*'

"The Nazis turned around, and I grabbed her and held her to me very tight, smothering her, covering her face, and said, 'Shh,

468

shh, it'll be all right. Mama is here, right here, baby.' You know, I don't think they believed me, or Anya, I remember the way they were looking at me, holding the baby. But they left the girl with me. For the next three days Olenka sat by our frosted-over winter window waiting for her mother to come back."

The two women sat side by side on the couch, not speaking, not touching. The house was quiet except for Lily's anguished cries.

"Did we ever find out what happened to Anya?"

"No. I suspect it was what happened to all the Jews in the Warsaw Ghetto."

It was a long time before she could speak again. Lily got up, said she had to be going. Thanked her grandmother for a cup for tea, which she slowly cleaned up, for an enjoyable afternoon. She said she was going to call her tomorrow, tell her how her blood work turned out. And before she left, at the open door, with her voice breaking, she said, "Grandma, I think my mother is still sitting in that crying room by that window."

She walked not to the F train, but in the other direction to the New York Harbor, and sat on the bench for a long time on the Promenade on the East River overlooking the mouth of the Hudson and all of Manhattan Island. It must be getting so late. Is DiAngelo even there this late? It's four o'clock. I might as well go home. Wait till Spencer hears. I can't even remember what I'm supposed to do anymore. My poor mother.

62

Lindsey

That night, Lily did something she could not remember doing since she didn't know when. She called her mother in Maui.

Her father answered. Her mother was back home, she was not feeling well at the moment, she was sleeping, no, no, everything was fine, she really was just sleeping, nothing more. It's been very good. She's been going seven times a week to AA meetings. They had the meetings right on the green lawns in front of the blue ocean for an hour a day. "Your mother is doing great. Shelly is so proud of her."

That Shelly was nothing but a troublemaker. "Well, tell her I called, won't you?"

"I will. She'll be happy to hear you called, Liliput."

When she hung up the phone, Spencer was looking at her. "She's still going every day," she said to him. "So there."

He said nothing, just opened his arms.

Lily tried painting the frosted window in Skalka, Poland, but ended up sobbing onto the canvas on the floor, and all the blue frost became gray blobs and dried with a briny texture like the dried-out sea.

In the comfort of her bed, Spencer heard about Olenka Pevny. Lily heard about John Doe.

Then they slept, woke up again in the middle of the night, tried to deal with things.

"Spencer, so this person is definitely Milo?"

"He is. I spoke to Clive, showed him the drawing you did. He recognized the eyes. He said the new Milo is much cleaner than the bum who was coming around last year. But you can't hide your crystal meth eyes. I showed it to Paul as well. He didn't know him."

"Well, how are we going to find him?"

"We? You are going to do nothing except go see DiAngelo in the morning. I am going to go see Jan McFadden tomorrow but alone—without Gabe, so as not to scare her. Maybe she can identify the mystery man from Amy's past, though I have my doubts. I've already talked to her until I'm blue in the face. She has no idea what her daughter got up to."

"Talk to her again, Spence. Use your finely tuned interrogation skills."

"I'll show you finely tuned." He kissed her prominent clavicle bones, all across.

Struggling to stick to the subject, Lily said, "I'm convinced this Milo is the reason that Amy is missing." She closed her eyes and moaned lightly with his mouth on her throat.

Still in her robe, unshowered, unhappy even to talk, Jan said, "Why do you keep coming back here if you don't have any information about my daughter?"

"Jan, I have a drawing here of a homeless man that Amy used to be friendly with. Do you recognize this man at all? I hoped you might know his name."

Jan glanced at the sketch of Milo Spencer was showing her. "Well, I certainly don't know his name. I don't recognize him. Do you have him in custody?"

"No. We've got an APB out for him. He's known as Milo. If we find him, I think we might find out where Amy is."

"Well, I don't know any homeless men! I can't believe

471

Amy would either, not my Amy."

"Her friend Paul said Amy was friendly with a lot of off-the-track people he didn't know." Spencer put the sketch away.

"You asked me this already! I didn't know them either!"

"Right. But perhaps—you knew somebody?"

"No matter how many times you ask me, I still won't know."

She stubbed out her cigarette, and said emptily, "Are they even looking in Central Park anymore?"

He didn't reply. They weren't. The police had searched for a year, combing 843 acres of wooded terrain and having found nothing suspicious finally stopped last month.

She asked if he wanted a drink.

"Coffee."

"Coffee if you want. I meant—"

"No, thank you."

"Just so I don't drink alone."

"No."

If only anyone but the demons knew with what effort his lips formed the words no. They didn't even form them. He managed to shake his head while his lips went dry.

He waited, thinking of something else to ask while she stared grimly into her glass of Chivas, while he stared grimly into her glass of Chivas.

He asked if Amy belonged to any clubs. Sports? Art? Choir? Jan said choir.

"Any political clubs? Did she run for student council? The treasurer? The president? Was she in young conservatives of America club?"

"Choir, I told you. Nothing political."

"Did she vote?"

"I don't know."

"You do know, darling," said Jim. He had walked into the kitchen earlier, still sweaty from running, and was fixing himself a drink of ice water as he listened. "She voted in the '92 election when she was a senior in high school."

Jan McFadden looked stupefied. "Did she? I know nothing about that. She was in choir. She sang. She was creative, artistic. She may have voted, but politics didn't interest her."

Well, they must have interested her a little bit, if she came in to see Andrew Quinn, thought Spencer. He wanted to say that to Jan, but didn't see the point, she seemed pretty high-strung as it was.

Jim said, "Maybe if you stop with the Chivas in the morning, you'd be able to recall a few more things that would help this man find your daughter."

"Oh, stop it! You don't think if I could help him, I would? If I knew anything!"

Spencer stepped into the breach.

"Did she know . . . Congressman Quinn . . . back then?" asked Spencer carefully.

"Of course not! God, what are you getting at? I don't even think she voted for him, she was so uninvolved in the whole thing. What are you getting at?"

"What I need from you is a single name, one of the people she traveled with, hung with, went out with? A name of a boy friend, anything." God!

"I told you a thousand times, I don't know! I forgot, or I never knew. Amy's senior year, I had two small babies in the house to take care of. And she was eighteen! I mean, honestly." She sat, nearly crying. "I don't remember. It was seven years ago. With everything that's happened, I'm surprised I can remember my own name."

"A single name. A first name of anyone you let your oldest child, your daughter, go traveling across America in a van with."

"Let her, who let her? I didn't let her! She just went. I wanted her to go to college."

"One name."

"Truth is," said Jim suddenly, "you didn't want to know. Tell the detective. Amy was wild, she constantly disobeyed, screamed back at you. You washed your hands of her. You had

473

the twins, you didn't want to be thinking about Amy. When she said she was going traveling across the U.S., you told her never to come back, as if you were glad to be rid of her. You as much as kicked her out when you heard she wasn't going to college."

"I didn't kick her out!" Jan shouted.

"That's why you don't know. You didn't *want* to know. You didn't care!"

"Lindsey!" Jan cried.

Spencer stepped back against the counter. LINDSEY!

Panting and lowering her voice, Jan said, "Lindsey was one of the girls she used to hang out with."

Well, well. "Lindsey what?"

"You wanted a first name, I gave you a first name. Lindsey."

"This Lindsey lived . . . ?"

"Down the road somewhere, here in Port Jeff Village." In a quieter voice still, and after a significant pause, Jan said, "Detective, if there's nothing else, do you mind . . . I'm very tired. I need to lie down."

Jim followed Spencer out to the car. "I'm sorry about her."

"Don't worry."

"She can't see straight.

"I know."

"I don't know how much longer I can do this, man. I'm at the end of my rope."

"You should do this for a little longer," Spencer said. "She needs you."

In New York City on 22nd Street at the hair salon, Paul said Lindsey? Lindsey who? Not Lindsey Kiplinger? I didn't think Amy was friendly with her, she was a year above her in school, and besides, I only know of her because she's dead, died a few years back in a car wreck or something, somewhere out west. New Mexico? Utah?

Spencer called the Kiplingers in Port Jeff. Their message machine said they were away on vacation.

474

Back at the station, there was a message from DiAngelo.

"Are you busy?" DiAngelo said, when Spencer called back. "I know it's the middle of the day. But she needs someone with her, and I've got to get her transferred to Sloan Kettering."

"I'll come. Sloane Kettering? What's wrong?"

"She's very sick, Detective O'Malley."

"Well, I know, but . . ."

"She's dying."

63

A Terminal Degree in Cancer Treatment

"Lily, where have you been?"

"I thought we were on a two-week test schedule."

"I haven't seen you for nearly a month!"

"I meant to come but then I was in Maui and then I was . . ." I was too busy living for cancer. "Just three weeks. So tell me?" She paused. "Are things not so good?"

"Things aren't so good."

She breathed in and out. "How not good? It's only been three weeks."

"It's been four. And before that you weren't improving, you were just holding."

"All right. And now?"

He said nothing.

"Is it back?"

"It's back."

"Is my blood black caviar again?"

He didn't say anything.

Three weeks of induction, thirteen weeks of consolidation, one of pneumonia, six more of maintenance, radical new leukemia treatment that was supposed to attack only the cancer cells and leave the rest unchanged, twelve months of my life, of Spencer's life, of Amy's life, of my family's life and after that effort, the doctor says nothing.

Lily sat silently for a few minutes in Dr. DiAngelo's office. "Well, now what? Consolidation chemo again?"

"No, the blastocytes are immune."

"Immune to *chemo*?"

"Yes. They were obviously immune to Alkeran."

"So what's left?"

"Well, there are two more things we can do."

Why did she feel so suddenly incapable of listening to him? What was happening to her? Her hands started to shake.

"I want you to have an open mind about this. It's not an easy thing after all you've been through. But I told you from the beginning this was going to be a tough fight."

"Yes, yes, you've covered yourself."

"I wasn't covering myself. I wanted you to know the truth. Didn't you want that?"

"You know, Doctor D.?" she said. "I'm finding out little by little that as it turns out, the less truth the better." She got up on unsteady legs.

"Come on, you don't mean it." He came around his table to where she was standing, ready to go, and put his arm around her. "Didn't I tell you that it wants you to give up first? But *I* don't want you to give up first."

"No."

"You have become my personal crusade. It's not going to lick us, Lily. Now sit."

But she couldn't sit. She wanted to go. She just couldn't hear it, couldn't take it. Couldn't take it alone in his office, sitting in his chair, telling her that there were only two more things they could do.

She couldn't listen. "Can I use your—can I just—"

And in the bathroom, she leaned facing the wall, her head pressed to the cool white tile, eyes closed. Her palms were pressed against the wall also. Lily slid down to her knees, breathing, breaking, so hard, so shallow, catching her losing breath, her forehead still pressed against the cold tiles.

What a foe. What a formidable opponent.

On her knees, she folded over, touching the floor tiles with her forehead, prostrate. She hadn't expected it—feeling so afraid.

"Arsenic?" She had managed to leave the tiles of the bathroom somehow, get back into his chair. He was still at the edge of his desk. "Arsenic, the deadly poison?" she said incredulously.

"Yes."

Lily tried to remember all she learned about arsenic in school. "Doesn't continued exposure to arsenic cause cancer in human beings?"

"Yes. Remember? We treat poison with poison. The cancer cells are also susceptible to being poisoned. So we're going to poison them."

"The drug cocktail didn't work. Alkeran didn't work, your wonder drug."

"Don't worry. This will. A new study just completed over at Sloan Kettering showed that patients who have failed all standard treatment for advanced acute promyelocytic leukemia and relapsed, like you, have had a near complete remission when given arsenic trioxide. I think we should try it."

"Do we have much choice?"

He paused, before he said not much, no.

Lily withdrew into a study of her hands. They were covered with indelible black 8B pencil from drawing Milo that even a shower couldn't get out. "How big was this study?"

"Lily, come on, it's experimental therapy!"

"How big?"

"Ten people."

"Ten people?" she repeated, looking up at him. "*Ten?*"

He nodded, rolling his eyes.

"How many of them achieved remission, doc?"

"Six. Out of those, four continued to test negative."

"And the other two?"

"Died."

"From the cancer or from the arsenic?"

"Lily!"

"I'm just asking," she said calmly. "So what you're telling me is in this broadbased study of ten whole people, six people died?"

"What's the matter with you? This isn't a court of law. Forty percent remission when all else has failed is very encouraging."

When all else has failed.

"What's the second thing we can try? You said two things. What's the second thing?"

"A bone-marrow transplant."

She perked up a little. "Oh, so what's wrong with that? I've read some good stuff about that on the Internet."

"I told you to stop going on the Internet."

"I know, I know. But it sounded pretty good. Where do we get good marrow from?

"Your two sisters. Your brother. They're the most likely match for a donor. It's good you have so many to choose from."

"So what are we waiting for?"

Now DiAngelo was quietly studying his hands.

And now Lily was quietly studying her Milo hands again.

"A bone marrow transplant is extremely invasive and debilitating," he said at last. "BMT patients need to be in good health, free from disease, infections. Liver, heart, pancreatic functions all have to be fairly normal. Your white cell counts are through the roof again, I've never seen them so high, like your body has been fighting an infection for weeks. Your platelets are non-existent. The malignant cells are in record numbers. What have you been doing with yourself? What has your body been doing since I saw you last?"

"Nothing," she said. Who have I been without cancer, without Spencer, without my mother, without my brother? "It's a Catch-22 what you're telling me."

479

"Quite a pickle, Lil."

"Quite. Arsenic it is then."

"Arsenic it is."

She stood up, holding on to the chair. "How are the side-effects to having a poisonous solid injected into your veins?"

"Surprisingly mild."

"Well, that's a relief. When do we start? Tomorrow?"

"Right now."

She tried very hard to be brave. "Blast crisis, Doctor D.?"

"Blast crisis, Lily."

Joy came back into her life. She didn't live with Lily again, but she came when Spencer was at work to take care of her. She took her to Sloane Kettering on 68th. Paul and Rachel came on days they weren't working to be with Lily when she received daily infusions of low doses of arsenic, administered intravenously into her newly re-installed Hickman catheter.

Her family was overwrought. Every time they came to see her, alone or in pairs, they cried. DiAngelo finally forbade them to come until Lily felt a little better. He himself was there every day, even though it wasn't his hospital or his arsenic to administer. She felt so close to him, she donated two hundred thousand dollars to DiAngelo's Mount Sinai children's cancer ward. On second thought and with the eleven-million-dollar apartment receding into the horizon of her lost dreams, she wrote a check for a million dollars to the cancer ward, and DiAngelo renamed it Lily's Ward, and she even cut the red ribbon at the renaming ceremony.

Arsenic was a slow poison then? She began to smell metal in her brain, in her mouth, on her arms, on her pillow. Her tongue felt like a steel gray lollipop. The side-effects of tiredness, of light-headedness she barely noticed, but the poisonous taste in her mouth she couldn't help but notice.

DiAngelo came every day. There were no days off for him. If Lily had to take arsenic seven days a week, then by God he was

480

going to walk five blocks to Sloane Kettering even on his off days.

"You don't have to come every day," she said to him. "The million dollar check cleared."

Her body a metal spring of raw nerve endings, there was no touching her, no love for her anymore, but there was for Spencer, and so one night, after she gave him some love, they were lying in bed together, covers pulled completely up, cozy and warm in the dark underneath, she said, "Spencer, you have a choice, you know. You can stop drinking."

He smiled. "Quid pro quo, huh, Lily Quinn? All right, let's talk about it. You think I choose to drink?"

"Yes. Of course you do. When you're sober, and you take the first drink. That's your choice. We choose what we want to be, how we want to live. It's my grandmother who didn't have a choice. My mother's mother." Her voice broke. "But it was war then. You understand the difference?"

He didn't turn away from her, he didn't even prop up to spirit himself for a defense. He remained lying down with a small smile on his lips. She couldn't resist, she leaned over and kissed him. "You're lucky you're so cute," she whispered.

He kissed her back and then pulled away. "The choices you talk about are theoretical things. Nice to talk about, nice to discuss. This is real, like your illness, this isn't a conversation over a poker table with five septuagenarian women."

"Octogenarian, but whatever."

"Lily, you think I choose this? Not to be able to drink at weddings, at Christmas parties? Not to be able to sit with you at dinner and have a cocktail? No more drunk bowling, fun with friends, no mimosas in the middle of Palm Court? You think I choose to drink so that I'm unconscious through a sixth of my life?"

"Oh, Spencer."

"I know who I am, Lily. I have no illusions. I'm a cop. I'm an Irish drunk. That's who I am. You want to know what my choice

481

is? Where my free will comes in? It's where I struggle every day, every week, to stave off the need for whisky until I can't take it anymore, until the staving off becomes in itself the reason to reward myself with Glenfiddich, for being so *good* for so long. The longer I keep from it, the more I feel I deserve the most expensive Scotch there is. A month off? It's Johnny Walker Blue Label for me. No AA, no God, no reason, no fear, no threat is going to keep me from wanting it. From craving it. That's ancient war, that's modern war. You willing yourself to grow healthy blood, to keep going, to keep living even though you have nothing left, that's war. Me at home every Sunday, desperately trying to keep my idiot brain from convincing me I can have just *one*, me getting up every Monday and going to work, that's war. What your mother goes through, tell me that's not war—against herself, against you, against your father."

Lily squeezed her eyes shut. "She didn't do so well."

"No. No, she didn't."

"You're doing better."

"A little better. Since you, I've been doing better, there's no denying it." He smiled. "But I wouldn't be doing better if I were living in Maui. I'd be just like her, sprawled out on my patio, wondering where my next drink was coming from. You think now that she's without a foot she wants drink less? You think she's seen the error of her ways?" Spencer exhaled skeptically. "She wants it, needs it more than ever. Her whole being is concentrated on that single need and she will not rest until she figures out a way to hobble over, peg-legged and all, to the drugstore to get it for herself. She does it the way we all do it—because we are weak and human and cannot help it."

Lily watched him.

He stroked her face.

"So what's the subtext of what you're telling me?" she said. "After I'm all better, and our passion hour has passed, you want to be just friends again, Spencer? You want me to find someone else to be with?"

482

"No. I just want you to understand that no matter how much we repair each other's damage, and we do, I cannot be without the drink. That crying room? I can't leave it. Rather, I leave it, but I can't not return to it. And that's no life for you."

"What do you know about what I want, what I need for my life? You don't know. Staying with you, is that at least *my* choice, or has *that* also been removed from me?"

"That's your choice. Don't be upset with me. This life is not just the only life I know, it's the only life I know how to live. I'm being as honest as I can."

"I wish you were a little less honest," said Lily.

He fell silent in the dark. It was the worst to have him fall silent in the dark.

"Spencer, tell me, do you think this arsenic stuff will work? Forty percent chance. Will it work on me?"

"Of course it will, Liliput."

She tried to move away, crawl away from him on her bed, but he wouldn't let her, holding her to him from behind, caressing her breasts, his lips nuzzling her head.

The two of them, in their own *pas de deux*, lonely, isolated, softly knocking on each other's souls, in their own Hungarian Dance, she with cancer, he full of a naked and desperate desire for drink.

I'm exercising my free will, she thought, rolling over and wrapping the wraith of herself around him. And I choose you. However, whatever, halved, damaged, wounded, bleeding, dying, drinking, in the crying room with the wolf forever at our door, it's you I choose.

Spencer was not around Friday night, Saturday night. Lily didn't discuss it with him. She didn't bring it up. She didn't say, Spencer, I'm having arsenic injections and you're doing God knows what. She didn't say that. What she did say with an ahem was, "Spencer, DiAngelo needs me to come in on Friday for an injection and some blood work."

483

"On Friday?"

"Yes. Arsenic seven days a week. Blood work three times a week now. Is there any way at all you can come and take me home? Paul and Rachel are working."

And he would come.

And with another ahem: "Spencer, I'm feeling so weak, I can't carry my paintings downstairs on Saturday morning. Look how many I have now that you're back. Is there any way you can come and help me carry them down? Maybe put them in the car for me? Help me set up my table?"

And he would come on Saturday morning drained like low tide and help her, and then sit wanly in his own folding chair at her table, and the women who would buy her paintings would say, "There he is! There you are—her muse."

There I am, Spencer would mouth.

She painted a series—seven small oil on canvas paintings that went together called "Whisky in the Hands."

Monday, Tuesday, Wednesday, Thursday, Friday, Saturday, Sunday, and each day different hands clutched around the glass of whisky, or around the bottle, the glass empty, full, broken, the hands bleeding. An extremely well-dressed, serious man bought the whole lot without saying anything to her other than, "I'll give you ten thousand dollars for all of them."

"Spencer?" Ahem. "Do you know I've never seen Bruce in concert? He's doing ten shows in Madison Square Garden. I hear Saturday nights is the best time to see him. Ah, well. Tickets are completely impossible to get."

And because the NYPD was providing police detail for Bruce, Spencer got seats, in the first row to the right of the general admission pit, and took Lily on a Saturday night on the First of July to see Bruce Springsteen play his last concert in Madison Square Garden. For three and a half hours, she jumped for joy, she sang along to twenty-eight songs, she danced through two encores, she was wiped out, she was alive.

But all of it was nothing, NOTHING, compared with the best

one of all, the charm of them all, even better than cancer. "Ahem, Spence, I'm so scared to be here in my apartment alone. After seeing the face of that Milo, I'm just sick in the stomach. What if he comes? Do you know the other day, I needed milk and had to go to the supermarket, and I was so scared, I nearly called the police to escort me."

"Liliput, I am the police. Call *me*."

Pause pause pause. "I'm calling, Spencer."

When he came he brought his clothes.

At the start of July, DiAngelo did not come for her Sunday arsenic injection. Lily felt his absence acutely, it was like spending a whole day without a glass of water.

The following Monday morning he came early without Joy, without joy, his mouth barely able to form into a smile. But it formed somehow.

"Let's call your sisters and your brother, Lil. Let's see if they can match marrow for you."

Many things have left me, she thinks, in the present tense, as she looks at the doctor, at her doctor, who is looking so beat, and she doesn't know what to say because he doesn't know what to say.

Lily's white blood count is increasing in exponential mathematical equations, inversely proportional to how fast her platelet count is decreasing.

The war still rages where you think you can't see it, in the middle of a summertime New York, a beautiful, comfortable, peaceful life, and the drum roll please! warns of impending bloodshed ahead. She closed her eyes. She held her breath.

"Spencer invited me to the Benevolent Patrolmen's annual picnic in a few weeks time."

"I wouldn't make too many plans, Lil," were the words DiAngelo finally spoke. "The marrow transplant is the most important thing."

He stopped the arsenic, moved Lily back to his own hospital and started with outpatient moderate combination drug therapy again—to have something in her. Moderate because it was the only kind her body could take.

Spencer shaved his own head again, and then shaved hers. Difference between then and now—when he was done and she was bald, he held her head between his hands and kissed every square of her bristly scalp.

She was not allowed to go to the movies, sell her paintings, walk in crowds, go to restaurants. She painted when she could get up, and Spencer put up a chair in front of her easels. When she couldn't get up she painted on the floor. On Saturday morning it was he who went down to 8th Street, and sat at the table and sold her art, and some of the women who came, they cried. "She's going to be okay," he said. "She's just on bed rest. Look, she's still painting."

Lily's love—Spencer on the couch, very big, and Lily on his lap, see-through and receding, and exceedingly small.

Lily's love—A brown-haired beautiful woman, sitting on a bench in an overgrown village, in the summer, with a small blonde girl, faces pressed close.

Back home on her bed she lay, surrounded by clocks ticking time away. July. Warm July, the trees full of summer.

Oh, life. Riddle me this. Who am I? I don't want to die and not find out.

I don't want to die.

Amanda returned early from camping in Montana to give her marrow sample.

Anne came in to Mount Sinai but not before she cornered DiAngelo and asked for Lily's prognosis.

DiAngelo couldn't get her counts right. She was all topsy turvy—in the double digits for platelets, in the seven digits for white blood cells. Her red cells were kept steady with near constant transfusions. Why did DiAngelo not want to utter a single word of this to Anne? "She is a brave girl. She doesn't complain," he said.

486

"What's the prognosis, doctor, what's the *actual* prognosis?"

"Mrs. Ramen, your sister needs a sample of your marrow to see if you can be a possible match for her transplant. Let's deal with the vital, and then deal with the trivial." He sped her on to the hospital's blood lab.

"Prognoses are now trivial?" Anne said. "Since when? Isn't prognosis essential in determining treatment?"

"Yes, we have only one thing to do, and that is to get her what she needs to live—a transplant. So let's get going with that."

"But the odds, doctor, the odds?"

"I think the odds, despite a difference in temperaments, are very good for a donor match, very good indeed."

Lily, calm, even tempered, takes it all in stride. She is a stoic. She is Marcus Aurelius, hands pressed together at the fingertips in a zen-like teepee.

Flinch not, neither give up nor despair.

Suit thyself to the estate in which thy lot is cast.

Remember this: the longest lived and the soonest to die have an equal loss, for it is the present alone of which either will be deprived.

Until one afternoon, after the Fourth of July weekend, Spencer comes during the day, while she's getting her outpatient chemo, and brings her flowers, white lilies, and his white Lily takes them and hurls them on the floor, and says, "Don't ever give me flowers again." And then turns her body to Marcie.

Spencer asks Marcie if she can give them a minute. When the door shuts behind her, Spencer picks up the flowers and throws them in the garbage. There are tears in Lily's eyes as he turns to the bed. "What happened?" he says. "Andrew is coming tomorrow to give a marrow sample. Everything is okay."

"Everything is not okay. It's not okay. Where have you been? Have you seen what's been happening to me?"

He is so sad for her, his shoulders quake with it. "I won't bring you flowers anymore," he says.

"That's right. And get your things out of my apartment."

487

Pause. "Okay."

"And don't come here anymore. I've got Joy, I've got Marcie."

"Okay, Lil."

She tries to sit up on the bed but she can't without his help. He helps her, and she clenches his suit jacket in her fist and shakes him feebly. He sits with her on the bed, holding her while she thrashes against him.

"Tell me this, Spencer O'Malley," she says, grasping him around the neck, pressing her head to him, and then pushing him away and looking desperately into his face, "tell me this, you sit here and pretend in front of me that oh ho ho all is well, and this transplant is going to work, if we ever find a match and everything is going to be just sooo hunky dory, but tell me why did you refuse to sell my art on the sidewalks of New York last Saturday? You hide behind your bottle, but tell me why you refused to go and sell it?"

He blinks—and gets off the bed, taking a step back from her, and feels that this is too much for him, that he can't take it either. He couldn't sell her art. After he learned the arsenic was a bust, Spencer can't sell Lily's paintings anymore. He wants to say, I'll sell them this week, Liliput, but it's a lie, he won't, she knows it. He won't, and didn't, and can't, because he fears that that art will very soon be the only thing left of her.

With gritted teeth, she says, "I wish I was hit by a fucking bus. This is worse than anything. I wish I vanished like Amy. Instant, immediate and irreversible. In many ways I feel like I have been, yet I continue breathing. The people around me have been acting like I've been dead for a year, and they're just waiting for my body to catch up."

"I act like that?" He takes another step back.

"When you bring me flowers though I'm still living, when you bring my art here instead of selling it there, when you tiptoe around me, not touching me, yes. Yes. You're thinking, only a little while longer. And then all will be normal again. Well, go to hell. I'm not your penance, Spencer."

"Lily . . ." he says, barely able to speak.

"What, I'm not being fair? I know—this is excruciating. Give me a car crash, a plane crash, Amy's sudden and permanent disappearance. Give me that any day, so you can get on with your life and not be burying me with white lilies."

"Amy's mother has gone on with her life?" He doesn't mention himself.

"If Amy is ever found, she will."

"Death is death," says Spencer, mentioning himself obliquely. But she doesn't hear.

"You know, DiAngelo is going to stop chemo for me. He says it's not doing me any good, and is making me sicker. That's right. Did you give him some of your advice? Didn't you once tell me that if I wished to drown, I shouldn't torture myself in shallow waters?"

"That wasn't my advice. I was telling you a story about something else."

"You must have told it to DiAngelo. Because he listened. No more chemo. And look at me, I'm not alive, I'm not dead, what am I? What am I without my Hickman? They feed me intravenously, they give me transfusions every five minutes, I can't make a single red cell on my own anymore. My liver, my kidneys are not failing fast enough. Talk about shallow waters. I'm on dialysis, on electrical monitoring of my heart, I just—! I know—this is how I spent the first twenty-three years of my life, at arm's length away from all feeling, but I was so happy then! God, I would have lived another hundred-and-twenty-three years not having life be this close to me. All I want is—" She broke off, her hands no longer in a zen-like teepee but pressed together in prayer. "To be stupid and unknowing," she said finally. "Go to the movies, sleep, paint, sit in Central Park on Sunday, smell rain, live like everyone else, as if I'm immortal. I don't want this anymore." She sinks into her bed. He can't come near her.

"What do you want, Lily?" says Spencer.

"I don't want anything. Just to live."

64

Amy and Andrew

Andrew came to Mount Sinai to have his marrow drawn, and then knocked on her door to visit her. Miera was with him. Two Treasury agents were by his side. He was thinner than ever before, very gray, and he turned ashen when he saw her, and she must have been thinner than ever before and very gray also, and ashen.

He brought Miera with him!

I mean, this was just unbelievable.

Lily and Spencer stared at each other, and then he stared into his hands.

Lily pointed at the Treasury agents. "Why are they always with you now?"

"For my protection. I've stopped feeling safe," said Andrew.

And Spencer said, "I think that's wise."

Andrew without even acknowledging Spencer, asked if they could have a *minute* alone, and Lily said, "Andrew, can Miera give *us* a minute alone?"

"Miera is family," Andrew said.

"You know what, Spencer's not leaving."

"Then *I'm* leaving."

"This is just great, Andrew," said Lily. "I haven't seen you since November and you're *leaving?*"

Spencer got up. "I'm leaving."

"No!"

"Lily, I'm just outside the door." He leaned deep in to her and whispered, "If he knows what's good for him, tell him he better not upset you."

"Shh," she said, but by the way Andrew glowered at the departing Spencer, Lily wasn't sure he hadn't heard.

"Lily," said Miera, coiffed and high heeled and Armani-clad, "you're not looking too bad."

"You were expecting worse?"

"I don't know what I was expecting. We knew you were sick. But you don't look—" she broke off. "I'm just trying to be nice, Lilianne."

"Thank you."

"So how are you, Lil?" Andrew said, taking her hand.

"Fine, thanks." She sighed. "How are *you?*"

"I'm okay. I'm hanging in there."

"Me too." She struggled to keep her voice even. "I'm glad to see you."

Andrew sat on the edge of her bed and embraced her. "Liliput," he whispered. "Liliput."

She was calm. On slow cytarabine drip today. Sick. Tomorrow home. She patted his back. She waited.

"Miera, could you give me a minute, please?"

Thank you, Andrew.

"Andrew, but you said—"

"I know. Just one minute, Miera."

After she left, Andrew lowered his voice and an audible groan came from him. "I've made a horrible mess of things, Lily. It's *all* my fault. I hope my marrow matches. Look at you. I'm so sorry. Can you forgive me?"

"Forgive you for what?"

He pulled back. "For not coming all these months."

"Oh. That. I forgive you."

"I've been too ashamed to come, Lil. Too ashamed to face you. I would have come if I could've. I just couldn't."

491

"I knew that. I told Spencer that."

"Stop talking about him."

"You mustn't be so hard on him. He's just doing his job."

"No, he hates me beyond all call of duty."

"Andrew, that's not true."

"Look I don't want to talk about him with you. You're sick, let's just get you better, and then we'll see about everything else."

She turned her head away from him, despising herself for her weakness, wishing herself strong, unable to talk to him about the only thing they needed to talk about. Why did she think Andrew would tell her anything?

He wasn't letting go of her. "What are all these things going into you?"

"Well, my heart is attached straight to the poison in that little bag right there."

"What's in the other bags? Attached to your arm IV?"

"Antibiotic, glucose, morphine."

Andrew started to cry.

"Please," said Lily, patting her brother's back. "It'll be all right. Really. Don't be upset."

"Can I pick you up? Can I pick you up in my arms?"

"You'll yank my chains off of me."

He picked her up very carefully, and sat on the bed, and cradled her, and rocked her. Her head was against his shoulder.

"Liliput, do you remember how I used to carry you?"

"Andrew, please . . . my heart's not strong enough."

"Oh, Lily," he said. "There are so many things I can't talk to you about, because of him. I know you feel I've betrayed you, I know that, but you must know that I have felt betrayed by you, no, no, don't protest, you're a child, how could you understand the motives of grown men. I came here with Miera as protection against you, but I didn't want to leave, seeing you now, without letting you know one important thing about me and Amy."

"What thing?" she said inaudibly.

His voice low and throaty, he said, "Lily, how could you have

492

been so blind? Haven't you figured it out yet? I was in desperate love with her! I was going to leave *everything* in my life for her. I loved her more than I have ever loved anything. More than my job, my career, my future, my family. All I loved in the world was her."

Clarity was still myopic, amblyopic in just one uncorrectable eye.

"You did?"

"Of course I did. She came into my life, and altered it beyond recognition. I didn't expect it. She certainly didn't expect it, I don't think, me to fall for her like that. I think it surprised even her. She thought she was strolling in to have a little affair with a powerful man. Everything under control. And suddenly there it was."

"So if you loved her, why did you end it?" She struggled. "Did you . . . end it?"

"I didn't. In April she told me she didn't want to see me any more."

"She did?"

"Yes. Completely out of the blue. She said . . . she didn't love me anymore and didn't want to continue."

"Did you believe her?"

"Not at first. I thought it was a ploy. Perhaps to get me to leave my wife faster, or not run for the Senate. I didn't know. I was devastated. But, eventually, I came to believe her. She convinced me that she didn't love me anymore."

"How?"

"She just did. With her actions. She was very cold. She cut me out of her life. With her words. She said some things that made me believe it."

"Like what?"

"Stop it, Lil. You're my sister, not a detective. Stop talking like one."

"So why didn't you tell this to him?"

"I don't know if you know this about him, but he manages to

493

turn every single personal thing I've ever said and use it against me."

"Oh, Andrew."

"Lily, trust me when I tell you my side—me and Amy had nothing to do with you. I know it's hard to believe, and you feel betrayed, we did deceive you for so long. But I just fell in love—and lost my head. Everything else fell by the wayside. If you tell your friend anything, tell him that."

"You know, Andrew, Detective O'Malley keeps his own counsel on all matters."

"Frankly I think that's probably best under the circumstances."

"Me, too."

They smiled.

"I'm sorry, Lil. That it's all gone to hell like this."

"Me too, darling Andrew. Me too."

"Is the policeman with you all the time now?"

"When I'm not here, or with Joy. Yes. More or less."

And then another incomprehensible out of Andrew: "That's good, Liliput. That's good."

After Andrew left and Spencer walked back into the room and sat on the chair next to her bed, Lily reached over, took off his glasses and pressed her hands to his eyes.

"What are you doing?" He didn't move away.

"Get that detective look right out of your eyes, detective. I'm not letting go until Spencer returns."

He kissed her hands, he pulled away, he smiled, he put on his glasses.

"Stop looking at me," she said.

"Your eyes are closed. How do you know I'm looking at you?"

"Because you're always gawking at me for this, for that. Stop it."

She lay on her pillows quietly. He sat in the chair by her side.

"So what are you doing now?" he asked.

"Nothing." There was a smile on her face. "Following your

heartfelt advice, I am freely exercising my American right to remain silent."

Spencer brought a sandwich for himself and soup for Lily, and she ate slowly, sipping teaspoons of her soup so as not to upset her intestines, so easily upsettable.

After she was done with the soup, she said, "All right, you want to know what he told me?" She closed her eyes, trying not to get upset. These days she was so easily upsettable.

"Dear Lily." Spencer brought her hand to his lips. "You want me to tell you what he said, coming in here? He told you that Amy reached down his throat and grabbed his heart, pulled it out, threw it on the floor, stepped on it with her high heels, spit on it, shoved it in the oven and cooked the shit out of it. Then she sliced it into little pieces, slammed it on a hunk of toast and served it to him, and then expected him to say, thanks, honey, it was delicious."

She opened her eyes. Stared at him in disbelief. Spencer, his piercing blue eyes piercing her, trained on her, was thoughtful. "Spencer . . ."

"Lily, I never thought Amy loved Andrew. I always suspected it was the other way around."

"Why? Why did you think that?"

"A number of reasons."

"Give me one."

"Because she gave away the jewelry he bought her."

"What?"

"Yes. You don't give the Tiffany jewels the man you love bought you away to a bum in a homeless shelter unless you don't love the Tiffany giver and love the bum."

"Okay, you have gone mad. Amy loving Milo is the most absurd thing I have *ever* heard."

And then she said, "You know what else is wrong with you? You don't understand women at all."

"Thank you for that."

"*You* may be immune to my brother's charms but no woman

can resist him. Amy may have flung her auburn hair into his heart, but he has tricks too. It's impossible not to fall for him."

"So what are you saying? I'm just not seeing the love?"

"That's right."

"Show me Amy. Find me her. In any form, and you'll make a believer out of me."

65

Nathan Sinclair for the Last Time

"I can't *believe* I'm here again," Spencer said to Liz Monroe.

"Well, we have some more sworn affidavits we wanted to talk to you about."

He looked around the room. She said *we* but she was alone this time. Just him and her in the rectangular air-conditioned conference room.

"Why don't you sit?" She opened up a letter. "This one here is from a Constance Tobias."

"Okay." He sat.

"Do you know who she is?"

"Well, obviously, Ms. Monroe."

Monroe cleared her throat and buried herself in the letter. "Her sworn statement says that a few weeks before Nathan Sinclair's death, you came to see her at the New Hampshire maximum security prison, from which she has just been released, having served six years for a crime she says in this statement she did not commit."

Spencer had no comment.

"Do you want to add anything to that?"

"No. Should I? There is nothing so far I need to respond to."

"For a crime *she* did not commit."

"No, Ms. Monroe. For a crime she *says* she did not commit.

Two different things. The jails are full of innocent people, if you ask the inmates."

"Are you convinced she is guilty?"

"I'm convinced that she pled down to a manslaughter from a murder charge, saving herself from life in prison. I'm convinced that she balked from being tried by a jury of her peers because the evidence was overwhelmingly against her. I'm convinced that though there may be a few innocent people in jail, she is not one of them."

"She says in her letter that you seemed disturbed by your conversation with her."

"No more or less disturbed than I am by many things of that nature, Ms. Monroe. Is there anything else?"

"Let's stay with this for a moment. Miss Tobias's letter alludes to the fact that you might have also believed she was not guilty of murder, in which case you might have sought out the one who you thought was guilty of murder and who got away scot-free. Is that possible, detective?"

"Is it possible?" Shrugging, Spencer raised his eyebrows. "It is not *impossible*."

"Well, let me say this, while we're on the subject of sworn affidavits, I have two here from your co-workers. One from your former partner Chris Harkman, and one from Gabe McGill. We interviewed them—"

"Detective Harkman, retired from the force, is still giving interviews from his hospital bed?"

"I don't see how that's relevant, Detective O'Malley. This is what Detective Harkman told us. He told us that once or twice a few years ago when you had been drinking after work, you told him, and here I quote him, that 'the Greenwich bastard got what was coming to him.'"

Spencer laughed. "Hang on a minute. When I've had a few to drink I've told my partner that the Greenwich bastard got what was coming to him?"

"Yes."

"All right, even supposing that I had said that, you think that's proof of guilt of capital murder?"

Impassably, Monroe went on. "I'm just telling you what I have in your file, Detective O'Malley. Gabe McGill, however, who has also been drinking with you and who has known you for five years, swears to your unimpeachability, drunk or sober. So does your captain."

"That's nice," said Spencer dismissively, "but getting back to my drunken rantings. I'm asking you again, how does that statement constitute a confession?"

"It doesn't per se."

"Oh, per *se*."

"But it's just one more thread of circumstantial evidence against you."

"Very thin circumstantial evidence, Ms. Monroe, if you don't mind me saying so. I don't think it's going to hold up in court, that I had something to drink and said some guy in Greenwich got what was coming to him."

"Detective O'Malley, moving on for a moment, do you consider yourself the kind of man who would set up an earlier daytime and public visit to his future victim, knowing that fibers belonging to you, or hairs, or fingerprints might be found at the scene, and you would need plausible deniability complete with witnesses, which is how the Suffolk County Police Department began investigating this matter to begin with?"

"No."

"No? Well, do you consider yourself the kind of man who would buy dark clothes and boots that were too big for him on purpose, and a dark bag he could throw the clothes into and throw away, or bring a gun untraceable and easily dismantled, or park in a public place, or provoke Nathan Sinclair into firing first?"

"No."

Liz Monroe sat across the long conference table, staring at Spencer. "Detective," she said, "let me ask you something. Do you consider yourself the kind of man who would kill another man for some vigilante sense of justice, if you thought that justice had not been done? Would you be tortured, made crazy by the thought that someone got away with a murder of an innocent? Would you risk your job, your professional credentials, your standing in your police community, your very freedom and livelihood, to take the law into your own hands?"

Spencer's palms were calmly on the table. "Ms. Monroe, I spend every day of my life watching people get away with all kinds of things. People who sell drugs to little kids, parents who sell their children into prostitution to score some H, fathers who abuse their children so badly that the children would rather run away and be exposed to unimaginable predators than face their own parents. Mothers who drown their toddlers in lakes and then report them missing. Men who drop the girls' dead bodies into oceans from chartered planes. Tell me, are all those people behind bars? Certainly not. I'm only one man, I can only do so much." He stood up. "I do what I can. But what you're accusing me of does not reflect my record, my history, my twenty-two years on the police force, or the recommendations of my superiors and my co-workers." Spencer paused—for emphasis. "So the answer to your question based on everything you know about me or can infer from observing my work for nearly a quarter century is *no*."

He remained standing, she remained sitting. Her eyes were on him, his eyes were on her. Her gaze was so steady, so penetrating.

"Detective, I have spoken to your commanding officer, Chief Whittaker. I have spoke to his commanding officer about you. I have spoken to the president of your PBA union. I have spoken to your co-workers. You are right—you are highly regarded. Your direct supervisor cannot say enough about you. In over two decades there has not been a word against you—except this one. You have not been involved in any other sustainable complaint, not in the suspicion of excessive force, nor bribery, nor extortion. But these claims just won't die down. Not at Suffolk County.

Not here. I know that you transferred out of SCPD because of these rumors. Nathan Sinclair for one reason or another seems to be the albatross around your neck."

"The fact that Nathan Sinclair came to a bad end, I will admit, does not leave me with much regret. I do not cry at the death of the wicked. I am barely able to cry at the death of the virtuous." Spencer's throat caught a little on those words. "Now, is there anything else I can help you with?"

Monroe closed his file. "No. I will evaluate and then make my recommendations accordingly. You will remain on duty until and unless you are notified otherwise."

"I look forward to seeing your report when it crosses my desk, Ms. Monroe."

She gave him her hand and without taking it away, she said, "Harkman mentioned in his affidavit that he thought you drink too much. Be careful."

Spencer let go of her, and for some reason thought she regretted having said the words she must have meant as a caveat, not a rebuke. "Thank you, I am always careful."

"You certainly are, Detective O'Malley."

"Please," he said. "After all you've put me through, do call me Spencer."

66

A Boat in Key Biscayne

"Lil, I think I'm going to lose my job."

"What?"

He told her what had happened with IA. She listened intently. "It's so ridiculous, no?" she said at last.

Spencer remained silent.

Lily studied his face and then looked away.

Later, hours later, with night there and Lily drifting in and out of sleep, she pulled him to herself and whispered, "Spencer Patrick O'Malley, I trust in you completely, I believe in you completely. The angels already know the truth. And I don't need to know anything."

"Good. You know too much as it is."

She said, "Maybe the way Liz Monroe hounds you, you understand how my brother feels, being pursued by you."

Spencer didn't say anything for a long time. She thought she had fallen asleep, he had fallen asleep. The breaths he was taking were breaths of a thousand whiskies, breaths of sepulchral suffering.

"What I understand is this," Spencer said. "The ground swells up. Lies, secrets, deceptions, untruths rise to the surface, the universe rights itself, the demons burst open, truth is uncovered."

It was deep summer, and the window was open, and July was blowing in. Pollination, nectar, life was blowing in. Lily didn't want to think about cold things. She wanted warmth. Spencer, naked in her bed, across from him on the wall was her *Girl in Times Square* painting that he had moved into the bedroom, her corkboard full of her young life, the life she had when Amy was still with her, the life she had when she wasn't dying. And stuck onto the corkboard with thumbtacks was her lottery ticket they gave her back as a souvenir, 49, 45, 39, 24, 18, 1, and near that was a photo booth black-and-white strip of four silly pictures of her and Spencer.

Her voice weakening at the feel of his hands on her lower back, she lay in his arms, but didn't look at him because it was easier to talk to him without watching his face close up, shut in, tighten, and she said, "If you lost your job we could leave here. We could leave New York and go somewhere warm."

He didn't say no. He whispered, *you're the sweetest girl, you're a beautiful girl.* Then he said, "Where are you thinking?"

"Like south of Miami maybe. Somewhere in the Keys? Key Biscayne? I hear it's nice. We could get a place, build a place right on the water. You could have a boat."

"I could have a boat," he said slowly. "And what would you do?"

Be with you, she wanted to say. Kiss you. Learn to cook maybe. I'd make you Irish Stew and spaghetti and meatballs and maybe something Polish from my grandmother, though she never did learn how to cook so good in Ravensbruck. I'd paint you and paint for you, and clean your fish if you learned how to fish. We'd swim every day, and the water there is warm year round, and so is the air, we'd be outside all day. We'd make furniture and bicker about wood or wicker. We'd be together. We'd be alive. I'd be alive.

It was a beautiful dream.

She didn't say any of it. We're supposed to be at peace now, have peaceful choices. We're not supposed to be at war any more, she wanted to cry. Didn't Tomas already do that? We can pick up and move to warmth, we can get new jobs, we can make our lives better, with just the boxes in the trunk of our car and our free will, we can make them better. We don't need to go fight the Germans. Tomas already did that. We don't need to go to Ravensbruck. Klavdia Venkewicz already did that. We don't need to deny our children with all our hearts as they run to us. Anya Pevny already did that. They did it so we can have a choice of New York or Miami, of police work or boat work.

To Love or not to love?

To Drink or not to drink?

To have Cancer or not to have cancer?

It was occurring to Lily with startling clarity that perhaps even peace was an illusion. Perhaps they still and constantly had to fight and pay a price for that simple joy of living. And perhaps even the simple was an illusion. The struggle was all.

"All right, no boat," she said, shifting from despondent to mock cheerful in a pained breath. "But we can open our own gumshoe agency in Florida, the *Spencer and Lily Private Investigations, no case no matter how trivial will go unsolved.* We could chew tobacco and have snakes in a tank, and punctuate every sentence with a spit into the urn. I could wear those cute cowboy boots, and a little skirt, and walk around on high heels, saying, will that be all Detective O'Malley, will that be all?"

"Now, that," said Spencer, kissing her, "is a beautiful dream."

67

Cabo San Lucas

DiAngelo stopped chemotherapy for Lily. He gave her Vicodin for pain, antibiotics for infections, and sent her home. "If the pain gets too bad, come back, we'll give you morphine."

"What about the results for the marrow samples?"

"Need a little more time on them."

"Really?"

"Really. We're also looking into the International Donor Registry, just in case. And your Detective O'Malley, we'll take a sample from him."

Lily watched DiAngelo. "Is everything all right?"

"It's as good as it can be." He smiled pastily. "Don't worry. We'll get you a donor. We just need to wait a little bit longer for the results."

Without chemo, Lily wasn't as nauseated, and her mouth stopped bleeding. She was getting bruises all over her legs again. They looked like her mother's legs. She was tired. She was fading, a day at a time.

She knew she was fading because she stopped painting.

Still she went with Spencer to the Benevolent Patrolmen's annual picnic, thrown and funded by Bill Bryant.

It was on a warm New York summer Sunday, at the Great Lawn in Central Park. Spencer gave her his glasses to hold and his shirt and his weapon, and played a game of soccer with the patrolmen from Brooklyn, and a game of baseball against the robbery detectives from Queens. The officers were all there with their families, and there was popcorn and cotton candy, and a trampoline pit and Frisbee, and beer and nuts. And the music was LOUD.

The mayor of New York made an appearance. The Police Commissioner stopped by. Bill Bryant, the New York City councilman and a friend of the NYPD—the one who provided Spencer with his Kevlar vest—was not feeling well and couldn't make it, but he sent his gracious wife Cameron in his place.

Lily sat in the shade under an oak, a glass of orange juice in her hands, and Spencer's glasses. Even though it was warm, she was wearing white capris to cover her legs, and a white, long-sleeved blouse to cover her shrinking arms. On her head was a straw-brim hat. She was avoiding the crowds and talking, feeling a little light-headed, but watching Spencer in the field with the ball at his feet. She was thinking about him, about how he had once been this man, this boy, and played like this all the time. She had asked when the last time was he had come to one of these things and he said never. Yet, he was running around the field, kicking the ball, laughing, as if he were still twenty himself. Twenty with his whole life in front of him.

A woman walked over with a mimosa in her own hand and sat down on the bench with Lily. "I'm Cameron Bryant," she said. "My husband pays for this little shindig. Everyone is having a good time, right? It'll please him. He's not feeling well. Like you."

"I'm having a great time," said Lily.

"You're sick?"

"I'm sick."

"Is this the beginning?"

Lily breathed in and out slowly before she spoke. "No."

Cameron was in her seventies, a well-groomed, well-presented, soft-spoken woman. Cameron told Lily all about her own bout with

506

cancer. Lily commiserated. People liked to talk about themselves, and Lily liked to sit and listen. Cameron told her she herself had had breast cancer twenty years ago. Had a radical mastectomy, one course of chemo, another, another, fought it on and off for ten years, and here she still was, clean now for the last ten years.

"I'm happy you're well," said Lily.

"You'll be well, too. You'll see. So whose wife are you?"

"I'm not anybody's wife. I'm only twenty-five."

"When I was your age, I was already married and had three of my four children," said Cameron.

Lily smiled, drank her juice. "Well, you know how we girls are in New York these days. We don't get married young anymore Or have children. We are too busy finding ourselves."

"So did you find yourself, darling?"

"Yes," Lily said. "I found myself with him." She pointed to the field, and motioned Spencer to come over. "He would love to meet you. He'd like to thank you personally for the vest. But I don't think he can see me without his glasses. He's near sighted. Spencer," she tried to yell, but she had found recently none of her words ended with exclamation marks anymore.

But Spencer saw her and heard her and came over, all perspired, panting, and happy. He put on his shirt, and Lily introduced them. Cameron said to him, "You know the doctors told me when I wasn't feeling well like her, that to go away is the best thing. Sometimes you just need to get away for a few days."

Spencer said, "Well, that *is* a good idea. I told Lily, as soon as she's a little better, I'll take her to Maui." He grinned. And Lily laughed.

Cameron, not in on the joke, said seriously, "Oh, no, why there? I mean, Maui is nice, we've been there many times, but if you really want paradise on earth, you have to go to Cabo San Lucas. Now that's a place for the gods."

Spencer had never heard of it. Cameron told them about it, how it was at the very southern tip of the Baja peninsula, surrounded by water on all sides, and she and Bill had a little cabin right on the ocean. "Yes, Bill and I have traveled all over the world, but on our anniversary, we go only there, it's just magical." She smiled. "We just celebrated our fifty-first, in May. Can you imagine, being married for fifty-one years?"

And Lily said, "To the same man?"

And Spencer laughed, and then carefully took his glasses from Lily, and put them on. "Did you say your anniversary is in May?" His eyes focused on Cameron.

"Yes, May 15, the Ides of May."

"Ah," said Spencer. "So you go just for that one day? A long way to fly, all the way to Mexico, no?"

"Oh, no we go for the whole week. We get there two or three days before, and stay two or three days after."

"It does sound great," said Spencer, not looking at Lily, who put her hands on his forearm and said in a tiny voice *spencer, please*. "Every year, you go? Last year, too? Around May 14?" He stared blinklessly at Lily.

"Of course." Cameron frowned. "Last year was our fiftieth! We went for ten days. From the tenth to the twentieth, I think. Had a bit of a family reunion there, too." She smiled. "We have seven great-grandchildren, they had a blast."

Lily wasn't letting go of Spencer, digging her fingertips into his arm. "Well, thank you, Mrs. Bryant," she said quickly, her mouth tight. "We have to be going now. It was a pleasure to meet you."

Spencer said, "Oh, yes. I learned so much about Cabo San Lucas that I didn't know."

"The pleasure was all mine. You're a good listener, Detective O'Malley. You both are. And I always believed," said Cameron, "that if you aren't listening, you aren't learning."

"You are so right," said Spencer. "Especially in my line of work."

After she left he stood blankly, and Lily turned to him, holding on to his forearms. Her hands were squeezing him, grasping him, nearly all her weight was on him. *Spencer please*, she kept repeating. He peeled her off him gently, sat her back down, sat down beside her. For a few minutes they both just sat there, collapsed on the bench. They didn't speak. Slowly they walked to say goodbye to the guys, to Gabe, and took a cab home.

At home, they laid their keys and guns and wallets carefully upon the dresser, they made tea, they got Cokes, they sat on the couch. He asked what she wanted to watch, and she said what is there that's mindless. They watched *Ace Ventura* and even laughed. They got ready for bed, they got in, and he turned away and she turned away, but only for a moment.

"Spencer . . ."

"I knew you'd break first."

"Come on, turn around."

"No. I know you."

But he turned to her.

"Spencer . . ." Her voice was supplicating. "I'm not saying don't go talk to my brother. I'm not saying that. All I'm asking is that you look for Milo first. That's all. Go see the Kiplingers, they must be back from vacation. They'll lead you somewhere. Find Milo. Maybe you'll find something else that's helpful. Please, Spencer, just . . . a couple of more days, to look for Milo. It must have slipped the councilman's mind when he penciled Andrew into his personal diary on a day he was not in his office in New York City."

Spencer was silent.

"I know what you're thinking," she said.

"You have no idea what I'm thinking."

"I do. I do. Andrew's alibi is bust. I know it looks bad, very bad, I know, but please. Please. For me, just a couple of days to look for the man to whom Amy gave Andrew's jewels."

Spencer was silent.

At last he said, "You know who knows who Milo is? Your brother. He knows, and twitches in agony every time I say his name out loud. He knows but he's not telling."

They slept.

The next bright and early morning, Spencer and Gabe were on their way to Port Jefferson to talk to Lindsey Kiplinger's mother.

"Prepare yourself," Spencer said. "We're dealing with a grieving mother. Fix up your tie, look sharp and solemn."

Lindsey Kiplinger's mother was not happy to see them. She showed them into her kitchen, but she moved as if she wished she could call the cops on them. She was wary and confirmed it by saying belligerently, "I don't know what kind of questions you could possibly have. My daughter has been dead for five years."

"And we're very sorry about that, Mrs. Kiplinger," said Gabe, solemnly, as instructed. He was terrible at the straightened tie and sympathy. He always looked and talked like he wanted to knock somebody's block off. When the mother turned around, Spencer elbowed him, whispering, "Shut the hell up, will you?"

"Just trying to help."

"Help by shutting the hell up."

They sat down at the kitchen table. Reluctantly she offered them some coffee. Gabe accepted, Spencer declined for both of them. "No, no, Mrs. Kiplinger, thanks but we really have to be running." As if to prove it, he got up and made Gabe stand up too. "Look, losing someone so young is terrible, especially in a drunk-driving accident. Was it a hit and run?"

Mrs. Kiplinger looked at them as if they were speaking Russian.

"What are you talking about?" she said. "She didn't die in a drunk-driving accident."

"No? I'm sure that my notes say . . ." He took out his blank notebook and started flipping through it.

"You can flip through *War and Peace* for all the good it'll do you. I know what my daughter died of and it wasn't drink." She clasped a mug hard in her hand. "It was some kind of hallucinatory drug. They did an autopsy on her, she had large amounts of something called mescaline in her blood."

Slowly Spencer closed his notebook. Gabe said, "That's terrible. But mescaline doesn't usually cause death, car crashes . . ."

"It does when the person who's on it drives the car off a precipice in the Superstition Mountains."

"Oh. I didn't realize she—"

"She didn't. What kind of notes do you have, she didn't drive the car, her damn boyfriend did."

Spencer opened his notebook, this time for real. He actually needed to write this down. "That's awful. Do you have his name so we can pay respects to his family?"

"Respects? The bastard didn't die."

Spencer looked up from his notebook. "No?"

"No, *he* lived, the son of a bitch. He's never come back home. They did some kind of a weird drug trip, crashed, my Lindsey died, and he suffered serious injuries, I don't know. I wouldn't put it past his family to lie about the injuries so we don't sue. But he hasn't been back, that I know." She narrowed her eyes at them. "What's this about, anyway?"

"Was it just him and Lindsey in the car?"

"In the car, yes. I think there was a group of them involved in the—whatever."

"Tell me, Mrs. Kiplinger, do you know anything about the Native American Church?"

"Oh, some tomfoolery thing them kids was involved in. I only heard about it afterwards."

"Lindsey was involved in it?"

"Why do you want to know, anyway?"

"Because we're trying to find him." Spencer showed her a picture of Milo. She recoiled, squinted a little at the eyes, and then said that she would have remembered if she saw a face like that. But Spencer could tell that something in Milo's eyes looked familiar to Mrs. Kiplinger.

"If you give us the last name of your daughter's boyfriend, we'll be on our way."

"Clark. They live off Old Post Road. Why do you want to know?"

Spencer didn't understand why people had to ask so many questions. Gabe, who was suddenly the less brusque one, replied. "Nothing serious. Just a couple of questions. Thanks so much, you've been real helpful. Have a nice day now. And good luck."

After they were in their car, Spencer said, "Have a nice day, and *good luck?*"

"Oh, I just freeze up in those situations. I don't know what to say. All I want to do is ask my questions and go. All those niceties get stuck in my throat."

"No fucking kidding."

"O'Malley, what do you think the Native American Church has to do with all this?"

"Not sure. If they joined the church, they could get peyote, or mescaline, legally and for free."

"How many kids are we talking about?"

"Well, Lily told me there were six of them. Lindsey and her boyfriend. Amy and possibly Milo. And two others. Out of the six of them, the Clark kid, Milo, and Amy are missing. Amy told Lily the other three are dead."

"Man, that's one rough joy ride," said Gabe.

"We'll find out. Let's go and talk to Mrs. Clark. Do me a favor though. Smile and nod politely, but whatever you do, don't speak."

Mrs. Clark was even more reluctant to talk to Spencer and Gabe than Mrs. Kiplinger, and wouldn't open the door for them until they threatened her with a warrant. The scene thus set, she walked outside and with her arms tightly folded stood on the porch in the middle of a suburban Long Island neighborhood, with well kept lawns and double car driveways.

She didn't look at them but at her freshly cut lawn as she said, "His life has been ruined. He has only a little peace now. Why can't you leave him alone?"

Spencer tried to impress upon her that a crime could have been committed. Gabe McGill from HOMICIDE added weight to that nebulous statement.

"A crime was committed," said Mrs. Clark. "Against my son."

"By who?"

512

"By the losers he went traveling with. They poisoned his mind, they brainwashed him."

"Did one of the losers look like this?" Spencer showed her Lily's Milo picture, and then the mug shot of John Doe.

"I don't know who that is," she said, with barely a reaction, as if Milo's face was not the scariest thing she had seen. "Never heard of any Milo." She seemed on guard.

"How well did your son know Amy McFadden?"

She raised her eye brows. "So that's what this has to do with?" She snickered. "The missing McFadden girl? You think she's visiting my boy?"

"I couldn't say. How well did he know her?"

"Not well, she was a year younger than him in school. They may have been friends."

"Do you know who else Amy went with?"

"I don't know, I only met her once or twice because she used to hang out with that Lindsey, who used to hang out with my son."

"Is that why your son wanted to go?"

"Oh, he pretended he liked the Kiplinger girl, but she meant nothing to him. He was too good for her."

"So why did he go?"

"Brainwashed, I told you. Got involved with some bad people. I told him, too. I told him, and told him it's not healthy not to tell your parents about the things you get up to in high school. I think this Amy was up to no good. Jerry never talked about what they did. It was always so hush hush. What did you do, son? Oh, nothing." She huffed. "And then he left. Left, and we never saw him. When I didn't hear from him for the first year, I knew he was doomed. I said to my husband, just you wait, the phone call in the middle of the night will come. We waited another year for that phone call."

"And what did the phone call say?"

"I would have never let him go if I had known what I know now. I thought they were just kids, playing around, wanting to see a bit of the world."

"What do you know now?" Spencer couldn't get anything concrete out of her.

"They all died, I heard."

"Well, you know they didn't all die. Your son is alive."

"If you can call it that. But the rest of them are dead."

"Well, Amy didn't die. She came back to New York."

"Where is she now?" said Mrs. Clark.

"And Milo didn't die."

"I don't know anything about this Milo."

She steadfastly refused to say where her son was being kept. She didn't want him "bothered." First Spencer was gentle with her, then he insisted, then he threatened to subpoena all her bank records, for surely the monthly payment to the place that was keeping her son would be on her statement. Only that explicit threat forced Mrs. Clark's tongue to tell Spencer and Gabe that her son was "remaining" (her term, not Spencer's) in a St. Augustine convent in Mexico, just south of Nogales, Arizona. To the question of why the mother wouldn't bring her son home, Mrs. Clark said, "Are there any Catholic missions here on Long Island that you know of, Detective O'Malley?"

"Does your son . . . need a Catholic mission, Mrs. Clark?" Spencer said carefully.

"It's either the Augustinian order or a psychiatric hospital for him."

That did not sound promising.

In the car, Spencer said, "Gabe, I think we have to take a little trip."

Gabe had a good laugh about that one. "Yes, Whittaker will instantly approve—a child who belongs in Bellevue is instead being taken care of by Mexican non-English speaking nuns, and we are going to go twenty-five hundred miles to ask him . . . what? Where Milo is? How his final peyote trip was? I'll tell you right now and we don't have to fly all the way to fucking Mexico. It was baaaaaad, man."

* * *

514

Whittaker did not approve this one. "It's not New Jersey, or Pennsylvania, or Delaware, or wherever else you go on your wild goose chases, O'Malley." He declared that if Spencer wanted to go on a wild goose chase to Nogales, he would have to go on his own time and his own dime. "Ah, you feel different about it, don't you, when you've got to put your money where your mouth is?" He grinned. "Suddenly seems a lot less important? Though I must admit, I'm impressed that you're finally following a lead on the McFadden case on something other than Quinn."

"Yeah, well . . ." But Spencer said nothing. He was going to keep Bill Bryant to himself for just a few more days.

"Why don't you call this Jerry Clark on the phone?"

"He's in a *monastery*."

"What, they don't have phones in a monastery?" Whittaker shrugged. "Oh, what do I know. Perhaps they should. Nevertheless, can't go, O'Malley. You do have some vacation time. Would you like to put in for it? You haven't taken a full week's vacation in five years. Take some time off—go to Arizona, have a good time, get some sun. You need it, you look terrible."

Spencer didn't know what to do. Even if he could go, there was the issue of . . . Lily. Could he go and leave her when she was so sick? What if they found a donor? What if she took a turn for the worse?

When he told her about Jerry Clark, she said, oh my God, go, of course, you have to go. "You go and you get answers. And we haven't had any answers for so long. Go. I'll be your Bill Bryant, your own personal benevolent patrolmen's benefactor."

He hemmed, hesitated. "What about you?"

"What about me?" She smiled. "How long do you plan to be away, detective? I'm only approving Thursday to Sunday. You'll be back for our Sunday comedy. I'll be okay. I'll be fine. Ever since the chemo stopped, I'm not as miserable, have you noticed? No more throwing your white lilies on the floor."

515

"I don't think that was the chemo," he said, hugging her. "I need Gabe to come, too."

"You do what you have to do."

"But you, you don't go far from the house."

"Like I would."

"And don't go out at night, for anything. I'm going to ask for a patrol unit outside while I'm gone, just in case, but please, take reasonable precautions for your own safety."

"Okay." She was sitting on the couch gazing at him with a melted face.

"I mean it. I'll get you everything you need beforehand. Otherwise, call Joy. Call Anne, old Colleen down the hall, anyone."

"I know the drill."

"And beep me if you need me. Try not to forget the number this time."

68

A Day at the Abbey

The hues in the Sonoran Desert were beach sand below and blue sky above, the air was warm though it was evening, and the white flowers were fluttering on the tips of the spires and arms of the giant saguaro cacti. Spencer saw something in the landscape beyond the desolation, something embracing and holy and tranquil. Perhaps this wasn't a bad place for a broken boy named Jerry to be. He loosened his tie in the car, and took off his suit jacket, rolling up his sleeves and rolling down the window. A shirtless Gabe was sleeping in the passenger seat, oblivious to the desert.

The small Augustinian convent called Asuncion was comprised of a small adobe church, and through an oval passageway, arranged around a courtyard, the buildings of a sixteenth-century monastery. It was in northwestern Mexico, forty miles south of the U.S. border, two-and-a-half thousand miles away from Lily. The abbess, a small woman with a black veil covering her head and an acute inflammation of the eye, and two stern reverend mothers all in black, came out to meet them. Turned out they spoke quite good English.

The nuns to the one were unimpressed with Spencer's credentials as either a detective or a Catholic—particularly a Catholic, he thought. While making quite a judgmental sign of the cross on him and Gabe, the diminutive abbess refused to give him any

517

information on the state of Jerry Clark, except to tell him that Hobbit was the only name he now responded to.

"We don't answer to you, detective," said Mother Agnes, unafraid of him.

Spencer clammed up. They were told it was late in the day and there was "no way" that Jerry was going to be disturbed. The nuns would revisit the issue in the morning. Spencer and Gabe were taken to their quarters with all deliberate speed, especially when they passed two open double doors that led to a dining room where thirty or so young nuns were sitting at long tables breaking their bread. The nuns looked up, "indelicately inquisitive," Gabe whispered, and the reverend mother, said, "Don't dawdle, please." They were hurried to their rooms, where chorizo with beans and rice and some tequila and tea was eventually brought to them. There was plenty of chorizo, not nearly enough tequila. "Spence, do you feel something in the air?" Gabe asked, finishing the last of tea, after all the other food and drink had gone.

"No, what?"

"I don't know. The erotically-charged air of the breath of three dozen young girls who have not seen a man, much less two men, in years?" Gabe grinned. "Other than the inmates."

"I think you're blaspheming in a holy convent," said Spencer, grinning back. "Go to sleep. We have a long day ahead of us."

"It's going to be a long night," reflected Gabe.

Night passed slowly indeed, with Spencer all the black lone hours of it wishing for more tequila.

The next morning, when they convened with the abbess and the reverend mothers, the first thing out of Gabe's mouth was, "So what's wrong with him?"

"We'd like to see him now," said Spencer, less confrontationally.

There was no answer from the nuns who squinted reprovingly at Detective McGill. Spencer, in sudden throes of deep apprehension for the nuns of his strict Catholic childhood, hemmed and hawed and said with hands knotted into prayer, "Abbess, this is very serious. I know your patient is sick, but a young girl's life is at stake. We think he might be able to shed some information that will help us find her."

The abbess was unmoved. "Did the girl just go missing?"

"Yes!" Spencer said, thinking that would help her see the emergency of it, but instead the abbess replied, "Well, there you have it. He hasn't been out of his room for four years except to get some fresh air in the courtyard. He knows nothing."

Letting out a breath, Spencer tried again. "This girl was someone he knew five years ago."

"He's had no visitors, except for his parents on Christmas. He has not talked on the phone, he has barely talked to the doctors. He seldom speaks of the experience that brought him to us, or his past life. You're looking in the wrong place, detective. You will find no answers here."

Spencer prodded and pushed and cajoled, and became more frustrated, and finally had to persuade them by threatening a court order to get Hobbit out of the convent and into a Nogales hospital where he would be under the jurisdiction of the Arizona State Police. Then and only then did the abbess relent, but not before she imposed on Spencer strict orders not to upset him ("he has been making such good progress"). On the way up to the third floor, Gabe whispered, "O'Malley, we better get the answers we need from him. I can't stay here another night, this place is about to corrupt me. I'm too much of a sinner, plus I haven't been willingly inside a church in ten years."

"You've come to the right place to beg forgiveness," Spencer whispered back. "I'd get started if I were you. Ten years is a long time." He hadn't been willingly inside a church in twenty.

On the third floor in front of an unpainted canvas wall covering, the abbess stopped. "Detective, he is a soul on the brink."

Aren't we all. Spencer became peripherally interested in the canvas. Lily could do wonders with it. Why was it left deliberately blank and then hung on the wall, as if it were art? Why was it left blank? So *he* could supply the content?

"He has no more protections, he is raw, he has no defenses. They've all been stripped away from him. We use prayer and soothing voices to bring him back from the abyss. But he hovers there all day long. He doesn't know who he is anymore. He spends his day either in catatonia or in a deep state of panic. He imagines himself being killed, being buried alive, he sees poisonous snakes in his room, adders in his bed, scorpions on walls, everything is supremely frightening to him. Sometimes when he sees new people, doctors, social workers, even nuns, it triggers a memory sequence, in vivid detail, of his original trauma. That's why we usually don't allow visitors. It can take him weeks or months to recover from the flashbacks. He flogs himself with his terrors. We comfort him with prayer."

"How has that been working out, abbess? Five years now. Is his ego healed?"

"It's a process, detective."

"A long process, I imagine." His eyes were on the blank canvas.

"He has not recovered. He may never recover. I'm telling you this because he is not much of a talker, and he gets upset at the smallest things. I'm going in with you, I need you to be easy on him. Detective, are you listening?"

"Understood, abbess." He turned to her. "I heard every word you said, and I will be as soothing as I can. But we need to go and speak to him alone."

"He needs me there."

"He's going to have to do without you for five minutes. If he talks to me, I'll need no more than five minutes of his time. By the way, is there any cell phone reception here?"

"Cell phone reception?" she said, as if he were asking for reception to Lucifer.

Spencer sighed. Even his beeper was working only intermittently. He hadn't heard from Lily since he got into Tucson early yesterday. He hoped everything was all right.

The bare room was small and overlooked the mountains that for some reason were not majestic but monastic. A white-linen bed, a white lamp, a weave throw-rug, a chair by the window. In the chair sat a small, emaciated man, appearing smaller because he had no legs. Though he was supposed to be only twenty-six, still a boy, Spencer was distracted by how old he looked, how aged. He began to wish he hadn't left Lily alone.

69

An Anarchist in Action

Lily had gone out to get some cherries in the afternoon; she actually felt like eating something. No mistake about it—maybe her blood was like corn syrup, but Lily was better without chemo. She waved to the patrolmen sitting outside her building, and slowly trudged the stairs to her apartment, taking them one at a time. Lily thought it was definitely time to move. The stairs stank. Fifteen-hundred dollars a month, and the place smelled worse than ever, like the homeless that were once outside were now squatting inside with no place to go. The odor got worse as she climbed the stairs, Tompkins Square Park brought home. When she opened the door to her apartment, the stench hit her full blast. She breathed out in revulsion and gasped and tried to scream. The man with the glass eyes sat on her couch, his filth draped over her blankets, over her cushions.

She turned instantly, to run, to run, but he jumped up, spry and agile, and in less than one second was on her, his hand over her mouth. His face, his broken swollen nose, his insane glass eyes were next to her. Words were tattooed in blue above his eyebrows. Now that she was close, she could read them. *Aryan* over one brow, *Honor* over the other. *Hammer and sickle* inked over his throat, *Aryan Honor* over his face. He dragged her inside and shut and bolted the door. The reek was devastating—as if a thousand unwashed men were throwing themselves on her—and, with some small subconscious satisfaction she retched and threw up against his foul hand.

He let go of her then, in visible disgust—at *her!* He shoved her into the kitchen where she cleaned up as best she could. He wiped himself with a paper towel and sat back down on the couch. Well, that's it for the couch. His eyes were fixed on her.

She managed to speak. She said, "What do you want?"

He sat motionless, rigid, his ice crystal eyes locked on her like firing sights. What could this person have to do with her fun-loving friend who liked to dress up, who chose her perfume for the lightness of its fragrance? He carried his stench with him like a curse.

He spoke. He said, "Where is Amy?" in a guttural American voice. She understood what he said though he garbled some of the letters, the *s* sounded like a *zh* and the *r* whirred. He sounded as if he had something in his mouth.

"What?" It was a gasp, not a response. His question pounded like cymbals on her heart.

"Whish part did I not enunshiate? Where izh Amy?"

She stammered. "I don't know." We thought *you* knew. How could *you* be asking me this? If *you* don't know, then who knows?

He sighed theatrically. He sat forward and looked at her with dead eyes. "Lizhen carefully," he said, and spoke slowly so that Lily understood every word. "I like that you've left her things on her door—" he pointed to Amy's small engraved plaque that still hung there, though Lily's gaze didn't follow his pointed finger—"but you've made her bedroom into your studio. All that *art*"—so derisively—"you've been selling on the street like a vagabond, done here. Now I know. You're using her room. As if she's not coming back. So you must know something. Where is Amy?"

"Who are you?" How did he get in here? The cops were outside! He must have come up through the back door, the basement.

"When you saw me in the park that night, you recognized me.

Amy must have told you about me. I am Milo. Now what have you done with her?"

She was staggered back against the wall across from him, next to Amy's door, next to Amy's plaque. "We've been looking for her for over a year," she finally got out.

"Don't lie to me. I know what you've been doing—you haven't been looking for her. You got a little sick, been taking care of yourself. You got a little money from somewhere, been spending it, investing it with Smith Barney. You've been playing a little comedy with that detective of yours, like he could find the truth on his ass. But I'm tired of playing. This is the end game. You tell me now where Amy is."

"I don't know!" Her voice was high pitched and shrill. She glanced at the fifty clocks arranged on a wall above his head. What time was it in Arizona? It was late afternoon here.

He laughed, a harsh choking sound. "Yes! Very arty of you to have the clocks ticking out your time. And by the looks of you, I don't think you've got much. You might want to buy some more clocks, and set them back, set them slow, see if they can give you a couple of extra minutes."

Lily's eyes measured the distance to the door.

"He's not coming. Friday is his day off from you. Tonight he drinks, carrying his mistress in his arms all the way from Soho." Milo smiled, showing his rotting teeth. "I follow him, too. I follow you, him. But let me tell you something, I'm not interested in him or you. I'm interested in only two people. One of them is Amy. Do you know who the other one is?"

Lily shook her head, sinking down on the floor before she could hear about the other.

"And the other is your brother, the honorable congressman, Andrew Quinn."

Oh my God, where are you Spencer, where are you? Lily felt light-headed.

"You think your brother knows where Amy is? Because if he knows, you must know."

"He doesn't know. And he tells me nothing." He told me nothing, Amy told me nothing. What am I going to do? Spencer, Spencer.

Lily did the only thing she could do. She fainted.

When she came to, she was on the wood floor and he was still sitting on the couch looking at her with detachment. "Would you like a drink of water?" he said. "I would offer you some drugs, but I'm afraid the only thing I've got will be no good for your condition, though it happens to be very good for mine." His rag sleeves were rolled up. Lily wished the afternoon light weren't so bright, exposing the vicious black and blues on the inside of his forearm. His other forearm was swallowed up in a tattooed mosaic of symbols, black swastikas intermingled with blue Stars of David and green Islamic crescents and red hammer and sickles.

He had a rubber band already tightened around his upper arm, and the needle was in his hands. "You're not squeamish about needles, are you, Lily? Probably not, since the needles are keeping death at bay from you." He exposed his teeth again. "Though not *too* far away. Just in the corridor."

The needle went inside his flesh, and his thumb depressed the plunger. Nearly instantly, his eyes glossed over and his head tottered back. His mouth started to make gurgling noises.

Maybe he'll OD here, she thought, the panic inside her very great. While his head was still back, she crawled to the phone, hid it under her thin shirt, kept moving toward the door, but his head came up, eyes half closed, and she froze, pressed TALK on the phone under her shirt and dialed Spencer's beeper number by feel. She waited a second, her fingers at the microphone blocking the sound of his voice telling her to leave a number and then pressed 9-1-1-9-1-1-9-1-1-9-1-1.

She decided to call 911. She managed to dial but not to speak, because Milo now glared at her. "What are you doing?"

She pressed OFF on the phone and remained on the floor. "I told you, I don't know where Amy is. You think if I knew we wouldn't have found her?"

525

He sighed again, but he looked happy now, happier. His body was as relaxed and dazed as his beaten face.

"What do you want?" she whispered.

"What, Amy never talked about me to her best friend Lily?"

"Who are you?"

"We are the revolution, Amy and I", said Milo, with ludicrous triumph. "We came to change the order of things."

The phone rang. It rang under Lily's shirt where she was hiding it. Spencer!

Milo raised his eyebrows. His glass eyes narrowed, he looked like an apparition, ghostly white, permanently beat up, scarred, tattooed. He looked like he had come from the netherworld for Lily, as if he were a horseman of the apocalypse. Lily couldn't read the caller ID. She just pressed TALK and cried, "Spencer, help me . . ."

Milo stood up slowly as if in a dream and hit her across the face, knocking her out.

70

Massacre Grounds

The abbess was right—Hobbit didn't want to talk. He sat by the window and made no sound, did not even attempt to surreptitiously glance at Spencer and Gabe. They sat down on the bed to appear less threatening to him, but that seemed to threaten him even more, because his body started twitching spasmodically until they stood up.

So they stood, and he sat, calmer, and looked out the window. When they asked him about Amy McFadden, he blinked but did not reply. When they asked him about Lindsey Kiplinger, his eyes welled up but he did not reply. When they asked him about Milo, he started to shake. When they showed him Milo's picture, he started to cry.

Finally! Somebody recognized Milo! Oh that Lily.

But he cried silently. No words. Spencer told him they would not leave until they got the information they needed. "We're here because Amy has gone missing, Hobbit. Suspicion has fallen on this man, known to us only as Milo. What we need is for you to tell us who Milo is and what relationship he had to Amy." This was as simple as Spencer could make it for the wreck sitting by the window. He waited for his answer, the silence stretching. Gabe had no patience, he was seething with frustration. He wanted to threaten the answers out of Milo and be on his way.

He dealt with too many people in homicide with whom nothing but menace worked. But Spencer knew that each interrogation was different. You had to identify with the subject, and sometimes if that meant standing around in a convent until the sitting subject got comfortable enough with you to speak, so be it.

Gabe and Spencer paced, Hobbit didn't like that. Spencer sat on the floor, lotus style, next to his chair. Hobbit seemed to like that a little better.

His hands in a teepee, sitting cross-legged, Spencer asked again, "Who is Milo, Jerry?"

Hobbit spoke his first coherent phrase of the day. "Hobbit's my name."

"Who's Milo, Hobbit?"

It was five long minutes before Hobbit replied.

"The church said Milo was the anti-Christ."

"The Native American Church?"

"Milo was thrown out of it."

"Why did the church call Milo the anti-Christ?"

Silence.

Hobbit had clammed up. He did not make eye contact.

"I didn't know the church followed Christian precepts," Spencer said, calmly pressing his tense fingertips together.

Seven minutes passed. Spencer felt himself churning inside. Something was welling up in him, a little dervish snowballing into a scream in his throat. GET IT OUT!

As though obeying Spencer's thought, at last Hobbit said in a quiet voice, "Yes, it follows Christian precepts. Which is why Asuncion took me. The church reads from the Bible, it incants Christ. It takes communion. Just not in the form you Catholics understand."

Ah. So, surprisingly eloquent when pushed to speak. Ego, no ego, psychosis, no psychosis—language, like bike-riding, was not forgotten. "What form does it take then?"

After a long pause Hobbit said, "A different form."

Gabe said, "A peyote form, perhaps?" Gabe was not sitting on the floor and his fingers were not pressed together but his fists were being clenched and unclenched. Spencer motioned to him to calm down.

"The peyote," said Hobbit haughtily, "is the incarnation of God. Just as Christ came in the form of man and was resurrected after death as God Himself, so in the Native belief was God re-incarnated as peyote. When we take peyote, we take in God. We are not supposed to do it for the visions. We do it for purification, as a form of communion, to be one with God. Through the peyote we receive the body of Christ."

"Hobbit, Hobbit," said Spencer, himself growing impatient. "I don't need your blasphemy, you explaining to me how mind-altering drugs are now the Eucharist. What I need is . . ."

Hobbit said, "I'm telling you why the shaman in Nogales said Milo was the anti-Christ. He said that Milo's only belief was non-belief. Rejection of belief. He said Milo was a nihilist." Hobbit smirked. "And he didn't even know us."

"How did you and Milo know each other?"

"From high school."

"What was his name before he was Milo?"

"His name had been Ben Abrams. But Ben Abrams died when we took our new form, and Milo was born, just as Jerry Clark died and Hobbit was born."

Spencer and Gabe exchanged a look. Was the name familiar in some way? His mind was reeling. He wished he had cell phone reception so he could call in the name before they continued the interview.

Hobbit said. "I thought Milo was . . ." and stopped there, but Spencer hoped it was just a pause, and it was, because the boy said another word: "Dead."

"Why did you think that?"

"His injuries." Hobbit shuddered.

Injuries, Spencer wondered. They would have to get to that later. "Well, he's not dead. What about him and Amy?"

"He and Amy were the center of it all."

"Center of what?"

"Our little band of revolutionary brothers and sisters. We went out to see and learn about the world that we had hoped to change." He didn't want to say any more.

"Amy as well as Milo?"

"Oh, yes. Amy as much as Milo."

"They were together?"

"Yes."

Spencer showed him the picture of Milo again.

"You mean this pulverized, crazy-looking guy and regular, middle class attractive Amy were together?"

"He was our shaman. He didn't always look like this, detective. Milo was superlative once."

"With this hidden underneath."

"No one saw it. Least of all Amy. She was completely under his spell. Her home life was a mess, she was wallowing, unfocused, not knowing anything, she was younger than us, I think. And he pulled her in good. He pulled her under his sway."

Hobbit was becoming agitated. Spencer guessed Milo was like that with everyone, and Jerry Clark had been very much dominated by him also.

"Hobbit, what were you doing with your life on the road?"

"When he said go here, we went here. When he said listen to Bane, we listened to Bane. When he said, join ATWA—Air Trees, Water, Animals—we joined ATWA. Join American Nihilist Underground Society, we joined. When he said, learn about the Russian Nihilists, we learned. Read about Libertarian Communists, about Pentii Linkola, about rational humanists, we read. He said join the Native American Church, we joined the Native American Church. He said go to Nogales, we went to Nogales. We were free, young, exploring, we hated all that absolutist bourgeois morality shoved down our throats, and didn't want to live that life. We believed in other things. And we followed Milo."

"ATWA," said Spencer slowly. "Isn't that Charles Manson's little Death Valley group?"

"And American Nihilist Underground Society," said Gabe, "Isn't that ANUS?"

"Whatever, man. We were experimenting." Sensing hostility, he fell mute and would not reply to any more questions.

Spencer frowned. Getting up off the floor, he sat on the white linen bed. Hobbit flinched, but Spencer didn't move this time. "Jerry," he said, "I know you don't want me to call you that, and I know that you don't want me to sit on your bed. But I'm out of patience. Open your mouth and speak to me. I'm not leaving until I know everything. Did you join the church so you could worship peyote?"

Hobbit finally spoke. "Don't say peyote as if you're spitting the word out. I told you, peyote is instrumental to the church. It is the god of the church."

"Mmm. Doesn't leave much room for actual God though, does it?"

"Yes it does. You become closer to Christ with—"

"What Christ, Hobbit? Christ didn't teach nihilism, which seems to be what all of you learned so well."

"What do you know about nihilism?"

"As a lapsed Catholic, I know something about Christ. He didn't teach that life was pointless and all human values worthless. He was not a skeptic who denied all existence."

"He did, however, call for the rejection of the established religious and moral practices at the time," countered Hobbit.

"Yes, through *more* rigorous application of personal morals, not less rigorous." Spencer almost wanted to laugh at the absurdity of it.

Fidgeting impossibly, Hobbit spoke. "We wanted to achieve a new level of consciousness."

"Stop it, Hobbit, stop this nonsense!" That was Gabe. "Nihilism, ATWA, ANUS, Bane—just cut the bullshit. You were on a headlong acid trip. Two years running around the country, getting up to absolutely no good. We're not your believing accepting nuns. What happened during your last peyote trip when you killed Lindsey?"

The twitching in Hobbit's arms and torso became a convulsion. His eyes rolled up into the back of his head.

Spencer cast a troubled glance at Gabe. He said in a quiet voice, "Hobbit, were you all thrown out of the church with Milo?"

"We were with the Oklahoma Comanches for a long while. Sixty, seventy people. We sat around the fire, and the peyote was shared, and the amount each person is given was tiny. It wasn't enough for Milo. So he got a great idea that we should go down to Nogales, Arizona, and have our own peyote hunt where we would find all the cactus we'd need just for the six of us."

"What are you telling me?" said Spencer. "Peyote is not heroin." *Or alcohol.* "It's not addictive."

"It's not . . ." he paused. "But . . . everybody is different. The cactus just helps you see what's inside *you* but what you cannot see on your own. The mara'akame or the shaman said that the visions you have when you take peyote are the visions you bring with you. And those visions are quite something. We all became enarmored of ourselves, we saw beautiful things, magnificent things, ourselves as eagles, as dolphins, as leopards. If you have never taken it, I highly recommend it."

Spencer rolled his eyes, exasperated. "You know what, thanks for the advice. But I've got all the visions I can handle at the moment. Get on with it. You went to Nogales, and then?"

"That's when Milo was thrown out of the church. He wanted to go for the hunt immediately, and he wanted to know where to go, but the mara'akame told him not everyone could go, not everyone was deemed worthy of freshly-found cactus. So the shaman, who was in contact with Tatewari, or the grandfather-fire, and who seemed wise and calm, said we had to wait, but Milo didn't see it that way. He wanted to go the next day. That's when the shaman deemed him not worthy. He said that Milo's visions had nothing to do with becoming one with God, with

532

'finding his life.' He didn't trust what Milo saw inside himself. He thought what was inside Milo should not be brought out. He said Milo was corrupting the peyote, he was not embodying the Creator's heart. He said the contempt for all mankind inside Milo had no place in the Native American Church."

Spencer appraised Jerry grimly. "Did Milo have contempt for all mankind?"

Hobbit didn't answer. "We were all told to leave, there would be no peyote hunt, no more dance for us." He was distraught as he spoke. "Milo went into a rage, and in a fit of this rage, he forced the shaman to take us into the desert at dusk to hunt for peyote."

"*Forced* the shaman?"

"Yes. Took him against his will into Mexico. What is that called?"

"Aggravated kidnapping."

"Um. I thought so."

"Did the police get involved?"

"I don't know. This is the first time I'm talking about it. I don't know if they got involved. I don't remember everything that happened before, and nothing after. Didn't the sisters tell you how long I've been here?"

"Five years."

"Yes. Just the beginning of my penance, detective."

"Penance?"

"Look, we were young and stupid, and unfortunately we made some irreversible mistakes. We got so involved in our philosophies, in our anarchic travels, in the things that the drugs helped us see clearer, better. So for one depraved flinty twirl of our free will, we forced the shaman to help us find the peyote in Mexico. We thought the church owed us that. We thought we could handle the peyote. Milo told us we could. He was extremely forceful, Milo; he was our mara'akare. He was like our peyote. He could convince the angels out of heaven. So we took the shaman and drove out into the northwestern Mexican plateau, not too far from here, and spent the early evening before the sun set hunting peyote. Have you ever seen peyote?"

"No." He'd seen other things though, *single malt, rare and magnificent from Speyside.*

"It's quite a thing to find it. A few miles south of Tubutama, we walked through the barren trees and the shrubs and in a matter of half an hour found a cluster of hundreds of them. Like tiny light-green pumpkins, each with a little white flower on top. It's quite a sight. The shaman said to take only what we could carry in our hands, a few at most. But we brought sacks, and could carry everything. We took it all. The shaman said we were perverting, subverting the will of God." Jerry lowered his head. He wasn't looking out the window anymore, but at his gnarled hands. "After we got what we wanted, we let him go—Milo wanted to kill him, but Amy convinced him otherwise—we left him back in Nogales. The shaman warned us when he was freed, he said, oh the hubris of man, you think you can control the uncontrollable, the forces you don't understand, but they will control you."

Spencer got a chill down his spine on this hot day. He wished for a dusty breeze off the pampa grassland brush.

"We drove up north to the Superstition Mountains, a four-hour drive—"

Spencer interrupted. "Why so far? All the way to Phoenix?"

Hobbit smiled. His teeth were black. "Superstition, detective. We drove the *Superstition freeway*, we went deep into the hills, in the night, along an unpaved trail called Massacre Grounds, and we had ourselves an all-night peyote dance. We built a fire, we broke apart the peyote and ground up its insides and caught its liquids in adobe crocks, we chanted and sang, and danced and prayed. We played the drums and the gourds, we confessed our sins, we worshipped . . . but I think back to it now, there was a point when all of us knew there was no return for us, and when we tried to turn away, it was too late."

71

The Cancer Chick
and the Revolutionary

When Lily came to, she was in a dank cold place and her limbs were aching. She was sitting unpropped and falling to the side against a cement basement wall. Milo was sitting on the ground across from her. They were in a hallway, the distance between them was a few feet. There must have been a plumbing leak, or something else equally distasteful, because standing swampy water was pooled underneath them. The floor was uneven, they were in the hollow. He could have set them down a few feet higher where the concrete was wet but unpuddled. Milo, however, didn't even seem to notice—the expression on his tattooed, tainted face was detached from this world.

Something was dripping from her mouth. She wiped it—blood from where he hit her. She was still attached to this world.

"What am I going to do with you, Lily? You were in your own home, we were sitting, chatting, and now look what you've done, calling the police. You're wet, uncomfortable. And bleeding."

"I need to get to the hospital," she muttered.

"Oh, I know." He said nothing after that, just eyed her. "I think where I'm going to have to take you is to see your brother. Don't you think? Do you have a cell phone? We should call him.

Tell him you're in great distress. Tell him you were abducted by Amy. See what he thinks of that."

She licked her lip. Her blood was thick.

"Tsk, tsk," he clucked, not sounding quite right when he did. "You think everyone around you is blind. But even the walls have eyes. Amy told me about your family. Your one sister is always working, the other is too busy with her halflings. Your mother doesn't know who you are. Your grandmother has nothing to barter with. And so we come to your brother."

Amy, her Amy, discussed Lily with this person. Her feeling of violation was complete.

"What do you want, money? *I'll* give you money for me. How much do you want?"

He laughed soundlessly. "Amy and I are revolutionaries, Lily. Revolutionaries are not interested in money. Did you ever read a book called *Catechism of a Revolutionist* by the Russian nihilist Mikhail Bakunin?"

She shook her head. They were sitting in sewage! What the *hell* was he talking about? It must be the H talking. When was that going to wear off? And when was her lip going to stop bleeding? She licked it again. Never, that's when. Never. Until all the blood was gone, seeping drop by drop onto the foul basement floor.

"Bakunin was the antithesis of Marx, of Lenin, of Tsarism, Imperialism, Colonialism, Islamism, Fundamentalism, of every *ism*. He abhorred them all for their chains around man. In his book, Bakunin wrote that the revolutionary is a doomed man. '*He has no private interests, no affairs, property, not even a name of his own.*' Which is why I became Milo, instead of who I was."

"Who were you?"

Milo continued. "'*His entire being is devoured by one purpose, one thought, one passion—the revolution. Heart and soul, not merely by word but by deed, he has severed every link with the social order and with the entire civilized world; with the laws, good manners, conventions, and morality of that world. He is its merciless enemy and continues to inhabit it with only one purpose—to destroy it.*'"

Lily sat up straighter. There was a tinge in Milo's voice, a posture in his demeanor that spoke of something other than narcotics or homelessness. Whose world did this Milo want to destroy?

"That is who I am," he said. "You want to know who I am? That is me." He coughed. "With one proviso."

Lily was afraid to hear.

"That's right. Amy. She was my passion. She was my muse, my desire, my alms and my church. I could not live without Amy. I still can't. Where has she gone to? Where has she disappeared to?"

"Whose world did you want to destroy, Milo?" whispered Lily. "Mine?"

He laughed. "You are so small potatoes. I was going to start with something a little bigger than you."

Lily raised her eyes at him, she stared right through his wounds, through his mangled body. "I have to get to a hospital. Look, you broke my lip, and I can't stop bleeding. My blood doesn't clot. I'm sick."

"Right now, believe it or not, this isn't about you."

"If I don't get to the hospital," she said, "you won't have anything to barter with."

"First we go see your brother. Maybe he can tell us where Amy is."

"He doesn't know."

Milo emitted a hollow laugh.

"And if he did, he wouldn't tell you. My brother loved her—"

Lily had to stop because Milo emitted such an excruciating groan that it seemed to come not from his throat but from his dissected spleen. The cry was so guttural that Lily, despite her weakness, tried to crawl in the standing water, away from the creature that could make so wretched a sound.

Unblinking, eyes as big as plates, Lily mouthed a conciliation, but it was too late—Milo, fully re-attached to his world, lunged for her, all filthy hands for her, grabbed her around her elongated, emaciated neck and started shaking her. "Don't lie to me, Lily," he hissed. "Why do you speak such lies?"

She tried to say, "All right . . ."

"They were not in love!" he cried. "*She* wasn't in love with him! She was in love with me, do you understand? With me."

"All right . . . let go . . ." Inaudibles.

"Say you understand."

"I understand . . . let go . . ."

"She wasn't in love with him." He brought his face closer, and opened his mouth and Lily's angle was just so, and the dim light was just so, and when he opened his mouth and hissed, she saw that Milo had no tongue.

Lily screamed—mutely.

"She wasn't in love with him," said Milo in a sibilant groan. "She was going to kill him."

72

The Peyote Dance

"What happened during the peyote dance, Jerry?"

"Milo kept telling us we weren't taking enough. I don't know how much we took in the end. The usual dose back in Oklahoma was tiny, micrograms. Very little. But we took . . . I don't want to think about it, not now, not ever, but after what happened, I need to believe that our visions became distorted because we took too much. That we were misguided and behaved excessively."

"Obviously that's true. What visions?"

"Well, I suddenly believed that I was tall and lean, not short and squat like I am, and had wings and could fly." He shuddered violently. Even now sometimes a voice goes off in my head, and the voice is saying, can you fly, Hobbit? Did you ever want to? Did you ever think you could?"

"Whose voice is it?"

"Milo's."

Spencer sat like a stone on the bed. Even Gabe sat down next to him.

"I wonder now if he plied us full of mescaline deliberately, poisoned us with mescaline . . ."

"Why would he do that? You were friends . . ." said Spencer.

"But what if he was done with us? Wanted us out of the way,

perhaps was afraid we'd tell someone about taking the shaman, and other things we were up to? I know he and Amy wanted to return to New York, what if he didn't want us running around the country knowing about him? I don't know. But what remains, remains. Petra slit her wrists and watched herself bleed out. We all watched her. We saw her bleeding, believing it was right and she was dancing—or laughing—and we were dancing as she bled—and laughing. Simon beat himself with the gourds and rocks and then hanged himself off a dead mesquite tree. He was swinging so gently, he looked like he was in a child's playground, on a swing, it was so calm and seemed so right, just the rope moving, his body moving, barely a night-time breeze, and we were still eating peyote."

"Who were these people, Simon and Petra?"

"Don't really know. Just some couple we picked up in California. He was from England. She was from Germany."

"What happened to Amy?"

"Don't know. In my memory she seems fine. I think Amy didn't take as much as the rest of us. She seemed still in control."

"Milo?"

"Milo—I can't, no, I can't." Jerry suddenly fell to the floor from his chair, writhing, the stumps of his destroyed legs in a seizure, his hands over his face, his head shaking, his torso in spasms. "I can't, I can't. I can't see it, can't, please."

Spencer was on the floor with him. "Tell me, talk to me. You'll never have to talk about this again, but talk to me now."

With his hands still over his face, Hobbit said muffled words that Spencer thought he had misheard. "Milo took the hunting knife Petra used for her wrists and cut off his tongue."

He convulsed on the brown stone floor.

"But he didn't end there. He pulled down his pants and sliced off his penis."

It was Spencer's turn to turn away from Jerry and stare with stupefaction into Gabe's stunned face.

"After this the laughing stopped. That's how I remember it. The laughing stopped, and there was screaming, Amy's screaming. Milo was not, he was spluttering in his throat, there was a black fountain gushing out of his mouth, and I thought it was his tongue rising up to heaven, and Amy was trying to— I don't even know—hug him, help him, stop the bleeding? I remember her pouring what was left of the peyote over Milo's groin. I thought that was ingenious, like the starfish regenerating itself, the peyote is supposed to heal the sick. Her shirt was off, she was pressing it to his stomach, he was lying down on the ground, and she was bent over him, and we said, is the dance over, and she yelled something through my haze, something about driving him away. I think she drove us down the dirt trail back to the highway, she was a very good driver, Amy. And then she got out with Milo, left me and Lindsey in the van, somewhere on Highway 88. Lindsey and I drove off. We were still fully under the spell. We drove up the winding Apache Trail, to get some more, to find some more, I don't know. I think we were lost. I believed I wasn't in a van but in a plane and we were so high up in the mountains, the oxygen was thin and it was going to my brain. I thought Lindsey and I were flying, you see. When I drove off the edge of the cliff, I had no fear, only exhilaration. We flew. I *flew* into the ravine with Lindsey."

Hobbit's hands remained over his face. "And here I am."

Spencer could not believe what he just heard. "You know for sure Milo cut off his dick?" he said dully.

"I remember him throwing it in the fire and dancing around it and then dropping to the ground. I remember it falling in the flames and burning and how the human flesh smelled—pungent and bitter, a choking overbearing scent, and I can't eat meat to this day— then him falling and I remember Amy trying to pull it black out of the fire and failing . . . and crying, Ben . . . oh Ben . . ."

"You were under an extreme hallucinatory spell. You could have imagined it."

"Perhaps. But I've never smelled cooking human flesh before. And I didn't imagine flying off that cliff."

Spencer's beeper went off suddenly, making Jerry shriek. It was the station. It said urgent.

73

The Lessons of the Russian Tsar

What are you talking about, kill him? But she couldn't say it. She spluttered down, coughed down her fear and pain, sank down to the ground, coughed up blood with her terror. She wiped her mouth on her sleeve, felt fainter, fainter, more disconnected from him, as if her lifeblood were being drained from her body by leeches. Andrew! Her mind wasn't working. *Kill her brother?* What was he talking about?

"I don't know what you're talking about," she said. "Amy and he were . . ."

"They were nothing!" he snapped. "Nothing to the end, I tell you. She sought him out, befriended him, for one purpose only."

Once again—Lily's whole life, all of the things she supposed and believed and accepted as true were being forcibly torn away in shreds of skin from her body.

"Amy was non-political. Amy didn't know politics. What are you talking about?"

"Lily, the universe is so vast, and you are so small, and you barely even know about your corner of it. Amy was radically, wholly, intensely political. She was political in high school, she was political in Hunter, she lived what I lived, she believed all the things that I believed. She was supremely loyal. To me. The art was just a ruse, Lily. And what a good ruse it was."

He snickered. "Didn't you ever notice that Amy couldn't draw?"

Oh my God.

The world in the wet basement had stopped making sense. Life was not being righted, Lily didn't know how to right it. She wiped her mouth, and couldn't speak for many minutes.

There were things like this. Her life had shown her these things in the last year—which were unfathomable. You go merrily along, believing one thing, not even believing so much as just living—unthinking, blissful—and suddenly all the things that once held you together are gone. Suddenly you win the lottery. Suddenly you get cancer. Suddenly Spencer tells you that the single imperative of his life has been a thing you had never even *suspected*. Suddenly your mother has frost-covered windows in her soul. Suddenly Amy goes missing, and the ground keeps rising and rising, swelling and swelling, and Lily is blindsided by the eruptions, sitting with her back against the basement wall.

Oh my God.

"But what did *I* have to do with anything? Why move in with *me*? Why single me out?"

Milo grimaced. "You were Amy's just-in-case, Lily. She never knew how things were going to go, and she wanted you on our side. And look how handy you've become. You're my last resort and I'm going to get to your brother because of you."

"So why didn't you do it then?" she said dully. "Get to him. What were you waiting for?"

"Who said we were waiting? We tried. We tried to harm him, to show him what it was like to have your life be destroyed by another human being, like he destroyed our life. We just didn't succeed. We failed in our one planned attempt. Then in another. And then I got unlucky and went away for a couple of years. But we were getting right back on track again, until Amy disappeared."

"Milo, you're sick."

"No, you're sick, Lily."

"You were in prison for two years. Why didn't Amy slip some mescal beans in his coffee if she was going to kill him? Why didn't she kill him while you were away?"

If Lily wasn't seeing the whole picture, she was sure Milo wasn't either.

"She was waiting for me to show up. We were in it together."

"So why did she break up with him if she was going to kill him?"

"It was stupid of her," he snapped. "Oh, I know the game you're playing, Lily, trying to sow seeds of doubt in me. But it was just stupid of her, nothing more."

"It wasn't stupid, Milo," said Lily, becoming less afraid between the bloodletting and the speaking and the *not* understanding. She shook her head. "No. It wasn't stupid, it was deliberate. Why'd she do it?"

"I don't know what you're insinuating."

"Milo, you were in prison. And while you were in prison, isn't it possible that Amy and my brother fell in love? Maybe once when she was with you a long time ago, she believed what you believed, but somewhere along the line she stopped believing it. She didn't want to kill him. She didn't kill him. When you turned up again, she broke up with him to protect him. Couldn't that be true?"

"No! It's a lie! IT'S A LIE!"

Lily remembered something else Spencer had told her. "Not only did she break it off with him, but she pushed me to go to Maui last year."

"Yes, she wanted you out of the way."

"That's right, Milo. No alibi. No offense, no defense, but *out of the way*. I'd be safe in Maui."

"She didn't want you safe! She didn't give a shit about you."

"That's not true," gasped Lily. "That's not true."

Time ticked away in a theoretical sense only. Time stood still in the wet basement in a building off 9th Street, where Lily sat on the damp concrete pressed against the wall, trying not to faint, and Milo crouched across from her, drumming fingers on his knees, drumming out what remained of Lily's life on his homeless rags. "I have to go to the hospital, Milo," she said. "I'm not collateral, I'm not an alibi, I'm not a hostage. I'm sick, and I will be no good to you in five minutes. I need to get to the hospital now."

"You're not going anywhere."

There was something wrong with him. Something other than the partial tongue. Lily wished she were strong, were healthy, had red blood instead of Beluga blood, had oxygen pumping through her brain instead of maple syrup, she wished she could jump up, hit him with something, maybe with that fire extinguisher that was hanging three yards away from her, strike him, then run, run for her life, screaming.

"He is armed, he's protected," she said. "He never leaves the house alone, he has two Federal agents with him at all times. You will never get to him. Never. They wouldn't let someone like you within half a mile of my brother. There's an APB out on you, they're looking for you everywhere. Where are you going to turn, Milo? How could you get to him?"

Milo laughed and Lily got a glimpse of the blackness inside his mouth. When he finished making his sloshing mirthless cackle, he said, "Lily, did you ever take history in school? Did you ever hear of a Russian tsar, Alexander II? The story of his assassination is a lesson in persistence, a lesson that teaches you that you can kill absolutely anybody, as long as you persevere. Alexander II is a classic study in revolutionary determination."

Lily was quiet, waiting for the depleted blood to work its way into her brain. "Why—are—we . . . talking about a Russian Tsar?"

"Because he gave birth to the modern revolutionary, he gave birth to nihilist zeal, to ideals that were more righteous than mere human life, to an ideology that was more noble, more visible, and more permanent than mere humanity."

546

"Is there such a thing?"

"It's all around you, wake up!" said Milo. "Have you not seen it? It shapes everything this world turns on. It's everywhere in the modern world, it's everywhere in the old world. And the Russian Tsar gave birth to it. You wouldn't understand it now, Lily, wasting your life with painting human beings kissing in your little primordial cave, but you'll understand it soon."

"I think I'm beginning to understand it now," said Lily on wet concrete, edging toward the fire extinguisher. She moved her legs an inch and then her torso followed. Another inch. And another. Milo didn't seem to notice. The extinguisher was three yards away. Nine feet. A dozen times perhaps to edge her sitting body sideways. She was nearly diagonal from him. Soon he would notice and she needed to be prepared for this. How could she get prepared? She lay down on the damp floor. He didn't mention it, notice it, mind it. When she lifted herself up, she was another half a foot closer.

"In 1879, a school teacher tried to assassinate the Tsar," said Milo, "He failed and was promptly hanged, as were sixteen of his co-conspirators. A teacher, Lily! That's how bad things got."

"Even teachers can be subverted, even teachers are not infallible," said Lily.

"A few months later," Milo continued in his rasping drawl, "a faction from the original nihilist group called the People's Will was determined to succeed where the teacher Soloviev had failed. The People's Will put nitroglycerine on the Tsar's train, but they had miscalculated and blew up the wrong train. Then they tried to blow up a bridge over which the Tsar was passing and failed there, too."

"A bumbling terrorist group then?"

"Not terrorist! Revolutionary! Radical. They were scientists, scholars, engineers, fighting unabated for a new political order."

"A new political order terrorizing innocent people?"

"Nothing innocent about your brother."

"Completely innocent, Milo. What did he do?"

"Stole an election for one."

"He didn't steal it, he won it. In a horse race by a nose in a photo finish, but a win is a win, even a close one."

Milo growled like an animal. "A hundred-and-twenty years ago, a carpenter started work in the Winter Palace, close to the Tsar, and he smuggled small packs of dynamite with him and hid them in his bedsheets. Finally he built a shaft under the Winter Palace dining room, and the bomb went off just when it was calculated that the Tsar would be having his dinner. But again, the dinner had been delayed and the Tsar wasn't there. Sixty-seven other people were killed or maimed in the explosion."

Lily was quiet. "Just collateral damage?"

"Completely irrelevant. No one remembers them. They're dust. But everyone remembers Soloviev, everyone remembers the carpenter. One of the main members of the People's Will was caught during this brief time and he told the police that nothing they could do would save the life of the Tsar." Milo stopped. "And that's what I'm telling you, Lily. Nothing you can do will save the life of your brother. Nothing Amy can do will save the life of your brother."

Lily lay down again—because she had to; the listening, the adrenaline, the panic was too much for her. What would Spencer do? she thought. Ah. Spencer carried a 10mm automatic weapon, one of the most powerful pistols ever made. Spencer would not be sick, Spencer would be strong, would be healthy. Is that what she was supposed to do now? Get healthy fast? She moved another inch or two while lying down on the ground. Milo, absent-mindedly, because he was so intent on his words, moved sideways along with her on the opposite side of the wall, to be closer to her, to be heard better.

"On March first, 1881," Milo continued, "Alexander II was traveling in a closed carriage from one palace in St. Petersburg to another. When the signal was given, members of the People's Will threw bombs at the Tsar's carriage. And missed."

"Really, the most inept group," muttered Lily, using it as an opportunity to move once more.

"Inept or not, the bombs burst among the Tsar's guards, the Cossacks. He got out of his carriage to inspect the damage, and to check on the state of his wounded soldiers. While he was standing out in the open, another revolutionary threw his bomb, and this one, my dear Lily, did not miss. The Tsar was killed instantly, and the explosion was so great that it killed his assassin as well."

Lily stopped inching over for a moment. "Is that what you want?" she said. "Is that the price you're willing to pay for your beliefs? You're willing to lay down your life for my brother's life?"

"Anything for your brother's life." Milo hit his head against the wall, from side to side.

Lily was under the fire extinguisher when she stopped.

"There is no justice in American politics," continued Milo. "Have you noticed? When a congressman is brought into power with only fifty-two votes that he steals, where is the justice in that?"

"You want more people to go and vote against my brother? Go rock the vote, Milo."

"He stole that election!"

"Oh, please. Stop. And what do you care? What do you care? Since when does dull Edward Abrams inspire such passions in high school kids—" She broke off, staring suddenly open-mouthed at him.

"When his wife Bernadette Abrams kills herself because she can't take it any more."

"Oh, my God," groaned Lily. "Oh, my God. You're—"

"Ben Abrams. Very good, Lily Quinn. Nice to meet you."

Lily stopped listening. Milo was Ben Abrams! Amy was with Ben Abrams, the son of Edward Abrams, Andrew's opponent! She remembered his mother because after the recount and Andrew's victory she was made to carry some of the blame for Abrams's defeat. Lily remembered that Mrs. Abrams had been compared unfavorably with Mrs. Quinn, she was not as gracious as Miera Quinn, as attractive, as young. Miera took this to mean

549

that she deserved more of the credit for Andrew's victory, which made her even more insufferable. But Bernadette Adams, unfortunately, already had problems with depression and addiction to diet pills. Three or four months after the election, she overdosed on her medication.

Her son must have gone into some spiral. And he took Amy with him.

Milo smiled, horrible, almost toothless. "I am going to get him. With or without Amy. Her faith had wavered a little bit but I told her with or without her, with a little perseverance, Andrew Quinn would become Alexander II." He blanched, made a noise of profound anguish. "Oh, how she was when we came back to New York from Phoenix. She was more determined even than I! The forcible retirement of your brother from politics was the focus of our whole existence. It gave our lives meaning, it was our beauty and our joy."

"Plotting to kill my brother gave your life joy?" said Lily. "The ancient Egyptians would be unhappy with you, Milo." She was single-mindedly focused on the extinguisher mere inches from her hands. But she would have to jump up, grab it, turn to Milo, run to him maybe, and strike him with it. Did it seem far-fetched? "Plotting to kill my brother, a husband, a brother, a son, a father of two children gave your life beauty?"

"Oh, yes," said Milo. "Everything that has happened to me is because of him. *Everything*."

The fleeting moment of her own existence flew by Lily like a wounded sparrow. Flew and fell to the ground. She sat up, she got up on her haunches, she crouched. When Milo didn't move from his sitting position, she stood up. Still he didn't move. The extinguisher was to the right of her. Was it attached to the wall? Was she going to have to struggle with it, pulling at it, tugging at it? Her heart, pumping tar through her veins at 200 beats a minute could not take the pressure anymore. Lily's knees began to give out and her arms trembled. Her lip continued to drip congealed blood. The terror and the threat of Milo were being removed from her.

"You *lived your only life* for killing my brother?"

"Solidarity with murder is critical! Without it, apathy sets in, complacence, acceptance. We reject authority because authority forces us to measure our words, draining them of meaning. We want change, we want radical monumental change, we refuse all compromise. And because of our beliefs, our actions dictate our lives. To have a life without measure," said Milo, "*we must act without measure.*"

Lily swung to the right, and pulled the extinguisher from its supports in the wall. Standing, she yanked it out, and it remained in her hands, and Milo, strung out, doped out on heroin, didn't move from his sitting position, his passionate and acute life was to be lived slumped in the puddle in the basement. Lily held the extinguisher in her two hands like a weapon, but she held it in her hands for only a moment, because the thing was so heavy, made of cast iron, made of bricks, made of sand and cement, it was a cinder block in her hands, and she held it for seconds— and then it fell to the floor and she fell with it. Milo watched, still drooping over, his head bobbing, and then he opened his mouth and laughed at her.

74

Acting Without Measure

Milo wasn't getting up, but Lily, having undertaken a course of action that precipitated her latest predicament, was feeling that whatever *else* happened, one thing that could *not* happen was her becoming a leverage in any negotiation between Andrew and the unhinged being in front of her. But, and also true—she could not lift the fire extinguisher. Kneeling over it, feeling for the release mechanism, leaning it towards her so that when she turned, panting, the rubber hose was aimed at Milo, who still sat suspended looking at her with cold amusement, wholly unaffected and unthreatened by her antics, Lily screamed and pulled the pin out of the extinguisher and squeezed the trigger. *Please* don't let it be just water.

It wasn't water. It was a dry chemical powder that shot into Milo's open throat from less than five feet away at what seemed to be a speed of two hundred miles an hour. The stream didn't just knock him back. It hurled him back, with his head popping against the concrete wall. He stuttered once with his whole body and then lay unnaturally still. Lily didn't stay two seconds to take another look at him. She let the extinguisher fall with a dull thud to the concrete, got to her legs and ran. Ran was probably too strong a word. In slow motion, she wobbled forward, stepping over Milo's legs, shielding her eyes, panting, crying, she rushed, trying all the doors in the long basement corridor until she found one that led from the boiler room to the laundry facilities. From there, she made her way outside into the rain, ran across the street to the three police cars with their lights flashing, and collapsed unconscious on the wet ground in front of them.

She came to, lying in a familiar beige room with lousy curtains, but with sunlight from the window. Spencer was by her side, and Dr. D. and Grandma, and Gabe McGill, and the sheets smelled snugly of bleach and the hospital, nothing smelled dank and wet, and she tried to mouth some words, but the only thing she could muster was, "Why oh why do they make fire extinguishers so heavy?"

Spencer, who was sitting so close he was practically on top of her, said, "Yes, we'll have to make them weigh less than two-and-a-half pounds."

Lily smiled and slept—almost in his arms—and remembered a slight raising of consciousness one night, and Spencer sitting by her, and he told her about the peyote dance, and she said, I think I killed him and he said, I hope you killed him. Did you find him, she mouthed and he said no. You didn't find him? But I killed him.

She had more questions. She took his arm, brought him close, right to her ear, snickered lightly, said, is it wrong for me to feel a small glee that he cut off his own . . .?

"I think it's wrong for you to feel a *small* glee, yes," said Spencer.

"I'm scared for my brother."

"He'll be fine, Liliput. The man lives in a fortress."

So did Alexander II, Lily wanted to say.

She opened her eyes again suddenly. Her mind was clearer. "Spence, have they found a bone marrow donor for me?"

"Not yet, Lily . . ."

"My brother? My sisters?"

"They're still looking . . ."

Lily fell back to sleep without asking Spencer: with all the things they now knew and thought they were so smart about, one disheartening, gaping hole remained:

If Milo didn't know, then where was Amy?

Marcie, still smelling of Milky Ways (though not nicotine: she must have quit smoking) would open the windows in her room and Lily would smell the arid midsummer air.

Joy would sit by her and knit. Joy was knitting? "Joy, are you knitting?"

"Hmm."

"Who *are* you? Madame Defarge? What are you knitting?"

"It's going to get cold soon. I'm practicing on you. You need a sweater."

One morning Joy ushered in a man. She said Lily knew him, but Lily didn't know him. Who was he? He was an older gentleman in a very well-pressed suit. He told her he was the one who bought the *Whisky in the Hands* paintings. "Oh," said Lily. "What happened? Did the colors run?"

The man introduced himself as David Lake of Lake Gallery in Soho. "I've been coming to 8th Street for three Saturdays in a row. Someone who knew you in the deli told me about you, told me you were sick. I took a chance you'd be in Mount Sinai. I did try Sloan-Kettering first." He told her that her seven small paintings sold for $78,000 in his gallery last Monday.

If she knew how to whistle, she would have.

"And you know what? It was my eighteenth offer for the lot. I finally had to accept. You must have touched a nerve with those displaced hands around a drink. So intensely personal."

She said nothing, acutely remembering one girl and one man to whom she was nothing but a speck of insignificant, intensely impersonal pollen in the faraway air. Means to an end to Amy—whom Lily had loved so much.

David Lake had a proposition for Lily—if she offered him thirty or so pieces of her work, oil on canvas only, he would have a show of her art in his gallery, and they would split the profits fifty-fifty.

In the background Joy was vigorously nodding.

Lily, up against the pillows, didn't know what to say. She said, "I've put my paintbrushes away, Mr. Lake."

"Why?"

"I don't need them anymore."

75

The Postman

Lily hears Grandma come and sit by her side.

Lily's mouth isn't moving, and she suspects her eyes are closed. She can feel her grandmother near, and the mind's eye is supplying the other details, the gray hair, the elastic comfortable pants, the clean tennis shoes that have not been out of the Brooklyn brownstone, the small gold cross around the neck. Tell me something funny, Grandma, she thinks. And Grandma, as if hearing, says, "Lily, a woman was on a Qantas flight from Wellington, New Zealand to Melbourne, Australia, and do you know what she found perched on a green cucumber in her salad?"

I don't know, what?

"A live frog. An airborne amphibian. Qantas is very unhappy with the lettuce supplier. They feel the quality control is not what it should be."

If Lily could laugh, she would. Was she in coach or first class, she wants to know.

Her grandmother presses her lips to Lily's head. "You hang on, there, baby, DiAngelo is working on you. He'll fix you all up, you'll see. He's full of pride, that man, he doesn't trade in failure."

Lily hears quite well.

"Lily," says Grandma, "remember I told you about your mother under the boards in Ravensbruck?"

I remember, Grandma. Ravensbruck—sixty miles north of Berlin. You hid my mother in your skirts to shield her from the German guards. You gave her all your rations. You hid her in the floor of the barracks while you went out to work with the other women. Ravensbruck, the first and only all-women's prison in the Nazi camp system, but you were in Germany, you were hoping for salvation. The Americans were rumored to be coming. The Soviets, too. You wanted to hang on just long enough. So you hid my mother in the planks in the floor with another small girl. One evening when you came back to the barracks and lifted the planks you saw the girl lying there immobile and you started to scream, but it wasn't Olenka, it was the four-year-old girl Olenka was hiding with, lying there dead. And when you realized my mother was still alive under the floorboards, you were so relieved.

"Lily, that's your doctor, that's what he's doing, hiding you under the wooden planks."

But what if I'm the other girl? thinks Lily. Someone was hiding her, too.

The rumors got louder that the Soviets were coming, the Americans were coming. The louder they got the more frequent the executions got. It was blind luck that you and Mama managed to live just long enough, though Mama caught scarlet fever and nearly died. You gave yourself to a German guard in return for some chicken stock for my mother. In March, 1945, the Soviets must have gotten very close, because the whole camp was evacuated and all the women sent on a trek south deep into Germany, sent without shoes, without food, without warm clothes. It rained the whole month. The Germans stood by the side of the road and threw rocks at you, "they who were without sin," you always add ironically after you tell me this; they threw stones at you, hoping you would fall.

"I turned my body to shield her," said Grandma, "I carried her because I loved her, because she was my own, and I love you, because you are my own . . . Liliput, I have no other."

557

I hear you, Grandma.

Small tears trickle out, and her grandmother leans over her and kisses her eyes, whispering, "Ah, my angel, my child, so you *can* hear me. DiAngelo said to me that unconsciousness doesn't mean you can't hear, and he was right. I'm growing a newfound respect for him."

Grandma is crying as she is telling Lily another story. And this one Lily has never heard. Grandma is telling her about Tomas. Lily thinks it's about Tomas, though she can't be sure because it begins on Montague Street in Brooklyn, in 1992. Why do so many things begin in 1992? Why wasn't that year on her lottery?

Montague Street, Brooklyn Heights, 1992. Claudia runs into her postman—the one who used to bring her no letters from the front, the one she used to wait for every day by the fence, along with a pregnant Anya.

Claudia had been out on Saturday morning doing a bit of fruit shopping, when she heard a voice from behind her. "Klavdia?" No one has called her Klavdia since Skalka.

The postman. They stopped on the street and chatted. She remembered the day well because it was an Indian summer October morning and it was warm, and they were standing near a church while the leaves were changing. The air smelled bitter-sweet, like sad nostalgia, and he said to her, *I'm going to tell you something, Klavdia.*

And Claudia didn't want to hear it.

I know how you feel, Grandma. There are so many things I would have liked to never hear. These are so many things I would have liked to never be true.

The postman said that Tomas took him aside before he went off to the front and asked that if a death telegram was ever sent to the house, not to deliver it. "He made me promise." Tomas told him that neither his young wife nor his ailing mother would survive that news. "If there was ever a telegram either about Tomas or his three brothers, I was supposed to just walk by your house, and if you were out in the front yard by the fence waiting, I had to put on my happiest face, and smile. I promised I would do it." The postman looked at the church, and said, "And that's what I did, Klavdia. I threw four telegrams away, one for each of the Pevny brothers, and as I walked by your gates, I waved to you and smiled."

Claudia paled then, and the air stopped smelling ripe or fresh.

"Don't be upset," he said. "It's been forty-three years. I did it because your Tomas asked me to."

Claudia asked if he had read the telegrams.

"Yes. They all said, *died of his wounds in battle*."

That's why she stopped going out. Who knows who else she might run into, who else with tattoos on their arms might tell her tales of horror about telegrams of death. She is too old for such surprises, she can barely lift her load as it is.

Claudia emits an awful sound, and Lily opens her eyes. She is on a respirator. She can't speak. Only her eyes move, looking at her grandmother's face for a sign, for a gesture, for something, her eyes pleading, asking, hoping.

Claudia swallows down, lifts her hand, waves to Lily, and smiles.

76

The Only One

DiAngelo debated with himself, trying to get up his courage, waiting for a miracle from the marrow registry, but finally he went into his small office on the hospital records floor and dialed Lily's mother's number. Spencer reluctantly gave it to him, saying he didn't think it was a good idea. But Lily was getting to a point where a successful platelet transfusion was no longer an option. Her organs were becoming clogged with detritus. Dialysis wasn't helping, her salt levels were abnormally high, making her swell, and her blood wasn't circulating. Lily was slipping in and out of consciousness, spending more and more days in a deep sleep, in a stupor from which she could not awaken. The International Marrow Donor Registry for four weeks had been unable to find a marrow match closer than four out of six enzyme markers. DiAngelo needed at least five.

He didn't want to call Allison Quinn but he had no choice. It was blast crisis time.

After a few rings she picked up. He introduced himself, explained who he was and how long he had been treating her daughter. He told her how sick Lily was, how they had tried every combination of drugs to kill the cancer cells and could not. How they had tried experimental treatments, and Vitamin A therapy, and Alkeran, and even arsenic, and how now the only option left was a bone-marrow transplant, which involved replacing her diseased marrow with a healthy marrow from a suitable donor. Allison listened carefully to it all.

DiAngelo said, "Mrs. Quinn, here is my problem. Marrow donors are not like blood donors. We cannot get matching marrow from just anyone. There is an international registry that lists all possible donors but at the moment no suitable match can be found for Lily . . ."

"You know, I don't understand all of this medical stuff very well. I had a perforated stomach operation and a gall bladder removed, and I've had sponges left in me by careless nurses, and I don't know if you know this, but I had an infection in my foot that was so terrible, I had to have the foot removed—*amputated*, doctor! but I don't know anything about this cancer stuff, this bone marrow. Frankly, I've never heard of it. I think it would be better if you spoke to my husband. He understands these things much better, he used to be a journalist. I'm just going to go and get him—"

"No! Mrs. Quinn, I don't want you to get your husband, what I have to say, I have to finish saying to *you*. I don't want you to get your husband. Please let me finish."

"All right," Allison drew out. "But I really don't understand . . ."

"What I'm trying to tell you is that we have tested all her siblings, who are often our best bet. But we cannot find a match among them for Lily."

Allison was mute on the other line. DiAngelo suspected that though she didn't know anything about the "cancer stuff," she perhaps knew more than she wanted to say at the moment about why Lily's brother and sisters were such bad marrow matches for Lily.

"I don't understand why you're calling me here," she said through her teeth into the phone. "Who are you? I didn't know she was still so sick, I thought she was better. I just saw her, she came to visit me, and she was all better. What kind of trouble are you trying to cause here?"

561

"She is not all better. Have you not spoken to your . . . your—mother, to your other children? She is much much worse. And what I'm trying to do here is save your daughter's life. Her siblings' marrows don't match." He paused, swallowed and just came out and said it. "Without even testing him, I will have to assume that your husband's won't match either."

Allison did not speak.

"The only one who may be a possible match is you, Mrs. Quinn. I'm calling to ask you to come to New York and let us take a sample from you, and if you match even five of the six necessary markers, to let us harvest your marrow and give it to Lily."

"Are you out of your mind?" Allison hissed into the phone.

"I'm begging you. I'm pleading with you. You are the only one who can help. You are her only hope. Please. Please come and help her."

"My blood might not match either," Allison whispered. "Did you ever think of that?"

"Was she adopted?"

"God, no! She is my child."

"Then come. It will match better than anything else we have. Get on the next plane and come to New York."

"Do you understand what you're asking me? I can't. I lost a foot. I had gangrene and lost a foot, had my foot amputated. I'm an invalid now. Didn't you hear me? I can barely walk through my own house."

"Have your husband help you. They have wheelchairs at the airport, and Lily will pay for everything."

"I thought she was unconscious in ICU, how is she even going to know?"

DiAngelo was fitfully rubbing his forehead. "I thought you didn't know how your daughter was doing, Mrs. Quinn? Never mind that. Trust me, I will work everything out. You will fly first class, you will stay at a first-class hotel, everything you need will be taken care of."

"I can't just come. I can't. I have to think about it."

562

"You will have to think about it on the plane. Your daughter has days to live. She needs you not five days from now, not a week from now, not tomorrow, but yesterday. Please come." DiAngelo paused, steeling himself, drawing from within him everything he could think of to convince her. "I know you've been sick. I know how hard life has been for you. You've been depressed, you've been unhappy. And you have difficulty traveling. But a mother is all the hope that Lily's got left in this world. If I had a choice I wouldn't've troubled you, I know you've got troubles plenty."

"What is that supposed to mean? I'm fine, just a foot problem . . ."

"Of course. I apologize."

"Give me your number, I'll call you back in ten minutes."

She called back in an hour. DiAngelo hadn't moved from his desk. "I will come," she said, "under one condition."

"Name it," he said. He would have promised her all of Lily's money if she had asked.

"That you will not breathe a word of what you think you have found out about me. The woman who brought me here went through too much to have my one indiscretion tear apart my family."

"Not a word out of me."

"They simply didn't match, that's all, and I've come to help. Mine might not match either. It's simple."

"It's very simple." He could barely hear her, she was so quiet.

"Until an hour ago when you called, I didn't know Lily wasn't my husband's. She could have been, couldn't she? It was very possible that she was his."

"Yes. Absolutely. You have four wonderful children. You should be proud."

"They don't love their mother, but I am proud of them. I love *them*."

"Time is running out, Mrs. Quinn. There will be a ticket waiting for you and your husband at the United Airlines counter for an eight p.m. flight tonight. I will also book you a

563

room at the Pierre on 61st Street and Fifth. It's an excellent hotel, and just a few blocks from the hospital. Ask for me when you get to reception, and don't be afraid to request a wheelchair."

"Fine, fine. I'm footless, doctor, I'm not incapacitated."

DiAngelo squared everything away with Spencer, who used Lily's American Express card to get the tickets and the hotel room. But Spencer was who he was, and nothing anyone said got by him. "I thought bone marrow matched best in siblings?"

Taken aback for just a second, DiAngelo glanced away, but it was all that Spencer needed. "Not this time."

Spencer sat down. "Oh Mother of God." His hands were in his lap. He got up after a minute. "Them hits, they just keep on coming." He sighed. "She might be able to live through the stem-cell transplant, but she won't live through this."

"I don't know about you, detective, but in my experience, human beings manage to live through quite a fucking lot."

Spencer didn't disagree. "Doctor, assure me that not a word of this is going to leave this room."

"I assure you."

"Though you cracked like an egg on marble, didn't you?" said Spencer. "I barely even opened my mouth to ask a question."

"Detective O'Malley, I'm hoping it's the last time I'm going to be interrogated by a professional investigator."

"*That* was being interrogated?" Spencer smiled. "Not a word to anyone."

"Don't worry."

They shook hands. "Though the mother knows, doesn't she?" said Spencer.

"You think we should knock her off after we harvest her marrow?"

"Well, not you. But I haven't taken the Hippocratic oath. Perhaps put something in her drink? Maybe arsenic?"

And they laughed softly at that, at the irony of it.

* * *

Lily could have painted this: The father by the side of his wife on the airport conveyance. She had refused a cart, and now stood holding on to the moving walkway rail, her prosthetic leg limply propping her up. And the father had his hand on his wife's back as they were silently propelled forward. And at the other end of the walkway, past the stairs, past the luggage carousel, three of her children, two daughters and one son, stood together waiting for their mother, to take her to the hospital where their sister lay dying.

77

Wollman's Rink

Lily is trying to form a word on her lips. The doctor is adjusting her respirator mask. She is laboriously breathing. He lets her breathe without the oxygen for a few minutes every hour, to see how she does. And this time before he reattaches it, she forms and forms the word she wants him to hear. The only word she wants to see in front of her.

"Spencer . . ." whispers Lily.

And he comes. He is sitting by her. She can tell that every time she takes a wheezing breath, it twists his heart, but he sits calmly despite it. Only his mouth is twisted.

"Spencer?"

"Yes, Liliput."

"You know what I think? About Amy?"

"What do you think?"

"I think she may have gone away to be rid of both of them."

"You think so?" he said quietly.

"I think she just had enough, you know? Enough! And she didn't know how to solve it. How to end it. She didn't know how to spare Andrew. How to get herself away from Milo, he was so dependent on her, especially after everything that happened. Amy didn't want to be part of Milo. She didn't want to hurt my brother. I think she loved him. You look skeptical, but I truly believe it. And I think she went away to save him, because she didn't know another way. I think she disappeared the same way Hobbit disappeared. A new identity for Amy somewhere around the bend of the Mississippi, a new life without them both. But maybe, in this new life, she is still waiting for him. Waiting for my brother to come to her. She came to him with malice in her heart, and she didn't expect love, it was the last thing she expected. And maybe she's waiting for him somewhere, to tell him this."

Spencer stayed silent.

"What do you think?"

He squeezed her carefully. "Maybe you're right." Then was silent again.

"Remember Oliver and Jenny?" she asked.

"Yes."

"Who do you feel more sorry for? Him, sitting by the ice skating rink, or her?"

"Her, Harlequin," said Spencer. "I feel only for her."

She held his hand. "And I feel only for him," she whispered.

He was watching her, and then bending so that she felt his lips graze against her cheek, he sang in a cracked low voice: *"Tomorrow my love and I/Will sleep neath auburn skies/Somewhere across the border/We'll leave behind my dear/The pain and sadness we found here/And we'll drink from the Bravo's muddy waters/Where the sky grows gray and white/We'll meet on the other side/There across the border . . ."*

"Bruce is not just for lovemaking anymore?" Lily whispered.

"He is for all seasons," replied Spencer, his forehead pressed to her cheek. "Like you."

DiAngelo had to give Lily massive transfusions to get her counts up and then pump her full of chemicals to empty her marrow completely.

In a hospital room, DiAngelo took healthy bone marrow from the hip of an anesthetized Allison Quinn, who matched five for six of her daughter's genetic markers. He harvested almost four pints of soupy, healthy matching marrow, leaving Allison with weakness and heavy bruising where the needle had repeatedly gone in. Then he injected the thick liquid into Lily's central venous line, right where she lay, without even an anesthetic.

And they waited. Would her body reject it? Would her body accept it? Would it start to regenerate again, like a starfish?

Her vital powers began to pool at her feet, the blood was coursing slower and slower, molasses-like, the saline in her body fluids depleted, the heart slowing down, pumping forty difficult beats a minute, pushing the molasses through her body.

Thirty . . .

Twenty . . .

Nineteen . . .

Eighteen . . .

Seventeen . . .

Fifteen . . .

Ten . . .

They gave her electric shock at ten.

Twenty . . .

Fifteen . . .

Code blue. Code blue. Electric shock.

Seven . . .

Six . . .

Another electric shock.

Five.

Four . . .

Five . . .

Six . . .

Four . . . one beat every fifteen seconds.

One beat every twenty seconds.

One beat every thirty seconds.

One beat.

I didn't paint enough, I didn't dance enough, I didn't love enough.

Spencer!

Life lived as exclamation, instead of desperation.

She thought she heard someone singing, someone close by, nearby, whose voice was so familiar and so beloved and so desperately desired. Lily thought that she had opened her eyes, and on her bed, by her side, holding her hands sat her mother. Her mother, dressed and coiffed and made up and sober. She sat and her eyes glistened, but she looked strong and beautiful like she did when she was young, and she was smiling. "Shh, shh," she said. "Shh, shh. Liliput, my baby girl, my baby, my child, my daughter, everything is going to be all right now. Everything is going to be all right."

Lily smiled, and with her eyes closed, she heard her mother singing a song from long ago, from deep comfort, from childhood.

> . . . *When you wake, you shall have*
> *All the Pretty Little Horses . . .*

78

DNR

"We can't stabilize her," DiAngelo said. He said this to both the mother and father in the waiting room, though he was having trouble looking at the father, afraid that his pitying gaze might betray him. Waiting with the parents sat Anne, Grandma, and Amanda. And in the corner by himself, as far away as it was possible to be and still be in the same room, was Spencer. Andrew was not there. DiAngelo thought it was to Spencer's credit that he was not afraid of the family's contempt, though Spencer looked right now like nothing was to his credit.

Anne stepped up. DiAngelo tensed. "What's happening to her right now?"

"Every hour or so she keeps going into cardiac arrest. Her pulse dropped below twenty. We keep resuscitating her. She is on oxygen, on IV fluids, antibiotics. Her body seems to be doing okay with the new marrow, we just can't get her organs to normalize, so no new platelets or white cells are being made. She keeps needing transfusions every four hours. Her liver function is down, her lungs aren't working on their own, her heart is not beating on its own. Dialysis, transfusions, electric shock, that's how she's being stabilized."

"Sounds to me it's how she's being destabilized," said Anne.

It would to you, wouldn't it, DiAngelo thought.

Her mother was in front of him, listening with clenched hands. He thought it was brave of her to stand. He could tell she had once been a beautiful woman, she still was if you didn't look at what she had done to damage herself on the outside too—the prematurely-aged skin, the puffy bloodshot eyes, the swollen face. Taking two quarts of her marrow had sapped her—she looked frail and depleted. "So what do you think we should do, doctor?" she said.

"We'll keep doing what we're doing. I'm just giving you a heads up."

"What's her prognosis?" Allison clutched George's arm.

DiAngelo glanced at Spencer, off in the corner. "Bleak," he said.

Anne patted him (!) gently. "You've done all you can, doctor. Really, no one could have done more. She's been comatose now for over two weeks."

"Yes."

"Don't you think she's suffered enough?"

"No," he said. "I don't think she has. I think she can suffer a little more."

Anne sighed. Allison frowned. Claudia rolled her eyes. Amanda put her arm around her grandmother and stayed out of it. George, *as always*, stayed out of it.

DiAngelo said tightly, "I will keep you apprised of her progress."

"There isn't going to be any progress! Two weeks in a coma! She's a vegetable, we don't know if she has any brain function left."

But DiAngelo was ready, no, not just ready, itching for a fight. "She has brain function left. She had a brain CT yesterday. She's holding up."

"Her heart would stop if *you* would stop those infernal electric shocks!"

"Would is a subjunctive case, Mrs. Ramen. Are you implying that you would like your sister's heart to stop?"

"I would like her to have some peace, for God's sake!"

The mother and the father tried to shh shh her—for comfort, not quiet.

"She'll have peace enough when she's dead," DiAngelo said.

"If you leave her be, she'd have peace, wouldn't she?"

"Once again, Mrs. Ramen, what are you implying?"

"I'm *saying*, not implying, that we've had a year of this, a year! A year of her body being done, a year of you fighting off the inevitable, and the only one, the only one who benefits from his ungodly mess is you! Her family has been grieving for months, she has been suffering for months, fighting a losing fight."

DiAngelo looked through Lily's chart. "Right here," he said, pulling out a standard hospital form. "Very clearly says keep alive by any means necessary. Signed by Lily Quinn. Who is not a minor and was of sound mind when she put her John Hancock to it."

Anne stepped closer to the doctor. She grabbed the sheet out of his hands, and before he could make a motion, ripped it into tiny pieces and threw it in his face. "That's what I think of your fucking form," she said. "You should have told us in the beginning this was a fatal cancer. I've read up on it, nobody makes it out alive. The bone marrow is the last straw, and she has fallen into a coma even before the transplant. Her body has given up. I'll go to court if I need to, with the full support of my family to give her what she needs."

"Death is what she needs?"

"To stop suffering is what she needs! Why are you the only one who can't see it?"

"All right, Annie, now, all right," said Allison. "Calm down."

"Ma, you tell him. You are her mother. She doesn't have a husband to administer her health. Tell him you don't want her kept artificially alive, tell him you want her to have peace, to stop suffering. Tell him, Ma."

"Why did I come seven thousand miles to give my marrow if we're just going to remove her respirator?" Allison said huffily.

Spencer, stepping up at last, said, "Mrs. Ramen, this is not about making her family more comfortable in their grieving process. This is about Lily. She wanted to be kept alive. She will be kept alive."

"Oh, shut the fuck up," said Anne. "No one asked you. No one is speaking to you. I can't believe you have the nerve to be here."

"I have the nerve to be many places where I'm not wanted."

"You're wanted here by Lily," said DiAngelo. "You are the first person she asks for when she wakes up."

"Well, he should have the decency to wait somewhere else," piped up Amanda, letting her feelings for Spencer be known. Claudia kept quiet with a lowered head.

"He has every right to wait here," said DiAngelo. "And you need to stop bickering. Why are you here, Mrs. Ramen? Why don't you go home yourself, where *you'll* be more comfortable?"

"I'm not going anywhere till my sister gets what she deserves."

"Your sister stipulated no DNR. Go spend your money suing the hospital to stop the resuscitation. You'll be broke long before we are."

"Well, of course—you're making millions of dollars on my sister."

"To keep her alive."

"Millions of dollars!" screamed Anne. "Of her money, when you know she's got no chance, no chance in the world. She is going to lie here for twelve years on your fucking dialysis, while you'll be collecting on your golf course, sitting sipping champagne in your country club, paying for your Bronxville mansion with her money. I will sue you, you bastard, and I will win . . ."

"Anne, you won't win, now stop this. It's your sister, for God's sake." That was George, leaning towards Anne, but he glanced at DiAngelo as if begging him to stop.

DiAngelo turned to go, but then, as if in afterthought, turned around and said, "It just occurs to me, Mrs. Ramen, that I forgot to mention something here that might be of some help." DiAngelo glanced at Spencer, who stood behind the family, vehemently shaking his head. But the good doctor would not be stopped. "Your concern for your sister is admirable, and you're so close to her, I'm sure you must know that if she dies—if that heart you want stopped is stopped—all her remaining money goes to Detective O'Malley."

The stunned silence in the waiting room was worth it.

"That can't be true," said Anne tonelessly.

"No? Turns out she did make a living will, Mrs. Ramen. And she left Detective O'Malley everything. Isn't that so, Detective O'Malley?" DiAngelo asked in an off-hand voice.

"Hmm," said Spencer, shaking his head at DiAngelo.

"Ah, yes, There you have it." DiAngelo took a step toward the ICU's double doors. "If we DNR her, *he*, whom you hate, gets all her money. The ironies just pile up. But perhaps to ease her suffering it'll be worth it? Well, good day now. I'll be out to talk to you again after my evening rounds."

DiAngelo made his exit and an incredulous Spencer inched away back to his seat in the corner. On second thought he decided to go out for a proverbial smoke. This was a very good time to start smoking. Either that or . . .

A voice called after him. Anne.

He reluctantly turned around.

Her voice was shaking, and hands were shaking. She was shaking all over. "You bastard. It's not enough that you managed to ruin my brother's life, you've taken from us the easing of our financial burdens?"

The language of tragedy! Spencer thought, as Anne closed in on him, quaking, talking. "You think you'll be able to keep that money? You and she are not married, you are not living together, you have absolutely no right to that money."

"I'm sure that's true," he said tiredly.

"You will spend the rest of your natural life in court," said Anne. "I will fight you, you crook, until I'm unable to stand. I will get that fucking money from you if it's the last thing I do."

Spencer gritted his own teeth and into Anne's livid face said, "No use threatening me. Your sister is not dead—" He didn't know how he kept himself from saying the word *yet*. He had to leave the room immediately and go outside to clear his head. He walked from 66th Street across Central Park to Wollman's Rink and in the humid September sat high in the blue bleachers looking below at the empty-of-ice rink. He took off his jacket. It was hot.

Lily, he prayed. I lost my pregnant wife at 23, and I didn't think I would ever recover. Perhaps in some ways I never have. In my thirties I met and fell in love with another girl, and she too died, murdered at barely 21. And now there is you. I seem to be so unlucky for all my women. Please. Don't die and leave me, too, Lily.

He sat there a long time. He thought of going back; perhaps there was some news. But DiAngelo knew his beeper number. He would have called.

His cell phone rang. Instantly he picked it up.

"O'Malley!" It was Gabe. "Get your ass over to the *reservoir* right now. You won't fucking believe this. We found her."

For a moment Spencer didn't know what Gabe was talking about.

"Stop being so Irish-dense, O'Malley! A dog owner running with his dog-pound mutt called in, says the pooch uncovered something that looks suspiciously like human bones. I'm betting my month's salary it's your McFadden girl. Go there *stat*. 87th Street on the West Side, off the bridle path."

79

And Now—About Amy

Buried bones were found under a tree in the deepest, densest part of Central Park off the Bridle Path. Horses went on the Bridle Path, not dogs, not runners, not policemen. It had rained for days, and the bones became unseated in the muddy earth. A man and his dog stumbled upon them when the dog ran off into the woods and the man followed, uncovering the gray shapes against the dirt and dead leaves. With the bones were found a jogging suit, a bra, sneakers, a pair of diamond earrings.

It took forensics eight hours to identify the dental records positively as Amy McFadden's.

Her mother cried as if Amy had died yesterday and not sixteen months ago.

The 57/57 Bar was up the wide marble staircase off the lobby of the Four Seasons Hotel. The bar itself was ultra mod, with crème marble floors and walls that stretched up forty marble feet into the marble ceiling of the lobby. The patron tables were light oak tops on brushed chrome legs, and the flower centerpieces were white roses and white lilies. At the farthest corner next to a narrow window with his back to the bar, sat Andrew in a chrome chair, with a full drink by his side. Across from him sat his wife. When the waiter came to ask if she wanted a drink, she shook her head but didn't speak. Andrew and Miera did not speak. She was dressed in a gray gabardine suit, and her neatly brushed hair had not been colored. She fidgeted with her purse. From his demeanor, one might have thought Andrew didn't know she was there, until he said, "How are the girls?"

"Fine."

"Have there been any problems?"

"No, everything's been fine. He is not going to show up, Andrew. He is a derelict and a heroin addict who has no money. How could he take a train to Port Jefferson?"

"Somehow he'll manage. Never leave the house unprotected." He glanced at the detail standing by the bar watching them.

"We live under a Praetorian guard," said Miera, slowly. "And in any case, why would he come there"—she paused—"when you're here?"

Andrew nodded. "You're right. I'm hoping to deflect him."

"Not just deflect. You've been gone from the house a month," she said. "You're not coming back, are you?"

It was a long while of waiters and bar-clanking and smoke before Andrew answered. "No, Miera."

"Andrew . . ."

"Mi, please. Please. I can't do it. Not now. I just can't."

She made to get up, as if she were done, then abruptly sat back down. The waiter came by to ask—"No!" she said, "Nothing, thanks."

She wasn't done with Andrew. She moved close to get his attention. "You're not coming back? Fine, then. So do you want me to call our lawyer? Draw up some papers?"

"That'll be fine," he replied, in a voice that said, *yes, I'd like an olive in my martini. Whatever.*

"I can't believe you've resigned from Congress."

"Yes, well."

She fussed with her purse, with the buttons of her suit jacket, with her hair. Andrew sat in profile to her; he did not turn to her once.

She said, "That girl's been found."

He was mute.

"Andrew . . ." she lowered her voice.

"Don't."

"I have to ask you, I have to. I haven't talked to anyone about this. And once I turn and go, it will all be over between us, I won't ask you anything again—" She forced herself to go on. "I don't want anything anymore from you, Andrew. I just want you to answer me. Over a year ago, one Friday night, for some reason I couldn't sleep, so I came downstairs to find you and I heard you in your office. When I opened the door to look in, you didn't hear me, your back was to the door and to me, much the same way it is now. I saw you sitting in your chair, and your shoulders were quaking . . . you were crying so hard, I became afraid that something terrible had happened to a member of your family. I said your name, but you didn't hear, and then suddenly . . . I felt that I was intruding on something you didn't want me to see. I don't know why I got that feeling, but I did, and so I tiptoed out and shut the door, and thought that you would tell me the next day, morning, night. But you never told me." Miera fell quiet.

Andrew was quiet. He gave no response.

Miera said, "Do you want to tell me now?"

"Tell you what?"

"As the last thing you do for me in our marriage." She clutched her purse.

"I was crying for her, Miera," said Andrew.

"It was the night of May 14, 1999, Andrew, wasn't it?" Miera's voice was nearly inaudible. "The day they said the girl disappeared." And then she left, stumbling slightly in her three-inch leather pumps on the slippery marble floor. One Treasury agent went with her. Two remained behind with Andrew.

A few hours after Miera left, Spencer walked up the same marble staircase to the lounge bar, in his clean dark blue nondescript suit and his black dress shoes, and Spencer didn't slip and he didn't have a purse to fidget with, nor was fidgeting his habit. He didn't know why he didn't bring Gabe with him. He didn't know why he wanted to talk to Andrew Quinn alone.

This from Elizabeth Monroe from three weeks ago that he had been carrying around in his jacket pocket: "*Internal Affairs have conducted a thorough and concrete investigation into the allegations against Spencer Patrick O'Malley and apart from vague circumstantial information found no sufficient evidence of abuse of his badge or his profession or of any other crime being committed on his behalf either in civilian or professional capacity to sustain the complaint against him of serious misconduct. Matter is summarily dismissed with prejudice.*"

One of the federal agents by the bar, there for the purposes of protecting the former congressman, told Spencer that "the guy has sat like a block all day at that table—almost as if he's waiting for someone."

"Thanks. I'll go talk to him now."

"Do you want a drink, detective?"

"Yes, a Coke," said Spencer. And with his "drink" in hand, he went and sat down at the table across from Andrew, who turned his head slightly to Spencer.

"I was wondering when I'd see you," Andrew said. "I'm surprised it took you this long."

Spencer took a sip and said nothing. His hands went around the tumbler. Coke in the hands.

"Do you want a drink?" he asked.

"No, thank you, I've had plenty," replied Andrew. "How is my sister?"

"The same."

Andrew sighed painfully.

"I've been thinking," Spencer said, "of certain things, of things we talked about, things I know, things I'm guessing at, the pieces I try to put together, and I always feel that I'm missing some pieces, here, there."

"Yes. And what has all this thinking led you to?"

"Certain things you said to me that I remember now that go with the things I've learned since we last spoke. For example, when I asked you if you knew Amy back in 1992, you replied that you did not know of her then. I hear the emphasis now which I didn't hear then. 'I did not know of *her* then,' is what you said to me." Spencer didn't take his eyes off Andrew. "As if you knew that she knew of *you* then."

"I was running for Congress. Of course she knew of me." Andrew was clipped.

Spencer cleared his throat. "Did Bill Bryant ever call you? Tell you Lily and I spoke to his wife?"

"He did, gave me a heads up. One of the reasons I've moved out of my house. I've been waiting for you ever since. Figured I'd see you soon."

"Your sister hasn't been well. I've been busy."

"Yes."

"I thought you might be interested in some of the coroner's findings. He is going to do an inquest in ten days and make a formal deposition, but do you want to hear the prelim?"

"Go ahead." This said in a dead voice.

"At the back of her skull the coroner found some blunt trauma, as if she had been knocked out perhaps after being violently pushed against a solid object, perhaps the tree under which she was buried. There were no other injuries. Perhaps she was suffocated. Her upper vertebrae, her neck, remained intact. Her skull, aside from a three-inch fracture in the blunt trauma area, remained intact. Her otherwise unharmed bones were found together." Spencer fell quiet, as if to give Andrew a chance to speak, but by the shut in, closed-up look of him, he might never speak, so Spencer continued. "Since there is no flesh left to examine for tell-tale signs of morbidity, the coroner supposes any number of things could have killed her. Do you know what's most distressing? He does not dismiss the possibility that she was knocked out and *not killed* but buried unconscious in the soft muddy ground under the oak tree. There is no way to know. He does not dismiss the possibility that Amy McFadden was buried alive."

Andrew's shoulders rose in an effort to square, and shook in an effort at self-control. "She couldn't have been buried alive."

"No?" said Spencer, ever so casual, taking another sip of his drink.

"Detective . . ."

"Congressman—"

"No more," Andrew said. "Just Mr. Quinn. Or Andrew."

"Andrew," said Spencer. "Why did you make up an alibi? You have a good friend in the councilman. All of us should have good friends like that. But why did you need an alibi for these hours? You met with her, didn't you?"

Without turning to Spencer, Andrew said, "She wasn't buried alive. Did you hear me?"

"I hear you."

"She called me on Thursday, May 13. I hadn't spoken to her, or seen her in four weeks. She called to ask me to meet her. Not here, like always, but in Central Park, in the woods off the bridle path. I had been out of my mind without her. I went to the bridle path like a man who'd discovered his life again." He was not looking at Spencer. "I was so happy to see her. I asked her why she wanted to meet here and not in our hotel, and she said because she was about to tell me some things that might make me upset and she didn't want me getting upset in public. And you know what I said? Nothing you can tell me will make me upset, Amy. I'm so happy you called me. I'm so happy to see you. I've missed you more than you'll ever know.

"It was there, in those woods that Amy told me she had voted against me in 1992. It was in those words she told me about herself and Benjamin Abrams, about herself and Milo. Oh, the things she told me. She had been in love with him. The only reason she came into my life was to help him kill me. And do

581

you know what my reaction was?" He quickly continued before Spencer could supply an answer. "I didn't believe her! That was my reaction. You're being absurd, Amy. If this is a ploy to get me away from you, it's not going to work. But she said it wasn't a ploy. She said she was never going to tell me, but Milo had been released from prison, and was now fomenting and pushing her towards something she said she could no longer do. She told me she was telling me this to warn me, that Milo had said he was going to stop at nothing until he got to me again." Andrew took a deep breath and stopped speaking.

"Do you know what the word was, detective, that struck out at me just a little bit," he said at last, "just enough to stop disbelieving her? It was the word *again*. What do you mean, *again*, I said.

"And she told me Milo was the one who shot out the windows in my SUV a couple of years earlier, nearly killing my wife, my daughters. We were all in the truck. It was the intention of harming of my family that I reacted to. Amy knew where we were going to be—because *I* told her where we were going to be. I told her and she told Milo. And then it dawned on me—she was telling the truth."

When Spencer remained mute, Andrew continued. "Detective, my whole family was in danger, living under their poison microscope. The things I had shared with her! I told her the most private things about my wife, my children, my *sister*. For years stalked by them. I screamed Amy, Amy, don't you know how much I love you? She said she knew. That was why she was here, warning me about Milo . . . I lost my mind. All right, I understand about me, but what about them, what about my family, my wife, my children, Lily, what were they, incidental accidental victims? I asked. And do you know what she said? *Not even that. All just tools against you, Andrew. Ben's mother is dead, Milo is the living dead; but your wife, your children, Lily, they're still alive.*" Andrew's head was down. "I must have grabbed her. I no longer remember it clearly. I must have grabbed her.

My reason left me." He didn't look up. "I broke her skull, I think, on the tree behind her, I bashed her against the tree, I took her and pummeled her against the trunk, and when she crumpled to the ground, I covered her with the leaves, and left. I didn't bury her, I didn't check to see if she was breathing. She simply fell, and I threw—heaved—dirt and stones and leaves on her and left, and that was all. I washed my hands in the Central Park Lake, I brushed the dust off me, pried the wet leaves off my shoes. It had been raining for days, the ground was wet. My shoes were muddy. I washed the soles off in the lake, and then walked back on dry pavement to 57th street and sat here in the bar for four hours and then I went home."

Spencer's drink was long gone. How he craved another.

"What she had told me was diabolical. While I was dreaming of her, she was dreaming of killing my children, to bring me suffering for something I had no direct hand in. Oh, there was some ideological bullshit. She turned a face to me that was funny and kind. I betrayed my wife for that face, and all the while, she was betraying me. She said she had changed, her heart had changed, but everything was shattered now that I knew the duplicity and malice of that beloved face."

Spencer ordered and finished another Coke. He and Andrew sat side by side at the same table. He fingered his handcuffs in the pocket of his suit, he felt for his gun, felt for his whirring tape recorder.

For a very long time, Spencer sat with Andrew at the little round table in the 57/57 Bar. Evening fell. The tape had long finished.

Spencer stood up from the table, finally. "The inquest is in ten days," he said. "The coroner is ruling this death an aggravated homicide because of the skull trauma. Someone else might have questions for you. Probably will have questions for you."

"I don't understand."

"But I myself am going now. I suggest you go too."

Andrew looked up at Spencer. "Justice is at hand?"

And taking out his recorder, Spencer pulled out the tape and handed it to Andrew. "Not from me," he said. "Mercy from me. Because of Lily. Now do you understand?"

80

The Other Side

The superintendent said later he first thought it was a mischief of dead rats. For weeks the hallway had been increasingly fetid. Finally he opened one of the fireproof steel doors leading to a small storage room, gasped and started retching even as he was running down the corridor. He had to stop and vomit before he could continue up to the street level to call the police. The stench was awful, he told them, almost like a room-temperature morgue full of bodies. The police with gas masks on discovered it was one decomposing body. The smell of wretchedness and nihilist zeal in high relief was the same odor that still clung to Lily's apartment, even weeks after Milo had absconded with her (and himself, and Amy, and Andrew). He must have regained consciousness just long enough to crawl away into a closet to die and rot in darkness, and his flesh began to fall off his bones. No one even knew he had been long dead and gone. The rats had gnawed on what was left of him.

Two police cars, three ambulances, and a fire truck were pulled to a stop on the Palisades Parkway north of George Washington bridge on the way to Bear Mountain. Part of the highway had been sealed off to traffic. Spencer parked his car at a sharp, expedient angle and he and Gabe made their careful way down the near vertical cliff to the Hudson River below. They stopped about twenty paces from the wreck that had just been pulled out of the water. He and Gabe slowly walked to the car, their eyes adjusting to the night, trying to discern what shape the car was in, and who was in it.

Spencer had a lot of experience with wrecks, after spending years patrolling the Long Island Expressway on Saturday nights. Within a few feet of the car he could usually tell not only what shape the passengers were going to be in, but also what injuries they were going to have. Gabe, never out of grid-locked New York City, was green in this area and was going to be of no help, self-evident by his stunned whistle and, "Oh, shit."

Spencer shushed him. When he got ten paces from the car, he realized things were going to be pretty bad. It was a blue sports car, a Mercedes 500SL convertible. He hated convertibles. He wished he could explain the laws of physics to every idiot who thought it was so cool to drive a convertible at night on the highway at ninety miles an hour. This convertible he thought had been going faster than ninety. This one seemed as if it had been going at a hundred-and-ninety when it met the immovable force of the concrete divider, careened once, twice; spun once, twice, flipped over, screeched to a sliding stop on its convertible hood, and then went over the cliff into the water below. The car was now unrecognizable as something that once had metal around leather seats, perhaps a dashboard and a windshield. Though the windshield could protect the driver from wind, it wasn't as good at protecting him from physics. Invariably it was almost always a him. Women tended to drive tank-like Volvos and to drive their Volvos slower, as if they still remembered the kids they had left back home even when the glorious night wind was whipping through their hair.

Spencer and Gabe stood silently by the wreck trying to process what they were seeing. Even the inexperienced Gabe might be able to point out the thing about the convertible that didn't make sense.

"Hey," said Gabe. "There's no driver in it."

"Shh. Don't say anything."

"You think there were passengers?"

"Gabe! This is not a remote-control car. Of course there were passengers in it."

It was a two-seater car. And it was empty. "Well, where are they?"

Spencer looked around. It was so dark with only the police flares and floodlights illuminating the wreck, and up above, over the cliffs, the occasional light whiz of passing cars at midnight. But whether it was dark or daylight, one thing was clear—there was no driver.

There was no driver in the car, and the car was demolished.

"Why did you bring me here?" said Gabe. "Why are we looking at a car accident in New Jersey at midnight? I can't even believe that sentence is coming out of my mouth! Why us? Why me at midnight?"

And Spencer replied. "Because, McGill, Mr. Homicide Detective, this is Andrew Quinn's car."

Andrew was not found.

THE PAST AS PROLOGUE

"Spencer, do you see this?"

"Katie, I do."

"Her investments are shooting out of the sky. I've never seen anything like it. Her fund is growing at rate of thirty-four percent a year."

"Joy, should we have some lunch?"

"Stop smiling at me like that, Larry, I know what your lunch entails. I can't. I'm knitting."

Giggling.

"Did you read the paper this morning? In Ethiopia, a grenade exploded at a wedding, killing the bride and three other people."

"Mother, please!"

"What? Apparently it's custom for guests to fire their guns at weddings in wild jubilation, though grenades are apparently more rare."

"You'll have to excuse my mother, Detective O'Malley."

"Thank you, but I'm quite entertained by her, Mrs. Quinn."

"Mrs. Quinn, how are you feeling?"

"I could be better, Dr. DiAngelo. I'm tired all the time. And I wanted to show you this." There is a pause, the sound of shoes walking across the floor. "What do you think this is? Some kind of a weird rash, right?"

"Allie, do you think you can stop showing the doctor your ailments with the police in the room?"

"Oh, Detective O'Malley has seen worse than this, Mother. Haven't you, detective?"

"Much worse, and please—call me Spencer."

"No, Allie, I just don't understand you at all. Why do this now? It's just a rash!"

"Oh, you can talk about your Ethiopian exploding brides, but I can't show the doctor a real problem? The doctor is here, I might as well take advantage, right, Dr. DiAngelo?"

"Absolutely Mrs. Quinn. Let's see what you've got here."

There is sighing, clothes rustling, a silence, an ahem, a "Well, what is it?"

"Well, Mrs. Quinn, it's very serious, I'm afraid."

"Oh, no, what is it, doctor?"

"I'm afraid—I think—I can't be sure, but I think it's the Baghdad boil."

There is silence, a slight familiar snicker from a man's throat.

"A what?"

"Yes. A tiny sand fly from the Middle East with a fierce parasite stewing in its gut that causes stubborn and ugly sores that linger for months, sometimes years."

There is a shrieking of incredulous disgust. "Doctor, what are you talking about? What sandflies from the Middle East? We're in the middle of New York City! It's just a little chafing, that's all, very normal, just a little chafing."

"Larry!"

"Yes, Joy?"

"Stop torturing the poor woman, this is completely unacceptable. Tell her you're an oncologist, not a dermatologist. Allison, don't listen to a word he says, he knows nothing but cancer. He is just trying to rile you."

"Oh." And then, "I find that completely unacceptable."

There is laughter everywhere.

No one even noticed when Lily opened her eyes. She was propped halfway up in bed, in her clean hospital room with beige walls, and her paintings everywhere, and white lilies everywhere because they just don't listen. It seemed like mid-morning. In front of her was the TV, to the right of her was the open window with white lilies in front of it, with a bit of sky beyond them, her mother and grandmother were on that side, and on the other, to her left, sat Spencer. Behind him stood Katie, looking over his shoulder at the financial statements. To his right sat Joy, still knitting, the yellow sweater sizable now. Next to her was DiAngelo, standing close. Lily didn't move, just her eyes blinked. It was Spencer who looked up from the statements, lifted his eyes, and noticed an awake Lily.

Spencer said, "Lily, I think your broker deserves a raise. Because while you were lying about in the hospital, grafting marrow, she made you seven-hundred-and-fifty-thousand dollars."

"Sleeping Beauty is awake!" said her mother.

"Lily, finally! I mean, we always said, oh, but did that child love to sleep, but I think you've outdone yourself," said her grandmother.

She couldn't speak. The breathing tube was in her mouth. She moved her hand to remove the tube, and immediately started choking. "Good God," she croaked. "How long have I been in here?"

DiAngelo put the tube back in her throat, adjusted the mask over her face, the clip over her nose, placed her hands back down on the blanket. "Since your transplant? Eighteen days. Don't speak. Write it down on the Magna Doodle."

She pulled the mask, the nose clip, the breathing hose out again. Breathing, gasping. "Where's Papi?"

"Oh, you know your father," said Allison. "He can't sit still for a *second*. He's out smoking. He told me this morning, let's just go for an hour, Allie, and then we'll take a walk in Central Park. He's impossible."

Lily and her mother looked at each other for a few moments, Maui in their eyes.

"It's a good thing you woke up. You are about to miss your twenty-sixth birthday," said Allison. "You can sleep through anything."

Lily said between breaths, "Do you see the picture I made for you?" She pointed to the oil on canvas of a little blonde girl in the close lap of a brown-haired woman on a bench in a village yard.

"I see it," said Allison. She said nothing for a second. "I don't know who that's supposed to be. Doesn't look like me at all."

"Lily," said Joy. "Come on, get up. You can't be lying around all day. We booked a very large room at the Plaza to celebrate your birthday."

Lily turned her head to look at Joy inquisitively.

Marcie came in. "Oh, look at this, I'm gone for five minutes and Spunky wakes!"

"Yes, Spunky," said Spencer, "get up. Because Keanu is playing in *The Replacements* and *The Watcher*. You've got double Keanu waiting for you."

Lily took the tube out. "Hey," she mouthed. "Can you give him and me a minute?"

They gladly filed out of the room, and Spencer came close to her, putting his head in the space between her opened arm and her neck. She held his head, caressed his grown-out hair. There were tears in his eyes he didn't want her to see. This time it was she who said, "Shh, shh."

"Tell me," she said, taking quick breaths of oxygen between her words, "did I miss anything?"

"Nothing," he replied, his caressing hand on her face. "It is all as you left it."

In October Lily was off the respirator. By Thanksgiving, she was released from the hospital. She never went back to 9th Street and Avenue C. She stayed with Spencer until they found a floor-through apartment in one of the buildings in brand-spanking-new Battery Park City, all the way down town overlooking the Hudson River, with fourteen-foot ceilings, two bedrooms, two bathrooms, plenty of closets, and a huge living room that became an art space appropriate for a girl preparing for her first gallery show. The living room had a 39th floor view of the sun rising in the east and setting in the west. The whole shebang was quite something and didn't set her back eleven million. "That's because it has no crown molding," pointed out Spencer.

Once Lily asked him what he would have done if she had died, and he mumbled and joked and equivocated his way through an answer, but in the dark of night in their bed, he said, "I would have taken your money, given a quarter to your family, a quarter to the American Leukemia Foundation, and retired from the force. I would have moved to Florida, and opened a gumshoe agency on the waters of Key Biscayne. I would have been warm all the time, maybe built a Spanish contemporary home. That way I would have lived where you had wanted to live, in a house you would have liked. I would have planted palm trees for you, and gone out on the sea for you and thought of you as my last rose of the summer."

Spencer drank less. The intervals between his bouts got longer, and once he went for four months without. He told Lily that he couldn't expect more out of life than being with a girl who made him go four whole months without whisky in the hands. "Well, because now Lily's in the hands," she said. "Your hands are full."

Lily continued to go to Paul at Christopher Stanley for her color, despite Spencer's maintaining that anyone who changed his own hair as often as Paul—from bleached blond to brown and back again constantly—should not be trusted.

Spencer still cuts Lily's hair.

To continue to be partnered with Gabe, Spencer asked Whittaker to transfer him out of missing persons and into homicide. At the celebratory lunch at McLuskey's Gabe maintained to Lily it was all so that Spencer could finally proclaim, "This is Detective O'Malley from *homicide*."

Grandma left her house and came every Thursday to meet Lily for lunch. Afterward she and Lily went to the movies, and then Lily took Grandma back to Brooklyn where Spencer came to pick her up after work.

And sometimes while Manhattan Island twinkled across the river, Lily and Spencer still parked at their Greenpoint docks in his Buick while Bruce Springsteen rocked on the radio.

Anne left *KnightRidder* and found a new job as a financial writer for Cantor Fitzgerald. She had an office on the south side of the north tower of the World Trade Center, on the 105th floor, and on a clear day she thought she could see all the way to Atlantic City. The New York Harbor, Ellis Island, Statue of Liberty, Verazano Bridge, and the Atlantic Ocean stretched out before her. She had her desk turned around so she could sit every morning when she got in at eight, and sip her coffee and get ready for her day. She told everyone that she had started a new, happier life. Her sisters came to visit her every Monday for lunch. That's how they repaired their sisterly bonds. Lily left her painting, Amanda left her children with a babysitter, and they met at noon, taking turns choosing a restaurant. Anne wouldn't let anyone else pick up the tab. "It's the least I can do," she said to Lily. And every other Tuesday morning, Anne took Lily to Mount Sinai for her blood work. When Cantor complained about her coming in at eleven on alternate Tuesdays—despite the fact that she stayed in the office until nine those evenings—Anne said they could fire her if they wished, but it was a deal-breaker: she was going to take her sister who was in remission to the hospital.

Cantor Fitzgerald didn't fire her.

George and Allison sold their Maui condo and came back to the continent, buying a small house in North Carolina, near the Blue Ridge Mountains. Their house was on a little lake where George had a dock from which he fished, and a row boat that he took out every once in a while. He had a vegetable garden and planted a hundred times more than he could eat, praising America for its bounty. He gave all of his vegetables to his summer neighbors. He bought a TV and a satellite dish, and watched sports live and movies galore and went on the Internet, and cooked for Allison, and for his brother and his wife, who lived nearby. He had a busy life. He didn't travel much, and Allison didn't either, having learned how to buy gin right off the Internet and have the UPS man deliver it straight to her front door.

George misses his wife. But the tomatoes are very good in the summer. And there's fishing.

Larry DiAngelo married Joy. They adopted a baby girl from South Korea, and they called her Lily. Joy retired from nursing and stayed home with her baby, in unrepentant daily bliss, cooking and watching Disney videos.

Jim left Jan McFadden. She had no choice but to get into shape and raise her twin children. Every Saturday she goes to the Port Jefferson cemetery on Route 112, and sits by the purple stone with the lilac flowers, easily the most decorated grave in the cemetery, the most colorful, the most vibrant, you can see it from the winding road half a mile away, the purples and violets shout like animated billboards against the gray of the rest. *Our beloved daughter and friend, Amy Jean McFadden, 1975–1999.*

When Lily talks of Amy, she still says "She has left." Or, "She has gone missing."

When Lily can bear to speak of Andrew, she still says, "He has left." Or, "He has gone missing."

A small plaque, a favorite quote, written in calligraphy by Amy: *When senseless hatred rules the earth, where will redemption reside?* hung on the door of Amy's studio as a last remainder from Amy's life on 9th Street and Avenue C, and then was stored, deep in Lily's large closet in Battery Park City, at the back of her summer T-shirts, until Lily found it one day and gave it to Anne, who liked it so much she hung it up in her office on the 105th floor of the North Tower.

* * *

One of these New York mornings—it was too beautiful to stay inside, even for Lily who usually liked to go back to bed after Spencer left for work. But she saw the bright and clear skies and seventy-five degrees and no wind—it was a magnificent Maui morning in her New York, when everything seemed not only possible but attainable—and she decided to walk with him two miles to the precinct and then maybe head on to Madison Square Park and sketch the Flatiron while the light was this good. She waited for him, basking on the warm side of the street while he went inside the deli to get them coffees. They really must get a coffee maker that worked.

Her blood tests had been so good lately that DiAngelo finally approved a vacation, and Spencer—who'd never been anywhere—finally and with a little convincing, approved one, too. Not to Maui, not to Cabo San Lucas, not to Arizona, but to Key Biscayne for two weeks, alone with Spencer! They were leaving in a few days and would stay through her 27th birthday.

A convertible buzzed by on the quiet Albany Street heading to West Side Highway. The entire downtown Manhattan was in her view from north to south. A man was putting up flyers for the Mayoral primary elections, on this second Tuesday in September, 2001, tacking the posters up on the pole right next to her. Her heart caught on the memory of the poles, the posters, the convertible, the long gone, the long missing.

She lowered her head for a moment, then raised it up to the sky and breathed in the air. It was too glorious a day.

Spencer came out of the deli and smiled at her, motioning for her to cross the street, as in, come on, I don't have all day. She smiled back and waved, lingering just a little longer with the sun upon her face, her sketchbooks in her hands.

She knew that Spencer, always glad for small mercies, was glad for this: that she had been comatose and near death when Amy's bones were discovered off the Bridle Path, because this let Lily remember Amy only as she once had been—wholly imagined and loved—and not as she really was, a person Lily never knew.

And Lily Quinn, now living each last day with first joy, could continue to hope with a great enchanting hope that maybe her brother Andrew and her friend Amy looked for each other in a place where there were no other lovers, that maybe she had waited for him until he became lost himself and abandoned his convertible after church on Sunday in the waters of the Hudson and she was waving to him from the other side, across the river. The girl slowed down, the man hopped in, and they sped away in a little rented Honda. Amy and Andrew, Allison and George, Claudia and Tomas, and Lily and her Spencer could maybe speed away, forever looking for a place where they would never be found. Without demands, without dead ends, without alcohol, without protocol, a safe place with no sorrow, no monocytes, no blastocytes, no whisky, no war, just a little bit of mercy, a wet and sunny life, and the remains of their fathomless frail free human hearts.

ACKNOWLEDGMENTS

Heartfelt thanks to Joy Chamberlain for her very own mediation of calm and dedication to the cause.

To Pavla Salacova without whom the adored offspring would be street urchins.

To Kevin, the guardian angel, the husband, the man, the everything.